My Memories of a Future Life

Roz Morris lives in London. From the earliest age she had a compulsion to express herself on the page. Let out of London university, she was soon working as a journalist and writing novels. You'll have seen her books on the bestseller lists but not under her name because she ghostwrote them for other people. She is now coming into the daylight with novels of her own.

When not at a qwerty keyboard she enjoys the 88-key kind, though she readily admits she handles the instrument with even less tact than the worst pianist in this novel.

ISBN-13: 978-1463784904
ISBN-10: 1463784902

Copyright © Roz Morris 2011

All rights reserved. No part of this book may be reproduced or transmitted in any form or by any means, graphic, electronic or mechanical, including photocopying, recording in audio or video form, taping or by any information storage or retrieval system, without the express, written permission of the author. This permission must be granted beforehand. This includes any and all reproductions intended for non-commercial or non-profit use.

All events in this book are fictional, as are all the characters. Any resemblance between persons living, dead or not yet born is entirely coincidental and the author assumes no responsibility for any such resemblance, nor from damages arising from the use of this book, or alleged to have resulted in connection with this book.

www.rozmorris.wordpress.com
www.mymemoriesofafuturelife.com

Published by Red Season, London
Cover art by Bonnie Schupp Photography/iStockphoto and Roz Morris, with thanks to Frazer Payne

My Memories of a Future Life

Roz Morris

THANKS

To John Whitbourn, Jane Conway-Gordon, Catherine Pellegrino, Ron Abramski, Frazer Payne, Porter Anderson, Victoria Mixon, Joan Morris and most of all to my husband Dave Morris. All novels need their believers. Thank you all for believing in this one.

1:

THE RED SEASON

Chapter 1

Within the soundproofed walls, the candles knew the truth. This wasn't nirvana. It was a building in the grimy backlands of Clapham Junction station. In the yoga studio all was hushed, but the candle flames stirred to agitated vibration as a train passed. Delicate instruments, shivering to an influence none of us could hear or feel.

The truth was I shouldn't be here, lying still on a purple slip of mat in a row of people who looked like they'd all fallen from the sky. Being told by a barefoot girl to empty my mind. To quiet my thoughts. And just be.

Quiet was something I'd had too much of in the past few weeks.

If this were a proper day I'd be at my Yamaha grand piano, sending glorious noise out of its black wing. For hours I would see only the black and white keys. My reflection in the lacquer-black bodywork swaying across the gold lettering. My hands lifting and falling. And today, being the first Monday of the month, I should have been at my tutor's house.

That was before the pain.

Now, on this first Monday, instead of dancing up a storm of demisemiquavers on his Hamburg Steinway, I was lying on a wooden floor on a sticky mat, trying to be – quiet.

I hadn't done yoga before. I was trying to like it. I'd heard so many people say they loved it with a passion, but so far I didn't get it. We'd been here for ages and all we seemed to be doing was lying down. Although the instructor didn't call it lying down. She called it a posture.

'Shavasana,' she intoned as she passed me at a serene pace, toes spreading with each step. 'It means corpse pose.'

In the mirror I could see the clock. We had been here only ten minutes. How time drags when you're a corpse. But I'm not good with things that need to be done slowly.

It must be the pianist temperament. Pianos are percussion instruments. They can't give you long swelling notes like strings or woodwind. You need to keep moving; keep the pulse.

The instructor continued her slow tour. 'Think of nothing,' she said. 'Absolute nothing.'

The rhythm of her feet suggested a tempo, and then the slow movement of Beethoven's Emperor Concerto. That moment when the orchestra goes quiet and the piano comes in with a languorous, meandering scale –

No, that wasn't nothing. Try again.

I looked at the white ceiling tiles and tried to be blank like they were. Ah, they weren't blank. They had a pattern, like they'd been designed to resemble something – what? Wood grain? Crazy paving?

No, that wasn't nothing.

The candle flames trembled. They knew, even if we didn't, that another train was passing. With somewhere to go. I studied the orange tongues, tried to pick up the iron beat drumming into the topsoil, the bedrock, the bricks that made this building, the boards of this wooden floor.

For heaven's sake. Was this all we were going to do?

I'd expected yoga to be more enthralling. Overwhelming. Engulfing.

The instructor reached the front of the room and folded into a cross-legged position between the candles.

'Feel your chakras aligning,' she said. 'Feel your chi. Flowing through your meridians.'

Meridians.

In the last few weeks I'd had my stuffing searched inside out. They'd found arteries. Veins. Nerves. Muscles. Tendons. Ligaments. Joint capsules. Synovial fluid. Long bones and the hollows in their core. Carpals. Metacarpals. Phalanges like witch talons. I'd been ultrasounded, CTd, x-rayed, y-rayed, z-rayed. What they didn't find, ever, was chakras, meridians or chi.

'Time your breathing with your heartbeat. Feel your heartbeat. Through your temples...'

I heard a sound behind me. A sort of muted rasp.

No, surely it couldn't be, not in the holy yoga class.

'Yes,' smiled the instructor. 'Let go of everything. Let go of self. Let go and just be.'

It was well past time for me to let go. I stood up and folded my mat. I tried to do it quietly but the purple plastic made a sticky slapping noise which earned irritated looks from some of the corpses. No one scowled at the corpse who'd farted, though.

I dumped the mat on the rack and grabbed my shoes. Being trainers, not slippers or hobbitty clogs like everyone else had, the teacher had placed them reprovingly at the door. And I left.

The club was windowless like an airport. I passed from yoga studio to changing room to reception without a clue what weather to prepare for.

When I reached reception the front door swung open and the horrible truth greeted me. Heavy, hissing rain. Oh great. I had a twenty-minute walk home.

I zipped up my inadequate fleece and prepared for a miserable journey.

'Are you walking?' said the receptionist. 'Do you want to borrow one of the club umbrellas?'

'I can't,' I said. 'I've got RSI.'

'RSI? Is that a class?'

A woman pushed in through the doors, her grey tracksuit streaked with rain, her hair in dripping straggles.

I hesitated, looking at the jolly brolly propped by the reception back office. But I couldn't take it.

In medieval times there was a kind of torture where your hands were bound in soaking cloths. As they dried they squeezed your hands like little birds in a vice, an inescapable ache hammering in the bones. If I carried an umbrella for half an hour, that's how it would feel.

I'd tried yoga because my specialist had run out of other solutions.

The pain began a few months ago. As I finished my work at the keyboard, as the last chords left the iron frame and steel strings, the penalty came creeping in. Persistent, neon flashes, deep in the structures of my wrists, fingers and arms.

If you were gardening and you felt pains like that you'd stop and take yourself to the doctor. I ignored it.

All musicians had aches and twinges. I had seen violinists put down their instrument after a long rehearsal and take two entire minutes to uncurl their necks.

Music is physical. Playing a concert grand is hard work; the action is much stiffer than a household upright. To bring out their big sound takes real strength. You might play a passage of sixteenths at a tempo of 120 beats per minute, which is four notes per second, every second, and you might do it for hours. So of course we get sore.

I thought it was just a bad patch. I started to be careful away from the piano. Umbrellas were avoided. I stopped opening jars. Tins likewise. But instead of relief, each week needed another sacrifice. Years before, the gauze of short sight had descended like a set of veils until I couldn't read the music in front of me. Now this damage closed down my whole life in millimetres.

Sometimes I woke in my bed at night, with a feeling like my arms were long gloves stroked by wire brushes. A horrible, painful prickling that went on for hours, as though my nerves were a crackling storm.

A month ago I was on my way into the ENO rehearsal room. Three mornings a week I played accompaniment for opera and ballet rehearsals. I gripped the door handle and gave it a good twist.

Then I was standing still, paralysed, because it felt as though my entire wrist was about to snap.

The conductor found me by the door, waiting for the courage to move. He looked straight at my hands.

'Just warming up,' I said. Musicians don't talk about injury.

If a concert organiser or an ensemble suspects you might not play, they'll find someone else.

'I used to be a pianist,' he said. 'Now I can't touch a piano. Go and see a specialist.'

I did.

The specialist did his tests, said I had repetitive strain injury, and told me to rest for a month. For three weeks now I hadn't touched a piano at all.

I reached my road: two facing rows of 1930s Tudor-looking houses. The hood of my fleece was clinging to my head like a wet sheet. Each footfall pumped freezing water around the inside of my trainers. I pushed through the gate and the overgrown hedge whipped me with wet fronds.

Parked in the porch was a bike, its saddle covered with a Sainsbury's bag.

My housemate, Jerry, must have Tim over again.

No way could I make small talk with a visitor. And the bike had fallen across the door, a stupid place to leave it. I'd have to move it before I could get in. I leaned on the wall and hooked my foot through the cross-bar. What I'd intended was that the bike should move neatly aside but it perversely crashed onto the porch, handlebars pointing backwards. The front door was snatched open.

Jerry stood there, his shaved head grained with stubble and his black eyebrows horrified. 'Why are you kicking Tim's bike?'

I waved my hands at him. 'Because I'm not allowed to pick it up.'

Of course I could have picked it up, but the specialist had said everything I did with my hands had to be rationed. I'd denied myself an umbrella, so why did an unwanted visitor deserve precious hand time?

And I was worn out and worn down and the wind was gusting on my skin as though the rain had dissolved all my clothes.

'Tell him if he's going to park his bike like a clown he might as well ride a unicycle,' I added, just in case my mood wasn't clear, and hurried into the hall.

'Glad to see the yoga's working,' muttered Jerry.

In the lounge, Tim the offender was sitting on the sofa, peering at me with curiosity. Looking at the foul-tempered prima donna pianist, as well he might. I rushed upstairs.

'Wow,' I heard Tim say, 'she's got an artistic temperament all right.'

I locked myself in the bathroom, turned the taps on. The strain of that simple action felt like a Chinese burn. I should have asked Jerry to help. He would have, too, despite me snapping his head off.

Water thundered out of the central spout into the bath. The noise was cathartic, like the howl that had been churning inside me all day. I sat on the bath's rim, exhausted and cold. The spray from the taps sent hot mist over my back.

On the radiator was a pair of white cotton gloves, drying. The specialist had told me to wear them so that I would realise every time I used my hands. I certainly did; they made everything slippery. I couldn't type emails, or write longhand, send texts or even hold a mug of tea. I'd sniggered at the suggestion when it was first made, imagining Victorian gentlewomen and dandyish hip-hop stars. Now I'd lost my sense of humour about them.

I peeled off my clothes. As they slapped onto the floor I saw a lime green Post-It note with a calm face drawn on it.

Jerry had them all over the house. I must have dislodged it when I came up the stairs.

He was prone to panic attacks. He'd had them for years but recently they'd been getting worse. He'd gone to doctors, who gave him things to do like sticking green smileys everywhere. I was forever finding one stuck to my foot as I walked out of the house, or opening the fridge to see a green grin. Painful as it was, I'd find a pen and annotate them. The one in the fridge had a slurping tongue. The one in the microwave had gone cross-eyed. Jerry, strangely, never said anything about how they were acquiring personalities.

I turned the taps off and slid into the bath. Sat in the water gazing at that green face – which I'd given a blindfold to, under the circumstances.

I don't know what it did for Jerry but it made me furious. I wished someone could prescribe me a cheery face to take everything away.

I couldn't go downstairs again. I couldn't think of how to get us all chatting normally and passing cups of tea around or glasses of wine. I stayed in the bath, the water turning tepid like my anger, until I heard Tim and Jerry go out and I could tiptoe back into my home.

CHAPTER 2

Four weeks' waiting were over. I was in the office of Dr Johnson Golding, consultant in rheumatology and rehabilitation, high up the tower block of Guy's Hospital.

I'd spent a lot of time in this room, sitting patiently while machines examined, scanned and scrutinized. But all those tests had involved some polite ray doing invisible detective work while I studied the anatomical charts on the walls.

Not today. Electrodes were taped on my forearms, one on the wrist and one in the crook of my elbow. These were connected by red and black wires to a machine with dials and lights. When the switch was thrown, an electric current fired down the main nerves and the doctor watched my thumbs twitch. It was painful and peculiar in a sickening way, like grabbing an electric cable and not being able to let go. Not the million volts they use to fry murderers in Alabama, of course. This was a spider-leg scratching, an electrical rasp, a dance of millipedes under the skin that you felt could do bad things to your heart but only if given the long leisure of a professional torturer.

Now it was over I flexed my fingers, checking they belonged to me again and only moved when I asked them to. Dr Golding peeled the sticky tape off the electrodes, discarded it into a yellow dump bin and rolled the leads into a coil. He gave his verdict. 'Nerve conductivity seems within normal ranges for both arms.'

'What does that mean exactly?'

'It's normal.' He looked at me and blinked, as he always did when I asked him to translate his diagnoses. 'Each nerve is working fine.'

'And that means?'

'Your symptoms are not caused by nerve compression.'

I rolled down my shirt sleeves and put my jumper back on.

Another test negative. They were always negative. No swellings, no anatomical abnormalities. No explanations. Just mysterious pain.

Jerry had had this too. He'd had tests for asthma, cancer, HIV, his heart wired up to ECGs. Nothing wrong, the doctors said when they'd examined him. Just panic attacks. Have a green smiley.

Dr Golding wheeled the machine back to its parking space, between the ultrasound and some other scanner I'd also had a close encounter with. He sat down at his desk and nudged the mouse. The screen came on, showing my notes and a series of numbers from the electrocution test. He checked them and flicked to another screen which showed how my arms would look if sliced up like salami, in gaudy colours like Andy Warhol prints.

I knew every patch of grey in his salt and pepper hair, or at any rate, those on the left-hand side of his head. I'd watched this view of him, interpreting my case notes, for at least as long as I'd studied his charts and the green paint between them.

When Dr Golding spoke he looked at the screen, as though those diagrams and read-outs represented me as adequately as the flesh and blood in the chair. 'You've been resting your hands now for – how long? Four weeks?'

'Four weeks exactly.'

'And how's the pain?'

'A little better.'

It was, a bit. I could open jars if they weren't too tight and carry light bags of shopping. The mundanities I'd phased out in favour of important things.

Dr Golding opened a drawer and stirred the contents with his finger. He pulled out a thing like a nutcracker and handed it to me. 'See what happens when you squeeze the handles together. Right hand first.'

I did as he asked. As my fingers closed on the handles I felt the familiar pain, as if all the tendons in my wrist were shifting like a points change on a railway track. I was going to pretend nothing was wrong but he was watching my face carefully.

He took the handles from me and put them in my left hand. That was even worse. He returned the device to the drawer and pushed it shut with his knee.

'Maybe it's painful because I'm a little bit stiff,' I said. 'I haven't been playing.'

He typed more notes at rapid speed. 'I think you need to rest more.'

More rest? Was that all?

'Can't you do anything?'

'Not really. You need to rest. Come and see me again in another month. Try to relax.'

Jerry had been told to relax too. He'd tried a brief flirtation with Buddhism. Herbal pills and weird diets. But it hardly mattered what he did. Several times a month I'd hear him wake with an animal gasp, then he'd pad down the stairs to his studio. I'd hear the rumble of casters on the bare floorboards as he rolled his chair to the computer. As I drifted back to sleep he'd be pounding the keyboard, checking in with other sufferers around the world. In the morning he would still be there, preferring to stay awake than risk the horrors that waited for him in sleep.

And besides, I only knew one way to relax.

If I'd had a hectic day before I sat down to practise, I didn't start with scales or arpeggios. I played my current piece, slow as treacle. The enemy of good playing is hurrying. If you take your time, you feel how one note wants to move into the next. You understand the function and organisation of the rhythm. Then you bring it up to speed and every note is perfectly placed. If I started my practice like that, I was relaxed immediately. Sit down, slow down, and you're in the zone.

The trouble is, to do it you need a bloody piano.

I walked out of Dr Golding's office. Miles of lino stretched into the distance, in stifling medical green. It had a pale streaked pattern like rain marks on a concrete building. I passed wards where people sat in dressing gowns with washed-out faces that never saw the sun, the dialysis suite where a man with a bloated abdomen like a pregnancy waited for treatment. The place reeked of helplessness.

A nurse bustled past me. The green walls sucked all the colour from her face too. I found myself walking faster, as if to prove I was still fit, to stop the green mile draining me too. Look, I told the walls, I'm able to walk around and I'm a lifelike colour. It's only my hands that are wrong.

And soon they will be all right. There's nothing structurally amiss, the scanners said so. The nerves are working fine, we found that out today. This is only temporary.

At the end of the corridor was a door to the stairs. It had a twist handle, the kind I found difficult. There were footsteps behind me and I stood aside to let a figure in a white coat pass me. He opened the door and held it for me with his foot, then slipped into a side door marked *Staff cloakroom*. I mumbled thanks and started down the stairs.

He called to me. 'You dropped these.' I turned. He was holding my white gloves.

I walked back up the stairs. I wasn't looking at the doctor's face. The white coat made him part of the hospital furniture. I focused on those limp gloves, mumbled thanks again.

'Carol?'

I looked at him for the first time. About my age. Slim, darkish hair with a side parting that went into a high V on one side of his forehead and made his features look elegant. Eyes emphasised by shadowed creases; that haunted look doctors sometimes have, but quite attractive.

Yes, I recognised him, but only vaguely. It wouldn't be from college; since the age of sixteen I'd been in music academies. Earlier then. Not my original school because it was girls only, so he must have been a friend of somebody's friend.

'It is Carol Lear, isn't it?' he said. 'I remember you playing Rachmaninov at Kate Rafferty's...'

Today, of all days, he couldn't have said anything more wounding if he'd tried.

I took my gloves. 'Thanks.' I hurried away.

CHAPTER 3

I escaped the hospital's mini-city and joined the Friday night hordes advancing into London Bridge station. I squeezed onto a carriage and a fat guy fell against me like a sack when the train moved off.

I was clinging to the rail and my wrist took his weight in a sharp spasm. We both ended up staggering, held up unwillingly by the people around us. A man saw I couldn't grab the rail and gave me his seat. I sank down and nodded gratitude, massaging my wrist. He stood where I had been. We travelled on in uneasy deadlock. Him staring at this odd thing I was doing, me wishing I could stop.

He looked a bit like the doctor from Guy's. The one who had recognised me from Kate Rafferty's party.

Kate Rafferty. That was a name from nearly two decades ago. She'd been at my first school, which I left after GCSEs for sixth form at Chet's School of Music. It had been a relief to leave because life as a music swot was tricky. But that party changed everything.

Our classroom rivalries had vanished. School was over and we were giddy at the thought of our shining futures. Kate's older sister had gone to RADA and Kate was hoping to follow. At the party she performed speeches from Shakespeare. A year before, that would have earned ironic sneers but we raised the roof with heartfelt applause. Her parents had a white grand piano; very Barry Manilow. I played a storming piece by Rach and they didn't drown it with the hi-fi, they stomped for more.

But who was the doctor from Guy's? Somebody's brother? I seemed to remember he had an unusual name, something that made you start a conversation with him to see if he was from somewhere exciting, like America. Or did everything that evening seem a little extraordinary?

Ah, it wasn't Rachmaninov I played; it was Grieg. The

piano concerto in A minor. The thundering opening that takes you down the whole keyboard. Great for showing off with if you're seventeen. Although I remember everyone starting to look at their fingernails when it got past the well-known figures, so I rolled it into *Rock the Kasbah*.

God, fancy remembering it so clearly.

That guy. I had a memory of him wearing glasses and peering over the top of them as though he didn't want to admit he had to use them. He wasn't wearing glasses just now; he must have got lenses or laser surgery.

What on earth was his name? For some reason I was thinking about a nuclear holocaust –

Winter. His name was Gene Winter. It could have been why Kate invited him. It would have made a hell of a stage name.

And now there he was. A doctor, handing me my invalid gloves. Remembering Rachmaninov at Kate Rafferty's party and drawing fascinating conclusions.

I got out at Clapham South, let the escalator carry me up. My phone bleeped. A text from Jerry.

U still in town? Call me.

I ran outside and dialled.

He asked how it went with Dr Golding. I told him. He tried to say things to make it better. Then he said: 'Can you meet me at Sloane Square at eight?'

'I thought you were meeting Tim.' Tim – of the porch bicycle – was a nearly-boyfriend. Jerry hadn't said as much but it was obvious because he didn't hug Tim the way he did everyone else. As if he was afraid of being wrong.

'Tim changed his plans,' said Jerry. 'I can't do this on my own. Can you come?'

CHAPTER 4

I looked for Jerry's blue and grey striped beanie hat in the crowds who were jumping off the number 11 bus. He spotted me first and grabbed me in a hug, his leather jacket creaking like an old ship.

Not only was it a big hug, it was a long, still hug. Troubled.

'Spill the beans,' I said. 'What's going on?'

He turned and, hooking his arm through mine, steered me across the traffic. His arm in the leather sleeve felt tense. Was it one of his bad days?

We set off down King's Road, dodging past the revellers who were taking their time. I only just kept up. 'Where are we going?'

He kept checking the names of side streets. 'It's one of the roads off here.'

'You're not going to get a tattoo, are you? If it's a rude one I'm going home right now.'

He laughed but only for about one second, then bit his lip nervously again. We manoeuvred around some people going into a pub. That looked like a normal Friday scenario; so busy chatting they weren't even in a hurry to get through the door. Jerry looked as if he was on his way to the dentist.

He hadn't even noticed I wasn't wearing my white gloves. Normally he'd have nagged me to put them on.

He stopped and squinted at a street name. Took a piece of paper out of his pocket; a printout from Streetmap. Stuck to the top was a green smiley Post-It. A virgin one, without my additions. He folded the map deliberately around the smiley and slid it back in his pocket.

'So why do we need a calm face?' I said.

He gave a sharp sigh and walked on again. 'We'll be there soon.'

A taxi stopped in front of us and a group of girls wearing bunny ears tumbled out, laughing. One of them was wearing L

20

plates and a tiny mini-skirt. She straightened her skirt while one of the bunnies paid the cab, then they all tottered into All Bar One.

'Jerry,' I said, 'it's eight-thirty on a Friday evening. We're not going to a doctor, are we?'

He took a breath. 'You remember I told you about Anthony Morrish?'

I didn't. But the way Jerry said it made me think I'd better not admit that. 'Was he the guy from that recital...'

Jerry gave me a tight smile. 'Recital!' He stuck his hands in his pockets and marched on.

Now I thought about it I did recall him talking about a kind of therapist. Was that Anthony Morrish? I'd had a lot on my mind. I wasn't very good at remembering names.

'Tim was going to go with you?' I said.

Jerry noted the name of another side street and consulted his map again. 'Yeah but something came up. I'm seeing him tomorrow instead.' He stopped. 'This is the road.'

Shawcross Street. It was an avenue of smart town houses with Farrow and Ball front doors and bright brassware.

'We need number 16.' Jerry set off, counting the numbers.

A figure in a long coat was walking ahead of us, paying careful attention to the numbers too. He opened a gate and went down a path.

'There,' said Jerry, and started to run.

As we ducked in through the open front door, more people arrived behind us.

Inside was a tall hallway and some stairs leading up, which were cordoned off by a thick black rope. The arrivals were heading down into the basement.

The basement had been converted into a small theatre. A semi-circle of raked seating pointed at a stage. On the stage was a velvet chaise-longue, and beside it another chair, but not in the same style; more like an office chair. There was also a low table with an iPod and a microphone.

It looked like the set for a play about somebody seeing a psychiatrist. There were already quite a few people there, and more were arriving. The theatre would be full to capacity.

'So what is it?' I said. 'A play?'

If so, why weren't there any signs outside advertising it?

Jerry didn't even hear me. He had taken his hat off and was searching the crowd, scrunching the hat in his fingers. He then became very still and took a deep breath. I tried to see who he had spotted but it was all heads, talking and nodding.

'You get a seat,' said Jerry. 'I'll see you later.' He made to move away, then stopped and shrugged his leather jacket off. 'Can you look after this?'

I took it and stuffed his hat into the pocket. 'Jerry, what's going on?'

'Just be here. I want a witness.' He pushed back his non-existent hair; his nervousness gesture. Then he made his way to the front.

A witness? To what?

I found a seat at the back, next to a black metal post. It supported spotlights that pointed at the stage. I folded Jerry's jacket onto my lap. The arms retained the shape of his limbs.

At the front, a group of people greeted Jerry with welcoming smiles and eager handshakes. He smiled, but it disappeared immediately. I saw his chest rise and fall as he took another deep breath. As he talked to them he lifted a hand and ran it over his head. There was sweat on the back of his red shirt and under the arms.

I wished I could hear what they were saying.

The lights dimmed. The ones trained on the stage became brighter. A tall man in a suit and open-necked shirt walked on from the wings with a microphone. Before he even spoke, the room hushed.

'Good evening, ladies and gentlemen. Thank you all for coming. For those of you who don't know me, I'm Anthony Morrish and I use the power of the mind to heal people.'

There was a smattering of applause. Morrish smiled and nodded until they were quiet. Then he extended a theatrical hand towards the front row.

Jerry stood up.

He smoothed his hands over his head, then climbed onto the stage.

'I'd like you to meet Jerry,' said Morrish. 'He's thirty-five and he's an artist. Jerry, will you tell us in your own words why you're here?'

Jerry took the microphone. 'Hi,' he said, and his voice croaked. He cleared his throat and smiled. 'Oh look at me, my mouth's like sandpaper.'

The audience didn't laugh. They regarded him with silent attention.

Jerry shook himself and had another go. 'Okay, I'm here because I've had panic attacks since I was very young and I don't know why.'

Morrish took the microphone back from him. 'And the doctors say there's nothing wrong with you?' He tilted the mike for Jerry to answer.

'They say it's all in the mind.'

'That's not very comforting to you, is it?'

'No.'

What was this?

'Jerry, some of the audience may be familiar with panic attacks, but for those of us who aren't, can you describe what it feels like?'

'I can't breathe,' said Jerry. 'It feels like something dreadful happened to me and I'm reliving it, or it's about to happen again. But when I tell doctors they just say, that's why they're called panic attacks. I've ended up in hospital because I thought I was having a heart attack...'

I remembered that night. It was just after we started renting the house. I heard a scream and found Jerry wide, staring awake, huddled like a primate in the corner of his bed. When I touched him his heart was thudding so hard it shook every bone in his spare frame. They do say fear can kill you, make your hair turn white. It just doesn't show up under a doctor's microscope.

Anthony Morrish said: 'And you must have tried so hard to find a cure.' Pointed the microphone at Jerry.

'Yeah. I haven't drunk caffeine for years... cut out wheat and dairy and artificial additives. I've tried crystal healing and at the moment I'm having cognitive behaviour therapy.'

'Did any of those help?'

'Maybe.'

Morrish addressed his next comment to the audience. 'Maybe. We all try to look on the bright side, don't we? But it didn't help enough, Jerry, or you wouldn't be here now. My friends, this kind of problem can rule your life. Panic attacks are not common in the general population, but there is a section of society who does get them frequently. They are special, sensitive people.'

There was a murmuring in the audience. Morrish waited for it to die down then spoke again.

'But there is another important piece of the jigsaw.'

He looked around the room, making sure we were ready for the answer. 'Panic attacks happen when people have suffered a trauma.'

Another beat. In the front row, a few shadowed heads were nodding.

'Jerry, has anything traumatic ever happened to you?'

Jerry leaned over to reply. 'No.'

Morrish turned to the audience again. His face was grave. 'Ladies and gentlemen. Panic attacks. So bad that our poor friend Jerry ended up in hospital with everybody thinking he was having a heart attack. He says nothing traumatic has ever happened to him. The doctors say it's all in the mind. But there's no smoke without fire. He says he feels as if something dreadful happened to him. What was it?'

The audience was silent, spellbound.

Morrish put a hand on Jerry's arm and scanned the room. Playing the silence, making sure everyone all the way to the back row was paying attention.

He spoke again, quietly. 'Maybe something did happen to Jerry. Sometimes a very bad experience can be buried, so that it is completely inaccessible to the conscious mind. I'm going to put him into a trance to explore this further.'

This couldn't be real. Was this man going to hypnotise Jerry, while an audience watched? If Jerry was going to try something like this shouldn't it be in private? What if it triggered an attack? Were we all going to watch that too?

How could Jerry think this would help?

On my knee, the green smiley was poking out of Jerry's pocket. If I'd had a pen it would have been chomping a £50 note.

Morrish turned to Jerry and spoke to him away from the microphone. Jerry nodded and went to the chaise-longue. He looked out into the audience. Was he looking for me? I smiled back.

Just be here, Jerry had said. *I want a witness.*

CHAPTER 5

Jerry seemed determined to go along with it. All I could do was watch.

Morrish turned back to the audience. 'My friends. As usual, we record the session, so Jerry can listen to it at leisure.' He peered up at the back row, no doubt to connect all the way to the cheap seats. 'I see there are a few new faces here, so I'll explain the ground rules. As always, the first part of the session will be just between Jerry and me and you won't be able to hear us. I'd ask you to try to remain as silent and as still as possible. Once Jerry is under, I will turn the microphone on. Even then, you must stay absolutely quiet or you might interfere with what the subject sees.'

He paused. It looked staged, as though he was reading a score and had come to an instruction to rest.

'You may hear and see some shocking things but on no account must you talk. You must not say a word – in any language: ancient or modern.'

All around me the faces were serious, earnest. And silent.

If a stray word could upset it all, why do it in front of an audience? Jerry was looking for real answers. What was everyone else here for? A cabaret?

Jerry settled back on the chaise-longue. He fidgeted, trying to get comfortable. He ran his hand over his head and a fine mist of sweat sprayed onto the floor. He grinned. 'Oh look at me, it's like I've run a marathon.'

He nodded at Morrish.

Morrish spoke. 'All right, Jerry, if you're ready we'll find out what your past trauma is.'

The stage lights dimmed and put us into darkness. A small window let in a little light from a lamp in the street above. I craned forwards and saw Anthony Morrish sit down. The light made a faint halo around him. I couldn't see Jerry at all.

I heard Morrish speaking. It was an indistinct murmur, too quiet to hear actual words. I hugged Jerry's jacket on my knee.

No one in the audience moved. For five minutes the only sound was Morrish's concealed conspiracy with Jerry. A rising and falling of the tone of his voice like a muffled tune. The concentration in the silent people around me was like heat. All directed at the stage, trying to pick out the words.

Suddenly the chaise-longue was illuminated in a circle of light. At the same moment, Anthony Morrish's voice was all around us, whispering out of the walls in surround sound. The big authoritative voice that used to say, buy a Kia-Ora and an ice cream, in a few minutes you'll be spellbound. Several members of the audience jumped.

Jerry looked relaxed on the sofa, his head lolling on one side as though deep in thought.

'Now Jerry,' said Morrish, 'I want you to go back in time. Way, way back, to before you were born, before the people you know were born. I want you to seek out the life you had before. Go back to your past life before you were Jerry.'

I knew it was showmanship. But nevertheless a shiver went down my spine.

Anthony Morrish said: 'What year is it?'

And Jerry answered. '1888.'

'What is your name?'

'Ruby Cunningham.'

Jerry's voice was different; softer. Coming out of the walls in surround sound it didn't seem like him at all.

'Where are you?'

'The east end of London. Whitechapel.'

'Describe what's around you. What can you see?'

'It's dark. I'm standing in front of a wall. It's Christian Street. The wall is big and white. Someone has carved letters into the brickwork: Violet loves B. I'm holding a piece of charcoal. I've been told to write on the wall.'

'What are you writing on the wall?'

'The Juwes are the men who will not be blamed for nothing.'

There was a loud gasp.

Anthony Morrish darted a warning look into the auditorium.

He went back to Jerry. 'What does that mean?'

'I don't know. I've been told to do it.'

'Who told you to do it?'

'A man. He's a doctor or something. I've never seen him before. I was out walking near the hospital when a black carriage pulled up. The door opened and the man stepped out. He was wearing a tall hat. I couldn't see his face. He asked me if I wanted to earn some money. I said, I'm not one of those girls. But he said, no I don't want a prostitute. Can you read and write? I said yes. I was terrified. That girl was killed here only last week, you know, by the Ripper.'

Another intake of breath from the crowd. But wordless. Nobody dared break the rule.

Morrish seemed to command our obedience as tightly as Jerry's.

'Go on,' said Morrish.

'He told me to write these words on the wall. He gave me the charcoal. He smelled funny, like birth.'

'Like birth? Can you explain?'

'When Rosie, my sister, gave birth, there was a lot of blood. That's what he smelled like.'

Out in the dark seats there was another murmur. Like a breeze passing a message around the trees.

'Ruby, how old are you?'

'Fifteen years old.'

'And you're writing on this wall?'

Jerry's soft Ruby voice started to shake. 'Yes. It's a wall on a corner near Whitechapel Road.'

'Ruby, what is the matter? Is something wrong?'

'The carriage has followed me. They're watching me. The cab is there behind me, waiting like a black bird. I have to finish this job and then they'll pay me and I can go.' On the chaise-longue, Jerry's head tossed from side to side. His arms were stiff as though he had been chained to the chaise-longue.

Morrish made his voice powerful, like a baritone summoning his deepest note. 'Ruby. Come forwards; come forwards in time. Where are you now?'

Jerry's head was stiller now, but the set of his neck was tense.

'I'm hiding.'

'Hiding where?'

'With my sister and Mary Kelly. The men in the carriage are following us. I don't know what they want but I don't want to talk to them.' Jerry began to shake his head again. His voice began to rise. 'Don't let them get me, don't – '

Pain vibrated in my fingers. I was digging my nails into Jerry's leather jacket.

Morrish's voice was all around us. 'Ruby, it's all right, you're safe. Come forwards; come forwards in time. Where are you now?'

Jerry's voice was anxious and fast. 'I'm in the carriage. I was in Mary's house. The man came to see her and she let him in. He cut her. Mary is... He's put me in the carriage. He's staring at me. Mary's blood is all over his shirt and splashed on his face. On his hands. It's Mary's blood...'

Jerry was gasping and struggling, as though trying to free himself from his curiously pinned body. Was this an attack starting? Even though he wanted it, could I let it continue?

Morrish called out, like a priest exorcising a demon. 'Ruby, come forwards in time. Come away from there. Come away from there now.'

Jerry fell silent. His head lolled onto his chest.

Morrish spoke to him again, more gently. 'Ruby, what do you see now?'

Jerry said nothing. His head remained where it was, tilted and unaware, like a very young child in sleep.

'Ruby,' repeated Morrish, 'are you there?'

Jerry lay still. I craned forwards, examining him. He was still breathing. And peacefully.

Well that could only be a matter of luck. Did Anthony Morrish have any idea what damage he could have done?

'All right Jerry,' said Morrish. 'I want you to come forwards.

Come forwards through the years, all the way through the years, to now. You're safe, you're well and you're among friends. Five-four-three-two-one – you are awake.'

On the chaise-longue, Jerry raised his head, opened his eyes and blinked. Flexed his fingers. Eased himself into a sitting position.

I realised I was hunched forward, folded around his leather jacket.

Morrish sat back in his psychiatrist chair and smiled. 'Well, Jerry, how do you feel? Do you know where you've been?'

His voice was a normal speaking pitch; not processed now. They had switched off the speakers on the walls.

Jerry nodded and swallowed, as if it took a long time to think about the question. 'Yeah. I feel – I feel okay.' His voice was his own again.

'Do you remember what happened?'

'Yes, I do.' Jerry kept nodding, as though that simple move was all he could do. 'Thanks,' he said.

'Do you feel like that could explain your panic attacks?'

He thought. 'Yes.' He seemed to be parsing every question very carefully. 'I think it does.'

There was a murmur of agreement from the audience. Obviously for them, it explained everything very neatly.

'I knew there had to be something,' said Jerry. He reached for Morrish's hand and shook it. 'Thank you; this makes it all so clear.'

The audience gave him another murmur of approval.

Anthony Morrish let go of Jerry's hand, stood up and faced the crowd.

'Ladies and gentlemen, we have just seen another extraordinary journey. Jerry here has discovered that he was a victim of Jack the Ripper. He was a woman called Ruby, who knew the Ripper's last documented victim Mary Kelly, and spent her last days in fear being stalked by the most vicious killer Victorian London ever knew.

'We know from other regressions we have witnessed in this room that Jack the Ripper probably butchered many more women than the six who were so famously recorded in the history books.'

They had 'found' other Ripper victims? And it had never made the papers? Even World War 2 bombers found on the Moon got into the papers.

'Jerry has been carrying around for his whole life the legacy of a violent death. Wondering why he was living in dread. Wondering why he felt this irrational, consuming sense of fear. Jerry, we hope that what you have learned tonight will bring you a new sense of peace.'

The audience burst into applause. Morrish nodded and smiled. He'd put Jerry through a terrifying experience and he looked pleased with himself.

Morrish let them go on for a while, then raised his hands. 'My friends, it just remains for me to thank you very much for your attention and for keeping so quiet. This wouldn't have been possible without you.'

No, I thought. What you mean is it wouldn't have been worth the bother.

The applause erupted again. I kept my hands clenched on Jerry's jacket. No way was I joining in. I looked at the people around me, along my row. Among the hands clapping like a line of performing seals there was one gap. Hands that remained resolutely on denimed thighs.

How interesting; another sceptic. I peered further out to see what he looked like.

My eyes met another face, also searching. A forehead with a high V parting on the left, intense eyes and high cheekbones.

Gene Winter.

I looked away. What was he doing here?

The applause pattered away. On the stage, Anthony Morrish beckoned to Jerry. Both of them walked to the front of the stage. Members of the audience were on their feet, surrounding the stage, eager to talk to them. The hubbub of conversation rose.

Jerry looked bewildered. Was he still half-hypnotised?

A voice behind me said: 'Hello.'

Gene, in a leather bomber jacket. Without his white coat he looked younger and as slight as I remembered from school, but the V of hair was a little higher.

Jerry stepped down off the stage. He was swaying.

'Gene, you're a doctor. Will he be okay?'

'We should get him away from this stress. He'll be vulnerable and it could bring on a panic attack.'

I pushed through the crowd to the stage. Jerry caught my eye and looked relieved. I reached him and held out his jacket. He looked at it as though he didn't know what to do.

I turned and looked for Gene.

He was right behind me. He didn't wait for me to ask a question, but took Jerry's jacket from me and nodded towards the exit. 'Let's get him out.' He raised his voice. 'Can we give him some space, please?'

I slipped my arm through Jerry's. The crook of his elbow was soaked with sweat, from the stress of that awful regression.

Gene went ahead of us, clearing the way. The crowd parted and every person gazed at us, face alight with questions. Some of them looked annoyed that we were taking Jerry away.

Outside the auditorium was a display of books and self-help tapes by Anthony Morrish, presided over by a silvery haired woman. She was taking tenners and handing over bags as fast as she could manage. Gene cleared a path through the customers and I hurried Jerry past.

We guided Jerry down the path and through the gate. He looked at them as though he was seeing them for the first time. I stood with my arm around him while Gene flagged down a taxi.

A cab pulled over. 'Where are you going?' Gene asked me.

'Clapham,' I said. Gene leaned in the window to talk to the driver. Please don't let him be one of those sods who won't go south of the river, I breathed.

Gene straightened up and opened the back door of the cab. I pushed Jerry and he climbed in.

He was so obedient, like a living doll. Was it safe for him to be in this state? Anthony Morrish had warned the audience not to say anything while he was under because of what it might make him see or hear. What if he had a flashback? Or a panic attack while in a trance?

Gene handed me Jerry's jacket. 'Do you want me to come with you? I have some experience of hypnosis.'

I nodded. 'Yeah. Thanks.'

I climbed in, sat next to Jerry and clasped his hand tightly. Gene sat on the fold-down seat opposite me. The taxi began to thread through the back roads.

Gene leaned forwards, looking at Jerry. The amber lights in the street outside accented the hollows in his cheekbones and made his eyes more intense. He twitched his finger; a tiny movement but Jerry looked at him, like a well trained dog waiting for instructions.

'Jerry, can you hear me?'

Jerry replied. 'Yes.'

'Good. Jerry you're safe and we're taking you home. Lean against Carol and sleep.'

Jerry's head sank onto my shoulder. His eyes closed.

Gene sat back. 'He'll be all right.'

I looked at Jerry. He was absolutely still. 'What have you done?'

'Put him back under so he can relax.'

The slightly higher hairline made Gene's face look narrower than I remembered. Maybe he had lost puppy fat. On either side of his nose were two tiny marks. So he still wore glasses sometimes.

Now we had sorted out the immediate problem I didn't know what to say to him. 'So what's a doctor doing at a charlatan show like that?'

Gene glanced at Jerry and put a finger to his lips. He reached into his inside pocket, scribbled on a pad of paper and passed it to me.

Shh. He can still hear. Not doctor; physiotherapist. You allowed to write?

I scrawled my answer. *Why would I not be allowed to write?*

Have you been reading my notes?

He shook his head. Scribbled some more. *Dr G only gives white gloves to the bad ones.*

So he knew everything.

He scribbled again. *Sorry about the Rachmnv.*

Sometimes I felt so angry it was like having Tourette's. It took over me without warning. I only kept control because Jerry's weight against my shoulder reminded me to be careful. The fury became tears, too many of them. I turned away and rested my cheek on Jerry's sandpapery head, looking at the streets passing so Gene wouldn't see.

Gene had only come in the cab to help me. He'd been nothing but helpful ever since he'd first seen me. But I couldn't cope with it. There was a tsunami of energy inside me and I had no idea where it could all go. I couldn't cope with anything. Even kind people.

I didn't dare look at him again. We stayed silent for the rest of the journey. Once we delivered Jerry home and safe I'd get rid of Gene as fast as possible.

CHAPTER 6

The cab slalomed around the speed humps of Nightingale Lane, swung into our road and put the brakes on. In the doorway of the house opposite the owners were saying goodbye to a couple on the front step. They saw our cab and the woman tiptoed on high heels to the gate to bid for it.

I nudged Jerry.

He stayed still, didn't wake, didn't stir.

Gene took Jerry's hands and spoke to him softly. 'Jerry, when you feel me squeeze your hands you will wake up. Three-two-one – '

He increased the pressure on Jerry's fingers. Jerry's head snapped up, his eyes open. As though the weirdness of that Jack the Ripper business had snaked out of the basement like a wisp of fog and followed us home.

The driver called over his shoulder. 'You all stopping here or what?'

'No, just us two,' I said. 'How much so far?'

'Twenty.'

High heels clattered into the road from the house opposite. The cab driver saw the woman and shook his head. She turned away, arms wrapped resentfully against the cold.

I paid and helped Jerry out.

Gene climbed out after him. He handed me a ten-pound note. 'I'm getting out here too.' I must have given him a hostile look because he added: 'I'll walk from here.'

The cab driver pulled away and tooted to alert the couple from the dinner party.

Jerry made his way down the steps to the front door. Unlocked it, opened it. Dashed to the cupboard under the stairs to turn off the burglar alarm.

He seemed to be moving normally; or at least not as though he was sleepwalking. But he looked so quiet. Normally if we were coming home from a night out he'd be chatting and laughing.

Gene stopped at the front step. 'Jerry,' he said, 'how do you feel?'

Jerry looked surprised to be talked to. 'Fine. Do you know what, I think I need to be on my own. Carol, can you lock up?' Then he frowned. 'Oh no, that's silly, of course you shouldn't.' He put his hand on the banister. 'You might have to remind me if I forget something...'

Since my piano ban Jerry had usually locked up because the bolt on the back door didn't move unless you bullied it.

'I'll manage,' I said.

Gene was still on the doorstep, hands in pockets. 'Jerry, you ought to get to bed. Carol, if you tell me what to do I'll help you.'

Jerry went to the stairs. Whatever Gene said he obeyed without question. 'Good night,' he said, then went up. Leaving me there with Gene.

If Jerry was feeling normal there's no way he would have gone to bed and left me with a good-looking stranger, without so much as a flirty wink.

'Is he still under?' I said.

'Probably just disorientated,' said Gene. 'He's calm. He'll be okay now.'

He hadn't moved from the threshold. Like a vampire waiting to be invited in.

Rain began to patter through the trees. Gene looked at it and shrugged deeper into his jacket. 'Do you need some help locking up?'

'I'll deal with it. And I don't want you snapping your fingers and putting me under.'

It was a reflex: leave me alone. I don't want sympathy or curiosity, or to discuss where things went wrong.

I should have thanked him for getting Jerry home. We should have chatted about old times. I should have asked him about his life, what he was doing. That's the way people normally behave when they meet someone who is part of their past. But a reflex stopped me. It was as if by saying the words I'd be starting something I wouldn't be able to cope with.

Gene gave a half smile. 'Jerry was still half-under. I'd need a bit more time to do you.'

'You don't need to do me,' I said quickly, and put my hand on the door, ready to push it shut.

Propped by the front door were a couple of golf umbrellas. Gene looked at them. 'Do you use those?'

I spread my hands. 'What do you think?'

He took the black one, pulled the pen out of the bomber jacket, grabbed my hand and inscribed my palm. *45 Elliston Rd.*

Then he turned, jogged up the steps and launched the umbrella. His footsteps echoed as he walked around the corner and away down Nightingale Lane.

CHAPTER 7

Back when Jerry was at art college he was looking for a flatmate and I answered the ad. He always wore something red and had a wide-open smile that was charmingly at odds with the brooding characters he liked to draw. It turned out he had a powerful mothering streak and was soon checking on me like a minder, knocking on my door in the morning if I had to get up, mopping me up with hugs and analysis when boyfriends went wrong. I often thought it was a pity he was gay, he was such an affectionate soul. Although if I'd dated him I'd probably have got jealous as he was equally as protective with all his friends.

But I had the feeling all was not well in his boundless heart. I wondered if he'd had a tragedy at an early age, if a brother or sister had died – like me he was an only child. One night I got my answer.

We'd been chatting in my room, top to tail under the duvet. The bed fitted snugly against two walls and we'd make a nest with every pillow and cushion in the flat. Sometimes we used his bed, but it rolled and developed a chasm at one or other end, which would swallow first the pillows and then your backside.

We'd been grousing about love and luck until we decided we two were the only reasonable people in the world. We'd always go on until we fell asleep. Usually I'd wake to see his red-socked feet on my pillow like two Muppets waiting for faces and it would make me smile as I turned the light out.

This time I woke to a scream.

I thought he was having a fit or cardiac arrest.

That was the pit of anxiety he carried. Every few months it would happen. He couldn't explain why or predict when, but a depth charge would detonate in his soul and he'd wake, insane with panic.

We shared that flat for two years, then rented the Clapham

house. It was owned by an obscure trust and we got the run of it for doing it up. We painted the dingy rooms white and converted the garage to a soundproofed practice room. We built up freelance careers – he as an artist and illustrator specializing in gothic and Victorian styles, me playing for ensembles and orchestras.

We each had our coterie of college contemporaries, but mine scattered further and wider, or fetched up in other professions, started families. Other musicians took the place of these friends, but by then I understood they'd come and go.

Even if they became more than friends, they couldn't resist the law of the music jungle. That's what happened last year with Karli, a velvet-voiced baritone with black curls and a face so perfect for classical CD covers that he must have been drafted by Botticelli. We were playing at a concert, he was spotted by an agent and pulled away to a new life in the States. This life swallows your time. There's no space for transatlantic relationships.

As people vanished I'd sometimes feel I was on a boat whose moorings were being cut, one by one. Even my parents were now remote and retired in Northumberland, although we'd never been close. But Jerry remained, more permanent than anyone.

I lie awake staring at the darkness. I expected to be playing again from today. I've forced myself through every long hour of the last month, like a marathon, knowing that I can do it because I will never have to do it again.

I've killed time most lavishly. I've done all the admin I never usually get round to, mailed my CV to ensembles and concert venues, sorted out my accounts. I've helped Danya and Ed, two players from the Garland ensemble, memorise concert pieces, until it reminded me too much of what I was missing.

I've been like a tourist in a city I've always worn as casually as my own skin. Done the art galleries, the Tower of London, Madame Tussaud's. Tried ice-skating; spent an afternoon in a fuggy Soho basement where unknown poets smoked high-tar Spanish cigarettes and read out work in hectoring tones. I've tired of being an observer, found pointless walks to go on. Saw how many of the city's green spaces I could walk in a day; trekked the entire length of the Circle line, one day to the east, the next day west. Walked along the ley lines that cross London like a mad pentagram, not because I believe in them but because they're routes I hadn't yet tried.

All those hours of watching, waiting to be readmitted to life. All those miles, putting time in the bank for the invisible damage to heal.

Why hasn't it made any difference?

Corpse blankness. I would love to be able to do that now. Properly, with none of these thoughts.

So, another month of resting. What if it isn't? What if it's two, or three? What if this pain never goes away? What if I am another incurable, like Jerry?

What good am I if I can't play? It's what makes me feel like me. It's my – it's not my gift. I wasn't born gifted. It's how I've cheated with the unsatisfactory clay I'm made from.

When I started at Chet's, there was a particular moment that made me feel at home there. Someone told a fellow pianist they thought her trippy runs and airy arpeggios were a gift. Nobody gave it to me, she snarled, I worked bloody hard for it.

I haven't seen her for a good eight years. I wonder what she's doing now. Please tell me that all these people who vanished from my radar did it because music carried them to a new place, like Karli. It didn't abandon them.

A creaking sound.

I sit up, alert. Is it Jerry? Has it started?

I hold my breath, listening for his choking gasp, the click of a light, his footfall on the stairs. I'll join him; this night is too bleak to endure alone. I'll take the duvet down and we'll burrow into the sofa, top to tail, red socks and all. It will be like old times, before he talked to the message boards instead of me. We shouldn't have let that slip.

But the only sound is a far-off train, scouring through the

wet night air. Jerry must still be asleep.

What did he say in King's Road? He was going to take Tim with him to the hypnotist tonight. I wasn't his first choice of companion; I was second.

Or who knows, maybe I wasn't even that far up the list. I can't think of anybody for whom I'd be first choice of friend.

When love went wrong, when Karli was taken away, I turned to that intimate communion with ivory, iron, ebony and wire.

Take the piano out of my life and what is left?

Chapter 8

At three o'clock I put the light on. In the palm of my hand were hieroglyphs. I found my glasses.

45 Elliston Rd.

I hated the way this injury was making me behave. I should have treated Gene better, made more of an effort.

Maybe if I went for a walk my body would let me sleep.

I pulled on jeans, a jumper and trainers and went downstairs, stopping at the pad by the phone. In case Jerry woke up wondering where I was.

Instead I wrote a note to Gene. *Sorry about earlier. Thanks for getting us back in one piece. Great to see someone from the old days – what a coincidence! Get in touch sometime when I've learned to be a bit more civilised.*

No, that was too much. I crumpled it and redrafted. *Thanks for getting us back in one piece. Carol and Jerry.*

There was a fireplace in the hall. Above it was one of Jerry's paintings, a cover for a glossy art book on Dracula, featuring a demonic figure against a Victorian street scene. It went well with the walls, which he'd recently painted red. In the background was a newspaper vendor. The lettering on the paper was soft focus, but as I looked the letters made sense to me.

VB.

Violet loves B. As Jerry had seen on that wall in his regression.

I put the light on. The hall and living room were full of artwork; either bought by him or painted by him. I looked at a picture of a barbarian, from a Conan-type book cover. The scabbard dangling across the meaty thighs had a design on it that looked like lettering. And there it was. Heavily stylized, but clearly: *VB.*

At the bottom of the stairs was another of his pictures, a

creepy graveyard painted to illustrate a book of ghost stories. I scoured its details and there it was on one of the gravestones. Not at the front so that it was prominent; on a little one at the back. But it was there.

One of his books on the shelf. I pulled it out. On the cover was a mage in purple robes and immediately the letters took shape on the embroidered border.

Wherever Jerry needed to draw lettering or an ancient design he made it VB.

Was he aware he always used that? Or was *Violet loves B* beating away in his subconscious for all these years?

He'd never told me. If it had been happening in those early days of cushions and Muppet feet on the pillow, he would have said. We told each other everything then.

If you can't sleep, I wrote, *call me. I've popped out for a few minutes.* I put it on his computer and went out.

It had stopped raining. The streets were quiet and sparkling wet. Elliston Street was about 15 minutes' walk away.

I turned down the road that ran alongside Wandsworth Common. On one side of me was darkness, broken by the lamps on the footpaths, and, further away, a chain of lights that marked the road to Tooting. On my right the houses were dark. It was too late even for porch lights to be on. Burglar alarm lights pulsed watchfully over the doors.

A cab went past, carrying a passenger who dozed against the back window. The head rolled gently as the cab turned.

An urban fox slunk out of a hedge and trotted across the road. Cab engines and trains rattled in the distance. But nothing else moved. The whole world had gone to bed.

I reached Elliston Street, a quiet residential road. Identical Victorian houses stretched away, personalised by the make-up on their window frames and door arches. One lighted upstairs window stood out like a cinema screen against the other curtained oblongs. I walked along and counted the numbers until I stood in front of it. 45.

I put my note through the letterbox, turned and hurried away across the road. My footsteps echoed like tapdancers' shoes on the wet asphalt. Something made me turn around and look back.

I saw a difference in the texture of the dark at Gene's door. Then a downstairs light came on. He was a black silhouette in the doorway.

I didn't know what I'd say to him. But I couldn't duck away. He'd seen me.

He held something out. The black umbrella.

I crossed the road and went to him. 'Sorry,' I said as I got close. 'Did I wake you?'

Of course I didn't. Only a ninja would be woken by a slip of paper falling from the letterbox.

He had glasses on, small oval frames like an updated version of the John Lennon specs he wore at school. He was in the same jeans as earlier, so he probably hadn't gone to bed.

I grasped the umbrella and he held onto it, keeping me there. 'Is Jerry all right?'

'He's sleeping. I'd better get back in case he has an attack.'

Still he didn't let go. With the other hand he put a cigarette to his lips and dragged on it. His words came out on smoke. 'He won't. He's probably getting a better sleep than either of us.' He released the umbrella. 'Come in.'

Chapter 9

I followed Gene in and pushed the door shut. He led me through a narrow hallway to a staircase, and up to the first floor. The red tip of the cigarette swung from his hand, along with my note.

That note. I was glad I'd toned it down.

Even so I had that feeling again, of starting something I couldn't quite control.

On the first floor he opened the door to a small living room. I glimpsed bare white walls, rough floorboards that had recently had a carpet, a beige sofa and chair, and several large boxes, sealed with parcel tape. He must be just moving in.

The window was open. Footsteps echoed outside in the street, crossing the road. A figure in a big coat looked up at the window and stared at us. Its face was an open-mouthed drama mask for a moment, then it hurried on.

Gene turned the lights off. The street lamp and the moon outside turned him into a silhouette again. 'That's the problem with not having curtains. Everyone treats you like a TV.' He leaned against the window sill. 'So what can I do for you?'

It was like the first words a doctor says when you walk into their surgery. Except for the smouldering cigarette.

I forgot about parties and being eighteen and the guy with the holocaust name. Slipped into the role of patient. 'I don't know. I've had everything done. I've got to put up with it now, do my time. I just want to get the next few months out of the way as quickly as possible.'

He gave a faint smile, as if that confirmed something he already suspected. 'So what do you think of all that regression business earlier?'

I wasn't sure what he meant by the question. 'In what way?'

'Do you believe it? Do you think going back in time could change anything now?'

Another drag on the cigarette. Grey smoke blown out thoughtfully. Not going to speak until I reply.

'Maybe it would.' I shrugged. 'Until you woke up and it was the same old crap again. Then I think I'd want my money back.'

That cigarette smoke is like a truth drug.

He straightened up from the window sill. The end of his cigarette glowed as he took a drag. He said, on smoke, 'Do you want a drink?'

'Yeah. That would be good. You know, I hardly used to drink before. I always wanted to get up early and practise. If you meet me when I'm able to play I'm a completely different person.'

He looked at me with curiosity. Dropped his cigarette onto the carpetless boards and trod it out with his bare foot.

He didn't flinch at all, just pressed his foot onto the glowing butt and took his time making sure it was out. He picked it up, walked to an archway at one end of the room. I tried to look at the sole of his foot under the ragged hem of his jeans. Was there a burn? There wasn't enough light to see. He must have cheated somehow. But I was impressed. Even though I knew that was what he intended.

I heard fridge doors, then he came out holding a half-bottle of champagne and a long-stemmed glass as tall as a vase.

One glass. Champagne.

'Have a seat,' he said, and sat next to me on the sofa. The light from the streetlamp made his hair and eyebrows dark and turned the stubble on his face into a shadowy beard. Quickly he dealt with the foil, the wire and the cork, and poured.

The foamy liquid went all the way into the glass. The entire stem was hollow.

He handed the glass to me. It was ice cold; it had been kept in the fridge. The champagne gave off a biscuity smell. The bubbles sparkled and jumped over the rim of the glass, like cold breath on my hand.

I didn't question whether he was having any. I took a drink.

He put the champagne bottle behind him on the floor. 'I've

seen people walk over burning coals in a state of hypnosis.'

He knew I was still thinking about what he'd just done with the cigarette.

I replied: 'I don't think I'd better try that. I can't afford to knacker my feet as well as my hands.'

I took another drink. I felt I needed something to hide in.

'Wait there.' He stood up and went behind the sofa. There was a rasp of cardboard as he opened one of the boxes.

The champagne showered sparkles over my hand. I was trying to think of something to say. There must be all sorts of conversations to have with someone from that long ago but they all vanished from my head when he put his bare foot on that burning coal.

I took another sip and the bubbles misted over my face. The bottle was on the floor by the foot of the sofa. Only one glass. What was going on?

But I had the wine and the bubbles and I didn't care. If he had an ulterior motive I was sure I could cope.

Gene sat next to me again and put an object on the sofa between us. A Dictaphone. It had a tape in it and the red recording light was on standby.

I thought of the stage at Anthony Morrish's; the chaise-longue, the iPod. The secret instructions to Jerry and the voices out of the walls. Then Jerry fighting as the visions took hold.

I'd need a bit more time to do you, Gene had said to me, patiently from the threshold.

If he tried one of Anthony Morrish's tricks I'd resist.

But I didn't want to move.

I gestured towards the Dictaphone. 'I don't have a past life,' I said. 'I'm just me, living now.'

He leaned against the back of the sofa, his chin propped on his elbow. His face was intense; the shadow brows, the dusky beard, the sparely fleshed cheekbones.

I tried to remember the Gene I knew from that party and I couldn't see him at all.

'Not a past life,' he said carefully. 'Merely a past. What if you could go back and change what has happened now? What would you do differently?'

What an impossible question. I took refuge in another drink.

He reached down for the bottle and topped up my glass, still talking. 'With hypnosis we can go back in time, or we could even hop forward a couple of years, see what might happen if you carry on from now.'

I wanted to change the subject and get rid of the idea altogether but a tiny grain in what he was saying fizzed in my mind, like a crumb dropped into the glass in front of me. I laughed and it felt daring.

'If I had a time machine, I would fast forward through a year, until my life is sorted and everything's fine again.'

He gestured to the Dictaphone with its waiting red light. 'We have a time machine. Which one would it be? Back – or forwards?'

He made it sound like a Mephistophelean choice.

'What would be the point of going back?' I said. 'It has to be forwards.' I managed a half-joke. 'Then I can see it all turns out okay.'

'If it turns out okay. It might be the opposite.'

I took a drink, angrily. 'In that case, go way, way forwards. Scrap the next ten years. Drop me in when I've learned to cope again.' I needed good news, even if it was a white lie. A hope to cling to. I looked down at the tape. 'And make sure you ask me how I managed to survive.'

He refilled again, tipping the bottle high. I'd had nearly all the champagne.

He took the glass from me and drank from the opposite side. His eyes held mine over the metal spectacles.

It wasn't like school when he tried to look as though he didn't need them.

This look was intense and still.

'You must be very tired.'

The wine put me in a flamboyant mood. 'Yeah. Tired right through to the bone.'

He held the glass up between us. Amber light from the

streetlamp glowed into it and threw a column of glitter onto his face.

'Look at those bubbles. You'd think they'd all be gone by now, but they keep coming, on and on and on.'

I looked, and became quite happy to gaze into the glass. The bubbles formed slender towers, underwater volcanoes. A whole world in a column of golden liquid.

For a moment I forgot he was there. I forgot I was there too.

He spoke very quietly, barely above a whisper. 'It's like staring into a fire. On and on, always changing. Always simple. So relaxing. You could be anywhere. The years slip away. Go forward.

'What year is it?'

CHAPTER 10

It was a city, in a dome under the sea.

A voice like my own thoughts asked me what I was doing.

I was watching my companions and pretending I could do what they did. I copied their joyful smiles and lifted eyes. I imitated the way they stroked the air so lightly with their hands.

If I did this, maybe no one would see that I couldn't xech.

Outside the dome there were divers, working on the rockery of an underwater garden. One of them had a handful of eels, curling in his grasp like a bouquet of black snakes. The other planted the eels one at a time into holes in the rockery, where they stood tethered by their tails, swaying like long grass.

On this side of the dome was a wide plaza with stone seating, like a fossilised lounge. The city spread away on the ocean floor. Shopping areas, residential villas, through dome after dome to the grubbier regions deeper in.

The voice asked me what I was.

I said a soothesayer.

Soothesayers? he said. Do you mean soothsayers?

No. It was soothesayers. For the sensitive people who need their ennui calmed, and their meaning confirmed, and other discords quietened.

Shoppers in the plaza passed us, pleased to see four young soothesayers in action. Four of us were making the motions, but only three were xeching.

Xeching, I explained because the voice asked, was conjuring light seen without eyes.

I could never xech at all. I am waiting for a hand to land on me and say Stop. This is no good.

The voice asked my name. I told him it was Andreq.

The voice asked me what year it was.

We don't have years, I said. They don't like numbers here.

They prefer the ageless cycles. This is the red season. If you wait you'll see why.

Soon the sea turned from crystalline blue to red.

Crimson clouds moved in, crackling over the top of the dome. This, I informed the voice because I knew, was the time when the discarded shells migrated. Empty shells that creatures had outgrown, carried around the seas of the world in giant nebulae.

They made a noise. A concealed, scratchy whispering.

We finished our xech and walked to the monastery. Our new home.

At the entrance, people were waiting. To see the new soothesayers. They stepped back respectfully and applauded us

A senior stood in the doorway, hands clasped formally. He called out in a ringing voice. 'Before you begin your new lives here, is there any imperfection that will prevent you living productively in our soothesayer family?'

I looked at my shoes. Then raised my hand to confess.

Just at that moment, one of the bystanders staggered. I dived forwards to catch him. Other soothesayers rushed to his side. A chair was brought and he was settled in it.

'Welcome to the monastery,' said the senior. Another senior poured a line of smoke across the threshold. Each soothesayer was invited, in turn, to pass through it and the onlookers applauded.

When it was my turn, no hand fell on my shoulder to stop me. I was cheered, especially by the fainting man, who now sat comfortably in a chair.

The voice swelled into a command.

Five... four.. three... two... one... awake.

CHAPTER 11

'Where have you been?' said Gene.

I can't talk. I have to tune back into the room. The champagne bottle is on the floor. The glass is beside it, no longer in my hand. Gene still has bare feet. His arm rests along the back of the sofa.

I answer his question. 'I don't know where I was. Where did you tell me to go?'

He looks amused. 'I just set you running and asked where you'd gone. Clearly ten years into the future wasn't nearly far enough.' He picks up bottle and glass and goes into the kitchen.

The big sheet of sky outside the window is becoming paler. I've been sitting here all this time, but I don't feel like I have.

I remember Jerry's face as he woke up in Anthony Morrish's theatre. So bemused, like he didn't know where he was.

Gene comes back.

'It didn't feel like I was me,' I say. 'I was a boy. Why did you do that?'

His raised eyebrow is eloquent. 'Patients go where they need to go. You ran straight off the cliff without a moment's pause and started another life. If that's how bad it is you should get some therapy.'

Therapy? If this isn't therapy, what is it?

He lights a cigarette and takes a long drag. I remember burned feet. Not-burned feet. I can recognise he's being deliberately flip, or maybe a little bit, but I can't reply. My brain won't think that way, it's put up a skin, perhaps to recover. I look at the objects around me, try to make them solid like a crisply focused picture; the sofa; the blank walls; the paling sky. A telegraph wire is taking shape across the window, developing like a thick black line on a photo. Or should there be red shadows and fish there instead?

He's right. I don't think that was me. I was about sixteen years old. Why am I being so slow to catch up?

'Do you remember anything about hands?' he says.

'Why?'

He puts the cigarette in his left hand and tenses the fingers of his right. The tendons lift out of his skin like spokes. 'You kept doing this.'

Simply seeing it makes me pull my sleeves down to my knuckles, for protection. 'I can't do that.' I look at my knit-covered hands. 'Was I?'

'I don't suppose it's significant. It will probably hurt later.'

Gene goes to the window and opens it. He's a black shadow again, blowing smoke out of his mouth. 'Forget all that Jack the Ripper stuff you saw tonight. I've seen Anthony Morrish do Ripper regressions before. Your friend Jerry's the fifth one I've seen exactly like that.' He inhales; breathes out a long plume of smoke. 'His other party piece is patients with chronic neck and back problems. They usually say they were beheaded. The patient feels special. The therapists get rich.'

What's he trying to say? I let my hands emerge from their sleeve cocoon. 'Pain doesn't make you feel special.'

The shadow is inscrutable. 'A patient would rather believe they've got backache because they're a reincarnated spirit than because they have terrible posture or are too fat.'

My brain may have gone under the covers but I can tell he's not intrigued by me any more, not trying to play and tantalize. I'm a patient. It's like listening to Dr Golding, with his weary pronouncements. If your head hurts, stop banging it on a wall. If your hands hurt when you play, don't play. If you still want to play, that's just perverse. Try relaxing instead. I look at my watch. Nearly five.

Oh.

Gene probably intended to go to bed ages ago but he's had to deal with a mad visitor. I mumble apologies. Ask for the number of a cab company. He calls one, probably relieved. The phone's on the floor. He's had so little time to himself that he hasn't got round to unpacking a table.

As he gives the cab company instructions I wonder if I can stay awake until the car comes. It won't improve matters if I drop off to sleep.

He leans over the sofa and picks up the Dictaphone. I'd forgotten he taped us. It's as if the Dictaphone was put there a long, long time ago, like last year.

'Is it all on there?'

He nods.

'Can I take it?'

'I'll drop it round at your house. I'd like to make some notes first.'

'Why do you want to make notes?'

'I'll have finished with the tape tomorrow. Call round sometime.'

He's very good at not answering questions, says my brain, under the covers. I feel the tape's my property but I'm not up to arguing about it. It's hard to resist someone who's just been in charge of your subconscious.

A car pulls up in the street. Moments later there are footsteps and the doorbell rings.

Chapter 12

I awoke at midday. The house smelled fragrant with coffee.

Jerry didn't drink coffee; we must have visitors. I leaned over the banister and listened. The chink of plates being unloaded from the dishwasher, but no conversation. There was no one else down there but him.

I went down. He was wearing the red T-shirt, socks and jogging bottoms he usually slept in. He grinned at me and slid the drawer closed with a metallic clash.

'I have had,' he said, swinging the cutlery basket back into the machine, 'the best sleep of my entire life. Twelve hours straight, no waking up.'

I slept solidly too. Like a bulldozer. Although fewer hours.

Beside the kettle was the cafetiere. Judging by the grainy tide mark he'd already had a mug from it. I picked it up and inhaled. 'I suppose that's decaf, is it?'

The caffeine hit me like a rush of cocaine.

'No.' A challenging smile. Knowing what I'd understand from this.

Even instant coffee could give Jerry palpitations. And this stuff was strong – the packet by the kettle was labelled Java Meltdown.

I watched him pick up a mug and take a drink. 'Are you sure you should be doing that?'

A dark eyebrow rose. 'Time to see if I'm cured. Do you know I had no dreams? Just deep black sleep. As though my dreams had been emptied.'

My sleep had been dreamless – once I got back to my bed. But what happened before that lingered and nagged. As if I'd had a vivid dream about a real person I knew.

I could hardly compare it with what Jerry had been through, though.

And he was so chipper he'd soon be singing arias.

Jerry opened the oven. The buttery smell of croissants wafted out on warm air. 'Anyway, what did you get up to after I went to bed? You came back with some guy.'

'I thought you were a zombie by then,' I countered, although it was nice to see him so cheeky. 'He left as soon as you went to bed. I used to know him at school. Well, I met him once.'

Jerry picked up a piece of paper next to the kettle, waved it like evidence. 'A nice walk together in the moonlight?' It was the note I'd left for him.

I could have told him about what happened later but it seemed ... too slight? Too difficult?

Hardly worth mentioning.

'I went for a stroll,' I said. 'You creeped me out last night.'

I found myself pressed to his red chest. 'Thanks for coming.'

'Thanks for –' I didn't know where to go with the rest of the sentence – 'the ride. Where did you find a thing like that?'

'Someone on a chat forum had been to him. I've been on the waiting list for months.'

I would have asked more. But I suspected he'd told me about it before. I remembered his irritated remark as we walked along King's Road. I didn't want to deserve that again.

'I thought you were going to thingy therapy,' I said.

He released me and flipped up the lid of the bin. On top of the croissant packet was a stack of green smileys.

'Oh. I was getting used to those.'

'Therapy was a stop-gap but this is what I really wanted to do.'

'Do you think it was worth it?'

Jerry leaned back against the worktop. 'You saw what happened.'

I certainly did.

'I've always felt an affinity with Victorian London. Right from when I was small. I went through a phase where I had nightmares about Jack the Ripper. That must be why.'

He took a slurp of coffee. His eyes widened like a kid thrilled on a fairground ride. It galvanized him to check the croissants again. He pulled the tray out and turned the oven off.

I went to fetch plates. Next to the cupboard was a print of one of his pictures, a clever facsimile of a Victorian etching of a young lady sitting at a desk writing a letter. Among the cursive text of the letter there it was: *VB*.

Should I mention that? How many details did he recall from last night? And might he still be fragile if I reminded him of the wrong thing?

Or perhaps he'd told me about *VB* before and I'd failed to remember.

'Plates, my dear. Earth calling Carol.' Jerry was flourishing red oven gloves as though trying to demonstrate how well they went with his outfit. 'We need plates.'

I passed Jerry the crockery. While he picked pastries off the oven tray and squeaked at them for being hot, I poured some of the coffee. The fumes made my eyeballs tingle.

'Have you got any plans today?' he said, blowing on his fingers.

'There's a yoga class I could go to but after your x-rated coffee I might murder them all.'

'Come out with me.'

'I'm all yours.' I picked up plate and mug, went through to the dining room.

'Well I suppose you're not so busy these days,' said Jerry behind me, and I didn't know what to say to that.

'Where are we going?'

'Whitechapel,' said Jerry, putting his plate on the pine table. 'I want to find Christian Street.'

CHAPTER 13

We took the DLR to Shadwell. The train was full of Saturday people, muffled like children in bright scarves and fuzzy boots. They looked half the age of the besuited introverts who commuted home the night before. Jerry strap-hung, swinging with the movement of the train like a monkey. I wedged myself against the glass partition.

'Tell me more about your strange friend.' His eyes were buzzing with curiosity and probably also caffeine.

'You mean Gene?'

'He's a hypnotist?'

The train rattled over a set of points, which made a reply impossible. The word hypnotist conjured up swinging watches and spinning swirls. Anthony Morrish was a hypnotist. Gene worked with a finely judged gesture in a taxi cab, a casual chat about bubbles in a glass. And a bit of showmanship with a cigarette.

The train noise quieted to a dull drumming. 'Gene's a physiotherapist,' I said. 'At Guy's hospital.'

'At Guy's.' Jerry's eye had a cheeky twinkle. 'You might run into him again.'

'And he might run away. He wasn't actually a friend.'

'He seemed cute. You should branch out a little. Don't dismiss him because he isn't a musician.'

A pause while another set of points made a drum roll. 'He's not a musician but he is a medic. I've seen far too many of those recently.'

Our station glided into view, all blue and red metalwork like a Meccano set.

In the distance were the forbidding walls and roofs of the former Whitechapel Hospital, sandblasted into twenty-first century smartness. The foreground looked less cherished; a grid of low-rise, boxy flats built in the fifties and sixties.

Jerry zipped up his leather jacket and hurried down to street level, shaping his striped hat onto his head. At the bottom he waited for me, unfolded the page he'd printed from Streetmap, then crossed the road with purpose.

His whole demeanour was different now. He marched with nervous energy, taking seven-league strides in a hurry to get there. We passed a church, a modern chunk of red brick that towered over the flats. A learner driver was practising a shaky reverse manoeuvre around a corner. Up on the viaduct, the toytown DLR train rattled away.

Jerry, nose in the map, led me around a corner. We were here. Christian Street.

By a lamp post was a life-sized graffiti figure of a man with baggy trousers and a gas mask. Trails of green paint bled from its sleeves like chiffon streamers. The gas mask had been styled to look like the Elephant Man. Looking at the flats and the church, I thought that was probably as Victorian as Christian Street would get.

There was a school on one side of the road, its walls dark with soot and its window frames painted primary blue.

Its perimeter wall was white.

Jerry darted across the road and laid his hands on the wall, taking deep breaths. 'This is what I saw. Ruby wrote on a white wall.'

I thought about Gene, telling me as I tried to surface about those other Ripper regressions he'd seen. Five of them, exactly like Jerry's.

I walked away, letting Jerry take his time. Whatever the explanation for Ruby Cunningham was.

Had Gene seen any regressions like the one he did to me? Straight off the cliff and into a new life; that's what he'd said. He'd sounded surprised.

He would hardly tell me if other patients had done the same. Didn't he say we had to feel we were uniquely afflicted?

Forget what it looked like to him. What did it feel like to me?

It felt as though someone had shown me a video of myself

as a child, walking through rooms I didn't know and doing things I didn't remember. Not recognising a single thing, but wanting to know how it could be me.

Jerry beckoned me, with quick, urgent movements. 'Look.' He pointed.

I went closer. Carved into the wall was a piece of graffiti.

V loves B.

His voice was husky. 'You remember that? I saw it on the wall.'

'Yes; Violet loves B. I remember.' My voice came out peculiar as well. Small.

Jerry put his arm around my waist. The muscles under the leather sleeve were ropey with tension. 'It's really here. And I saw it in my regression. You remember me saying I saw it.'

'I remember.'

In a moment something would happen to make twenty-first century sense of this. Surely.

Jerry gave a nervous laugh and disengaged. He pulled his phone out of his pocket and primed the camera.

I started walking away. I didn't know where I was going. But there had to be a way to test this apparent proof of Jerry's reincarnation.

I came to some spiked gates. Very little of the school looked Victorian. There were green fire exit notices on the smogged walls. Yellow racks for tethering bikes.

Next to the main entrance was a black plaque with white lettering. *This building stands on the site of the Shoreditch Poorhouse, destroyed when the street was hit by a bomb in 1940.*

1940. That wall wasn't even there in 1888.

I went back to Jerry and pulled him gently away. 'Come and look at this.'

He stood in front of the plaque. Fingered his lip while his brain digested the words.

Then he walked back to *V loves B.* Traced the letters. 'I definitely saw this. How did I see it?'

I believed Jerry saw the wall. But there had to be a way to explain it. I squeezed his leather carapace. 'You may have come here before. You may have seen it in a picture. You're an artist. You've got a visual memory. When you need to flesh out details to make a picture authentic, you pluck them out of your head. You can't possibly remember where they all came from.'

He nodded, but as though he didn't understand.

I began to see other graffiti on the wall. They were fainter than V and B, but still visible as impressions in the paint. Initials in a heart: *DM*. And, near that, *Sarah*. Further along there were marks that looked like the initials of football teams. This was a place where people stood around and killed time.

I rested my chin on his shoulder. 'Jerry, you had me going there, but I think we are looking at an old bus stop.'

CHAPTER 14

We walked back to the DLR in silence and climbed the Meccano stairs to the platforms. A train pulled up and we got on. Back to the west, into the setting sun. The pointed towers of the City were turning black as the sky bruised into sunset behind them. Jerry looked back, trying to keep his eyes on Christian Street as it receded in the hotch-potch of shoebox buildings. The train descended, sinking between concrete walls into the Bank tunnel.

Jerry's face was a blank mask, as if he was diverting all resources inwards to grapple with ideas he found impossible.

I touched his leather-armoured shoulder. 'You okay?'

He nodded, then gazed at the black tunnel wall.

My fingers in my pocket found my glove.

I remembered another fragment of the previous night. Gene had told me I was clenching my hands. Was this what I was struggling to remember? I tried closing my fist in my pocket.

It was immediately unpleasant, just as he'd said it would be. Like one of Dr Golding's tests. And the flare of pain that remained in my hand warned me not to do it again.

It seemed the most graspable memory I had of what I did last night, and it was impossible. Like Ruby Cunningham.

Jerry was leaning on the glass partition, studying the floor. Maybe one day he and I would look back on this weekend with wry wisdom.

Do you remember the time when we discovered we had other lives?

Yeah, what a trip.

At Bank we climbed through the warrens to the Tube. Jerry turned and enveloped me in a hug. A sadder hug. 'I'm supposed to meet Tim and some of his friends in Leicester Square now. Will you be okay getting home?'

I nodded into his shoulder. 'I'll be fine. See you later. And go easy on the coffee.'

The crowds streamed around us, eager and bold for Saturday evening out on the town. Jerry smiled faintly and turned away, not quite moving to the same beat as the rest of them. He split off to follow the red signs to the Central Line and I went the black way to the Northern.

I emerged in Clapham to the mass Saturday homecoming. Cars stood outside every house, doors open and hatchbacks lifted as if co-ordinated by a military operation. People unloaded shopping and guided hesitating toddlers into open front doors.

I walked fast, eager to get back to the treat of an empty house, to open the door, to unlock my piano room, sit on the stool, lift the gleaming black lid of my Yamaha and spread my hands on the keys. Although my practice room was soundproofed, although Jerry always said my playing didn't disturb him, it was particularly delicious to have the house to myself.

I think it was Pavlovian, from when I was at school. An empty house meant liberation; no listeners to judge my experiments, no one who would automatically say 'that sounds nice dear' when I knew it was rubbish, no one who would mind if I repeated the same figure again and again. I didn't have to worry about listeners when the house was empty.

Then half-way down Nightingale Lane my brain caught up with my marching feet and said, why are you hurrying?

I reached my road. I walked on, up the hill, past the darkened common where a couple walked hip to hip over the railway bridge.

If Gene Winter was in, I could collect my tape and be out of his hair so I didn't disrupt whatever plans he had for the evening.

CHAPTER 15

I reached Elliston Road. The window in Gene's upper-storey flat was still curtainless. I could see the bare bulb of the central ceiling light and two arches leading into other rooms.

I rang the bell. In the room above, a shadow passed across the ceiling, then became footsteps on the stairs.

Did he have someone else up there? I looked for more shadows moving in the room but couldn't see any.

He opened the door in jeans and a knotty black jumper. The grey eyes greeted me with curiosity.

I said: 'I was on my way home and I wondered if you'd finished with the tape yet?'

The words came out sounding like I meant something else.

'Sure. Come on up.'

His feet were bare again. I remembered him stubbing out that cigarette and tried to look at the soles as he walked up ahead of me. But I was too close. If I stopped on the stairs and fiddled with my boot I might be able to look up and get a glimpse, but he'd look round with those penetrating eyes and I'd be rumbled instantly. So I followed at a normal distance.

They were strong-looking feet, the kind that went with his lean frame.

His living room looked as bare as the previous night. Maybe he'd been too busy today to unpack anything more. Two arches at one end led away to other rooms. He went through one of them and came back with my tape. It was tiny, the size of a matchbox.

'I listened to it this morning. It was interesting. You'll need one of those old Dictaphones to play it on.'

It was interesting. So few words, but they seemed sharper than all the others. I wanted to know what he meant. How, exactly, was it interesting? List the ways. What was it telling him? List those too.

What could I ask him about them? I could mention my hands, because that was concrete and medical, but would he give me a dismissive answer about gullible people believing in Ripper regressions? I knew all that logical stuff on one level, but I still craved answers. An expert's analysis. Or he might tell me I was way off the scale and should get proper therapy.

And so I also wanted to slip home with no fuss, maybe listen to the tape again by myself.

I took the tape from him and slipped it into my bag. 'I've got a Dictaphone at home for practising. I can play it on that. Thanks.' I turned to go.

'For practising?' he said.

I nodded, my fingers curling around the strap of my handbag as I prepared to move back down the stairs. 'I tape myself playing.'

'How narcissistic. Do you want tea?'

His response, apart from the offer of tea, was typical of non-musicians, although most people don't say it out loud. Musicians tape themselves to develop a critical ear. Often the way you think you're playing is not what you're actually playing – just as your voice sounds different on a tape from the way it is in your head.

And then there was the offer of tea.

I could go – back to an empty house I couldn't use – or I could stay.

'Tea sounds nice,' I said, 'if you can bear the company of a narcissistic artist.'

I slipped my bag off my shoulder, put it on the sofa and followed him through to the kitchen. I nearly walked into him; the kitchen was tiny like the cooking quarters on a ship. Like the living room, it was completely bare. There were no stray plates or teaspoons or even storage jars; just brushed steel units like a surgeon's scrub room. Even the champagne glass from last night wasn't in evidence. In our house it wouldn't be washed up for days.

I leaned against the arch. 'Okay, you've heard my secret. What do you use tapes for?'

'Oh I tape myself talking.'

He no doubt expected my blank reaction; and sure enough he got it.

'About patients. I use them for dictating referral letters.'

'That sounds more grown-up than playing the piano,' I said.

He handed me a white mug of tea. He didn't make one for himself, just indicated we should go back into the living room.

He put out the central light, switched on a floor lamp and sat on the window sill.

The street light from outside was stronger than the floor lamp, turning him into a shadow.

'When I heard you at Kate's party,' he said, 'I thought it must be fantastic being able to play like that.' Don't say it, I thought, but he did. 'Such a gift.'

Every time we talked we ended up in conflict. What happened to reunion protocol where you asked someone what they were up to, who else they'd seen and so on.

'What about medicine?' I countered. 'That must be a gift.'

'Why?'

'Why? You can make a big difference to people. They're actually grateful.'

'Maybe. So are you famous?'

Several phrases leaped into my mind, the usual stuff about bleak concert venues, the grind of careers and hard work. But he was obviously jerking my chain.

I said: 'You should take a leaf out of Anthony Morrish's book. He'll probably have his own chat show in a year.'

I moved off the sofa and sat in the opposite corner of the window, where I could see him in the light. So that it wasn't like being interrogated by someone whose identity was being protected for security reasons.

Gene's grey eyes under the strong brows narrowed. Telling me he knew what was in my head when I did that. As if I'd made an interesting move in a game.

I took a sip. The tea was fiercely hot. At this rate it would take me all evening to drink it.

Perhaps if I told him about Jerry being better, I could bring the conversation around to my hands. Keep it logical and medical; and then he could tell me what made him describe the tape as interesting, although perhaps I didn't want to know that.

'Speaking of patients,' I said, 'Jerry's cured.'

Whatever made me say it like that? I didn't think of Jerry as a patient. So much for my attempt to restore the power balance in the conversation; now it was as if Gene's thought processes had taken over my vocabulary. If he'd been in charge of that yoga class telling me to think of nothing, I'd have been well away; mind as blank as the white mug in my hands.

'Jerry's cured?' said Gene.

'He woke up this morning and said he was cured. He even drank coffee. He's avoided coffee for years but this morning he had about three espressos. I'm waiting for him to go into orbit. Then this afternoon I went with him to visit the scene of his death.'

Gene propped one foot on the table in front of us. It wasn't the one he trod on the cigarette with.

I had to stop thinking about that; he would be too pleased if he knew.

'Jerry doesn't look like your type,' he said.

How arrogant. I smiled over the mug. 'Oh yes? And who is?'

'His mind works in a very visual way. You don't.'

It seemed rather a personal remark. 'What do you mean?'

I had another go at the scalding hot tea. Why wasn't he having one too? Like with the lone glass of champagne last night it added to the feeling that I was being observed in some way. While he dug and prodded to see what wound me up.

Maybe when he met me at Kate Rafferty's party he didn't like me.

Gene bent behind the sofa to reach into a packing crate. 'Close your eyes.' He came out with his hands behind his back. I watched him with open-eyed defiance.

'Close your eyes.'

Nothing was going to happen unless I played along. I decided to humour him.

I heard him place something on the table in front of me.

'Keep your eyes closed.'

Actually, I couldn't have opened my eyes even if I wanted to. A cold little tremor went through me. What if he told me I couldn't see and left me like that? Don't be silly. I was at school with him – virtually – and anyway he's taken the Hippocratic Oath. Or has he? He's not on duty. Does it count?

'Without opening your eyes, pick it up.'

I pawed the air cautiously. My fingers touched the wood of the table, slightly rough. I walked them forwards, like a crab. A rattle of plastic as I knocked something and it skated across the wood. I grasped for it and it fitted my hand. A familiar shape.

'Keep your eyes closed. Let your hands tell you what it is. Let your fingers tell you what to do.'

Buttons along one side. Seams in the plastic. A deeper groove like an opening. A window of smoother plastic, through which I might see wheels turning.

I said: 'It's a Dictaphone.'

A musical phrase came into my head. One I'd been working on before my playing ban. Listening to on my iPod as I travelled to my tutor's house in Sutton.

I opened my eyes. The phrase was still with me. 'Did you know,' I said, 'the opening run from Robert Schumann's C Major Fantasy is the same as the beginning of *I Will Survive*?'

Gene sat opposite me on the window sill, one arm folded across his chest, one hand supporting his sharp chin. Watching me. 'Is it?'

I sang it to him to demonstrate and my fingers played the table, starting at the bottom of the piano and rippling up. My nails clicked on the wood.

A sound all pianists hate. I stopped and looked at them.

'You know, every time I look at my hands, my nails have grown. They don't look like my hands any more. I keep cutting my nails as often as I always did but they keep growing.'

'You're not wearing them down now you're not playing.'

I didn't want to be a person who doesn't play. My nails were getting long. Like corpses' nails, growing in the grave. I was going to seed. All the nerve pathways shrivelling, all the fast-twitch muscle fibres slowing.

I tried to laugh, put a brave face on it. 'There's an old saying. If you don't practise for a day, you know it. If you don't practise for two days your friends know it. If you don't practise for three days, the audience will know it.'

I tried the Schumann phrase again. My reactions were sluggish, a couple of seconds behind my brain. I lost the rhythm and finished in a pile-up of notes.

'I don't think you should be doing that,' said Gene.

I tried again. My fingers wouldn't obey me.

'Don't do that,' Gene shifted off the window sill, leaned across the table and closed his hands around mine. My fingers struggled in his grasp. I couldn't leave it until I'd got it right.

'Stop,' he said, grey eyes firm. 'You might make it worse.'

'I'm not hitting the keys, there's no impact.'

'It's not just impact, it's the whole system. The micro movements are as damaging.'

He squeezed my fingers together so I could no longer move them, stood up and pulled me away from the table. Across the room to the sofa. Guiding me to sit down. I let him lead me. I was wrecked. It wasn't even a difficult phrase but I was playing it like an amateur.

He was next to me, his hands still around mine. 'Look at me.' His grey eyes demanded my attention. 'That's good. And stop trying to play. I can feel it. Look at me. Imagine you've done it, you've played the piece well. You've played the last note and you've taken your hands off the keyboard.'

I tried but the little voice of perfection raged inside me. Screamed.

'Look at me.' Gene's voice was patient and calm. 'You've finished the piece. You're sitting at the stool, you've taken your hands off the keys. You feel good and calm. Think of the last chord you played. It's inside the piano, in its wooden body. You can still hear it.'

He had stolen into my head like a thief. I forgot I was in a room in a bleak flat. My perception shrank to his hands on mine, and those dying sounds inside the piano. I never closed the lid until they'd totally gone.

Gene didn't move at all; he kept my hands imprisoned.

'Hear those notes dying away. It's the end of the piece. You feel calm. You are happy to sit there, with the last notes hanging in the strings and the wood.'

I was.

'It spreads out, thinner and thinner. Even when you can't hear it, that last note is there, like a ghost. That note you sent into the world. Every event sends a ripple, however imperceptible, into the future.

'As it goes you can travel with it. Be somewhere else.

'Where are you?'

Chapter 16

Tape 2

Where are you?
    Visiting a client.
Tell me about your hands.
    My hands?
Tell me about your hands.
    They are small. Pliable.
Are they painful?
    No. Why?
Tell me what you are doing.

I am visiting a client in her villa. It has a private sea garden – a wall of coral and waving plants and, in the centre, a bowl containing a shoal of red dots. They are bloodfish; their bodies invisible so that all that can be seen is tiny red organs in a cluster. Kaleidoscoping, flowering, inverting, like a changing rose. If they become ill, their bodies appear in a ghostly outline.

These fish are the subject of my client's ennui.

The client is expensively sensitive. She is wearing a pink tracksuit and her satin-shod feet whisper on the marble floor. The pink is startling, but that may be because I've started wearing chromatic contact lenses. The blue sea light is harsh on skin tones and makes people look like ghosts. It's bad manners to behold a woman without colour correction.

The client doesn't say hello. She finishes talking on her cell, sinks into the sofa cushions with her eyes closed and addresses me loudly.

'I have had such a bad morning. My husband is being impossible. I've just bought those bloodfish and we had an argument about them. I said, look at them, aren't they beautiful, a cloud of tiny hearts swimming around. He said those little red dots are the spleen, not the heart. I said what would be the point of having the spleen showing, who wants to see that? How could he say that? He is so insensitive.'

Her husband is right. Soothesayers learn about biology and I know for a fact that the red spots in the bloodfish are the spleen, not the heart.

But my job is not to educate her. I stand with my hands folded into my sleeves, and play the opening moves of the soothe.

'It is so difficult sometimes. Life can be so upsetting. That is why it is so important to have this time to recharge and restore equilibrium.'

She stretches out her feet, expecting me to hold them. I kneel on the rug in front of her, supple my hands to reassure her I am prepared, then pick up her feet and wrap my fingers around them. This is to drain some of her negative energy.

She isn't looking at me. Her attention is still on the bloodfish in the bowl. 'Which would you want to look at? A shoal of hearts? Or a shoal of spleens? Spleen is offal.' She points at the bloodfish. 'These fish came from Kartorzes salon. They wouldn't sell fish that looked like a shoal of offal. Would they?'

Anatomically, both are offal, but it is not soothing for her to be told that. I say: 'Kartorzes sell such beautiful animals. And not many people realise that. You must have excellent taste.'

'They don't sell to everybody. I had to pass several checks before I was allowed to even look at the merchandise.'

This is an opportunity for a really successful soothe. 'I knew Kartorzes were very discerning, but I didn't realise how stringent they were. What did they make you do?'

She describes, with satisfaction, a succession of meetings with Kartorzes staff, from junior saleswoman up to maitre, in which she seems to have impressed them by being rude and boasting about her wealth.

Once she has finished I say: 'You clearly will do their reputation nothing but good. They will have been so very pleased to have your custom.'

She sits back in the creamy cushions, satisfied. But not for long. She sighs and puts on her sad, disturbed face again. 'This weather's been so changeable. There are too many of these red clouds. That shouldn't be happening.'

I am not sure where to take this and need to explore further. I open with a general reply.

'It is difficult for us all right now.'

'No,' she says firmly, her hand across her forehead as if a headache is developing. 'I really do find it difficult. My friend was complaining because she found red shells in her garden. But that's of no consequence, it's what you pay gardeners for. Those red clouds irritate my nerves. It's the noise. I simply can't function.'

Now I know what this is about. She doesn't want to be told that everyone finds it hard and therefore she is normal.

'You must be particularly sensitive. That is a rare quality.'

Our eyes meet. Direct hit. 'I think you're right. It is a rare quality. People have said that to me often but I don't think it myself.'

She sits back looking at the ceiling as she thinks about my words some more. 'Yes I think it is rare. Just the sight of those clouds makes me feel ill. I was shopping yesterday and I saw some and I had to come home.' She looks at me, my cue to say more.

I don't think the flattery will spin any further. I need a different route to continue this soothe. 'I think,' I say, 'you are also going through a period of mild melancholy.'

She receives this news with interest. 'Oh. Melancholy. I wonder what could have caused that?'

'Is there anything that's happened, anything that's bothering you?'

'Not that I can think of.'

'It might be something so inconsequential.'

She lists the tiny irritations in her life that might be making her melancholy. I listen, still holding her feet. She clenches and stretches her toes as she talks. When she has exhausted all the possibilities she says: 'I think I need a treatment'.

I nod. 'Metamorphosis would suit you. Have you had that before?'

'What is it?'

'It's one of the ancient therapies. You might have a short-circuit in your energy flow. This will help unblock it.'

I begin to rub her foot.

'When will I feel it start to work? It's not doing anything.'

'You may feel a number of things, but it's individual to everyone. After about a week you might have more vivid dreams.'

She pulls her foot away. 'I can't wait that long. I'd rather xech.'

Of course she would.

I reply: 'That's unwise. The energy block might go all the way back to when you were born and only be coming out now.'

'I'd rather xech.'

What I do in situations like this is try to get her to xech on her own.

'How did your previous soothesayer do it before? Did you xech and he watched? Or...'

'We xeched. Together. Like anybody would.' She smoothes her pink sleeves down her arms and composes herself with deep breaths.

I fiddle with my case of tinctures. Sometimes they start xeching without me. Then they get so well away they don't notice that I haven't.

She opens her eyes. 'When you're ready.'

I have no alternative but to begin.

There is a small moment when her face is serene. Then she screws up her eyes and her mouth.

I stop immediately. Not that I thought I was doing anything. But she blocks her ears and screams.

'Stop it! Stop it now!'

'I have stopped,' I reply.

I expect she will shout at me. Instead she slumps back against the pale cushions, breathing hard as if she's had a fright.

I'd better sort this out. 'You must be exceptionally sensitive. This is the hallmark of a truly gifted xecher. The melancholy can occasionally have these effects. That was why I felt metamorphosis would be suitable.'

She's looking dazed, as though she's been deafened. I try to add weight to the soothe. 'Episodes like this, although challenging, confirm to us the true nature of xeching. We all assume it is harmless and everyday, but we are using a power that is very potent.'

She nods, looking at the visor hand.

I can risk a little more. I add: 'Remember xeching comes from the ancient sensory passageways of the brain.'

She does not answer. I look at the time. We have had an hour. I close my case and stand up.

'This is a good place to end the session. If I were you I would not xech again for a few days and when you do, do it just for a short period and in the presence of good friends. It will probably be absolutely fine.'

'Goodbye,' she replies curtly, and shows me to the door.

I hope I haven't hurt her, or deafened her. Or whatever a bad xech can do.

I find a taxi. The city slips by in a blur of lights. I hope she won't complain. But the rest of the soothe was faultless, apart from the xech.

Some children are xeching before they learn to talk. I have no recollection of ever doing it. Did I miss a vital lesson? If that were true, it might give me hope.

Or is something broken inside me?

The rest of the day is art lessons. We work in a classroom, heads bent over desks, sculpting wet balls of clay. We are to make tiny busts as a new type of therapy for clients who wish to be congratulated by their deeper selves.

The classroom is at the bottom of the monastery, on a ledge where the sea floor plummets into the deep intercontinental ocean. Pearly globes throw soft light over the bowed heads of the other soothesayers.

The soothesayer next to me is bigger than the others. The roof of the room is low and she has to bow her head to fit between the desk and the low ceiling. The fabric of her robes stretches across her back and the bumps of her spine. Her name is Luna and she is having corrective sessions.

The slip of our fingers and thumbs on wet clay. The heartbeat boom of the shifting sea. The hair-scratch of fishbones on paper as we make notes.

The art tutor clambers between us, whispering criticism.

He inspects the work of the big girl, Luna. 'Too lifelike. Often the client will not be good starting material.'

He comes to mine. 'Very nice. Very soothing.'

The big girl glares at me. The tutor pads on through the room.

Something hits me. A piece of paper, scrunched into a ball.

The big girl is looking at me. A cocked eyebrow invites me to uncrumple it.

It's a note, written with a fishbone.

You may be a genius at soothing, but they know you can't xech. How long do you think you can carry on?

'Novices,' calls the tutor, 'the red season will be over soon, and the clients will be most soothed by being told they are nobler for what they have endured. Your sculptures must be a lasting testament to their bravery.'

I crumple the paper, look out of the window and lock my eyes into the liquid midnight of the abyssal plain.

It looks like the weightless dark of the deep ocean, except for the amber ball of light. A barefoot shadow walks in front of it, quiet but not as soundless as a soothesayer. Not as small either; tall and lean, its outline enlarged and roughened by a jumper.

'Are you back?' says Gene.

CHAPTER 17

He lifts the glass. Cut crystal catches the light like a Morse signal.

Car doors slam in the road below. Footsteps tap across pavements, crunch on gravel paths. There is a mug on the table in the window. Everything in the room seems like black paper cut-outs against a background of grey. No colour anywhere but the amber street lamps outside.

Gene clicks the light on. The window turns into a black mirror. I see my face, pale with big eyes, my hair a dark curly cloud in a vaguely triangular shape and a big pale scarf, which makes the hair look bigger and wider than it really is. Behind me the bare white walls.

I suppose I must be 'back'.

I feel hung over. Not in a painful way; the kind when your brain re-evaluates every sensation like a learning spy.

Gene is drinking whisky. He is pacing up and down, crystal glass in one hand, telling me the soothesayers are so true to life, the woman in the rich villa is exactly like some of the fussy, stupid people he treats time and again. That it is like I've been inside his head.

My reflection in the black glass smiles at me. Touche. Thought I'd return the compliment, after you told me about the notes fading through the body of the piano.

Where did it come from, he's saying. His voice roughens for a few seconds each time the whisky wakes up his throat. Have you been to someone like that? No I haven't. It just came from – well, wherever it all came from. Except I can't say that, it's too much to load into the brain and send out through the mouth. And I feel like I shouldn't discuss Andreq in that way, as if he might come back into the room and demand to know why we're talking about him.

I shake my head sagely while Gene paces up and down, my

white face in the window moving in curly dark hair. I'd like to know where he got the image about the piano.

He's amused, enjoying himself. It makes a change. Up to now, it felt as if everything he did was like a move in a chess game, calculated and the results observed. Right now it's all very pleasant and relaxed, even if I'm ninety per cent dumbstruck and he's pacing like he's on a sponsored walk. At least we're connecting somehow.

That's all a musician tries to do; connect. Send the spark to jump the gap in an unexpected synapse, create the twist of longing. Communication beyond words. I love music. It is a direct line into the emotional centre of the world.

'Have some,' he says, and hands me the whisky glass while he looks for cigarettes. It smells like caramel and tar. Is it all right to drink, I wonder, then try some anyway. It's a liquid blowtorch.

'How charming; you're a whisky virgin,' says Gene, blowing out a tower of smoke.

He volunteers, before I can ask, that this time I kept my hands still and didn't do anything therapeutically unlawful. It must be because I've settled more into it. I know he asked about them, how clever of him to know, but I can't actually say that. Listening to what he's saying is absorbing all brain power, like taking notes in a lecture.

He's positively garrulous, though; can't stop him talking. And then he tells me he's moving out tomorrow and I must visit him. Moving out a long way, apparently, to somewhere on the coast, part of a job swap where he can run a department.

And after that the details get fuzzy because my brain stops accepting input.

He's going; that's a pity. He says come to see him, but they all say that. Everyone knows we'll all be too busy to do it. The musician's social diary is littered with encounters that would have been more if we'd all managed to stay in the same place instead of buggering off to a faraway part of the country. Or, in the case of Karli, a different country altogether.

Gene calls a taxi for me and sees me out, giving me his

mobile number on a piece of paper and promising to post me the tape, but that's it.

'Good luck,' says my befuddled brain to him as I get in the taxi and give the driver my address.

The house is dark when I unlock the door. It still smells of coffee from this morning. That makes it seem like the wrong house because we hardly ever make coffee. Jerry is still out; hopefully that means the evening is going well.

I put the hall light on. A deluge of leaflets has come through the door from pizza makers, cleaning services and taxi firms. I take them straight to the bin. As they slither in, one of them richochets onto the floor. I pick it up.

Nobody can beat Maria. Born gifted!!!! Results: believable.

Maria, it goes on to say, *has the high knowledge of removing problems from people in SEVEN days. For example, business, financial, depression, domestic problems regarding husband, wife, children, exams, court cases, immigration, hair grow, lose weight and sexual impotence or several other problems. Maria's work is 100 per cent guaranteed. Breaking black magic and evil spirits in 48 hours. If any healer has left your work incomplete or unsuccessful see Maria immediate.*

Incomplete or unsuccessful. Your timing is uncanny, Maria, and so is your English, but no more spooky, gifted people for me. I crumple the card into the bin, hunch over to the sofa, lever my boots off and go to sleep.

I heard a key in the lock. Laughter. Jerry shouldered the door open and came in backwards, leading a dance partner onto the floor. On the other end of that guiding leather arm was Tim. I sat up, prising my eyes open and blinking away the grit that had settled behind my contact lenses.

Jerry noticed me as he pushed the door shut.

'Sorry for waking you,' he said, in a quiet voice like he was saying shhh. He was wearing a striped scarf I didn't recognise.

It must be Tim's. Tim was wearing Jerry's striped hat.

As they took their coats off and hung them by the door they bumped into each other a lot, laughing.

'Drink, Carol?' said Jerry.

'No I'm beat,' I replied, and said good night, saying it especially to Tim to make up for the banshee reception he got last time.

I went into the kitchen for a glass of water. Jerry, blissful with success, followed and hugged me with one arm as he got out glasses and a bottle of red. I squeezed him goodnight and went up.

I hadn't intended to listen to the tape that evening. But sleep refused to come. From downstairs I could hear *Mad World* sung very slowly like a lullaby. Jerry and Tim were no longer talking. I put the bedside lamp on, took the headphones from my iPod and loaded the Dictaphone with the tape of the first session.

There was Gene, talking about the bubbles in the glass. I don't know why but I hadn't expected that to be on there. But then I don't know what I expected instead.

His voice had total confidence, like I was an instrument and he was its player. I'd never heard anyone talk like that.

I tilted one headphone out of my ear. Café del Mar was still lulling in the depths of the house. I kept it that way, like having one hand on a lifebelt. Well suppose I fell into a trance again, who would get me out? I imagined Jerry dialling Gene's number: can you come and help, Carol's stuck.

Gene's voice stopped talking about the champagne bubbles.

What year is it?

It wasn't gently leading any more. It made me feel chilly.

And I jumped off the cliff.

We don't have years. This is the red season.

When the tape finished, I slipped the headphones out of my ears. Downstairs was silent. Trees rustled outside the window, like someone sighing in their sleep and turning over.

Where had it come from, Gene had said as he paced the room, swirling the whisky glass.

Jerry conjured Ruby from his history books, from training himself in every detail until he could draw Victorian London as authentically as his real life. But what on earth made Andreq?

Some of it was clear enough. The discipline, the anxiety. The extraordinary light in the rooms – I went to St Ives once and the streets had that same luminous quality. Living under the sea? Was that from too much media nagging about global warming?

Ah, though, Gene had said he was moving away to the coast. He could have put it in my head. Probably not in an obvious way, he was too clever for that. It wouldn't be something I could spot when I played the tape back.

So I was channelling Gene Winter. Should I feel duped? I would if he'd looked smug about it like Anthony Morrish. He'd actually looked quite surprised. But I've probably got a head start. When you work with duet partners you can develop near-telepathy.

Although it usually took a few weeks.

That was obviously the answer. And where did all that soothesayer, healer stuff come from if it wasn't from him?

I thought my voice on the tape might sound sleepy, but it was wide awake and lucid. And I wouldn't have known it was me. Normally when I've heard tapes of myself it's been embarrassing. I sound exactly like a posh girl who's been cosseted at music school. A Julie Andrews who's never acquired the street-cred rough edges that develop in a properly misspent teenage-hood.

This voice I heard on the tape had a different accent. It was a little bit foreign, but no region that I could identify. And deeper in tone; like hearing a violin part played by a viola.

I could think of logical explanations for everything I'd seen and heard. But not for this feeling it gave me. As if I'd been shown a video of myself as a child, and was wondering how it could possibly have been me.

CHAPTER 18

My school had a building that used to be a convent.

Some of my classmates remembered the nuns. Their older sisters used to watch them from the window of the sixth form common room.

Most of the convent was screened by trees. The watching girls saw only arrivals and departures at the front door, but that was enough. They fretted about why young women chose to deliver themselves there, to robe themselves like nurses from World War One, away from men and make-up, TV and university.

Once the school took possession of the building, we scrutinised every room. Stains on the French room floor must be evidence of abortions. A bricked up doorway in the language lab must have been sealed because a nun hanged herself.

The building certainly had an atmosphere. The thick walls were a hood of silence the moment you passed through the door. The staff loved it. Languages and drama on the ground floor and music on the floor above. You could have several pupils bashing pianos and the choir in full cry, and they could barely hear each other.

Those walls not only swallowed all sound, they kept the building cold.

The coldest room was the Broadwood piano practice room. I had special permission to practise in there, a privilege as the Broadwood was a fine instrument. Even in high summer, with fierce sunshine outside, I had to keep the light on and wear my blazer. There was a window, but it was high up the wall, narrow like a letterbox and nearly enclosed by ivy. As I played I could hear the rest of my class chatting on the lawn by the head's study, lazed out and sunbathing.

But there was no sun inside the Broadwood room. It was like a Druid tomb built with eerie awareness of where the sun rose and fell. I used to think as I played my scales that maybe there was one day in the year when the light would blaze in. It would be early one morning, at the winter solstice when the school was closed for the holidays. The dawn would rise and spread through the room in a heavenly flash. Then it would go dark for another year.

I was, of course, the biggest music nerd in the school. I was quiet at all times except when sitting at an instrument. By the age of eight, the teachers were saying I was gifted. The other girls didn't care about gifts, other than to resent them. They knew I was the only one who wasn't watching the new soap *EastEnders*. The only girl who didn't have an opinion on the merits of Jason Connery versus Michael Praed.

At the age of eight I played a star turn in the school Easter recital. In the interval the headmistress praised my performance to my piano teacher. 'It's a gift from God,' she gushed, 'Carol is so lucky.'

Kate Rafferty, much more feral in those days, was standing nearby, making barfing expressions behind the silly woman's back. I agreed with her, only I couldn't say because I had the head's eyeline. I endured these comments and more with a desperate smile, while Kate watched with a fomenting expression.

By the end of the concert, Kate's friends had been briefed about the prodigy in their midst and were acting on her ennui. To make it worse they saw me get into my piano teacher's car, as she was giving me a lift home. They whispered about teacher's pets and mummy's darlings.

I didn't want to get a lift with a teacher, but my mother and father hadn't come to the recital. They didn't come to school events. They refused invitations to parents' evenings, prize-givings and similar gatherings.

That was the way it was in our house. They ran a plastics factory, twenty-five miles away in a suburb of Manchester, and the last thing they wanted was extra obligations or meetings. I knew when I let myself in through the back door I'd find them sitting at their habitual ends of the Chesterfield sofa in the drawing room watching the news in uncompanionable silence.

The county music festival was coming up and I didn't expect they would come to that either. It was on Saturday morning, when they went to Sainsbury's. I knew that they would have to discuss soon who was going to drive me there and pick me up and I was dreading it because they usually argued about tasks like that. I wished I could get there by myself, but our house was at the end of a secluded road outside the village, too remote to walk from at the age of eight.

Despite the trouble that the festival would cause, they did seem to approve of me spending so much time on the piano. I think they liked it when I was occupied for long hours.

I played in the county music festival and won a prize. It was announced in assembly and the school had to applaud. Kate and the others were sitting along the row from me, clapping in a deliberate rhythm, a curl of the lip promising that later I would pay for those congratulations. I did, and for the other prizes that followed.

After a while we reached an equilibrium. They stopped bothering to trip me up or trying to break my fingers in games lessons, and there were a few of us loners who were always the last to be partnered in lab experiments. But then adolesence dawned.

While I used the Broadwood room at lunchtime, Kate and the others developed a taste for sunbathing on the lawn and an awareness of their tanned bodies – and a new curiosity about the girl who didn't do that.

They knew about each other's social lives, but they didn't know about me. Few of them had been inside my home. They were often asking me where it was and how big it was. Whether I was having a birthday party. When I replied that I wasn't, they would turn away smirking, making me feel I'd leaped into a trap.

Sometimes through the letterbox that led to the sunlit world, I could hear them. Wondering why I preferred to shut myself in the Broadwood room, as their older sisters before them had speculated about nuns shunning the world. They thought I couldn't hear them.

That's when I got my head down and worked like stink to get into Chet's.

CHAPTER 19

Victoria looked surprised to see me. 'You came!'

I handed over wine and a card. 'Happy birthday.'

She put a tray of mini-pizzas in the oven and knocked over a packet of oboe reeds which she tried to pick up, still wearing oven gloves.

Oboe reeds next to the olive oil. Scraps of manuscript pinned to the message board. It was so long since I'd been in the house of someone whose life was governed by music.

Her tiny flat was already crowded. People had spilled out of the kitchen and lounge and were standing in the hall chatting.

I dropped off my jacket in the bedroom. Most of the guests were in the Jubilee Orchestra, a small outfit I'd played with the previous year. The carpet was a sea of instruments, leaving a narrow walkway to the coat-piled bed.

All those black cases, battered from years of going wherever their owners did, kneecapping people on the Tube, bumping up escalators, sliding around the back of a tour van. Timelessly shaped pieces of luggage that shared their owners' travels like a sorcerer's familiar. They had been stacked in an orderly way, too. Violins, violas, cellos and basses propped together to make a bulbous family. The brass section, all flares and curls, like an archaeologist's haul of ammonites and ear-bones.

A Korean guy with small glasses and a wide pumpkin face arrived at the same time as me. He tossed a jacket on the bed and noticed my lack of baggage.

'You travel light too?'

'Pianist,' I said.

'Timpanist,' he replied.

At least I felt normal not having an instrument to drop off. So far, so okay.

In the kitchen, the second violin, Martin, was standing at the fridge and there wasn't room for anyone to get around him, so he was handing out wine. When he saw me he was eager to tell me what I'd missed since I left.

'You didn't meet Calum, the new musical director, did you? He has all this modern stuff he's composed. For ten minutes all I play is A flat in little bursts syncopated with the piano. It sounds like a car alarm.'

Fred, the cellist, reached over my head for a glass from Martin. 'Carol, why aren't you with us suffering Calum's Te Deum?'

'Tedium,' grunted Martin.

I tried to look triumphant to have been spared.

In the living room, it was like winding time back a year. The orchestra members decompressing after a heavy week.

'Trevor was so loud in the adagio that I couldn't hear myself.'

'Jo's going to the Halle next month and Calum doesn't know.'

Fred the cellist told me his duet partner was diagnosed with ME, did I know anyone who could step in? He meant me. I told some fibs about helping out Ed and Danya at the Garland Ensemble.

Always make it sound as though you're busy, gloriously fit and in demand.

Several glasses on, I'd acquired a lot of email addresses and phone numbers. And heard rumours about Fred's duet partner. She would be ill for two weeks, six months, was bedridden, had AIDS.

At least I was able to get out and speak for myself. I eked out my cover story about the Garland Ensemble.

The first line of *Happy birthday to you* came out of the bedroom, played on a lone violin. The double bass thumped a reply.

'The neighbours,' gasped Victoria, and bustled into the bedroom. There was a great call of 'surprise'.

I glimpsed instrument cases split open to reveal velvet interiors like lodes of amethyst, sapphire and ruby. About twenty players were in there, squashed in corners and standing on the bed, playing happy birthday to Victoria.

The Korean timpanist looked towards the players wistfully. 'Why didn't I learn the recorder?'

A skinny girl in a pink scarf muttered in an American accent about wanting to miniaturise her harp.

We kidnapped a bottle of acrid wine, formed a clique beside the oven, the exiles hunkering down to bond. I prepared to make more conversation about Ed and Danya and I couldn't do it.

So I said: 'Do you think it would be cool to live under the sea?'

'Where would you do that?' said the American harpist.

I said, 'I don't know. In the future. It's just an idea.'

The timpanist said: 'There was an article about it in *Scientific American*, did you see it? They were saying people might have to go under the sea because of the hole in the ozone layer. The water is a natural UV shield.'

'I've never read *Scientific American*. I was thinking people might do it as a back-to-the-womb lifestyle. Like those David Attenborough programmes. The blue light, the way the fishes move. It's soothing.'

'So would we have diving suits?' said the harpist.

'No,' said the timpanist, 'it'd be whole cities, all covered and sealed like the Eden Project. Or Centre Parcs.'

'What about global warming?'

'That too. They say that eventually the whole south coast will be below the sea.'

'Yeah, not for a thousand years or so,' I added.

'It's closer than you think,' said the timpanist, '*Scientific American* said it could happen in the next hundred to a hundred and fifty years.'

'Gee,' said the harpist, 'that might be our grandchildren.'

CHAPTER 20

I showed my postgraduate membership card at the front desk. The Royal College of Music was a time capsule in marble, granite and the aroma of floor polish. Its yellow walls, its columns the colour of salt beef, its mosaic tiles underfoot like a Roman bath. And the far-off sound of practising and lessons. Oboes, flutes, strings, guitars all having their separate conversations like guests in a restaurant.

My first port of call was the tuition notice board. I rearranged the cards on the green baize and made a space. *Singing teacher, all levels, particularly RCM exams. Must provide own accompanist or be happy to work a capella.*

Singing was my subsidiary subject. I wasn't very good but I was qualified. I might as well make use of it.

My second card had needed more soul-searching. *Soundproofed practice space in private south London home, 6ft Yamaha C3 in concert condition. Tozer stool. Price negotiable.*

I didn't want other people pounding my piano, but if I auditioned applicants carefully I could make sure it survived with minimal abuse. And once I could play again my tuner could sort it out. I would probably have no shortage of takers. There were never enough practice rooms in college.

One voice in the musical chatter began to come through more strongly; a piano. It could only be one. The Bosendorfer down the corridor.

Nearby on the board was a poster. *Leo Korda postgraduate workshop, 3pm until 5pm, Durrington Seminar Room.* I looked at the clock in the wood panelling behind reception. Quarter to three.

I'd been an observer at one of Leo Korda's workshops two years ago. I hadn't played for him, but watching what he told others had inspired my practice for weeks afterwards. My postgraduate card would get me in, if I wanted to.

No, I shouldn't. I should return the library books I'd brought, and go.

The quickest way to the library was from the entrance hall. I went back out through the swing doors and the Bosendorfer faded into the other musical dialogues in the building.

I ran up the stairs. The patterns in the marble balustrade under my hand were so familiar. In this section the veining resembled the muscled hindquarters of a Grecian horse. Next it faded like clouds into a mackerel sky. Portraits of former principals and college patrons stared down from the walls, exactly as they did when I was eighteen, and nineteen and twenty.

The Bosendorfer was no longer playing scales. Now it was Chopin's sonata in B minor, interrupted every few bars to play scales, repeat figures, work on the flow. I knew that piece. I had difficulties with the flow there too.

At the top of the stairs, I went along a corridor and through a set of swing doors into the library. As they closed a hush descended, book-lined walls muffling the music from outside. I headed for the desk and hauled my books out of my bag onto the counter.

A bored-looking woman with a librarian badge sat at the computer terminal, took my card without looking at me. She had been exactly the same when I was a student. She swiped the spines of my books along a reading device, still with the same dead expression as though she despised my choices or thought I would never read them. Her name plate still said *Miss M. C. Froy*. Miss. We always imagined her going home to a tiny flat in Haringay which she shared with a cat she probably disapproved of too. That probably wasn't very nice of us.

The clock over the doors said ten to three.

Miss M C Froy typed on her keyboard, inputting my returns. My ears adjusted to the quiet and I started to hear the Bosendorfer. It was muffled by carpets, walls of books, acoustic tiles and the mouse subways between ceiling and floor, but somehow I heard it as a radio telescope locks onto the tiniest beat from a distant star. Now it was playing a passage from the sonata straight through, without interruptions, and I could distinguish every note. Or my brain was filling them in.

Miss M C Froy was having trouble. She slid my card back and forth in a slot on the computer as though trying to carve cheese with it. She raised the card to her nose, squinting, and with her less dextrous hand began to type the numbers.

The pulse of the Chopin added an imaginary countdown to the clock in the wood panelling. Eight minutes to; time was running out.

Now the choice was out of my control it was suddenly essential for me to be at that workshop. Not everyone who attended had to play, there was much to be learned from watching while others were tutored. If there was only one tutor I could go to during my convalescence it should be Leo Korda. I could take notes and they would be my manifesto when I started playing again.

The computer bleeped and rejected my card. Miss Froy looked bewildered and readjusted her glasses.

With one eye on the clock, I said: 'Should I leave the card and come back later?'

'You won't be able to use any college facilities without it.' Miss Froy began to input my number all over again.

The Bosendorfer continued to call from below.

At exactly three minutes to, Miss Froy gave me my card. I stuffed everything in my bag, hared out of the door and down the stairs.

The piano had stopped. I turned left at the bottom of the stairs and ran along a corridor, expecting to go flying on the mosaic tiles. Leo Korda would be introducing himself, the masterclass would be starting. I reached the red doors of the Durrington Room and composed myself. It didn't do to barge in like the Sweeney.

In the room, several rows of grey plastic chairs were arranged in a semicircle, around the piano at the far end. The seats at the front were all taken; a clutch of students were giving their full attention to a diminutive, bespectacled figure who stood beside the piano stool talking in a Hungarian accent that sounded like he was chewing on springs. Leo Korda.

Sunlight streamed in through the tall windows, throwing window shapes over him and the gleaming black body of the piano.

I tiptoed across the parquet.

'Don't skulk at the back,' called Leo Korda. 'This is a workshop, not one of those formal masterclasses where nobody dares to speak.'

Fifteen faces turned and stared at me.

'Come on,' said Leo Korda, and beckoned me with quick movements of his arm. 'Music is for sharing. I want to communicate with you, not shout at the back row.'

There was quiet, respectful laughter. Nervous too.

I walked to the front.

My eyes devoured the Bosendorfer. Its black case, more than nine feet long, as sleek as the bodywork of a fast car. The keys, a unique shade of black and white that Farrow and Ball should have patented. The line of red felt where the neck of the keys met the wooden casing. The golden lettering: *L. Bosendorfer* in small capitals. The perfect line of golden hinges along its lid, burnished by sunlight.

'I think,' said Leo Korda, 'that we have our first performer ready.'

There are times when your body takes charge. My bag slid onto a chair and I put myself at the piano.

The master's eye was on me. All those postgraduates looked on, professionals like me, the harshest audience of all. They competed with me for work, for the attention of agents. They would judge me for every fluff, every missed note, every too-loud *fortissimo* and every disappeared *pianissimo*.

What to play? I hadn't prepared a piece. I didn't have any sheet music. I spread my fingers onto the white keys. The ivory felt warm under my fingertips.

My body knew what to play. The tiny, sub-aural notes that had sounded through my bones and wakened old pathways as I waited at the desk upstairs. Chopin's sonata in B minor.

My world shrank to the black and white of the keyboard,

the mirror-like wood and the red felt edge. The feel of the keys under my fingers, the brilliance of the right-hand more sweet than a soprano, the rich answer of the left. Chopin's gentle, tumbling phrases.

The language of notation is dictatorial and domineering. Every fraction of a second is documented. You don't think, you do as the score tells you. Play this note for exactly a sixth of a second, and at exactly this volume. You feel what the composer orders – *amoroso*, play it lovingly; *appassionata*, passionately. Sitting at that Bosendorfer I understood that in a way I had never understood before. Playing a piece is channelling the composer. You don't read a score, you let it in and you do what the composer did inside his mind and his heart.

I finished. I put my hands in my lap.

Slowly, I came into the room again.

Leo Korda was looking at me and nodding. The other students too. Their faces weren't critical. They were soft and open. Music, the language of souls. That was why we played. To do that to each other.

Someone began to clap quietly. The others followed. I sat still. To make music and be engulfed by it was all I ever needed.

Gradually the pains crept in. Shivering up through the long strings in the Bosendorfer's oil-slick body. I pressed the web of skin between my right thumb and my index finger but the pain sparked into the other hand too.

Leo Korda's face solidified into his teacher mask, like wax hardening. The other students had their criticism faces on again. Pens poised to take notes.

'Too many performers,' said Leo Korda, 'play too much of themselves and too little of Chopin. While there are points to improve technically in this musician's performance, the essence of the composer and the beauty of the piece are coming through. The classical pianist should bypass their ego and think of the composer's intention when interpreting a piece.'

Leo Korda looked at me. 'My dear, I don't know your name.'
'Carol Lear.'
'Miss Lear, it's a pleasure to meet you. Now we get to work.

Can you play from bar 17?'

I put my hands on the keys. Just holding my fingertips poised made me swallow a gasp. I bit down on my lip and conjured the score in my mind, identified bar 17 and began.

Pain shot burning needles up my left forearm.

But Leo Korda was waiting, and so were the other students. They would remember how I played. They would remember Leo Korda was impressed. They would know who I was when they needed another soloist or ensemble player.

I would not let them remember that I had to stop.

I put the pain somewhere else and let the composer flow through me. Let Chopin tell me what to feel. *Amoroso*, play it lovingly, and the pain isn't there.

2:

Rachmaninov and Ruin

CHAPTER 21

After the Leo Korda masterclass I went to the cafeteria with two of my fellow students – a Japanese girl and a roly-poly guy with a heavy Brummie accent.

My right arm was sore. I was not allowing it to be any more severe than that.

My left hand I cradled in my lap, keeping the fingers dead still.

I would deal with them both later.

For now it was so good to be talking about playing. Exchanging real experiences. Instead of getting them secondhand from Danya and Ed.

We swapped stories from previous workshops. The Japanese girl had been playing and Leo Korda snatched the score away from the desk. When she complained she hadn't memorised the piece, he told her to carry on and fill in by improvising, so he could see what she'd understood about the music. The Brummie guy had been at an ensemble workshop and Korda had made everyone put down their instruments and read their parts out loud in nonsense syllables so that they found the natural way to stay in rhythm.

We parted, a good hour later, promising emails and phone calls.

Outside, Kensington Gore was solid with traffic. Kensington Gardens was a dark space behind the Albert Memorial. The Albert Hall was decked in golden lights for evening. In the loading bay stood a pantechnicon, marked with the insignia of the Philharmonic Orchestra. Somewhere inside the Hall the musicians would be putting their tails on for the performance.

I could go to Knightsbridge Tube or South Ken. I chose neither. I wanted to linger as long as possible in this handsome square of red brick and golden stone. Here I was a practising musician again.

I walked into the sidestreets instead, past mansion blocks where cast-iron lanterns over black front doors continued the Albert Hall livery. In my first year I shared a grotty flat in Kennington with Evelyn, a violinist, and we used to swear that when our glittering careers took flight we would live in one of these grand apartments.

Evelyn retrained as an accountant five years ago and now seemed to have given that up to write Christmas letters about her twins.

My arms were aching, but in a manageable way. Maybe walking all the way home would do me good, get the blood flowing. And I could digest the masterclass. Leo Korda had made a number of valuable comments about technique and flow.

But most important was what had happened at the first run-through. I knew, even before Leo Korda confirmed it, that the essence of Chopin was truly there. I don't know what I did differently, but it worked.

Not that I thought Chopin was giving spooky direction from beyond the grave. But maybe those evenings with Gene had awakened something.

It was more than a fortnight since Jerry and I went to Anthony Morrish. With distance, those evenings had acquired proportion; a curious weekend that would dwindle into the past. I'd put my tape away with the Dictaphone, filed it like old photos once the novelty of examining them wears off.

But Jerry had still not had another panic attack. The house permanently smelled like Starbucks. Of course you couldn't take his unlucky, murdered predecessor at face value, but it had indubitably left its mark.

Maybe it was the same for me.

I hadn't thought that Gene could cure the pain in my hands. But perhaps he had helped with a different problem.

I reached Fulham Road. Each junction was a scrum of cars. I dodged across a fading box grid, hopscotching around vehicles that had ignored the yellow cross-hatches. A white van loomed up, horn blaring. I had to run to get out of the way.

Self-preservation brought me back to my senses. I might be thinking too much about the interpretation breakthrough. Perhaps it had just happened. Whatever was going on, once I could get back to practising there would be so many new ideas I could explore.

In the meantime, I would be a model patient and would rest.

On Battersea Bridge I remembered my white gloves and pulled them out of my bag.

Such an undemanding movement, but my arm jagged with pain.

In the river below, a boat chugged towards the bridge, passed underneath and went into the distance.

It took that long before I could consider moving again. Then I could only do it if I cradled one hand in the other, a sling to protect it while I walked.

I'd overdone the playing, that was all. I hadn't touched a piano for nearly six weeks and then attacked a concert Bosendorfer. The Bosendorfer wasn't an easy instrument, it had a stiff concert action. To go straight in and play a full piece was like an out-of-shape athlete going for a sprint without even a warm-up. Of course I should expect it to hurt. Perhaps it was a tad foolish but after more rest I should be fine. Dr Golding always said there was nothing wrong with me.

It was all worth it when I thought about Leo Korda's words after I finished for the first time. My audience's faces. My breakthrough; my new channel to true interpretation.

There was the time before Leo Korda; five dark weeks of running each day like a tap. Now there was hope. Soon I would be better – and my playing would rise to a new level.

This was the start of my real recovery. I'd wear those white gloves respectfully and gratefully. Tomorrow I should be able to get them on. I might even give the yoga another try.

An hour and a half after I left Kensington, I brought my key up to my front door and slid it into the lock.

The pain shot me. It held me staring at the tiles of the porch for several minutes.

Carefully, with my other hand, I tried again. The key and

the crooked hole wouldn't go together.

The door was snatched open. Jerry stood there, the tip of the black umbrella warning me off like a weapon.

He rolled his eyes and holstered the umbrella in its churn behind the door. 'Jesus, Carol. I thought the lock was being picked.'

I picked the key up from the mat, absurdly having to kneel for it so I could keep my arms stiff like a statue. Even that move became extra complicated because my bag slid off my shoulder and it was easier to let it fall.

I became aware that Jerry hadn't gone back to his study but was watching me. His hesitation before he returned to help me was as expressive as folded arms.

'So,' he said, 'what have you been doing?'

Chapter 22

Dr Golding switched off the ultrasound machine and passed me a tissue to wipe the gel off my arms. I went slowly, especially over my left wrist. I'm quite skinny but my bones had disappeared under pulpy swelling.

The doctor watched me, seeming to find that almost as informative as his high-tech machine. 'There's a lot of oedema. What have you been doing?'

'The pain suddenly got worse,' I said.

That was what I had said when I made the appointment. I don't think he was fooled for a moment.

But if I told him I had been playing, I thought he'd refuse to see me.

On his desk, among his prescription pads and doctorly paraphernalia were the white gloves. I'd brought them to try to demonstrate that I'd been taking proper care. Well, except for that one incident I had.

He scooted his chair on its castors over to his computer and typed. 'You need a complete rest. Positively no playing for six months.'

Six months. He must be saying that to give me a fright. And I probably deserved it for being cautious with the truth.

'Six months?' I repeated. I would accept my telling-off and then he could tell me what he really thought.

I looked at the grey patch of hair at his temples, which extended over his ear and then flecked into the darker hairs. So many times I'd sat here, looking at that pattern, waiting for my sentence. It was never in denominations of months, it was always weeks.

'Six months,' he repeated, and clicked his mouse to close my notes and seal his pronouncement.

I heard myself accepting his prognosis, still hoping he would take it back. 'And after that it will be all right? I'm only

35, I know players in their sixties.'

I didn't mean just the few famous masters in the Classic FM charts. There were plenty of others on the circuit. Leo Korda, for instance, still gave concerts occasionally. They might look less vibrant than the young talent, but they played up a cyclone. How fantastic to have that much performing mileage bedded in your biorhythms. If all the cells in your body are replaced once every seven years, those players must have been through seven or eight entire upgrades, each more attuned to music.

'Miss Lear,' said Dr Golding, 'for more than twenty-five years you've been putting your limbs under immense, repetitive strain. You must rest.'

He was bluffing.

'It will get better, won't it?' I picked my gloves up off the desk. Showing willing again.

Six months, a dizzying amount of downtime; it gave me vertigo.

But I didn't put the gloves on. If he saw how painful that was he might give me nine months. A year.

'Anything could happen,' I said, 'couldn't it? After all, all this is a bit of a medical mystery.'

Dr Golding gave a rueful smile. It was the first time I'd seen any expression on his face that approached sympathy. 'Miss Lear, you're not a medical mystery. The mystery is the players you talk about who never get injured.'

Chapter 23

I walked away from Dr Golding's office, down the green corridor. I went through a door, thinking it was the stairs, but not knowing where I was at all. Six months started from this moment and I was already withdrawing.

I registered that what was in front of me was a kind of sitting room. A man in a brown checked dressing gown was standing at the window smoking a cigarette. His face was like a cadaver. His eyes and mouth were black pits carved into putty.

'Are you lost?' he said, in a voice like gravel.

'I was looking for the lift.'

He gestured with his cigarette. 'Back three doors. I think. It's been a while since I last used it.'

I found the lift and followed another green corridor.

After some time, I don't know how long, I found the street. A canyon of office buildings. The sun was a nicotine stain across the clouds. People were hurrying past me to the station. They walked fast with their heads down, no one talking to anyone else, as though they hoped to escape from every living thing around them. A wind whipped up, blowing a bin over and pushing sandwich wrappers and a discarded *Evening Standard* past my feet. That's what I was doing; drifting through the streets like the remains of the day's newspapers.

I got home, I don't know how, and had a long soak in the bath. I must have dozed off because the doorbell woke me. I was surrounded by cold water like a Frankenstein experiment in a tank. I lurched out, tried to warm myself in towels. I heard Jerry downstairs let the visitor in. Sneakers squeaked across the floor of the hall, then went outside and I heard the door of my practice room open.

There had been no shortage of people ringing in response to my advert. I'd organised a rota of three people to share my C3 and already there was another on the waiting list.

I dressed. Downstairs I could hear the TV was on. Tim was a journalist and would listen to the news twenty-four hours a day if he could. Before he started staying over the house would be silent except for the click of Jerry's mouse and the clatter of his keyboard.

Now over the sound of Tim multitasking news channels I could hear it faintly. The sound of my piano. Playing figures from Chopin.

The girl lacked the easy flow; she was trying too hard.

How easy it is to lose technique if you can't practise.

Six months before I could channel Chopin again, draw him out of the score and onto the keys. It had taken me so long to find that effortless facility, and I'd only done it the once. After such a breakthrough you need to practise more than ever, wire it into your body as fundamentally as breathing. In six months' time, what would I have lost? What would I have left?

The answer was obvious: another hypnotherapist. There would be plenty in this part of London, with so many health clubs and borderline-medical therapists. Although I'd avoid the Gifted Marias.

The first hypnotherapist I spoke to put me off a little. She asked a lot of questions, then told me I should go back to the therapist I'd originally started with as she didn't want to tread on a colleague's toes.

So I was grateful when Justin Fordham, the fourth on my list, said yes. Even better, he was a convenient ten minutes' walk away, in the precinct near Clapham Junction.

By the time I spoke to him I knew how to pitch my case. I'd been having treatment for an injury. Did he mind continuing the work another hypnotist had started? No, he said, hypnotists often had to be flexible enough to take the reins from other experts.

I had the feeling his flexibility was lubricated by the £40-a-session fee he could take over too. No matter.

CHAPTER 24

Justin Fordham's directions were given with pedantic detail. 'Go down the paved street that leads to Clapham Junction. When you reach the travel agent, turn to your left. Walk for approximately fifty yards until you see the grey-painted door beside the charity shop.' Setting a tone of exactness and obedience.

No jokes were made about the travel agent.

He buzzed me in and told me he was on the top floor. I climbed a staircase of grey lino and dim walls. The first floor housed an accountant. The second, a solicitor. Third was an insurance agent. At the top, there it was: a door with ribbed glass etched with Justin Fordham's name like a film noir detective.

Justin Fordham approached through the washboard glass and opened the door. He looked manageable. In his fifties, wearing a black polo-neck and tightish jeans, as though he was trying to look younger than his years and smaller than his size.

'Hello Carol,' he said. 'Come on in.'

His quarters smelled of fan heaters and roasted dust. There was a reception area with a black desk overlooked by a Nostradamus print. No receptionist; obviously a one-man band.

'We will work in here,' he said, and led me to another room. It had two tall lamps and armchairs that retained the impressions of many previous travellers. A digital recorder stood ready on the coffee table.

Justin Fordham sat in the biggest chair, his hands on the arms in command position. 'So, you have back pain, is it?'

'Hands,' I said. Did he even remember our conversation?

'No worries. What I usually do is – '

'I've been working with a different therapist,' I said.

'Ah yes. Why don't you tell me about that.'

I took a piece of paper out of my bag, fumbling in my white

gloves, and passed it to him. 'This is how it was done before.'

I had transcribed some of the first session. No more than the beginning – and that had been an entire day's hand work – but it should be enough to guide him.

He read it, frowning. The heater crackled and ticked.

'It's unusual,' he said, and read it again.

Be flexible, I willed at him. It'll be easy. Think of your £40.

He set the paper on the arm of the chair with a certain amount of ceremony, as though demonstrating it had passed a test. 'Well, we explore past lives to heal present ones. This is just an unorthodox way around. Give me a few minutes to set up. Why don't you lie back and get comfortable.'

He was going to do it. I lay back, looked at the aureoles of Artex on the ceiling and tried to feel calmed by them.

Justin Fordham dimmed the lights and went to the other room. I heard him lock the outer door. I wondered if his clients often tried to make screaming, dramatic exits. He came back, started the recorder, then placed himself in the big chair.

'We begin. You're safe and warm. I want you to drift off, listen only to my voice. Imagine you're looking at clouds; something beautiful...'

He hardly had Gene's panache.

But it seemed to work. The Artex swirls receded. His voice drifted away.

I wasn't in the room any more.

It was dark. I could see nothing.

I could hear only a man's voice far away, like a radio turned down very low. All around me it was immense and quiet, like the sky, but there was no sky. The man was asking me where I was. I was nowhere at all. There was only the tiny compelling voice, which seemed to have no more sound than a puppet making shapes with its mouth. I was like a disconnected phone; an atom in the cold void of space; a blind primitive organism in the deep and lightless trenches of the ocean.

After a while I recognised I was hearing a countdown. I had a sense that light was returning, like dawn rising.

I was seeing Artex again.

Justin Fordham was in his chair, hands in command. 'Do you want to go to a point where the character is still alive?'

Like before with Gene, my answer had to swim up a long way.

'Alive?'

'You're probably disorientated.' He reached for the recorder on the table. 'Do you want to take a copy of this and we'll finish another time? I can put it on your iPod.'

I struggled with his words. 'Did it go all right? What did I say?'

Why couldn't I remember anything? It wasn't like this before.

'You didn't say very much,' said Justin Fordham. 'It's quite normal.'

The digital recorder was in his hand. His finger was poised on the buttons.

'Can you play it to me?' I said.

Fordham pressed play.

I heard my voice say: 'It's getting dark.' Then there was silence. Only the swell and ebb of the traffic passing four floors below.

After a while he pressed stop. The traffic sounds continued, but drier, subtracted from their recorded echo.

Fordham put the recorder on the table. 'I tend to find the people who are good at verbalising say "dark" or the word "nothing". Others shake their heads or even hum one long note.'

I stood up. Grabbed my coat and bag, which was too ungentle to my arms but I had to get out.

Fordham turned the lights up. It made the room bleak, like a back-street abortionist.

'Take a moment and calm down,' he said, but I was already at the fluted glass door.

Justin Fordham reached me, with the bill. 'I'll give you a credit slip for the portion of the hour you didn't use so it won't cost you so much next time.' He put his hand on the lock.

I handed over the cash and stuffed the credit slip in my bag.

The smell of burning dust was choking, like cremating hair.

Fordham unlocked the door. 'Some people find that part of a regression quite upsetting, but you mustn't allow it to deter you. Even past lives must come to an end.'

How rehearsed the line sounded.

I hurried down the stairs and out into the street.

It was the same bleak Clapham afternoon. Tawdry shops selling plastic tat for a pound. A health food store with dingy yellow tiles, the shelves stacked with pseudo medication. Pills for everything, it looked like a 1950s vision of what people would eat in the future.

I called Jerry. His phone was off. I texted him: *Call me*. My wrists cried at even this miserable amount of keyboarding.

By the time I pressed Send I didn't know what I would say if he did call. I was stumbling, like someone behind a blindfold, reaching for a familiar touch to restore my faith in the world.

A bus roared past, its horn blaring at a cyclist to get out of the way. In the windows the passengers had headphone wires trickling from their ears. Their eyes stared out blankly.

As I reached home, a Japanese girl came out of the gate, a leather case of music under her arm. She nodded at me and walked away. She had a red scarf so long it picked up the brittle leaves on the path.

Inside, the house felt very cold. I turned the thermostat up and put the TV on to fill it with voices and warmth. Children's programmes were in full swing, babbling cartoon people, popping weasels and clown colours.

Jerry had left something for me. In the middle of the floor was a printout of A4 pages, annotated with one of his green Post-Its.

Was he having panic attacks again? Had his bubble burst too?

No, this note was intended for me.

Remember V loves B. It worked for me. Did some research you might be interested in. J x

The pages were a printout of a discussion board with a kind

of past-lives agony aunt. I noticed the name Anthony Morrish, although the website wasn't about him. *For years I had suffered excruciating neck pain. Then I was regressed and found out I was guillotined –*

I couldn't read that now.

I tried Jerry again. Still unreachable. I longed for him to come in with Tim, koala hugging and spreading joyous vibes of love. Children's TV ended and the news stepped in. There was a picture of a pretty young woman, a snapshot from a family album, and the newscaster said: *A murder hunt has been launched...*

No. Off.

London was a brilliant place to be if you had a life that was going well, momentum to keep you going. If you stopped, you saw the horrors that were really there.

CHAPTER 25

Jerry and Tim tumbled in with wine and nibbles. They canoodled as they put tubs of olives and dips away. Tim went upstairs for a shower, and Jerry asked how my day was and oh yes he'd had a text from me, what was up?

'Nothing,' I said. 'I just needed a phone number.'

I couldn't explain like this, leaning on the cabinets in the kitchen, with Jerry glancing at the ceiling tracking his lover's footsteps.

And these regressions were obviously a waste of time; what you got depended on who was hypnotizing you.

When the shower stopped gushing Jerry nipped away. Just to make sure Tim wasn't running around without a towel.

Music started. It was trance, muffled into a liquid heartbeat by the bedroom door. Too freaky, like an out-of-body experience.

The hangovers I'd had from these regressions were monstrous and this was the worst yet. I had to get away.

I took a key from the rack by the fridge, went out the back door and unlocked my practice room.

I hadn't been in there for six weeks.

I stood at the door and inhaled. It smelled foreign; perhaps traces of perfumes and shower gels from the other players who now used it.

The Yamaha, under a padded cover, took up the entire space, nearly touching the blankets that hung against the walls for soundproofing. Heavy velvet curtains were closed across the window. On the ceiling was a mosaic of eggboxes. When we put them up Jerry had insisted on figuring out a pattern that made sense of their random colours.

I shut the door, put on the light. The acoustics felt homelike and snug. No more unsettling beat from upstairs. I couldn't even hear the eternal traffic in Nightingale Lane.

I pushed back the dust cover. The strings inside the piano sang a faint echo. A piano always greets your touch.

I scrutinised the polished case. If I saw anything as heinous as a coffee ring I'd hold a major inquest.

But my clients had treated my instrument with respect.

I sat on the stool and my reflection looked at me, the way I always saw it when I practised. A warning pain vibrated along the tops of my fingers and into my wrists.

But I wasn't intending to play. Just to be here.

I took out my phone and clicked to my contacts book. Angelica; if I phoned her she'd want to talk about the piece she was working on. Next was Charlie, a mad violinist I'd briefly dated from the Halle – I kept meaning to delete him. Then there was Danya – she'd want to moan about concert organisers. Ed – he'd try to persuade me to come over to help him memorise a piece because he was neurotic about forgetting. Evelyn – that was her old number, it didn't work any more. Next was Gene.

Why not? At least I wouldn't have to play musical agony aunt.

'Hi Gene, it's Carol.'

'I owe you a tape, don't I?'

No time to be wasted with chit-chat, it seemed. And I had to get him off the subject of that tape or somehow he'd fox out of me what had just happened. I couldn't imagine he'd be sympathetic.

'I'd forgotten about the tape,' I replied gaily. 'I just thought I'd catch up. How's the new job?' My foot doodled on the sustain pedal.

'The new job's okay.'

Judging by his tone, either the job bored him to tears or he was waiting for the real conversation to start. I shouldn't have called. I'd wind it up, then call Danya.

'It sounds like a bad time,' I said. 'Don't worry about the tape.' Slipping it in now was safe because I was about to go, and it didn't look like I was ducking the subject. 'I don't need it yet. Let's chat soon.'

'So how's everything?' he said.

I should have said I'm fine, how are you? And then, after he'd batted the same back to me, goodbye. But pretending seemed like such an effort.

'I'm barred from playing for six months,' I said.

'Why?'

I told him.

'You musicians have about as much sense as boxers. What have you done? Ruptured a tendon?'

My mistake for thinking a medic would understand. I should have rung off already.

'Not ruptured. I just need more rest. And I've had all the bollockings from Dr Golding.'

Behind me, the door opened and knocked against the stool. It was a guy with a round face, ruddy from the cold, a zip satchel under one arm. His name was Michael and he was being groomed by my tutor.

He made a ducking motion with his neck and shoulders as if to apologise for the fact that he was about to evict me.

We squeezed around each other to swap places and I went out. The door closed, leaving me in darkness.

The sound of scales began immediately, very fast and rippling. Michael was good, and he didn't like using the practice pedal to damp the noise. I walked along the pavement but I could still hear him.

'Where are you?' said Gene. 'Who's that playing?'

'That's my piano. I'm charging people to exercise it. Much less effort than playing it myself.'

He said nothing, reproaching my lame effort to sound cheerful.

'I'd never get very far as a secret agent, would I?'

A motorbike tore down the road. The echo shouted off the buildings.

'Do you know any singing teachers?' he said.

'Why?'

'There's a singing teacher down here who needs cover for a couple of weeks. She has to go abroad because her mother died.

There's free accommodation too because her sister's cat needs feeding.'

'That's too funny. Somebody told you I teach singing, did they?'

'Trained singers' voices are a giveaway when you hear them on a tape.'

I'd been forgetting how unequally we knew each other.

'That sounds tempting,' I said, although it didn't; it was crazy. 'But I need to be in London.'

'You're booked up?'

'I've had a few enquiries.' Although demand wasn't as brisk as for my piano.

My wanderings had brought me back to the house. In the front bedroom, the curtains were lit with moving colours from Jerry's lava lamp. I heard a fragment of Michael's scales. Jerry occupied, my C3 getting a workout. Me passing like a visiting satellite.

I turned and marched up the road again. 'You know what?' I said to Gene. 'It's a deal. Who do I call?'

CHAPTER 26

Such is the freelance musician's life. Where there's work, you go. Like Karli, off to adventures with people you scarcely know.

On the Saturday I packed a few clothes, woke up my ancient Vauxhall and pointed it south-west out of London. I'd inherited the car from Evelyn when she abandoned fugues for figures. It had belonged to her parents and was equipped to the plushest standards of 1988 – a tape player and automatic gearbox. The auto transmission used to be embarrassing. Now it was the only reason the trip was even possible. If I'd had a gear lever, the constant overtaking of lorries and slowing for junctions would have been agony.

Once free of London I had a choice. The M5 motorway: six lanes, wide visibility. Or the A303; the old dual carriageway. I took the old road. It rolled on for hours through valleys and over hills, further than I would have thought possible for a road so narrow. Signs pointed to Roman remains. Stonehenge forced the traffic into single file. As if I was not only travelling a long way in miles but in decades too, sailing a metalled sine wave back to a time before motorways. For a terrifying hour, fog closed in like a curtain so the fields around the car disappeared and I seemed to be gliding blind on an endless bridge across white space. All roads claim souls from time to time. When you travel the old road, you are lucky to land.

By the time I slowed to urban speeds, the sun was a crimson band in front of me and the night was racing in from behind.

I was to cover for a singing teacher, who had to go abroad with her sister because their mother had died. I could stay in her sister's cottage if I'd feed the cat. Jenny, the sister with the cat, was the connecting piece in this puzzle. She worked at the hospital with Gene.

Jenny had texted that morning to say she'd postponed her

flight until Sunday. Gene said come anyway. There were plenty of spare rooms in the nurses' home, where he was staying temporarily.

So here I was, a whole day early, with wine and cheese from the deli in Clapham. All set for a reunion with my old acquaintance from school.

I was looking for a town called Vellonoweth. Features from Gene's directions started to take shape. The long hill and the sign welcoming careful drivers. The schizophrenic town architecture – Victorian buildings with spinsterish gables, next to shoebox parades built in the 1950s.

At a roundabout I took the exit for the hospital and drove to the end of the car park.

The nurses' home was a tall, double-gabled house. I had expected it to look more populated but just one light was on, in the upstairs bay window. It looked as though Gene had the entire place to himself.

He opened the door. Polite kisses on the cheek, enquiries about the journey, feedback given for accuracy of directions. He led me along a passage lit by an inadequate bare bulb. Underfoot were tiles in terracotta, turquoise and black, which rocked and slipped like loose dominoes.

He was wearing trainers; no wild barefootedness here. He knew his limits. Unfinished floorboards and burning dog-ends: yes. Loose Victorian tiles: no. Or maybe he'd had a misfire putting out a cigarette.

The place smelled of mustiness and plaster, as if it had been abandoned.

'You can't be living here?' I said.

'Temporarily, until I can move into the flat I'm renting. The hospital wanted someone to sleep on the premises. Makes it more secure. At least the commute is easy.'

'Secure from what? Burglars?'

'Squatters. Drug users. It's all going to be knocked down next month anyway when they build the new radiology department.'

He unlocked a door and gave me the key. 'You can have the

caretaker's flat. I'm in matron's quarters upstairs.'

He went up while I dumped my bag.

I had a living room that was bare of furniture except for a meagre fireplace, kitchen cabinets and a yellowed Baby Belling. In one corner was a pile of newspapers and squashed cardboard boxes, swept into a heap like a bonfire.

In the next room was a bed with a pile of hospital linen and battered white rails at the head and foot. I peeked into the bathroom. A white, grubby basin; a loo with a black seat; bath taps weeping green tears into a giant tub. Above the taps an enamel sign said *Do not waste hot water*.

If Gene's flat upstairs was like this, he was probably desperate for someone to visit him.

Was this really the only place he could stay? I'd been in grotty digs on tour, but musicians expect that. It never mattered because you'd be run so hard by rehearsing. The digs were no more than a place to park your coffin, like a vampire.

The nomad life felt natural to me. I never felt homesick when I was at the College, unlike some friends who in the middle of term bolted back to their families for weekends. When the holidays started I'd rent extra days in my room, or cadge floors to sleep on. My availability got me some great jobs. One Easter I played in Harrods restaurant every day. I was happy on it; travelling from floor to floor, piano to piano.

Gene didn't have a nomad job. Maybe he didn't take much notice of home.

That was quite endearing, in a way. It made me feel more like I knew him.

I unpacked and headed up the stairs.

Matron's flat was scarcely less spartan. The sofa and chairs were shrouded in sheets. The lighting came from the red bar of an electric heater, like a student room.

I began adding up what this might mean. While he might tune his surroundings out, a girlfriend or boyfriend probably wouldn't. Which must mean he didn't have such visitors. Or they were so submerged in love that all they needed was a nest.

Perhaps tonight we'd fill these blanks.

Gene came out of the kitchen and I gave him the bag with wine bottles and cheese. He exchanged it for red wine in one of his tall glasses.

'That's a lot of white sheets,' I said as he went back into the kitchen.

'They're from the hospital. The furniture is out of the old waiting room and it's rather frightening. But I'm hardly here so it doesn't matter. Beware as you sit down.' Paper rustled as he unwrapped the cheeses.

I tried the sofa and realised why he'd given me the warning. It felt like sitting on wire and tree branches and made a faint crunching noise as I tried to get comfortable.

'So have you had any other friends visit here?' I asked.

'No.'

His tone was remote, as though I'd asked about something very unlikely. It also suggested he didn't plan any trips to visit people either.

Perhaps he was divorced.

Questions like that might have to wait until later, perhaps around bottle number three.

On a table by the sofa was a plate with hunks of baguette. The plate was white Pyrex with the hospital crest.

All his belongings must be in storage. There were no books or CDs to give any clues about him. The only personal possessions I'd seen were plain white mugs and these towering wine glasses.

He was like me with my grip bag, a nomad travelling where the work took him. But travelling in complete anonymity – there was nothing of his own in this room, not even one book. Even I had my cuddly Liberace bear when I toured – no, that's a joke, I don't have one, at least not any more. It was a Christmas present two years ago from my mother, who misjudged my taste, but then it was unusual for us to exchange presents at all. Even Jerry thought the bear was inexcusable. I sent it to Evelyn, who said her twins loved it.

Gene brought in the cheese, on hospital Pyrex. We dug in, shared what we knew about Felicity and Jenny, the strangers who were our anchors to this place. He'd quit smoking. So far, so superficial.

Time to nudge the conversation on.

'Vellonoweth's a long way from London. What made you come down here?'

'It was a change.'

'A change?'

He didn't answer. 'From London?' I nudged. 'You know what they say, when you're tired of London...' I couldn't believe I was going to bring out the cliché but we had to get started somehow.

'I think if I were Boswell, I'd get tired of Johnson.'

'When we were at school, where did you live? Your parents, I mean.'

'Macclesfield.'

A town five miles away from where I lived. An answer at last, though hardly revealing. 'Whereabouts in Macclesfield?'

He stood up, took my glass and refilled it, then came back and asked where I'd lived.

'How,' I ventured, 'did you know Kate Rafferty?'

'My sister knew her.'

So he had a sister. That doubled the information I had about him. 'Was she at my school?' I didn't remember a Winter in the school. I'd have noticed a surname so self-contained and windswept.

'My sister wasn't at your school. She's six years older than me.'

'And how did she know Kate Rafferty?'

'She knew Kate's older sister.'

Kate's sister who had gone to RADA. I was just about keeping up with the history. 'So you were the baby of the family.'

He stood up. 'There are more rooms upstairs. Let's have a look around.'

Well that conversation had been like trying to make gerbils sit still.

I followed him into the hall. The stairs up were illuminated by a weak bulb. The banisters were coated in green paint; the sick-room green of Guy's Hospital. There were holes in the plaster and some of the banisters were snapped. As though the removals had been done with no care for either furniture or building.

On the next floor, Gene stopped by a door and went in. I followed, found a light switch and clicked it on. Nothing happened. The bulb was gone. Gene walked to the window. He still had the big glass in his hand. The moon was three-quarters; it shone into the glass like a glowing torch of ruby.

The room had a mausoleum smell, as though nobody had been in for months. Dust frosted every surface. A broken chair stood in the middle, its back lying on the floor beside it like a beheading.

'Gene, if you pull a stunt with a sheet to try and scare me, you are a dead man.'

He wandered through to another room. It was in the same state – broken furniture, rubbish, a smashed vase, stubs of hardened Blu Tak on the walls. There was a mirror over the fireplace, with a message in marker pen: 'Goodbye'.

We both paused. Then, in the same instant, started to laugh.

For a moment we were in synch, shaking in front of the ridiculous doomy message.

Then Gene picked his way over to the window, kicking cardboard boxes out of the way. 'In my flat downstairs, there were initials in the bedroom. WG.' He took a sip from the ruby tower in his hand and smiled, white teeth in the moonlight. 'A barbarous inversion. I tried not to take it personally.'

'At least it didn't say Goodbye, WG. Then you should really start to worry.' I shivered – but only from cold. 'Gene,' I said, 'I'll see you back downstairs.'

He followed me back into the flat. It was warmer, and after the desolation upstairs, positively welcoming. I sat on the sofa and tried to negotiate with its garden-debris stuffing.

My wineglass had gone. Gene brought it in from the kitchen, refilled.

He sat beside me. As I took the glass he held onto the stem.

Maybe that was where this was going. Were his arched brows assessing how I'd react if he tried to make a move?

He'd gone to some effort to persuade me to come here. And he wasn't making it easy to have a conversation.

Go on, I thought. Put some cards on the table. I don't know what's going on, you tell me. Then I'll see what I think of it.

He released the glass. 'Shift over. I'll give you a massage. You'll be stiff from driving.'

He sat behind me on the sofa and put his hands on my shoulders.

I sat still, wondering what was coming. He squeezed lightly through the thin cotton of my shirt, as though feeling the contents of a parcel. Explored like this all over my neck and shoulders. Stopped in the middle of my back and drilled under my shoulder blade.

It hurt like a hot needle. Then it released into a pleasant warmth.

'You've got knots everywhere,' he said, and went prospecting for the next one.

This wasn't a seduction ploy. It was a straightforward massage. And it was painful.

He found a tender spot between my shoulder blades and got to work on it. 'Interesting,' he said.

He was pressing so hard I could only manage a grunt. 'What?'

'I thought you'd have muscles from playing. I thought pianists were built like channel swimmers.'

'Channel swimmers are built like channel swimmers. Pianists are built like pianists.' My voice went funny as he dug his knuckle in.

He finished with that muscle and started on another. He carried on kneading and drilling, finding tight points and releasing them. Not talking, merely settling into the rhythm of the massage. As if he was doing it to make himself relax, not me.

CHAPTER 27

I woke early. Saw the white jail bars of the hospital bed and wondered if I had had an accident and woken in a ward. I felt for my glasses. The room snapped into focus. The flowered curtains at the window, made thin by the rising sun. The green paint and my bag on the floor. It was seven in the morning.

I felt like my shoulders had been used as a punchbag. That was a very odd evening.

I must have dozed off again, because the next I knew it was ten o'clock. I dressed and ventured out of the flat.

On the crumbling floor was an envelope. I picked it up and a key slid about inside.

It also contained a note.

Jenny leaves at eleven this morning. After that number 1 Chapel Cottages is all yours. She says she's left some milk in the fridge, and you won't be able to get any in the shops as they're all closed on Sunday. Don't give the milk to the cat. She's left instructions about what it eats and what it doesn't. Try to talk to it – those are her instructions BTW, not mine. She told me what it was called but I can't remember. Probably doesn't matter because you're not taking it for walks.

PS Jenny has osteoarthritis of the hands and I told her you've got trouble. She said she'd leave detailed instructions about everything, including special can openers. Use them. That's an order.

PPS Go to the roundabout, along the high street and up the hill.

Vellonoweth high street was the row of flat-roofed buildings I'd glimpsed the previous night. There wasn't much traffic, so I was able to dawdle, identifying the music shop where I would be teaching. There was one chain retailer; a Spar. The other shops were a bakery, a butcher and a hardware store; old family businesses, judging by their names and the local-made look of their signs. All were closed.

The cottage was a white building at the top of the hill. It was divided into two. One side had been extended with a garage and had a burgundy-coloured car in front. The other had a concrete area around the side for parking, and a door knocker in the shape of a treble clef.

I let myself in. I expected a cat to ambush me for company and food, but the place was quiet. The decor was chintzy and politely antique – not my taste but far nicer than I was expecting. Especially after the horrific nursing home. There was a sofa and a coffee table, a mahogany dining table pushed to the wall, a mantelpiece clustered with nick-nacks. I put my bags on the mock-Chinese rug and explored the kitchen.

I found Jenny's notes. The cat's name, apparently, was Verdi. She'd listed every household item that was adapted for her arthritis, including an entire paragraph about her washing machine: *It's got a dial you need to twist; some days if I can't do it I go next door and Jean Dowman lets me use hers. She said you're welcome to do the same.*

My medical history preceded me, it seemed.

The kitchen was compact, with cooker, hob and cupboards. Getting to the first floor seemed an insoluble puzzle until I opened what I'd thought was the larder and found the stairs.

On the upper floor the bedroom and bathroom were a shrine to Laura Ashley, with sprigged flowers and frilly pelmets. A little fussy, but not bad for free digs.

I wondered again: why was Gene in that derelict place?

On Jenny's dressing-table was a cluster of framed pictures. Many were taken abroad – big-leafed vegetation, verandahed buildings in benevolent sunshine. People in sunglasses and bare shoulders, all sporting the same recurring nose; a family that lived in lands of summer. It was probably where Jenny and Felicity were now.

I went downstairs, found the catfood, made sure Verdi wouldn't starve. Now the day was my own.

I took the Vauxhall out exploring. Rain started to fall, a persistent drizzle that outsmarted my wipers. Intermittent was too slow; faster screeched in protest.

The rain sloshed dark shadows over the concrete of Vellonoweth's high street. The period buildings were no more cheery. An indoor market with grimy bricks and windows, and the Railway Hotel, a monstrosity the size of a Victorian mill. There couldn't have been that many people living in the entire town, let alone wanting to visit it. Half of the hotel was now an old people's home.

The station it had once served was long gone, a no-man's land of curling brambles like barbed wire. The old platforms were in a deep cutting, so that the Railway Hotel seemed to stand on a precipice.

I drove on and into the hills, still arguing with the drizzle. I tried the radio, but the reception was terrible. One tiny, local station came through clear, playing organ music.

Ixendon, the biggest town in the area, had a Sainsbury's and a warren of half-timbered shops selling crafts and antiques. All were asleep behind their blinds. The buildings looked Tudor, and the streets became narrower and taller the closer I walked towards the centre. In the middle was a cathedral, the stone darkened in the rain like wet hair. There was a pub called the Iron Horse, and up the alley from there a second-hand bookshop that occupied two entire buildings. The bookshop, at least, was open. A handful of other customers were in there, drifting between the crammed shelves, smelling of rain.

In the shop I found leaflets for other tourist attractions. There was an art gallery in the cathedral – closed of course. There were regular spiritualist events at the Iron Horse pub. And there was Vellonoweth Hall, the country's first nuclear power station.

Over the years I'd sent Jerry postcards of many enthralling tourist attractions in funny little towns. The house of the inventor of the stapler, the museum of pilchards. But never anything so grand as a nuclear power station.

It was built in the second world war, apparently.

Vellonoweth Hall was five minutes up the road from Chapel Cottage. I drove back that way and parked beside a wood. There was a visitor centre. It was, of course, closed.

The leaflet provided tantalising glimpses of its delights. Displays that looked like Open University programmes about the atom. Models showing how the landscape had changed. The hill I was standing on had once been a valley, at the bottom of which was the buried remains of the station. Under my feet were hundreds of tonnes of concrete and material dredged from the sea, muffling a little machine still ticking away nuclear time. Vellonoweth's contribution to the barrows and artefacts of more antique civilizations.

I walked further. The oppressive drizzle had made me forget this was the coast. Now the rain eased, the mist dissolved and from the top of that hill I saw it at last. Wide, glittering, grey and fading into the horizon: the sea.

My mind did a little flip and I imagined the sea from underneath, like a special effect blinking to negative.

It was an interesting game, but I wasn't going to do it again.

I thought of Justin Fordham and his parting line. 'Even past lives must come to an end.' He couldn't be bothered to alter his catchphrase so the details were right.

All these hypnotists were putting on their own shows. They pushed you into cabs with Jack the Ripper so their audience could applaud your screams. They wound you fast forwards until you dropped off the end of your life, they imprinted themselves on you and scrutinised the results, making notes you were never going to see. And while they've made their therapy point or pleased their crowd, you've spent real hours and heartbeats in there and you don't forget it.

Gene, how curious that you brought me to the sea. What do you want?

As I walked, I thought, don't be so dramatic. I was brought here by a teaching job. Gene certainly wasn't angling for more hypnotic games. He'd endured a chat the previous night and hadn't stuck around for more today, even though it was a weekend. I probably wouldn't even see him again before I went back.

Back in the cottage. Night outside the windows, with no street lights. Countryside darkness, dense and black.

The cat bowl was licked clean, but there was no sign of the cat itself. Jenny seemed to overestimate the amount of human company it needed.

If I was in London I would be rushing to my practice room. Or frustrated because I couldn't do that. But here it was different. I could read one of the books I bought in Ixendon, or see if there was a film on TV.

No, I didn't want TV yet. That would be too similar to what I'd left behind. I'd get to know the house. Jenny Tollderson might be flowery and frilly but she had a door knocker in the shape of a treble clef. Her sister was a singer. She and I must be alike at some level.

It didn't take me long to find the connection. On the sideboard was a pile of sheet music. Propped in the corner of the room was a violin.

I flicked the case open. The violin was wrapped in a cotton pillowcase; obviously looked after. Under the flap at the narrow end were spare strings and a block of rosin with a groove scrubbed by the bow.

Jenny had arthritis. Did she still play? The packaging was up to date; bought within the last few years. I hoped she'd been lucky. I closed up the instrument and put it back. Looked at the sheet music. Books for grade 3, annotated in pencil. Hard to tell whether they were written last week or years ago.

My mobile rang. I ran into the kitchen to grab it but by the time I did it had let go of the signal. I walked into the lounge, trying to catch it again. Finally it came alive again in the bedroom.

'Hi darling, how are the digs?' Jerry.

'House: ten out of ten. Town: one. Actually, three out of ten but I'm not going to tell you why, it's a surprise.'

'You sound relaxed. It's done you good to get away.'

Exactly at the moment he said that, the light went off.

I sat up. The room was coal black. Eyes open, eyes closed, it made no difference. The light from the stairs was off too. The only illumination was a tiny blue glow in my hand from my phone.

I clamped it hard to my ear. There was a sound of computer keys clicking, far away in a house in London.

'Jerry are you there?'

'I think so. Are you?'

'Jerry, all the lights here have gone off. How do you change a fuse?'

'How should I know? I get Tim to change mine.'

I rolled off the bed and peered out of the window.

Next door, no lights were showing at all. It was absolute, inky dark.

'I think it's a power cut. Damn countryside. It's like black armageddon out there. Keep talking.'

Thank God for Jerry, cheeky and in love, earthing me to our civilised house in London. To nights of red socks on the pillow and cushions around the walls. We should never have stopped.

CHAPTER 28

Before I started at the shop the next day, I bought a power cut kit. The Spar in the high street was admirably stocked for Vellonoweth's darkest hours, offering a festival of torches, batteries, wind-up lamps, solar-powered lights and candles.

At the till, a woman looked up from stamping price labels onto sacks of chicken feed. 'Got caught last night, did you?'

Shopping down here was not a wordless swap of goods and money, as I had found the day before in Ixendon.

I replied that I had indeed 'got caught' and she volunteered that power cuts happen all the time if you've got the old wiring. And had I been up to the park? So lovely at this time of year. She nudged a rack of postcards standing next to a tray of iced buns. She hadn't been in business all these years without recognising an out-of-towner who might buy a souvenir.

I considered a postcard for Jerry's collection, but something genuinely caught my eye; a box of blue badges in cellophane packets.

Radiation detector – colour will change to pink in the presence of radiation. Vellonoweth Hall is entirely safe but for your own reassurance keep this with you whenever you visit! Enjoy your trip.

'We sell a good number of those,' said my patron. 'Especially in the tourist season.'

'Do they work?' I said. I put my thumb over the blue to see if that would somehow make it change.

'My husband makes them,' said the woman cheerily.

I bought one and the necessaries to post it to Jerry. That took me to nine-thirty and the music shop.

My entrance was announced by door chimes like a snakecharmer's pipe. Inside, my eye went immediately to the racks of sheet music: simple school-grade pieces. The glass counter displaying violin and guitar strings like ties in a haberdasher's: budget level only. The violins and recorders on the wall, starter-level.

I felt a twist of disappointment. But what was I expecting? A place like this wouldn't have a professional clientele.

Somewhere in the shop, a singing lesson was in progress. The pupil was attempting to sing scales but they were too high for her. Her easiest notes were middle C to F. Above that she was straining to place the note and keep tonal quality. But that wasn't her fault; the teacher needed to go back to more basic work.

Nobody came to answer the snakecharmer's call, so I browsed a rack of CDs. It was already being inspected by a tall crisply-groomed woman in her fifties, with a neck that was slightly too long for her head. She made me think of Alice in Wonderland.

The singing pupil wound her way up through another scale and I winced. I noticed the woman wince as well.

'I don't like Christine's method of teaching,' she whispered.

'No,' I said quietly. 'She needs to go through breathing and vowel placement, and those exercises are too demanding for her level.'

The woman leaned closer. 'Christine is the owner's daughter. Careful.'

Her eyebrows formed a heavy V, which gave her the appearance of a male character in a Japanese Noh play.

A woman bustled out of the back of the shop. Her cashmere jumper sported a brooch in the shape of a treble clef. More treble clef novelties were displayed next to the till.

I went to introduce myself. 'Are you Sally? We spoke on the phone.'

We shook hands, exchanged the usual preliminaries.

'It's so good that you could help us,' said Sally. 'Felicity's got a lot of dedicated clients and they'll be so disappointed if they have to cancel.'

'Did you manage to sort out an accompanist?' I said.

Sally called out. 'Eleanor, come and meet Felicity's cover teacher, Carol Lear.'

The tall woman stopped browsing the CDs. Her Noh eyebrows batted upwards. 'So you're a Lear? Pleased to meet you. I'm a Lear too.'

'Oh I hadn't realised that,' said Sally. 'How funny.' She turned back to me. 'The clients are darlings. A lot of them are in the operatic society and they're auditioning for the spring show. They're all anxious about it. We can't let them down this late and Felicity wouldn't have left them but her father's in a state and she's got to go to him.'

A voice from the other room attempted an ascending line in Italian from an aria by Pergolesi. It was probably the teacher's voice because it was stronger than the previous one. As she crested the top E her soft palate blocked the sound and made a harsh screech.

Sally mistook my silent attention for admiration. 'Can you do as well as Christine in there?'

It's Sally's daughter, I reminded myself, and took a deep breath to arm myself with tact. 'I'll certainly give it a try. Where is your teaching room?'

Sally waved in a general upstairs direction. 'Eleanor will show you the way. Your first client is due in fifteen minutes. Don't worry about anything, Eleanor knows them because she plays accompaniment for Felicity anyway.'

In our teaching room, the first thing I did was inspect the accompanying instrument. It was an electronic keyboard, covered with buttons that promised entire string and brass ensembles. Its keys looked plastic and over-springy. Not likely to tempt even a casual tickle.

Eleanor took off her coat and unwound her scarf, revealing her long neck, which made me think all the more of Sir John Tenniel's Alice. 'So your name's Lear. How marvellous. The Lear family have, as you no doubt know, lived in this village for generations.'

My family hadn't, of course. Most of them were as northern as millstone grit. I said 'Oh really?', while looking for the music stand. I pulled it out of the corner and positioned it for the singer.

Eleanor placed herself at the keyboard and turned it on. It came alive with a carnival of red LEDs. She played some slow arpeggios, her hands spreading easily. I'd always yearned for hands that big and capable. However, hers were stiff and she was probably too old to supple them very much now.

'This keyboard has quite a nice piano sound,' she said. 'Is that what you like to work with?'

The noise it made was not in any way like a piano. It sounded like a wild west honky-tonk heard at the far end of a drain. But so long as it provided a pitch, that was all we needed.

'Whatever the clients like is fine by me,' I said.

Eleanor played a few scales, talking all the time. 'It's good to have more Lears in Vellonoweth again.'

She pronounced the name as though it was three separate words, Vellon O'Weth. Presumably to make a point, although heaven knows what.

'Did you realise,' she said, scaling up and down with bizarre fingering, 'the Lears built the original Vellon O'Weth Hall? It fell into disrepair and was sold because the baronet, Sir Bertrand Lear, spent all his time gambling and drinking.'

'Vellonoweth Hall, the power station?'

'The park, yes,' said Eleanor, in the same corrective tone she used to enunciate Vellon O'Weth. 'It was a manor house. It isn't there any more, of course. It had to be knocked down. Sir Bertrand squandered the family fortune.' She sat back, satisfied with her warm-up. 'Anyway, Carol, tell me about yourself. We haven't had many musicians in the Lear family before.'

She still seemed to imagine I was related to her. 'Actually,' I said, 'I don't think my family comes from here. We come from Cheshire. Can you play me an A?'

She put her finger decisively on the note.

'The tuning's off. It's a half-tone flat.'

'Felicity likes it like that,' said Eleanor. 'She starts them off a bit flat to give them confidence.'

'I can't teach like that. If they're singing top C I want them to sing C. If they can't sing it, we have to work on it. I'm not going to flannel them into thinking they can sing top C if they can't.'

'Ah,' said Eleanor, 'but we tune upwards during the lesson. That's the marvellous thing about these keyboards. You can twiddle the tuning up and down.'

'Sorry, I've got absolute pitch. I know it's off and I can't teach like that.'

There was a knock at the door. 'Come in,' called Eleanor.

Our first pupil, a mousy-looking lady with a puff of tightly curled hair like a brown dandelion clock, greeted Eleanor, then remained in the doorway looking doubtfully at me.

'Come in, Jean,' said Eleanor. 'Felicity's away so you've got Carol. She's one of the Lears, isn't that nice? Carol, this is Jean Dowman.'

I'm not one of your Lears, I thought. You're as woolly about listening as you are about tuning.

But there was Jean Dowman to welcome.

I realised where I had heard Jean's name before. 'We're neighbours,' I said to her. 'I'm cat-sitting for Jenny.'

'Oh yes,' said Jean. Her eye still held faint suspicion, as if she was worried about what I might make her do.

Eleanor perched Jean's music on her keyboard and played a broken chord of C major. Flat.

'Eleanor, just twiddle that tuning up to concert pitch, will you please? Then we'll start.'

An hour later, Jean left. The next pupil was already at the door. Her name was Anne Stubbings and she ran the Railway Hotel, in its now abbreviated form. She seemed to enjoy her lesson more than Jean did, or at least she smiled as she left. Jean had gathered her music and exited in affronted silence.

After Anne, Sally came up with tea.

'How is it going?' she said.

'Very well,' said Eleanor firmly. Which was decent of her.

After Sally closed the door I said: 'I think they wanted Felicity. Especially that first one, Jean Dowman.'

'Yes, Jean Dowman's on the committee of the horticulture society. A real busybody. But that's committees for you. You're like me. We Lears have never got on with conventional authority.'

She patted my knee. 'It's so nice to have a musical Lear. We've had artists and explorers but no musicians. Except for me of course.'

From the room below I could hear another pupil wailing through scales that were too high. And footsteps were coming up the stairs.

'That'll be Mrs Snetterton,' said Eleanor, and turned back to the keyboard. Her hand reached for the tuning knob again.

When I finished for the day I texted Gene. *Feel like a drink?*

Okay, he replied. *Railway Hotel bar, 6pm.*

He wasn't easy company, but he was the nearest thing to a friendly face.

I was slightly surprised he said yes, especially as I thought Saturday had exhausted his tolerance for company.

But I wouldn't need him to talk; just drink and listen.

The bar of the Railway Hotel had been themed as a New England railroad station. At least, that was how they explained the walls covered in crossed signs and lined with tongue and groove panelling like a sauna. We sat in tall-backed banquettes and leaned over a table like two people meeting on a 1950s train. American soft-rock provided just enough aural camouflage for me to have a good rant.

'Half of them can't read music. They've got terrible aural skills – sing a phrase to them and they can't get it right. Most of them didn't want to learn, they just wanted to show off and have me pat them on the head.'

Gene listened with thoughtful attention, his face flitting with microscopic reactions. I had a sense that although he was quiet, his brain was having a very lively time.

I took a drink, as I was falling hopelessly behind. 'I hate half-assed, amateur things. I don't do amateur. None of the people I know do amateur. I'm not saying I sing well, but if I went for a lesson it would be to improve. I wanted to learn piano from the best so I went to the Royal damn College of Music, not the teacher down the road who'd flannel me all my life. These people don't want to sing better. Mediocre is all right for them. Well it's not all right for me.'

Above us was a skylight. Rain had been pattering onto it all the time we were there. Now it started to drip onto the table.

Gene stood up. 'I think we'd better move.' His glass was nearly empty; mine was hardly touched.

'Sorry,' I said. 'I'll try to drink more and talk less. How was your day?'

He relaxed back in the seat. A secretive smile. 'Not as bad as yours.'

With such permission, I went on.

There was much that needed to be said about my clients' songs. The musical they were all auditioning for was about a man trying to find a lost hat. Although each song had different words, they were all identical in rhythm and melodic trajectory, as though they were all descants of each other – and, in fact, of *Singing in the Rain*.

I shut up while a guy in a Railway Hotel shirt cleared the previous occupants' glasses.

When he'd gone, Gene said: 'The musical was written by one of my patients. He teaches at the local school.'

'Please can you advise him to stop on medical grounds? If it's bad for me to play the piano it must be bad for him to compose like that.'

The wind picked up and the rain came down harder, thudding onto the banquettes next to us.

'It'll probably get its own special programme on Radio Active,' said Gene.

'Radio Active,' I groaned. It was the local station. 'I can't seem to get anything else.'

'It's something to do with shadows from the hills.'

'They're a real local treasure. Did you hear the man imitating an Irish fiddle this morning? With his voice?'

'Lucky you. Every time I switch them on they seem to be playing whalesong.'

'Jesus.' I scrunched my hair into handfuls, plonked my elbows on the table and looked up at him. 'How do you stand it here?'

His reply was an expression so subtle it was beyond unreadable.

'No really, how do you stand it?' And I also meant, how do you stand living in that nurses' home, and having no one you want to see. I'd never met anyone who was so isolated.

'I guess it makes a change.' He sounded like he gave it no thought at all. Perhaps he didn't, and it didn't matter.

I turned my glass around on the mat, thinking.

'You know, when we were eighteen, Kate Rafferty won a place with the Royal Exchange youth theatre group. No one I knew was going to settle for second best.' I leaned further over the sticky table. A challenge to discard his secretive mask. 'When you were eighteen, what were you going to do?'

A tiny, impudent smile. 'Change the world. Maybe.'

He didn't mean it in the slightest. He was just echoing back what I'd been saying. 'You're still not smoking. When you were in London you smoked like a volcano. I haven't seen you light up at all since I've been here. What's the secret?'

'I just gave up.'

'How? Nicotine patches? A dose of your own hypnosis?'

'I gave up.'

I took a drink of cider. 'You know that trick you do, putting a cigarette out with your bare foot?'

'You like that?'

'How do you do it?'

'You mean, what's the secret?'

'The secret.' I prodded my finger emphatically on the table. 'Spit it out.'

'You put your foot on the cigarette, tread on it, and the cigarette goes out.'

I decided I was way too sober. I drained my glass, picked up his and went to the bar.

The next morning, I made my way up the teaching room and an unexpected sound. Not a metallic honkytonk, but a sensitive instrument.

Not that it was being played that way. In fact, each key was apparently being bludgeoned with an axe.

I pushed open the door. Eleanor was sitting at the keyboard of a Clavinova electronic piano. She beamed at me, eyebrows high.

'Isn't it lovely? Sally said we can use this today.'

I closed the door. Eleanor did another jackhammer flourish, which staggered into the opening of Bach's *Toccata*. I folded my coat over my bag and stowed them under the shelves in the corner.

'Let's have concert pitch, shall we?'

CHAPTER 29

'Darling, thank you for the thingy.'

Jerry had received the radiation badge. I'd posted it only the day before. The town might be stuck in a time warp but when you sent objects away they fled with super-efficiency.

I'd escaped for a walk during my lunch break. The Vellonoweth Hall leaflet showed a beach, so I followed a fingerpost sign to some narrow stairs down the side of a cliff. And there it was; a pebbled bay enclosed by high cliffs, the sea rocking and heaving.

Further up the coast was a radio mast, where the bay spread an arm into the water. Right at its fingertips was a square building on stilts like a birdwatcher's hide. According to the Vellonoweth Hall leaflet it was the incomparable Radio Active, housed in an abandoned anti-aircraft tower because otherwise the hills blocked the signal. This morning it had been playing beginners' clarinet lessons.

Phone reception was good, though; the bar was full to the top. So I tried Jerry.

After I explained about the radiation badge he asked me how the teaching was going. I had plenty to say. Not only about the pupils, but also about Eleanor, who had clanged that poor Clavinova all morning.

'Darling,' said Jerry, 'you always hate your ensemble partners. You say they're not musical enough, or they haven't got perfect pitch.'

'Absolute pitch. It's not called perfect pitch.'

'And you end up loving them to bits.'

'No. These people are Neanderthals.'

'You always say that too. Remember when you were in that trio?'

'Ensembles are all about doing justice to the music. That's why it gets stormy. This isn't remotely similar.'

'Sweetheart, don't be too hard on your pupils. Remember they're doing it for fun.'

I dug my toe into the gravel beach. 'Why is doing something badly fun? They're happy to be humdrum, but they should be ashamed.'

'Chill. It's a different pace of life there. Have a casual fling. Make love, not war. You get so intense.'

Jerry was so love-drunk he assumed that was what everyone else needed.

There was a slurping noise at the other end of the phone. Probably coffee. No doubt he needed it with all the sleep he must be missing.

'Hey, I had another session with Anthony Morrish.'

My diaphragm tightened. 'Oh yes?'

'I wanted to know more about Ruby Cunningham. Some people on the message board said it was odd that she could read and write if she lived in the East End at that time. Particularly as she was a woman.'

Was Jerry admitting to the cold light of logic? Had he seen through Morrish and his cheap Ripper cabaret? Perhaps.

'And what did you find?'

'It turns out she was the daughter of an artist. How about that?'

Hearing him say that set my heart hammering. Don't be gullible, sweetheart, I wanted to say. Someone's using you.

'Did Tim go with you this time?' It would be interesting if he did.

'No. I haven't told Tim yet. The time's got to be right.'

I couldn't imagine the time would ever be right. Tim, non-stop newshound? He'd strip off the mumbo-jumbo like acid on old paint.

Carefully I said: 'Don't scare him.'

'I won't.'

'No really, Jerry. He may not have to know.'

The teaching timetable was relentless. As soon as Eleanor and I sent a pupil down the stairs the snakecharmer's pipe would toot and another pair of feet would trudge upwards.

These people were serious about their music. If only they wanted to learn.

I started all new pupils with exercises to check their pitch and breathing. One woman got confused as I asked her to pant like a dog. Her eyes begged Eleanor for rescue. I had no intention of letting her off as she'd arrived puffing like a stegosaurus from the stairs, which she shouldn't have been if she had any breath control.

After a few moments, Eleanor chipped in. 'This is Felicity's cousin, Freda. Usually I play and Freda sings.'

Freda squared her shoulders and adjusted her paisley pashmina so that it draped like highland costume. 'I've performed at the Ixendon recital for years. I don't need lessons.'

Eleanor lifted her hands, Freda nodded and off they went.

Normally when a pianist partners with a singer, you are combining two perfectionists who love their disciplines to distraction. And forcing them to compromise. The first rehearsals usually go like this: 'if you play that way, you'll drown me'; 'if you sing that way, I can't keep rhythm'. They battle and then they learn to blend, and sail the music as though they were one instrument.

Freda didn't sing. She yelled with red-faced aggression as though heaving a caber into the air. Eleanor walloped the Clavinova, progressively turning the volume louder and louder. I expected Freda to clout her, but they took precisely no notice of each other, grinding on like a pair of drunks having a sing-song.

After the lesson, Sally brought us tea. She looked pleased.

'That lesson went well. If you keep stopping them they get frustrated. They like it if they can sing a piece properly.'

Eleanor kept discreetly quiet as usual. After Sally went she even had the grace to apologise for butting in during the lesson. She just thought, she said, that I needed a bit of looking after.

Then she talked about another of her ancestors, an explorer

called Ronald Lear, who became stranded in the Antarctic when his plane broke down. He and his companion spent two months in a base camp, and Ronald said his ancestors frequently spoke to him while he was there.

Maybe, I ventured, this was what one would expect of two men on their own with nothing to look at but snow, and nothing to eat except snow.

On the contrary, said Eleanor, they hadn't gone mad at all. Rescuers found them in excellent spirits, having taken baths in melted ice each day and shaved.

What this was meant to illustrate, I haven't a clue. Except that enduring the intolerable was in her genes. I doubted very much that it was in mine.

I finished early, at two o'clock. I went to the Spar for bread. It was locked and dark. On the door a sign said it was half-day closing.

Half-day closing. Another bygone tradition, alive and well in Vellonoweth. I wandered along the main street as the sky glowered above me, threatening rain again. Not good as my car was back at the cottage.

Fat raindrops splashed onto the pavement. I looked more urgently for a welcoming reprieve. I spotted one; the Victorian indoor market. I dashed inside.

'Hello, Carol!' A woman in a bright red polo neck and thick, curled-under hair was presiding over a cash box and a book of raffle tickets. Her name was Bronwyn and I had taught her the day before. She had a breathy, weak voice and hit her cues late most of the time.

'Do come in,' she said, and pushed a leaflet towards me on the black cloth. It said *Welcome to the psychic fate*. The table was covered with a black velvet cloth.

I had been hoping for something a little more down to earth, like an antiques fair. But the rain was now a thick curtain, turning the road into a grey river.

'Shouldn't that be fete with an E?' I said.

'We wanted it to be more than just a feast or a festival,' said Bronwyn. 'It's about destiny.'

One last time, I looked out at the hissing street. Fate, it seemed, wanted me to go in.

I paid and was given a raffle ticket as proof. 'We have a musician in here,' added Bronwyn.

I hoped she wasn't psychic, or she would know how dubious that made me.

Inside, the building was a long hall with tables down the middle and a stained glass roof like a grand greenhouse. Bronwyn had certainly pulled in the punters; there were enough visitors ambling past the stands to make a slow tour compulsory. A fair number were in loose-fitting clothes like civilian versions of monkish robes; others were expressing their inner demon with head-to-toe black. Shades of the Anthony Morrish audience.

The first stall I saw was captained by a man with a demonic beard, who sat at a table with two bowls of water and a clutch of leaflets fanned out like a poker hand. *Internationally Renowned Clairvoyant and Occultist*, said the leaflets. He was in his own world, reading a Dan Brown novel. Next to him was a stall displaying a line of miniature bottles, also with no takers.

All the punters were crowding around a thickset woman with dark hair that stuck up as though it had been brushed around a wire frame. She was handing out slips of paper, heavy bangles rattling on her stocky arms. Someone passed a slip to me. It was mysteriously blank.

I watched one of the other recipients take her blank slip to a table. In a round hand she wrote: *Isabel, can you find me a set of runes, old if possible. Gladys.* She folded it and placed it in an earthenware bowl.

Beside the bowl, a block of business cards explained it all.

Death comes to all witches and psychics, who, with their passing, leave behind the debris of their faith and calling. Isabel Caswell will pay cash to relatives and others seeking to dispose of these often misunderstood magical artefacts and temple furnishings dedicated to the world of the beyond.

There was also an open photo album. The pictures showed a pottery candlestick with a moon drawn on it; a heap of purple velvet; a statuette of a woman with a pregnancy bump and a smugly fecund expression. All of them were on sale for £20 or £30 a go. They must have been the magical artefacts, but they looked like charity shop leftovers.

A white-haired man in a spry corduroy suit with a bow tie, like a dapper professor, called out in a high voice: 'Isabel, have you got an aurora?' I thought he must be making a joke, but the bangled woman – presumably Isabel – handed him an A5 booklet. Its cover read *Aurora – A New Age, Pagan and Occult Atlas of Ixendon, Vellonoweth and Nowethland*.

Isabel brought out more copies and waggled them with a clatter of her armgear. 'Anyone else want an *Aurora*?' Gladys Runes hailed for one.

Isabel put a copy on the photo album, which I was still investigating with slow horror, and said firmly: 'It's only a pound'.

I decided Jerry might like *Aurora* and paid up.

Bronwyn bustled past with a tower of polystyrene cups. 'Ooh, tea,' said the dapper professor, and followed her. I did too, to give myself elbow room to sort out where I was going to put *Aurora*.

At the end of the room was a serving hatch leading to a kitchen. I dumped my bag on the counter to organise a space among the petrol receipts and paperwork from the music shop.

A man came to the serving hatch. 'Oh, have you bought *Aurora*? That's good.' Around his neck he had a little bottle on a leather thong. He gave the bottle a shake. 'This contains spirit water. You can buy them on my stand. This bottle's quartz, which are a bit more dear. Glass ones start at nine-ninety-nine.'

I said no thanks.

The dapper professor put a cup under the nozzle of an urn and squirted tea into it. 'Trevor has spirits who bless the water personally. You should get one.'

I realised he was talking to me.

They couldn't be serious. Who could charge ten quid for a thimbleful of water in a bottle? At least Anthony Morrish gave his punters a good fright. This fraud hardly made an effort.

Even con tricks in Vellonoweth were third rate.

Saying no again, I reorganised my bag so *Aurora* could lie flat. I hitched the strap onto my shoulder and turned.

And then I saw it.

At the end of the room was a baby grand piano. A waif of a woman sat at its stool, with a distant expression like someone who had waited a long time for a bus.

There was something heavy about the front of the instrument. The keyboard looked too bulky. Not like a piano, but the bonnet of a van.

I excused myself to Trevor and the professor and edged past them for a closer look.

Above the black notes on the keyboard was a shelf of white.

No, not a shelf. Another set of keys, narrow and white, between the black and white set.

They were extra notes.

I felt a cold, delicious tingle.

On a normal piano, C sharp is the same as D flat, but musically the notes are distinct. On some other instruments they still are, but the piano averages them into one note.

This keyboard, though, divided them into two true tones.

I'd heard of enharmonic keyboards. They were rare and fabled, like unicorns. No one I knew had ever seen one.

A piano that allowed each black note to speak as its two hidden halves. Waiting to be played.

'That's Willa,' said the dapper professor. 'She channels music from the spirit world.'

Of course, this was Vellonoweth. It would be disappointing.

Nevertheless, my gaze was drawn back to the girl.

Although her clothes were wisps of black material like many of the other would-be witches, she was cut from different cloth. Her posture was light as a Siamese cat, and quiet. Like a musician who truly submerges in a piece, not these Vellonoweth hams who pickaxed their way through.

'Excuse me,' I said to Trevor, and made to go closer.

'You shouldn't talk to her unless you channel a spirit,' said the dapper professor in his fussy voice. 'She's in a trance. You could be very disruptive.'

'I might take her Flo, my midwife spirit,' said Trevor. 'I need her to bless some more water for me.' The dapper professor seemed to approve.

Willa turned her head in our direction and her expression was so familiar. The distant greeting of someone half in twilight. The people here might call it a trance but to me it looked no different from musical concentration.

I thought of the dreary possibilities if Trevor inflicted Flo the water-blesser on us all. Such an instrument deserved better.

'I channel a spirit,' I said.

I was talking to Willa but the dapper professor butted in.

'I meet a lot of channellers. They are usually very untrained.'

That really irritated me. I probably knew more about rigorous training than he ever would. And to hear her play that keyboard I'd sell my very soul.

'Actually,' I said, 'I'm Royal College trained.'

'Royal College where?' said Trevor.

'London,' I said with complete truth.

'Is that near the Spiritualists' Association in Belgravia?'

'Very near there,' I replied. The College was certainly a lot nearer to Belgravia than it was to here.

'So where's your stand?' said the dapper professor.

But I was already at Willa's side.

Her eyes focussed on me. 'Can you give me a token? Something you use when you talk to spirit?'

Gene's tape was still in my bag. He had given it to me the other night. I offered it to Willa, releasing it hesitantly. And prayed she had nothing to play it on.

Willa put her fingers around it as though cradling a bird. Her hands were those of a pianist, tough and stretchy. 'Who is here?'

How few details could I give?

'Me.'

'Another life?'

'Yes.'

I noticed the room had become quieter. The browsers had stopped their slow circuit of the stands and were watching us.

'From when?' said Willa.

Aware of the watching eyes, I replied. 'The future.'

I think I heard a few people repeat the word 'future'. But Willa kept her focus very still. Bravo, Willa. That doesn't matter if we understand each other.

She put my tape on the piano and the instrument yawned a soft echo. Lovely noise.

I heard the word 'future', still passing around the room like a fly.

Willa tilted her face upwards, lifted her hands and began.

The first notes were uncertain. She played middle C, then C sharp. As I'd thought, the C sharp was a sliver flat. Her fingers wandered to the bony key next to it. The note was a hair's breadth higher. True D flat.

Improvising is tricky. I can't do it. But Willa made it sound like something padded in and spoke through the piano in its own crooked voice.

She roamed through a series of chords, experimenting. On one she trod on the sustain pedal. And she was right to; harmonically it joined what had gone before.

Abruptly, she sped up, changing direction as if running between the cracks of a chessboard. Her technique began to falter, but her musicality carried it. Notes slipped out from her fingers and the piano sang in its divided voice. It was an impossible instrument but she coaxed it to make music.

When finally it ended, the room stood in silence. I was thankful for that. It's too abrupt when audiences applaud while the last chord is still hanging. As soon as it had properly gone, I started. She deserved it.

Nobody joined in. A few of the robed punters gave me irritated looks, then moved away to browse more stalls. Still none of them gave so much as a twitter of reaction. Not one.

I leaned down and spoke to Willa quietly. 'That was remarkable. Thank you.'

She was still in twilight. I retrieved my tape and moved discreetly away.

Trevor and the dapper professor were nearby. I said: 'She is so talented. Is she studying music?'

Trevor rocked back on his heels. 'Most of us find it helps to have something tangible like music to use with meditations and communion with spirit. The skill of being a medium is in how you use them.'

Unbelievable. This seller of overpriced water thought that he was the talented one.

'The skill,' I replied, 'is to play an instrument like that and make it truly musical. She worked miracles with it.'

The dapper professor gave a superior smile and shook his head. 'There are many tools a medium can use. I once used music but now I find my cleansing crystal confers more control of spirit.' He tweaked his bow tie. 'This spirit of yours came through well. But how does the channelling work if it's from the future?'

Trevor answered for me, with a rather irritating air of authority. 'I don't have a problem with that, Richard. If you have memories of the past, why can't you have memories of the future?'

The dapper professor frowned 'It's not very orthodox.'

Bronwyn bustled towards us with a clipboard. The dapper professor looked at her ample front appreciatively.

'Nice tie,' said Bronwyn, obviously hoping to get rid of him.

'I find they cheer people up,' he replied, and preened the tie. 'I am usually asked whether it lights up and spins round.'

'Oh?' said Bronwyn, and turned her bosom away.

'I feel,' said the dapper professor, 'that bow ties make the wearer appear distinctive, artistic and thoughtful.'

'Mm,' said Bronwyn.

He went on. 'But for me a bow tie is more than just a display of individuality. If something goes wrong with spirit you are less likely to be strangled.'

Bronwyn held her clipboard out like a racquet. 'Willa needs to be alone. There will be more spirits to play. Come away now.'

Trevor and Richard looked slightly surprised to be reminded Willa was still there.

As I headed for the door I took a last look back at her, a composed figure waiting at the heavy-jawed keyboard. Alone with a talent of her own that no one saw or cared about.

My phone rang, lighting my bag with blue ice. I took my eyes off the road to glance at the display.

Karli.

My old collaborator and brief paramour. Why was he calling?

I was returning to Vellonoweth from a supermarket run in Ixendon. A black and white chevron loomed out of the dusk, warning of a tight corner. I wrenched the wheel while the phone continued to announce my surprising caller. One more ring and it would cut to voicemail. Should I let it?

No. I grabbed it and answered.

'Hi Carol. How are you?' His baritone sounded like velvet even in the tinny handset.

We went through those predictable overtures while I cruised to a safe spot and turned the engine off. It was such a surprise to hear from him.

There was a delay each time he answered. He couldn't be in England. I asked him where he was.

'I'm still in Boston. But I'm back in London soon for a brief visit.'

I noticed his stress on the word brief. Not that I was hoping for anything else – we'd said our goodbyes. So this call must be business.

'Carol, I've got great news. I'm doing a CD of chamber music as part of a Sony series and they want our arrangement of *Dover Beach.*'

'Say that again – Sony want *Dover Beach*?'

His voice came back, two seconds later. 'Can you clear your diary?'

I could hear he was smiling. His face was always mobile, as supple as his singing.

A track on a CD. For Sony. Deals like that don't come along very often, particularly if you're not a well known name.

My words came out in a jumble before I managed to be coherent.

'That's great, Karli. Fantastic.' Whatever I said didn't seem adequate. This was an amazing offer. 'Is there a recording schedule?'

Please say there's plenty of time, that it's months away.

'They need it by the 22nd of next month.'

Less than five weeks.

But I couldn't refuse this. It was Sony. It was with Karli, who not only was a glorious singer, he had to be doing phenomenally well if Sony was letting him put such an obscure piece on his disc. *Dover Beach* wasn't standard repertoire and this was our own arrangement. That agent of his must be a rottweiler. And this could be a major break for me.

'Carol, are you there?'

'I'm here. That's great... Does it have to be so soon?'

'They want to release in time for Christmas.'

My right hand was clenched on the steering wheel. My wrist started to beat with an agonizing pulse, a warning to the hopes whispering in my heart.

I'd played for Leo Korda. Could I do this? It was just one song. But there would be rehearsals and multiple takes. We might be working for days to get the piece perfect. Look what playing at the masterclass had done. And that had been less than an hour.

'Carol?'

I forced the words out. 'Sorry Karli, I don't know if you heard but I can't play. I strained a tendon. I've been signed off.'

The transatlantic relay held onto his voice for a moment, and then: 'You're kidding. How long for?'

'Six months. Possibly more. I just have to see how it goes.'

When Karli's voice came again, it had descended three tones. 'Carol, you're joking, right? Sony want *Dover Beach*. I'm coming back from the States for this. Get up off your hospital bed.'

Another chance to take it back; to agree to play, which he so wanted me to do. The pulse in my wrist fired intensely, like a burn. It must be psychosomatic, a response to the stress of this horrible choice.

'Karli, I'm not joking. I'm not even in London. I'm teaching singing in a fleabitten town on the south coast. I can't play.'

Singers are so sensitive to the changes in a voice. He heard the catch in mine. 'Oh Carol, I'm sorry. Look – you take care, all right? Call me when you get back.'

Did he mean back to London, or back to music?

'Yeah,' I said. 'You too, Karli. Nice talking to you.' He was gone.

CHAPTER 30

I sat in the stopped car, looking at the black hills. It gets dark so early in winter.

Karli and I met last summer when a mutual acquaintance held a concert of Samuel Barber, the twentieth-century American composer. One of the pieces they performed was his arrangement of Matthew Arnold's poem *Dover Beach*. It's an eerie piece for voice and strings, and I'd often toyed with the idea of arranging it for voice and piano.

So, it turned out, had Karli. Soon we were spending the afternoons at my Yamaha with the windows to the garden open, reinterpreting Barber's uneasy melody for the keyboard. To spare the neighbours we worked quietly, Karli *mezzo voce*, me using the practice pedal. Searching for the way to melt the parts together, while the heatwave put the city into a stupor.

The first time we rode it all the way through, Karli's rich tonation sounded conspiratorial, like whispering; the muted piano like bells tolling under water.

After that he didn't leave my house very much at all. Until the recital in a church in Fleet Street, when the agent saw us perform it – and fell for Karli's singing too.

I was crying. I pressed the heels of my hands into my eyes but the tears scorched their way out. I saw my practice room in London, the Yamaha sealed under its cover. The windows closed and the garden dead.

My phone rang. No, Karli. Don't try again. I looked at the display. It was Gene.

I answered. 'Hi.' It came out sticky.

'I spoke to Jenny Tollderson this afternoon. She was trying to get hold of you. She and Felicity need to be in Spain for at least a month. Can you stay a bit longer?'

I mastered my voice. 'Yes. That would be good.' It wouldn't. It would be unbearable. But it was better than going back.

Keep me away from London.

The car was cold. I started the engine so the heater would come on. Twisting the key produced an explosion of agony in my wrist. To punish me for the very thought of playing.

'Is something wrong?' said Gene.

He knew, of course.

I turned the heater up and moved my wrist in the hot stream of air, trying to warm the pain away. 'My arm's really bad – do you think you could look at it?'

I hadn't seen Gene for a nearly a week. He'd moved. His new flat was in a row of buildings next to the hospital, above a furniture warehouse.

He showed me up the stairs, sat me on a sofa. The sofa had chrome arms, different from the one he had in London.

The pain slowed me down and made me notice every detail, moment by moment.

He felt up and down my wrists and forearms, squeezing along the long bones with his fingertips. He flexed my wrists backwards and forwards, watching my face, and tested my grip. Repeating Dr Golding's routine, even down to the questions.

'What were you doing when the pain came on?'

'Nothing. Driving.'

'Is the pain the same type as before, or different?'

'Same.'

'Is it more severe, or less?'

'Quite bad.'

Gene continued, feeling gently for abnormalities, trying each joint through its range of movement. It seemed to help. I stopped tensing for the next jolt and began to look around.

There were packing crates behind the sofa, the tops sealed with brown tape. What would come out of them to populate the blank walls?

'You haven't been playing?' he said.

I gave him a hurt look. 'Playing what? There's nothing here to play.'

He flicked an eyebrow up, waiting for the real truth.

'Honestly. Not this time.'

Gene let go of my arm and nudged his glasses up his nose. 'There's no heat or swelling. It must be the nerve. They sometimes fire randomly.'

My phone warbled from my bag. I glanced at the blue display and then stared at the five black letters.

Karli again. What more could he want to say? Should I switch it to voicemail?

Gene stood up, waving to me to answer it.

I put the phone to my ear. Hello.

'Hi Carol. Sorry to bother you again.'

He was nervous. There was a tremor in his voice. Singers always betray their feelings.

His hesitation was magnified by the transatlantic pause.

'Sony are really keen to go ahead with this. I was wondering... you'd get a credit in the sleeve notes... but the Barber estate have approved it and –'

Oh no, not a long preamble. Especially when it's so obvious what's coming. 'You want to use our arrangement with another pianist?'

'I didn't want to do it without consulting you.'

What did he expect me to say? Hip hip hooray, have my blessing?

'Carol?'

'That's fine, you go ahead.'

Silence, then: 'Thanks. It's just I didn't – you'll get a credit as co-arranger. I'll make sure.'

Don't start all that again. You're embarrassed, which is decent of you, but that's nothing compared to how I feel.

Another suspended moment, then: 'I really don't want to do it without you. I'm going to have to learn it all again and it won't be the same.'

Yes, I know. But you'll manage.

'Karli, I've got to go. I'm with someone.'

'Okay. I'll call you sometime.'

No you won't. You'll never be able to face me after this. I

can hear it in your voice. 'Bye, Karli.'

I cut the call and put the phone down.

Gene was leaning against one of the crates watching me, his arms folded across his chest.

'Boyfriend?'

'Duet partner.' I felt the tears starting again. I blinked fiercely and tried to put a brave face on. 'Duet partner with the offer of a lifetime. I don't suppose you can perform a minor miracle? Cure me so I can play?'

If I was with Jerry he would have given me a good hug.

Gene watched me with physicianly detachment. 'Do you want me to do something about the pain?'

He meant that suspended darkness. Where they all want to take you.

'No,' I answered immediately.

My eyes blurred. This was not the place to shed tears. I didn't even know why I was crying. Saying no should have been enough.

I fussed in my bag to have an excuse to look down. 'I'd better go. I've got things to do.' Like go back to a cottage that's furnished as though humans live there. Call Jerry. Or Danya, she had a fling with Karli once.

Gene seemed to become more still. 'Is there a reason why not?'

'I think it's bad for me.' I pulled my bag onto my shoulder and stood up.

He stayed exactly where he was.

'I was at the burns unit the other day. There was a kid with third-degree burns because he'd tried to cross a railway track. The skin on both his legs was scorched black. The surgeons had to cut it all away. That was even more painful than the burn. He'd taken drugs and couldn't tell us what, so we couldn't give him any analgesia. But they had to cut or he would have died. So before they worked on him they gave him to me.'

Through the material of my shirt my leather bag felt cold on my ribs. I had an image of Gene talking to a bloodied, burned kid, as implacable as he was right now. His composure never wavering despite screams, blood, struggling.

This room was so cold, it chilled everything. These blank walls. How could Gene stand it? A person who was comfortable here must have a soul of solid steel. A surgeon's soul.

I'd come to him like a patient and now he saw me as a problem to solve. A problem that belonged to him.

'Why do you think it's bad for you?'

I couldn't tell him, but he'd know if I tried to lie.

'I think it's bad for me because it made me play better. At that masterclass I was better than I've ever been. It's too tempting.'

'What was the piece?'

'The piece?'

'At the masterclass.'

'Chopin. The sonata in B minor. You probably don't know it.'

'Tell me about the sonata.'

'Tell you what? You're not a musician.'

'How does it make you feel?'

I hugged the bag closer. Both arms around it, like a hot water bottle.

'Warm. Light.'

'And now without it it's dark.'

I sat down, completely involuntarily, felled like a tree.

I'd given him that word. He'd got it out of me.

Gene went out of the room. He returned with a duvet, settled it around my shoulders, removed my handbag and placed it on the floor by my feet. He took his time. He had me, paralysed like a stretched pause in a transatlantic phone call.

The duvet smelled of fabric conditioner with a faint note of something spicy, like exotic wood. But I still felt cold.

He was going to make me go back there.

He sat beside me on the sofa. The oval frames of his glasses made the angles of his face look sensitive. His grey eyes invited me to look at him.

'Don't think about being cold.' His voice carried gentle authority. Like Karli's mezzo voce taking persuasive charge of

Matthew Arnold's words. 'Feel the warmth. In your sleeves. In your shoulders. Spreading all over your skin. Softening through your blood.'

I shuddered as though one of Dr Golding's machines had control of me. My voice came out as a small scared sound. 'I can't.'

He waited. His eye seeking my eye. So steady. 'Take your time. You're warm, you're safe. You won't slip into the dark.'

He pulled the duvet tighter around my shoulders. As his arm crossed in front of me I realised the smell of wood was the smell of him.

'It won't be dark. Just come and see.'

A tear fell out of my eye. It made a track down my cheek.

His breath as he talked turned the tear cold. I felt every millimetre that it moved.

'This tear falls and it takes the cold away. You feel it travel down your face. Every cell it touches. As it goes down the darkness lifts.'

Chapter 31

Tape 3

I wake as if someone has shaken me.

But no-one is there. The dormitory is quiet.

One side is a tall window into the sea. Seaweed strokes the water with black fingers. Fish with sequin eyes glide past. The rock building shifts and creaks.

All around me are sounds of slumber. In, out, breathing to soothe the world. Soothesayers sleep serenely on their backs, never tossing or turning. Our slumber is filmed so that clients can watch if they need it. There is no room for nightmares.

I do not have nightmares but my nerves are strings under a bow.

A groan above me in one of the bunks. Someone turns over.

An arm drops down, grey in the sea-night.

I know who the bad sleeper is. It is the big girl, Luna. She must have had another corrective experience. I don't know what they do to her but afterwards she fights in her sleep.

She and I are the only two sleepers who are not peaceful.

Her head lurches over the side, a heavy mass of hair. Her body twitches and her fingers clench.

Our dormitory is a tower. The bunks are stacked one above the other, reached by a ladder. We are kept in by the peace in our minds. If we roll over in our sleep we tumble out and the next thing is the hard rock floor, ten feet down.

If she moves any further she will fall.

Luna, who passed me the vicious note. Should I let her?

I can't. The result will not be soothing.

On the camera is a light. It is steady, indicating no clients are watching.

I clamber onto the ladder. Sounds of gentle respiration rise up the tower like a vapour.

The other soothesayers are composed, like carvings on tombs. I climb past them, get to Luna's bunk and give her a shove.

I expected she'd wake up. Not necessarily to thank me, but perhaps we could have evened matters a little. Instead her body gives a resentful jerk and nearly knocks me off the ladder. I heft her back in and climb down to my bunk.

I glance at the camera light again. No clients were watching.

Those few minutes of rescue were as secret from them as they were from Luna herself.

I lie back and assume a serene position. But sleep doesn't come.

Perhaps the water pressure here does not agree with me. I originally came from a deep-level dome, where the sea is heavy as oil. Giant creatures pass, dragging the sea into shock waves. Some people know because it gives them headaches. The creatures are rarely seen except in green flashes of phosphorescence, which are talked about for days.

This dark. This pressure in the head. The seniors in my soothesayer family thought that was why I couldn't xech.

So I was sent here, to the shallows.

The day I left, the head of my soothesayer family gave me a bitter speech.

'You are being sent to San Otanne. They have more soothesayers per head of population because they soothe to give themselves significance and to make their skin nice. They have their pampered children soothed when they are far too young to warrant it or treat it with respect.

'It is hoped that you can be sold to a family as live-in soothesayer for their children. A child performing a xech may produce something, but they have no control. Their efforts would deafen a well-tuned xecher, but won't trouble you at all.

'The abbot says you're oversensitive to the dark here, but I think it's more likely that you are incompetent, or perhaps don't want to xech. How can anyone be unable to xech? Still, you're not our problem any more.

'When you're in that gay, light city, think about us toiling here where soothing is lifesaving work. Many of us deserve a new start but they send you.

'Of course, no family will take you if they see how badly you xech, even though their savage children wouldn't care at all. So they might dump you and send for one of us after all.

'Now I will perform a formal xech to bid you goodbye and we will bend the rules and not have you participate. Put on a pleased expression and pretend you can see it, and I will tell you when I have finished and you can go.'

And so the head of my soothesayer family xeched. I feigned delight as instructed. We both knew she was conjuring the foulest xech possible.

A new day. My client says: 'Soothesayer, my Kartorzes bird has gone. It is a dreadful calamity.'

Birds from Kartorzes, the exclusive pet shop, are popular. They patrol your house as though deep in thought. This is accomplished by regular shots of tranquiliser. Some clients give so much that the animal can't move. Instead it stands still, as if wondering where it left its wits. Other clients forget the drug. Then their animal starts to regain its inconvenient urges.

The client takes me to her cloakroom. The cloaks are in a heap on the floor and the ventilation duct is open. She'd bent down to put in a new air freshener, the bird got in and escaped.

The client kneels down and peers into the hole.

'This must be so difficult for you,' I say, and adopt the same position beside her. If we look into the hole together, I am sharing the hunt in spirit. And then perhaps we will have some chants to calm the soul after a fruitless search.

'If you xech he will come to you. He's ever so good.' She turns to me.

'He'll hear us xech from here?'

'No. When you catch up with him.'

She expects me to run after her bird and catch it.

With a xech.

I fold my hands under my robes, assume an expression that is masterfully unperturbed. 'Have you spoken to Kartorzes?'

'They said it's not their responsibility. But now you are here. He will always come for a beautiful xech.'

I demur. She pleads. Complains her bad knee prevents her from going after the bird herself.

A soothesayer's duty is to ease suffering, never to exacerbate it. So I go after the bird.

Up a tunnel, bored into the undersea rock. Service lights like a chain of gems stretching into the distance. Puddles of white matter tell me which turn to take. Scrawled signs show I am passing villas, offices, restaurants, shops, backstage entrances to our civilised world. I see a sign for the exclusive Darli's silent restaurant and try to creep.

After a long time I see the bird. Its wings are clipped so it can't fly; it has spindly red legs like a flamingo. It is walking up the incline, a silhouetted shape in a circle of light, looking at its feet in astonishment.

Do I xech?

No, I take a bottle of sedative from my robes and throw it. The bird capsizes.

Above me the sea roars, like a cover flung over my head and dragged back, repeating, unceasing.

I run to where the bird has fallen. It lies in sand, on its side, blinking at me with a disc-like eye.

I am no longer in the tunnel. The opening is behind me, an O-shaped burrow, rising out of the sea.

The bird has brought me all the way to land.

Ahead of me are dunes. White sand blows off their peaks like smoke. Heat holds me like iron bars. I am a soft, fleshy thing in a burning, powdery world. Above me is a bright space that seems to have no end.

Never have I been anywhere without a surface above my head.

The sea stretches away into vast distance until it melts into the sky. Down under that silvery cover, like blisters in the sea bed, are the domes of our cities.

I sit down in the sand. I watch the water push up and withdraw. The roof of the sea meeting its floor. The edges of my world moving in and out.

I think how that same water goes out to the Deeps, becomes slower and colder, fills fathomless canyons with viscous, rocking dark. Here it tapers to one molecule thin, the very edge of the civilised world. I think how my travels have taken me to the edges of two infinities; infinite depth to the narrowest film.

I think of how I fit nowhere.

The bird lies beside me. Occasionally its legs attempt to cycle, puffing up dust, then the drug eats its energy again. The bird blinks together two eyelids like rubber lips and regards the sky.

CHAPTER 32

I wake on Gene's sofa, wrapped in duvet. The sun streams in through the big front window, illuminating every corner.

I feel as if I've woken too soon and there was something I had to say to Andreq, still sitting on the beach.

There's a day I remember, playing in the Broadwood room. Everything feels wrong. The room has been painted since I was last in there. The walls now have a faint gloss, like the face of a person in a fever.

Outside, the girls are discussing me, chipping away my concentration. It's summer, the time of year when they speculate about my birthday. They find it easy to remember because I'm the youngest. Last birthday of the school year.

Here comes the question that is always asked.

'Is she having a party?'

I couldn't have a party. I'd tried it in junior school. My mother supervised with stiff-backed ennui. As though she'd rather get back to managing the factory, even though it was Sunday. That's where my father was, after all.

Not long after that they started to say they didn't want people to come round. I said, why? They said, 'in case they see how much we've got'.

What were they hiding? The house was decorated in a tidy, grown-up sort of way; mahogany, leather Chesterfield suite. No Rembrandts, Ming vases or casks of treasure that anyone might want to steal. There were two BMWs, separate bedroom suites at each end of the house with walk-in wardrobes and gold taps. But apparently schoolgirls might blab to parents. Parents picking up might catch a glimpse and be struck with envy.

Envy of what? And why would that matter?

They didn't even like visitors of their own age. We don't have time to entertain, they'd say, and you need to practise.

In the Broadwood room, Kate Rafferty's voice drifts through the high letterbox window.

'I bet Carol isn't having a party.'

This time there's a difference in the way she says it. Not catty; curious. If she was invited she'd actually come.

Too late to start having friends around now. My fingers trip over an arpeggio and I ball my hand into a fist and punish the keys. I can't play the even simplest thing today. It all comes out wrong.

No more of that now. I'd survived. It was years ago. Now there was this room of white walls, sealed crates, thin sunlight.

I could see it all perfectly. I had fallen asleep in my contact lenses.

They sandpapered my eyes as I blinked.

I threw the duvet back.

The cold was a shock. Didn't Gene have any heating?

Next door there were sounds of footsteps and large objects being pushed across wooden floors. Next door as in the adjacent property, not the bedroom.

I remembered the flat abutted a furniture warehouse.

Christ, what time was it? I had to be at the shop.

My watch said eight-fifteen. I made a shivering dash for my coat, which was draped on one of the packing cases.

I called out to Gene but there was no reply. He must have gone.

Stuck on my coat was a piece of paper. *Tea/coffee in the cupboard. Sorry, no breakfast. Help yourself. G.*

I went into the kitchen. There was one mug – the white one from London, washed up on the draining board. A brushed steel kettle, not hot. He must have gone early.

Curiosity drew my gaze to the white cupboards on either side of the window. I glanced at my watch.

Five minutes longer wouldn't hurt. I'd see if there was anything to learn from his strict minimalism.

In the cupboard were the two flamboyant wine glasses and

the three Pyrex plates from the hospital. In another were tea bags, dried noodles and rice. Light bulbs and a cellophane pack of Dictaphone tapes. The fridge had milk, beer and the crags of cheese I brought from Clapham. The cheese had a bloom of bluish mould. It hadn't been touched since that night.

I checked my watch. Three minutes and I should go.

The silence in the flat tempted me to further bravery.

Bedroom or bathroom?

Bathroom. Just in case he was asleep in the other room.

Into the bathroom and a quick peek in the medicine cabinet. That could be so informative. Karli's was a compendium of throat elixirs and lozenges. Charlie's – the violinist from the Halle – had several kinds of migraine pills and lithium for his manic depression. If I'd looked in there earlier I could have saved myself a lot of trouble.

Gene's medicine cabinet had toothpaste, dental floss, shaving soap, razor. Nothing else at all.

The straightforward contents rebuked me. What did I expect to find? Hallucinogenics to help me on my way, prescription painkillers sneaked from the hospital?

Shame on me for thinking he might cheat in those regressions or have nasty addictions.

A glance at my watch again. I could look in the bedroom.

I shouldn't, I hardly knew the guy. Bedrooms were invitation only.

But how intrusive could I be in so little time?

My bag was on my shoulder and if he was in there I looked as if I was intending to leave.

I knocked. Listened. Silence.

I pushed the door.

A big mirror showed an empty double bed with white sheets and a blanket stripped back. I crept in.

My phone rang.

I jumped and retreated to the door. *Jerry*, said the display.

'Hi,' I gasped.

'Thought I'd catch you before work. Mr Fetcham called.'

Mr Fetcham was my piano tuner. 'Yes, yes, I'll phone him.'

Thanks.' My hammering heart threatened to suffocate me.

Jerry gave a peculiar laugh. 'Carol, what are you doing?'

I lowered my voice to a whisper. It seemed the right thing to do. 'I'll call you later.'

A giggle. 'Where are you?'

'Can't talk right now.'

'You're with a guy.'

'I'm not.'

'You naughty girl. Are you doing the fact-finding tour?'

'The what?'

'He left earlier than you so you're looking in his cupboards trying to find out about him.'

'For God's sake, Jerry.' I could see my reflection, a figure in a black coat and bed-hair retreating to the front door. Trying to pretend to the mirror that I hadn't been doing what I'd been doing.

'You are or you wouldn't sound so furtive. Just remember the three Ms, they tell you all you need to know.'

'Three Ms. What are the three Ms?'

'Magazines, medication and bedside toys. That last one doesn't start with M but it does make you go mmm. Happy hunting and report to me later. Mmmmmmmwah.'

I stuffed the betraying phone deep into my bag.

My face, when I caught myself in the mirror, was bright guilty red.

The mirror also showed something on the floor on the left-hand side of the bed. A small pile of magazines.

Three Ms. Curse you, Jerry.

Well, I'd checked out the medication. I stole around the bed. A quick look wouldn't hurt.

The magazine on top was *Pain*. The second was *The European Journal of Pain*. Titles that might have sent Jerry into a frenzy, imagining S&M orgies, except the covers showed Warhol-enhanced brain scans. There were other publications about neurobiology and anaesthesiology. All consisted of academic papers or reports of difficult case histories. There was one mainstream magazine, *National Geographic* – with a cover feature on the use of pain in the religious practices of African tribes.

Interesting bedtime reading.

I hadn't investigated the last of Jerry's Ms, but I did have limits. I tiptoed out and closed the bedroom door. It was definitely time to go.

Outside there was a line of cars moving inch by inch towards the roundabout. Rush hour was under way. The sunshine and cold air stung my eyes as I hurried up to the cottage. Sleeping in contacts was always bad, I'd have to wear glasses today. But at least I didn't have the heavy hungover feeling I'd had the other times.

Now I thought about it, I didn't remember Gene summoning me to wake.

Perhaps he'd let me drift into sleep. It seemed more peaceful, anyway.

I opened the front door, seeing little beyond my gritty eyes. A ginger cat was sitting in the middle of the rug. It flattened its ears and wailed at me.

I fed it, blinking in pain, then was finally free to go upstairs – and, thank god, to flip those lenses out. I forced some eye drops in to calm the redness, although I still looked like I'd been out all night.

I tried to compensate with eyeliner and shadow, peering closely in the mirror on the front of Jenny Tollderson's medicine cabinet.

In the time I'd been here I'd never opened that cabinet, or anywhere personal such as her wardrobe or the chest of drawers. It would be too invasive.

But when I searched Gene's flat it seemed like evening up the score, for the time he spent with that secret, half-sleeping me.

I wasn't sure I wanted to think about it like that. It was too predatory.

Perhaps I shouldn't worry. He was used to it. To him it was

merely a treatment. Random memories unpacking. He did it all the time.

If that was so, why did I feel I couldn't talk to him about it?

Now that was a good question.

No it wasn't. I'd been through this before whenever I started with a new tutor. When they'd unmasked an ugliness in my playing and I knew they could see the filthy row I had earlier. In a lesson you peel down to an uncontrollable, private you and show it to a stranger. No, worse than that, a fellow professional whose respect matters.

To start with, there's always a period of adjustment.

I teased a final lick of mascara onto my lashes and zipped my make-up bag.

I really had been surprised I didn't find drugs in Gene's flat. I'd known other manipulative, intelligent people, and they all had a safety valve.

When I came down the cat was curled on the sofa. I stroked it to say goodbye. It opened one eye and twitched its tail like a snake, warning me to go away.

At the music shop, Eleanor was waiting, clicking car keys in her hand. Anne Stubbings couldn't leave the Railway Hotel as she had staff off sick, so we were going to her.

Her car was a reproachfully clean silver Volkswagen Golf. A St Christopher on a chain hung from the rear view mirror. I moved a parcel off the passenger seat before I sat down.

'Oh that's for you,' she said. 'The postman hadn't known where to deliver it, so he asked me.'

I thanked her, pulled open the staples and peeked inside.

Eleanor observed this approvingly. 'I'm like that too. I can't leave a letter unopened for a moment.'

I could probably have picked my nose and Eleanor would have told me which Lear rejoiced in that habit.

I wondered what she would make of the Lears I really came from. My parents would have thought hers were not worth knowing if they didn't have a five-bedroom house and two executive cars. There were some Lear cousins who lived in a small town in the Peak District and taught maths, but they were despised because they were doomed to earn the same low wage all their lives. Eleanor's artists and explorers would have been blanked in the blink of an eye, especially the one who had a stately home he couldn't afford.

The parcel was a novel from Jerry with a note. *Thought you'd enjoy this. Love and hugs.*

Eleanor drove with her chin high. Despite this vigilant pose she nearly missed the drive for the Railway Hotel, then swung in fast so that the hanging pendant flew at my face, a silver demolition ball heading for my glasses. St Christopher, patron saint of travellers, but not of their passengers. Next, the back fence rushed at us. I gripped the seat, because it seemed inevitable that we would burst the wire and plunge into the old railway cutting. But Eleanor pulled the wheel again, the pendant scythed at my eye and we came to a skidding halt.

Her driving, it seemed, was rather like her piano playing.

After the lesson Eleanor offered me a lift back, but I said I'd meet her in the shop after lunch. She waved and accelerated out of the drive in a swirl of gravel. As she zoomed away, she no doubt noted in her rear view mirror that I was heading for Vellonoweth Hall, and probably ascribed it to the call of the ancestral nest.

On top of the hill the wind was tyrannically cold. I plodded like a dogged mountaineer past the visitor's centre, over the hill that hid the power station and down the narrow steps to the beach.

The landscape brought back Karli's voice.

The cliffs of England stand, glimmering and vast, out in the tranquil bay

Karli would be finding another pianist. He would be using our work. Our piece, which began as a stumbling experiment just for us. Karli was finding someone else.

I walked. My feet slipped like skates in the shingle. The

song replayed in my bones. The sea surged up, slowed to foam, then took itself back.

My phone jangled. A text, from Jerry.

Mmmmmmmm?

I called him. 'Thanks for the book.'

'You saucy minx, I've been dying of curiosity all morning. Whose bed were you in last night?'

I heard clashing crockery. He was unloading the dishwasher.

'Not a bed. I was on the sofa.'

'On the sofa in what sense, exactly?'

I looked across the bay at the mast with its red winking light on the tower. I hadn't thought before about telling Jerry. Now suddenly it seemed right.

'I had a problem with my hands. And Gene's working down here.'

The crockery percussion stopped. I think he understood already. 'Tell me everything, petal.'

'Gene did a hypnosis thing and... let's say you're not the only one.'

I didn't need to bother him with anything more tricky than that.

His voice had changed. It was warmer, younger. Eager. 'All this time I was telling you you're the type. Who are you?'

The waves pushed up and back. I looked at the foam, sinking down between the pebbles and vanishing. When Jerry talked about Ruby Cunningham it seemed as natural as when he talked about Tim. Could I sound as easy?

I gave it a try. 'Nobody famous. A healer. Sort of.'

'A healer.' He repeated the words slowly, digesting them. 'Does it make sense? With your hands and the pain?'

That didn't. 'There aren't any streets to search for and it's not as straightforward as Ruby, but there's something about it.' I twiddled a loop of my hair around my finger. 'How is she, by the way?'

I had inquired after Ruby before of course, but each time I had really been asking about Jerry. This time?

It's different when you have one of your own.

'Ruby's going in a book. It's going to be called *Voices of the Ripper Victims*. Anthony Morrish is collecting all the experiences he's had of Ripper regressions and he's working with a historian to identify who the Ripper was. I'm making illustrations from their descriptions. We're going to build up a picture of the Ripper's real face.'

'Terrific. Sounds like it'll be a bestseller.' The waves came up, went back. 'What does Tim make of it?'

'He thinks it's just another book. That's all he has to know for now. But he finds it a bit freaky because I've got my roughs up in the hall.'

Not so long ago it would have been Jerry who would find that too freaky. He'd turned down several illustration jobs because they were too dark.

'Wait until you see them. It's like an art installation – photofits of Jack the Ripper, a hundred years on, assembled by his victims.'

I heard him close the fridge door. Its tell-tale bounce; it never shut first time. I'd never noticed that before.

'Ruby and I are so alike. Get this – she always tries to wear something red. Anyway, tell me about this healer. When did she live?'

Too difficult to explain that. I'd have to do everything in baby steps. 'The healer's a he,' I said.

'Have you got an audio?'

I hesitated. Then thought, why not?

'It's on tapes. I'll send it by snailmail. Let's talk later, I have to get back to work.'

I cut the call.

I turned my focus back to the grey, heaving sea.

The grating roar of pebbles, which the waves draw back, and fling ...

up the high strand,
begin and cease, and then again begin...
And bring the eternal note of sadness in...

It was all right. The ache I expected wasn't there. I could let go of *Dover Beach*.

Maybe that would wear off. But for now I was grateful. Soothed, perhaps.

I climbed the steps up the cliff, shrugged deeper into my coat and walked down the road.

At the cottage I stopped to top up the cat's supplies.

A couple of texts arrived.

Jerry said: *What about the three mmms, Ms? And, hmmmm, the sofa!!!*

Gene said: *Same time tonight?*

I looked at the phone. Should I? The last time was relatively benign. In fact, it was like the old, simpler days. Perhaps that was his style.

Anthony Morrish had a clear style. He steered his subjects to Ripper deaths. Jerry had even seen this demonstrated beyond all doubt but it seemed irrelevant to him. There was Anthony Morrish with his agenda, and on the inside there was Ruby.

For me, there was Andreq and there was Gene.

If we looked at it with logic, I could guess where Gene was pulling strings. He knew neurobiology, anaesthesiology. Mysterious malfunctions of the human system. And soothing nonsense.

Medically, was it helping me? My hands felt much the same as they did when I was resting before. But what he had done was transform my playing. I was a different grade of performer when I interpreted the Chopin for Leo Korda. And now I could leave *Dover Beach* in the past.

Maybe that was why.

All musicians acquire a private ammunition box of techniques. Some of them you couldn't explain. If I was having trouble, as all pianists do, with my weak third finger, I imagined my tutor was playing, not me. In a way, the player you are is a gestalt of the people who have guided you.

The player I am is now absorbing a part of Gene. And he's keeping that player alive.

But on the inside, where Gene can't see, there is Andreq. Sitting alone with a bird on the edge of the world.

It felt better now I'd told Jerry. I pulled the tape out of my handbag, put it in an envelope with a note.

This is the other me. It's not what you were imagining but it's helping. So you were right. ;) PS Spare Dictaphone in kitchen drawer behind the screwdrivers.

I texted Gene. *Yes. See you tonight.*

More hours of clumsy music stretched ahead of me at the shop, but I'd go to Gene's afterwards and we'd work.

Chapter 33

Tape 4

It's started. What has started? The tumbling season. Much more upsetting than the secretive whispers of the red season.

Outside, the sea is in turmoil. Rocks and coral batter the dome like fists demanding to come in. A shoal of angel fish hurtle by, disintegrating into rags. Their mouths gasp and close, saying no no no.

A soothesayer whispers into a tiny camera. 'Here in the heart of the temple, we are xeching night and day, looking after your sleep to keep the tumbling away.'

Behind him, five soothesayers stand in a circle, xeching. Their eyes are half closed and they are performing light movements with their hands, as though weaving cobwebs into yarn.

As I pass them, a sound creeps up on me. Imagine a bang so loud you can't hear afterwards.

I stop. I'm almost surprised to find my two feet are still in the same room and nothing around me has changed.

The noise wasn't from the sea.

Did I just feel the xeching?

I hear thumping footsteps. Someone who walks as though her feet are bigger than she expects. It is the large girl, Luna.

As she passes me she gives me an open-mouthed leer and taps her forehead, where there is a small burn. But her finger is not as defiant as she would like it to be. It quivers.

She's just seen the surgeon. I guess it will be another rough night.

The chaos continues outside the dome. And I can still feel the ringing from the xech.

What has happened? Did I get burned when I sat under the open sky?

Am I sensitive to xeching at last?

'You have to teach my daughter to xech,' says my client. 'It's tumbling season already and she's upset because she can't.'

She and three-year-old daughter sit on the sofa. Daughter is cross-legged on a yellow cushion so large it makes her look like a doll being presented to a king. Mother is prim, upright and ratty.

Daughter certainly looks upset. Her eyes are red. She balls her hands into fists and rubs them. Mother pulls the hands away. 'Stop it. You're going to learn to xech.'

Daughter blinks, abnormally slowly. I glimpse a glint of gold in her eyes. She's wearing chromatic lenses. She's far too young for them. No wonder she's upset. But they will be a reprieve for me.

I fold my hands into a soothing position. Tell them that to teach her we must take the lenses out. Mother looks annoyed and says it took long enough to get them in. I feign a xech, tell them I can't open a channel, and advance on daughter. Daughter is not going to let a stranger poke her miserable, swollen eyes. Bad enough when mother did it. She squirms free, vaults over the sofa and scoots into a corridor.

The rest of the hour is passed with mother outside a locked door, begging daughter to let her in. While I soothe both of them.

I will not have to use these cheap evasions much longer. Xech is coming.

I am back in the temple. The sea cracks and booms. Schools of fish whirl backwards, pulled by a ripping current. The other soothesayers answer with xeches and express them with their fey hands.

Dumb, I copy their blissful moves.

The commentator murmurs to the camera. 'The soothesayers are sending their most golden xech out into the city. Into your streets, into your villas, into the chambers where you are sleeping, vibrating through every atom of air, to soothe the storm.'

I wait for their xech to reach me. The soundless, deafening

boom. But my hearing and vision stay in the room with all its noises and sights.

I cannot feel it any more. It has gone.

Andreq, you've gone too soon again. There was some more nonsense I wanted to tell you.

I was six years old, practising. I was trying to play one of Debussy's preludes. It was too hard for me; several grades above what I'd been set by my teacher.

But I'd heard it and I wanted to play it.

For a moment a phrase came right, as though it flew in through the window and sang for me. The next I came to a stumbling halt.

Instead of enchanted Debussy, there was only my clumsy fingering and the noises in the house. Male shouting, female screaming.

I went back to those impossible staves. Looking for the way to fall into them again.

It works if you keep trying, even if it seems impossible. Any moment, Debussy might fly in once more and you will soothe the storm.

As I said. Just a bit of nonsense.

CHAPTER 34

I opened my eyes. I was on Gene's sofa, under a blanket.

It was quiet. The outspread silence that says no other soul stirs in all the land.

Moonlight dappled the floor with moving shadows. Not tumbling debris, wanting to come in. The swaying limbs of the trees outside.

Again it was a shock to see clearly. More abuse for my contact lenses.

I pushed back the blanket, felt the bitter temperature and padded on boot soles across the boards. Retrieved my black coat, which was slumped on a packing case. Gene was still camping out of boxes. I burrowed into my sleeves, shook my hair free of the collar and buttoned it to the throat. Folded the blanket, shouldered my bag and stepped into the corridor.

I caught a glimpse into the bedroom, silver and navy blue in the moonlight. Slimy grit floated across my vision and I poked it away. When it cleared I saw into the mirror.

Gene was still awake, turned towards the window, propped on one elbow under the white duvet. White iPod wires crinkled out of his ears, over the black T-shirt he was wearing and into the Dictaphone beside him on the covers.

He must be listening to our tape.

I knew he listened to them; of course I did. After the very first time he'd mentioned that he made notes.

So what notes would he make about this one?

I waited for him to notice me. We were both awake, I couldn't slip away like I hadn't been here. But he never looked up. He remained still, inwardly focussed. He had no idea I was there.

I stepped away, down the stairs and out.

Frost sparkled on the hedge, the flagstoned path and the cars parked in the road. I carved a curved visor through the white on my windscreen, fled up the hill in my freezing car. Finally, back in the cottage and under my own duvet, I lay awake, so thankful to be thawing the chill in my bones.

Waiting for sleep, I listened to the trees rustling. The same sound had surrounded that cold flat down at the bottom of the hill. Was Gene still awake too, studying the tape?

Every time I drifted off, it tugged me awake as though I was seeing for the first time. Gene attentive as a held breath, with my voice a captured whisper in his headphones. Talking my Andreq dreams to him in the dark.

CHAPTER 35

I pulled back the flower-sprigged curtains and saw Gene's car in the road below. A black metallic VW, the little dent in the rear, doing 50mph in the 30 zone. Its noise rang on afterwards in the chilly air. A car came the other way and wiped the sound of his.

Moonlight turning his T-shirt and hair black. Picking out the white threads of his headphones, which were connected to the Dictaphone, which was playing my voice, which was connected to ... me.

I felt like I had thought about it all night.

I showered, fed the cat, drank coffee, wrapped up against the cold, locked the front door, sprinted down the hill to keep warm, arrived at the shop and taught two clients – and still the thought would not let go.

I had an early break, at eleven. I walked up to the Hall and down to my hollow of rocks on the shore. I phoned Jerry and got voicemail.

I didn't want to leave a message, I wanted the act of talking to him, the diversion while something else went on, like a healing or adjustment in a profounder level of my brain.

I climbed back up the steps, two at a time, to the visitors' centre on top of the hill.

Inside, the building was quite slick, with photos and diagrams, and displays in Perspex cases. Behind a desk, an attendant was working through a Sudoku, but when I walked in he jumped up to give me the personal tour.

First the guide showed me a case that contained a model of a building; the old power station as it was.

'Vellonoweth Hall power station,' he said, 'was built in the Cold War. The British were looking for a way to run an underground bunker. They never built the bunker but they built the power station.'

Half attentive, still deeply adjusting, I looked where he directed. The model showed two white buildings with a dome like an observatory, nestling in a deep valley, a short distance from a small bay. Next to it, another model showed the landscape I recognised now. The hill had swollen enormously; it not only filled in the valley, the summit was three times higher than the walls of the valley had been. Black and white photographs taken from a helicopter showed the burying of the reactor core. They looked like the discovery of an ancient tomb, in reverse.

'The turbine halls were demolished,' said my guide. 'The radioactive core was encased in concrete one hundred feet thick and the valley was filled in. Then they enclosed it all in this hill using waste from slate tips and dredged material from the sea.'

There was a sign by the models: *A monument to man's mastery over nature.*

The enlarged hill didn't look like mastery to me. It looked like panic. Nailing planks over the door because you know the lock won't keep the demons out.

'That's a good model, isn't it?' said the guide. 'People like to gaze at those thick walls and shudder. In the summer more people come here than go to Glastonbury Tor.'

The remark was probably meant to appear casual but sounded scripted. I imagined a succession of guides in the green Vellonweth Hall sweatshirt, repeating the same words.

He tried to interest me in a nuclear science exhibit, switching on red lights that orbited a model of an atomic nucleus. Equations were written beside the displays. The Roentgen level is x, the concrete thickness is y. The monster should stay asleep. Because this said so.

'Is it all safe?' I said. 'What about the radiation?'

'People always ask me about the radiation,' said the guide. His rehearsed tone conjured up the guide chorus, standing beside him, mouths all moving at once. 'Vellonoweth is a community. People bring up children here. How could we if we thought it was dangerous? There is no radiation here.'

Yes there is, I thought. It's buried a long way down but it's still there.

We finished with a series of sepia photographs, with another caption about mastering nature's forces. They showed the Curies and Ernest Rutherford, proud beside lab equipment made of rosewood, brass and bellows.

They looked like an orchestra posing with their instruments, unequal to mastering anything but a tune.

Jerry called at the end of the day, as I walked home.

'I got your tape,' he said.

Finally the world seemed to sharpen. I ducked into a bus stop to shelter from the wind.

'What did you think?'

'It's a bit worrying.'

There was a clattering noise in the background. He was on a train.

I sat on the bus stop's plastic bench and covered my other ear to block the sound of the wind. 'Why is it worrying?'

'Well you're the past life and –' He sighed, trying to delete the sentence and start again. 'Promise me you'll be careful.'

'Careful?' What did he mean? 'Do you think Gene's – '

'It's not that. Gene is good at this. He makes Anthony Morrish look like an amateur.'

This wasn't what I expected Jerry to say at all. 'Why?'

'I've been reading about hypnosis and I've heard a lot of tapes for Anthony Morrish's book. Gene's been doing this a long time. When you've talked about him he sounds practically autistic. I don't doubt that he's strange but on this tape he really knows what he's doing. The way he used the champagne...'

We will shortly be arriving at London Waterloo, said a voice at Jerry's end.

'Going somewhere?'

'I'm meeting Anthony Morrish and we're going to see a publisher.'

I heard the bleep and hiss of train doors releasing. Shuffling of feet, a scrum of bags, made tinny by transmission down the phone. People saying excuse me.

Jerry came back. 'What else do you know about Gene?'

There wasn't a scrap of playfulness in the question, or the slightest hint about three ms.

'A morbid interest in pain and a party trick with a cigarette. He keeps himself to himself.'

Footsteps now, echoed many times, announcements in the distance, the beep and shush of more train doors. Jerry must be walking along the platform.

'I don't know how he ... it's not – ' Jerry was floundering. He tried again. 'Carol, just be careful what you're doing.'

'Careful?' I repeated, for the second time.

'You're the past life and you're haunting someone... Don't do anything silly, okay? Call me later.'

He rang off. Tinny, tiny-sounding Waterloo disappeared.

A man arrived at the bus stop, stamping his feet against the cold. He sat beside me and opened a paper. It was the local rag. As usual, the headline was about a lifeboat rescue. Vellonoweth life plodded along, safe and humdrum, but beating at its door was the merciless sea.

I pulled my coat tighter around me and marched onwards. Briskly, because I'd got cold sitting around. Because I had a feeling like a dynamo inside me, charging up, with nowhere to go. Like I had been all day.

Gene really knows what he's doing, Jerry had said. He certainly does. And you haven't heard anything yet. Wait until you hear the second tape, when he talks about the note hanging in the piano and fading to nothing. It's like he reached into my head and pulled out one of the most private experiences of playing. And the one after that, when I was so scared that the last thing I wanted was for him to put me under, but he found the words and that was it. If I believed in ESP I'd say he had it.

I took my phone out and wrote a text, working fast before I could change my mind.

Are there any decent restaurants around here?
I sent it to Gene.
And then thought, what have I done?

A reply came later, when I was curled up on the sofa, reading the book Jerry sent while the ginger cat had a very involved wash.
Party tonight. Come along.
Don't think. Text back.
I'll be chauffeur.
He agreed.
Good.
I put the phone down.
If a duet partner was proving difficult to talk to, I found a reason to take them for a drive. Once they were in the passenger seat and I was at the wheel, I became more nosy, less willing to settle for an evasive answer.
Some people get road rage. I get road inquisition. Not in an aggressive way; you don't have to hare around at high speeds until they're a nervous wreck.
Road inquisition is more subtle than that. It's a patience game.
It had started with Charlie, first violin in the Halle. Charlie, who teamed his evening tails with a haircut like a chimney sweep. He liked every performance to be a battle, but one conducted under the waterline where the audience couldn't see. He would miss out bars and during his rests he twirled the end of his bow in his hair so that it looked like he would miss his cue. So I had to constantly adjust the tempo to keep him running after me.
Charlie was also paranoid when amputated from his instrument. Once when I took him to a wedding which was full of people he didn't know, he stuck to me like a second handbag, getting sulky when I talked to someone other than him.
The best way to have a verbal conversation with him was to go for a drive. I could ask the questions I wanted to and look

ahead at the road and not at the resentful silences. And the journey didn't end until I'd finished.

So Gene and I were going to a party. And I was driving.

CHAPTER 36

I pulled up outside Gene's flat and sounded the horn. I watched his shape move across the upstairs window, fetching keys and adjusting lights.

So, I asked his outline, you don't exist in a vacuum. You've been invited to a party.

Will I meet someone who knows you well? Do you often listen to those tapes of me? What do you think of those things I'm telling you? Why do you have magazines about pain? What do you do to chill out because there's got to be something.

Most of which I might not get round to in one journey.

Gene shut the front door, jogged down the path and snatched the passenger door open. He looked cold, which wasn't surprising as he was wearing just a black shirt and black jeans that clung to his slim frame. He pulled the seatbelt on and poked the dials in the dashboard, shivering.

'God, doesn't this car have a heater?'

'It's already up to maximum,' I said, and pulled out into the road.

The shiver amused me. How unusual to see him look so vulnerable.

He fiddled with the dial anyway. 'Look stop here, let's go in mine.'

I accelerated. 'It'll be fine once it warms up.'

Around the roundabout and away to the Ixendon road. He deserved to be cold after the number of chilly, bleak rooms he'd inflicted on me.

'So who's having the party?'

'Sadie at the hospital. She's an occupational therapist. She's dating a male oncology nurse and she's getting bored with him because he's getting fat. He used to go out with the cardiac rehab nurse but he dumped her because she nagged him about his weight.'

Well that was a more complete answer than I was expecting. Aggressively complete. Was he trying to put me off asking anything else?

Tiny spots of rain stippled the windscreen. I flicked the wiper stalk and my left hand hurt. I bit my lip for just a second.

'You shouldn't be driving,' said Gene, and turned the fan up. It roared like a hippo yawning. He turned it down again. 'Let's go back.'

'I'm fine. It used to hurt a lot more. It's getting better.'

He stopped fiddling with the heating. 'Yes, but it's still hurting, so you shouldn't do it. I could drive if you like.'

Now suddenly calmer, more persuasive. Strange how he could turn on that gentleness. It seemed to happen as soon as he had the chance to treat me like a patient.

I smiled. 'You can stop being a doctor now. Or a physio, or whatever it is you do. Is that what you do?' My audacity amazed me.

'Is that what I do?' he repeated.

From his tone I guessed there was an expression that added a twist to the statement. But I didn't get the benefit of it. I was timing my exit onto the Ixendon road.

'I've been to a few physios in the past few months. And they're not like you.'

He folded his arms.

Folding your arms won't help, my dear. I'm in the inquisitor seat.

Ahead, the orange street lamps disappeared and gave way to blackness. We passed the national speed limit sign, then the only light ahead was a faint constellation of amber on the horizon. That was Ixendon.

I put my foot down, the full beam headlights up, and accelerated into the true night.

'And what are other physios like?' he said. Carefully. Wondering where this might be leading.

'I've never known a physio who hypnotised people with burns.'

'You've got a good memory.'

A white chevron sign appeared out of the dark. The cats' eyes hooked around to the right. I steered around the bend and felt the back end of the car swing. Perhaps that was a bit fast, I should have slowed. I straightened the wheel and eased off the accelerator.

Pearly dots pointed the way ahead, rushing towards us and under the right-hand wheels.

'So how do you do it?' I said. 'You said the guy was coked up –'

'Not coke. We didn't know what he'd taken.'

I stole a glance at him. He was looking down and scratching his fingernail over a mark on the thigh of his black jeans. No longer defensively folding his arms.

That's nice; we can talk. Road inquisition starts to become beneficial when the passenger realises you're in control.

I glanced at the glowing instruments in the dashboard. The needle on the speedometer was waving at 90mph.

Normally 60 was my limit except on motorways, and on roads like this I wasn't even that brave. Especially not in the dark as my night vision isn't good.

I lifted my toe to release the accelerator. My recklessness shocked me. I took a breath, watched the speedo slow.

We hit 55. I continued. 'Anyway you said this guy was drugged. Screaming with pain. But you talked him into letting surgeons cut and prod bits of him? If I was him I'd be fighting like a maniac. Was that what it was like?'

'Pretty much.'

'So what did you do to him?'

He made a noncommittal noise. If I could have looked at his face it might have made more sense, but my attention was on a pale stone shape in the headlights, which became a stone wall jewelled with red reflectors, and the headlights of another car rushing up the other way. These roads were creepy, everything loomed up like a ghost train. I slowed, dipped lights, slipped between car and wall, then flicked the lights up and put on more speed for a hill.

'No really, I'm interested. How do you do it?

'You have to find a way.'

'How?'

'Whatever will get through to them.'

'You sound as if you do it a lot.'

'I do and I don't.' A movement out of the corner of my eye told me that came with a shrug.

The right-hand side of the car continued to eat up cats' eyes. They seemed to be closer together.

'What does that mean?'

'With pain, no two people are the same. Watch out, there's a corner at the top here. Do you normally drive like this?'

We crested the hill and another band of white chevrons appeared, begging for slowness. I touched the brake and turned.

This time I felt both inside tyres lift.

I glanced at the speedo. I'd just taken that corner at 80.

And that had been with the hill slowing us down. What was wrong with me?

I've seen stage fright make performers do very odd things. Nervous twitches, pulling funny faces, playing too fast are all ways that we show we really don't want to be up on a stage, exposed. Even though we've fought to be there. It's our body's way of trying to run away.

Another bend and Ixendon appeared. A 30 sign and amber lights opened up the road. I braked, hard.

Thank god we were nearly there. Because I think if I drove any more with him in the car we would end up dead.

Chapter 37

The house was easy to spot – in a terrace, the one with the front door left ajar and red bulbs in all the windows. The sound system was pumping a smouldering beat.

Gene moved into the crowd to say hello to someone and disappeared. The red light turned everyone's clothes to black.

I fought to the kitchen to leave my bottle of red wine. A row of glasses on the fridge made me regret volunteering to drive. There was nothing I felt more like than getting absolutely scuttered.

On the window sill was a packet of Silk Cut. I stole one. I wasn't a smoker, except occasionally when drunk.

Without a drink it tasted disgusting.

Next to the kitchen was a cloakroom. A girl came out. She had long dark hair and was wearing silver shoes. In her hand she had a note.

'Did you see who left this? It was pushed under the door.'

It said: *Your shoes give me goosebumps.*

'Sorry,' I said. 'I didn't see anything.'

The girl grabbed a can of Carlsberg from the ice bucket and pulled back the tab. 'Mm, how exciting.' She went out into the darker room, inspecting faces, looking for a signal.

I took another drag in case the cigarette had improved. It hadn't. I looked at the bottle of red wine again. One glass probably wouldn't hurt. I poured it and downed half immediately. The alcohol stayed in my throat like a warm echo, inviting me to throw some more down after it.

I went out into the lounge, away from temptation. At the far end, doors opened onto the garden. Perhaps fresh air would be a good idea. As I worked my way out, I passed Gene. He was talking to a girl with blonde bobbed hair. She was leaning submissively against a bookshelf, holding up a glass and twinkling at him. She looked like she was trying to get him to imagine her draped over a bed.

I didn't think he'd seen me, but as I edged past he grabbed my arm. 'Carol, this is Cherie, she's a nurse. She's interested in learning to sing.'

Cherie glared at me; she couldn't look more uninterested in singing.

'Hi,' I said briefly, and tried to move on to leave them to it.

Gene took my glass and plucked Cherie's out of her hand. 'You stay here and I'll find us some more drinks.'

He squeezed past the girl in silver shoes, who was showing her note to a girl with fierce glasses, then his black shirt blended into the forest of dark backs and red shadows.

'So you teach singing?' said Cherie. She was standing up straighter now.

'A bit,' I said. 'So you want to learn?'

She glanced past my ear to see if Gene was coming back. 'So how do you know Gene?'

'School,' I said.

She looked a good deal more interested in me then. 'Oh really? So you guys must be ... good friends?'

'Just friends.' Presumably that was what she wanted to know.

A guy with tousled hair walked past, holding a note like the girl with the silver shoes had. Perhaps he'd see her and they'd meet.

Since Cherie wanted to pump me for information, I could do likewise. 'Do you work with Gene?'

'Not really. He sometimes comes into my department.'

'I can never quite work out what he does.'

'The hospital's a big place,' she said, and waved to the guy with tousled hair. He came up and passed her the note. 'Cherie, whose writing is this?'

It said: *Your shoes are really cool.* It was written in capitals, like the other note. I checked out the guy's shoes. They were Converse trainers with a black brocade print.

'It wasn't me,' I said, 'but they are cool shoes.'

Gene didn't come back with our glasses.

I left Cherie and went to the front room to dance.

I needed a route to oblivion other than wine. I joined the shadows who were already moving in their own trance worlds. It wasn't social dancing, sexy dancing, dancing to bond; it was dancing to not be there.

As the music swept everything away I imagined that I could talk to Gene about what we were doing, that we could slip off our inhibitions like these people here, that we could talk about what was me and what was him and what was neither ... and just what, finally, might be going on.

When I came out, the party was spilling upstairs. I followed a cool breeze up to the landing. Cherie was sitting with two other girls in an open window, their feet on the flat roof to the kitchen below, smoking and passing a note around. I didn't see the message but the paper had a name on it in red, like an advert.

'That's a cardiology drug,' said Cherie, and passed it back to her friend. 'It must be from someone in cardiology. I don't know anyone in that department – do you?'

The note was written in those same capital letters. The house Cupid was carefully keeping themselves anonymous.

I felt a squeeze at my elbow. Gene was behind me. He had a glass of red wine in one hand and a joint tucked behind one ear. With his black shirt and jeans it made him look like a spy from a sixties film.

'How's it going?'

I nodded towards the window. 'Your friend Cherie's there, in case you're still avoiding her.'

'I've given her something to think about.' One-handed, he unfastened the button on the breast pocket of his shirt and held it open. Inside was a selection of Post-It pads. One was the same as Cherie's note with the cardiology drug. Others had different drug names. He fastened the pocket again.

Along the corridor the girl with the long dark hair and silver shoes was sitting cross-legged in front of a candle, chatting to a guy. Her shoes were arranged in the candlelight like a still life and he was taking a picture of them. It wasn't the guy with the Converse trainers, who seemed to be an obvious match, but they seemed to be having a good time anyway.

'Were they cardiology too?' I asked Gene.

'No. Oncology. Got to go.' He padded away along the corridor, past the guy photographing the silver shoes. He opened one of the bedrooms. The door shut slowly, deliberately, then the click of a lock made sure of it.

I went down the stairs. A guy in a NY sweatshirt was coming up. The sides of his head were shaved to downy stubble and the top was a floppy wave like a Chinese painting of the sea. He looked carefully at me, like a sergeant checking a soldier for neatness, then handed me a note.

Me: dark wild hair. You: about to make it wilder.

The bottle had spun and now pointed to me. Thanks, Gene.

Someone turned the hi-fi up. Husky vocals swirled up the stairs. Such yearning chords, you could drown in them. So why not?

I walked downstairs with the guy. The dance room was now packed. We went in, gradually pushed closer as other people joined, like passengers on a crowded Tube. Soon the guy and I were up close, heads and fronts touching. Obeying the beat, because everyone was. We tried a kiss – I hadn't noticed how thin the guy's lips were, like a fish's. I hadn't noticed anything about him really. I tried not to think about that room upstairs, where the lock was clicked so decisively, and kissed the guy again.

The beat gathered speed. We separated. Other dancers moved in and we were shuffled apart without ever even exchanging names.

In the kitchen I found another note, discarded beside some crushed Carslberg cans. It was on the oncology notepad. *My husband's nipped home to sort out the babysitter. He won't be back for an hour.* Gene's bottle-spinning was getting more daring.

Candles had been lit along the back of the stove. I had a conversation with a couple of girls who were also staying sober to drive home. Two guys came in listening to iPods and dancing to their own internal worlds. They were pogoing, while moody synthesizers swirled in from the main dance room. Like mischievous imps who had become frustrated with the slow music and candlelight.

I felt heavy and tired. I found a piece of paper – which said *Kiss me* on the back – and looked for a pen. When Gene went to unlock that door he'd find a note telling him I'd gone.

Someone put a glass down beside my hand as I was scribbling hard over *Kiss me*. The candlelight illuminated a glass of deep red.

It was Gene.

He reached towards me as though he was about to touch my face, and pushed my hair behind my ears. He brought a white iPod out of his pocket, put it into my hands and fixed a headphone in each of my ears. Then he picked up the glass and went out.

On the glowing iPod screen was a message. *Play me.*

I pressed play.

'Are you ready?' said a voice. His voice.

'Shall I take this off?' said a woman. There was a sound of shuffling, like fabric being moved. Clothes? No too heavy for that. Bedclothes.

I wasn't sure I wanted to hear this. And why did he want me to listen?

The corner of the kitchen was dark. I ducked down onto the floor. That way, if Gene was watching to see what my reaction was, my face would be in shadow. I'd learned that from him.

'If I start having a migraine,' said the woman, 'you'll stop, won't you?'

'You won't have a migraine,' Gene's voice said. 'Just sink. Feel the bed under you. Taking the weight of you. Taking everything; your worries, your fear. Let them slide out of you.'

It was so soft, his voice.

There was a sound of fidgeting.

Any more and I'd tear the headphones off, dunk the iPod in the kitchen sink with the beer dregs and fag ends.

The woman's voice, high and tense, cut through the sultry

mood. 'I find it so hard to relax. Maybe I can't be hypnotised.'

Gene said patiently: 'Some people do find it difficult.'

'No,' she said, 'I really do find it difficult. I went to yoga with a friend and they were all lying on the floor relaxing. But I can't. I find it so hard. I'd like to do something like this but I think it might not work.'

Gene said: 'You must be particularly sensitive. That is a rare quality.'

'Do you think so?' The woman sounded pleased.

'Hypnosis,' said Gene, 'is one of the ancient therapies. You might have a short-circuit in your energy flow that stops you relaxing. This will help unblock it.'

My soothesayer's lines.

I wasn't the only one learning some new tricks.

'A block in my energy flow,' repeated the woman. She was taking this very seriously.

'It might,' said Gene, 'go all the way back to when you were born and only be coming out now.'

Just what the soothesayer ordered.

The woman sighed. 'I think you're right.' There were more noises of scuffling and bedclothes rumpling. 'I think I'm ready to try again.'

'Feel the duvet around you,' said Gene, and began to talk her into a trance.

Of course it worked. When he asked her the question 'Where are you?' she replied that she was she was in the court of Henry VIII.

Some dark denimed legs were coming towards me. Gene knelt down and took the headphones out of my ears. The voices disappeared.

'I was just getting into that.'

Gene folded the iPod and headphones into his pocket.

'You've heard the best bit. From then on she had a fling with Henry and was beheaded on the orders of Anne Boleyn.'

I got to my feet. 'I thought that wasn't your style. Beheadings and stuff.'

There was a packet of Silk Cut on the worktop. He shook

one out and lifted the candle to light it.

'I wasn't allowed to say no. She's the hospital chief. She can fire me.' He inhaled on the cigarette, poured more wine and drank most of it down in one.

There was shouting out in the hall. The woman with silver shoes marched in and yanked open the fridge. She was tailed by a woman with a pink low-cut top. Silver shoes tried to ignore pink top, but pink top didn't like that. Then silver shoes turned around and yelled at her.

Gene and I slipped past them into the hall, while the women continued an argument that had obviously started elsewhere in the house.

The front door was open. There was a small group of smokers outside, leaning on the wall that separated the path from the house next door.

I followed Gene out and we found a spot on our own. He finished the cigarette and tossed it into a drain. The joint was still tucked behind his ear, but he lit another Silk Cut.

'Wouldn't the joint be more interesting?'

'It's Sadie's home-grown. It's rubbish.' He dragged and breathed out, long and slow. 'I think she grew parsley by mistake. But she's not a pharmacologist. That's her in the pink top, by the way.'

Above the wash of music I could still hear shouting. 'I don't suppose you know what that's about?'

'Can't imagine,' said Gene.

'Perhaps you should go and soothe them,' I said.

'Yes,' he grinned, and took a swig from the wine bottle. 'I think that went very well.' He took another drag on the cigarette and offered it to me. I waved it away.

I wanted to say, Do you often use my lines? Whose were they anyway, yours or mine? And so much more.

Instead I asked: 'What happened to giving up smoking?'

'I had until that bloody regression. That woman spent an entire minute screaming.'

Chapter 38

It was Saturday and I was teaching non-stop. My pupils had had their audition results and the lucky ones were keen to start polishing their solos. The others were consoling themselves with new material. With such relentless demand I was glad I'd stayed sober at the party.

Jean Dowman, the next-door neighbour and leading light of the horticulture society, was one of the audition failures. She was licking her wounds with a recitative about finding joy in Jesus. Recitatives aren't easy; they're like the spoken part of an opera and have very little tune. To perform them well, expression is all.

She bleated the song in a monotone, with less expression than the way she had asked to borrow a cup of sugar from me – or rather Jenny – that morning.

I stopped her and tried to explain what was wrong.

'Look at the words. This is about joy. Do you have joy in Jesus?'

'Yes I do.' She blinked at me as if she felt it was none of my business.

'Now show me in the way you perform this song.'

Her second attempt to share the joy was even more grudging than the first.

At least the work was easy. No need to warm up. No struggle with my stiff body and criticising mind until I tumbled into the zone and started to truly make music. No need to be producing my best. I didn't have to do anything. Just react.

Gene answers the door in shirt, jeans, wet hair and bare feet – and grey eyes heavy with exhaustion.

'Is that a hangover,' I say, 'or have you had an even worse day than me?'

He turns and leaves me to close the door. I follow him up, catching the scent. Skin fresh from the shower. Damp hair with a faint fragrance of exotic wood.

The living room is still full of boxes. The shelves in the alcove are empty. I try to joke about my day of musical purgatory. He picks up a cigarette from an ashtray and sucks the last mouthful, then takes another from a packet and lights it off the dying one.

That is seriously intensive smoking.

He turns out the main light so that the only illumination is from the kitchen and the street lamp outside. I put my bag on the sofa. The Dictaphone is already on the cushions, red recording light primed.

Next to where he expects I'll sit.

He walks behind the sofa, takes another drag from the cigarette then kneels down so that one hand and his chin are leaning on the back of the sofa. His face is close to me.

The semi light, as ever, makes his bone structure sculptural. He takes another drag on the cigarette and tilts his head away to blow the smoke, then turns to me.

Ready to start. And we've hardly said hello, talked about last night, or anything.

Something's wrong. I've never seen him smoke like that, one after another. I don't relax back on the cushions as he expects. I twist around and look at him.

'We don't have to do that.'

The grey eyes look at me. It's such a cold, judging expression that it actually scares me. What am I starting by saying this?

Like in the car the previous night, as soon as I put him under pressure my body tries to tell me not to. My throat is dry and there's a pulse trembling in my jugular. As if I'm going against some deep conditioning that says I must obey him.

For a moment he doesn't say anything and I wonder what he's going to do. Then he takes my left wrist. His cold fingers find my pulse. A few seconds of rapid beats and he takes his fingers away and starts to talk.

His voice is quiet, the whisper like Karli's rich mezzo voce.

'You're falling, you're falling very fast. The wind is scouring your face. There is nothing in your head, or in your body, but pure, blinding speed.'

I want to resist and tell him no I'm not, but the more I do the harder that pulse beats, like it's being fed back to me through headphones.

He goes on. 'This is what it feels like to fall out of the sky.'

And it does feel exactly like falling.

'Down you go. Then the parachute opens and you've stopped.'

Yes I have. Thank God because I couldn't take much more. He's caught me, got me as surely as if I landed in his hand.

'You've stopped in mid-air and are floating; in silence, clouds and brilliant sunshine.'

He gets up and pads to the kitchen door. 'Now you're starting to go down again. Not falling now. You're drifting. All around you is bright sunlight. It is dazzling and warm, like being in a cloud. At last you can breathe.'

Yes, I can breathe. I feel my chest slowing. There is an electronic tick-tick as he adjusts the thermostat on the wall. The gas flares up in response. It makes a sound like wind snatching a flag.

He moves quietly onto the sofa beside me. A smell of cigarette smoke mingles with skin fresh from the shower and exotic wood.

That fragrance smacks me back to the reality of us in this room.

I hear locks turning and the heavy slam of the front door in the warehouse that adjoins the flat. I erupt to my feet and go to the window, legs moving before I'm even aware they are.

Below, on the path, a figure in a checked skirt and a parka walks away from the house to the gate, a big cardboard file in her hands. I see street lamps, parked cars, indicators and headlights twinkling through bushes as cars circle the roundabout by the hospital, everything in urban amber monochrome. A Saturday night in Vellonoweth, England. I'm still in the world.

My nails curl into my palm; in case I slip again. Slip where? To where he wants to put me. The tendons in my left arm obligingly keep me grounded with a lance of pain.

I don't want to do that tonight. Gene, talk to me. Communicate with me. You're alive and you're warm; I can smell you. You're flesh and you're upset and if you were Jerry I'd put my arms around you.

I don't know how to say any of this to him. I'm breathing fast again. All I've done is get up and go to the window but it feels like I lifted a two-tonne car.

I turn around. 'Can I have a cigarette?'

He reaches down beside the sofa and tosses me the packet. I take one out, then have to go to him for a light. He ignites the end with polite care, narrowed eyes assessing what's going on.

Is he angry? Or just calculating his next clever move?

I don't want the cigarette, I just want something to be in control of. The nicotine gushes in, takes hold of my heartbeat. It's not pleasant but at least it's something I'm doing to myself. I'm in charge of me again.

'You look as if you've had a hell of a day,' I say, breathing out on smoke.

He drags his hand wearily through his hair. 'Do you really want to know? I have spent the afternoon hypnotizing people with Alzheimer's and senile dementia.'

I believe him totally. This is not calculated, he looks too tired.

The only thing I can think of to say is banal and obvious. 'You were working on a Saturday?'

He drags his other hand over his head again. His damp hair flops between his fingers, dark as his eyebrows, making his skin pale and drained.

'It's a thing they asked me to do at the care home. I put the patient into a trance and ask them to talk about their memories. An artist listens to it later and paints a picture for their relatives.'

He takes a drag on the cigarette and blows the smoke up towards the ceiling. 'After I'd done four of them the nurses told me no one else had ever managed to get through to them. They've got no attention span left. Poor old things.'

He takes a deep drag on the cigarette, and then one more, as though he's in a hurry to finish it because what he really wants to do is start another. Now he's not trying to hypnotise me he looks nervous. His bare foot across his knee is beating a fidgety rhythm.

I return to the sofa and sit next to him. If it was Jerry I would pull those slim shoulders towards me, stroke the fine hairs at the back of his neck. But it's Gene and I don't feel I can even touch his hand.

My gaze drifts to the packing crates. I am sure they are in exactly the same spot as the first time I came to the flat.

Perhaps if we do something practical that will take his mind off it. Break this stalemate.

I take another drag on my cigarette – unwanted now, it tastes disgusting – then stub it out in the glass ashtray beside the chrome leg of the sofa. I stand up.

'Shall I give you a hand unpacking?'

'No. I'll get round to it sometime.'

I roll up my sleeves, go to one of the boxes, inspect the lid. It's still taped, sealed. 'How long are you going to leave it like this? Come on, just one box won't hurt.'

'No. Or I won't know where anything is. Leave it.'

I give up on the box and wave my hand towards the Dictaphone with its waiting red light. 'We shouldn't be messing around with all this. We should be out in a bar getting smashed out of our skulls. Are you coming?' I go back to the sofa and reach for my bag.

Even if he doesn't come, I might as well go, he seems hardly aware I am here.

Before I can lift the bag he puts his hand on it. His eyes look at me, slashes of dark in his pale face. 'Please. Let's just go back to where we started.'

The appeal shocks me. He looks completely defenceless.

A cynical voice inside me observes that this is why he's so effective as a hypnotist. He will not give up. Drug addicts in appalling pain haven't been able to resist him when he gets going. Or people who can't even think any more. What did he tell me? You find the way. He can appeal to me, be vulnerable, spin a plausible yarn (yes I'm doubting that business about the Alzheimer's people). I believe he will do anything he thinks will get me to go with him.

His hand is on my bag. Pale skin, contours shadowed in the light from the kitchen, resting on white leather. Carefully manicured nails, fingers leanly shaped like the rest of him.

A devilish thought enters my head. How far could I push this? A frisky game of spin the bottle for two, perhaps? I think he probably would. He knows he's sexy. He takes care with his appearance. Those jeans he's wearing aren't just any old jeans, they're expensive and the shirt is Paul Smith. That haircut is West End too. *You find the way*, he said, and I bet there have been times when he's used his charms as part of the game.

He may even be hoping that's what I'd respond to.

But it would just be a game. Like the games he was playing all night at the party.

Which is why I wouldn't.

This obviously matters to him. Why? The challenge? But he doesn't look excited, he looks exhausted. Like someone who's cold and can only think about being warm again. Like me when I've had a bad day and all I want is my hands on those black and white keys.

Besides, when I turned up at his door looking for an antidote to my day, what did I expect? When you go to the house of a duet partner, you expect to play.

I let him put the bag on the floor. Lie back on the sofa. And let him talk.

This – this thing with the listening Dictaphone and the half light – is what we do.

3:

LIKE RUBY

CHAPTER 39

I push back the blanket, retrieve bag and coat from the crate. The familiar routine. The tape's gone, the bedroom door is closed.

Has Gene taken it in with him? Is he listening to me while the real me fastens the collar of my coat and hurries down the stairs into the street?

TAPE 5

The appointment begins in the usual way. 'Soothesayer,' says the client, 'I feel as ragged as that poor, torn fish out there.'

Out in the sea a fish's face floats past, a giant filmy mask of lips and empty eyes, with trails of muscle streaming behind like tails. Other parts of its skin follow; two fins like torn-off hands trying to catch it.

The client lies back, waiting for me to step up to the game. The lenses glint golden in her eyes.

I had intended to soothe her but suddenly I cannot.

The words are stuck inside me. If I soothe, I feel I will break something. I am an elastic band stretched to forever; it will not take any more.

I say: 'I cannot soothe you.'

She blinks, digesting this. 'Oh well, in that case we can xech. I've never had a xech from you.' She takes a preparatory breath.

I shake my head.

She stands up. 'I'm calling the monastery.' Her voice is crisp.

I don't know what they will do with me. But I have nothing more to give. I am at a dead stop, as though ahead of me is the edge of a cliff and I must turn away before it drags me over.

They send two seniors, who escort me into a taxi. They do

not speak, not even to each other. To an onlooker we appear to be in devoted contemplation. But none of us can find the words for this awkward, uncommon occasion. I catch a smell in their robes; they are carrying sedatives. But I'm not going to resist.

At the monastery they take me to a room where a man is waiting. The seniors are unable to find the words for this transaction either, and hurry past me to their more familiar duties.

The man who is waiting for me looks unusual. His skin is dark and his eyes are like raisins behind his cheekbones. His clothes smell of outside.

We leave the monastery. The marble entrance is deserted. There is no goodbye from the seniors, not even a malicious xech.

We go down a narrow alleyway and into a tunnel. Not the same one I went up before to get to the surface, but very like it.

Outside, under the wide open sky, the air is a hot mask.

Far away in the dunes, something is moving. The sand forms a cloud, travelling towards us. It comes closer. A shape develops at its head. First a black dot in a wake of sand. Then no bigger than a bug. It grows into a vehicle on skis and halts beside us in a rasp of dust.

A cover lifts. The driver pulls a cowled hood over his head, muffles a scarf around his mouth and speaks through the material.

I seem to be expected. As they talk, the sandy wind scours through my clothes. My hands and face tingle. I pull my robes tighter around me but the sand forces its way through the thin material. My clothes are not made to withstand the weather here.

I take a last look at the wide, glittering sea, which contains everything I know.

I jump into my car, shivering so hard it's difficult to stab the key into its hole. I swing across the roundabout and accelerate up the hill.

I have left behind everything I know. You just nailed my life, Andreq; or that grey-eyed wood-scented devil did.

It used to be so simple. I played and I tried to play better. I tamed duet partners and they tamed me. I kept freelance gigs ticking over. Then it broke and I had to leave. And now I feel like I'm caught naked in a dream, thrown out with just my thin skin while everyone else copes just fine.

So full marks for perceptiveness, and maybe even for repeating my mistakes through the reincarnation continuum. But what are we all going to do about it, eh?

It's gone two o'clock and there are few other cars on the road. The ones I do see are breaking the speed limit. It's after hours; normal rules don't apply. We're all wanderers, out later than we intended, trying to get home before we're beaten by the cold.

I pull on the handbrake in front of the cottage. The black windows reflect the two points of my headlights as I close them down. The Dowmans have long ago gone to bed. They are not night birds, they keep regular hours and get up for church.

I push open the front door of the cottage, grateful for the homely aroma of Jenny Tollderson's pot pourri, the sprigged comfort in her Laura Ashley collection. The Ansaphone light is on. I get ready with a pen at the A4 pad and press play.

A long moment of white noise like the ether breathing, then a voice. 'It's Andreq.' Then click.

I think I actually shriek.

The only reply is the wind rustling the trees and the sound of a car on its own business a long way away.

After a moment I laugh at myself and dial 1471. The last call was made at seven o'clock but the number was withheld. At that time I'd been at Gene's, although of course it wouldn't be him, such a trick was too cheap. It must have been one of the many people who phone up looking for Jenny. I add another message to the pad. *Andrew/Andrea? Saturday 9th.*

I turn the radio on. I pray that Radio Active is feeling cuddly and not playing another kooky whalesong experiment. Or, like the other day, when it had a programme where three guys discussed their rare records of railway trains.

Radio Active obliges with a lush American ballad. Cheesy as brie, but a relief.

Soothing the storm. Isn't that what we're all doing really?

No, I'm just trying to stay alive until I can play again. And that had better be soon or I'll be so shrivelled that I'll never get back.

CHAPTER 40

A sharp rapping on the door dragged me away from a lazy morning with the Sunday papers. I shifted my lapful of newsprint and went to answer, expecting from the murmur of voices next door that it was the Dowmans returning borrowed sugar.

It was not one of the Dowmans. It was a dumpy woman with shaggy black hair and shapeless clothes, like a monk in mufti.

'My name is Alice Swanley. I'm a clairvoyant and I would very much like to get to know you.'

In London you get the Jehovah's Witnesses canvassing. Here it seemed you got clairvoyants.

At that moment there was a whine of hinges and the Dowmans' door opened. Jean and William stepped out, fussing about locking up. They were dressed for church in neat coats accessorised with prayer books bound in red.

Jean gave me a guarded nod, which also took in my spooky visitor. William dealt with the door and they walked to their maroon Rover.

'Sorry, I'm not really interested,' I said to Alice Swanley.

'Miss Lear, I need to see you.'

Jean Dowman's eye was on me. She took a long time to fold the skirt of her coat around her legs and climb into the passenger seat. Her face in the dandelion clock of hair had exactly the expression she used when I was suggesting a modification to the way she performed a song. A look that said: we don't do things like that around here.

For goodness' sake, I thought. You should see some of the musicians I've worked with. Black back-combed hair and studded leather, singing *Ave Maria* like the heavenly host. Although they were possibly more stylish.

While Jean gave me the evil eye, Alice stumped across the

threshold. Without waiting for me to give permission. And without apology either.

She came to a standstill in the middle of the lounge and pulled her coat around her with a disapproving shiver.

'Where do you contact spirit?'

'Excuse me?' I said. And I also meant, did you just walk in uninvited?

Outside, the Dowmans' car was going down the hill very slowly. They were still watching. Then another car beeped them to move on.

Alice Swanley turned so that her back was towards me, looking like a squat purple candle, with her dyed hair forming the burned wick. She addressed the room.

'This kind of journey can be very dangerous without expert guidance. You have no experience with spirit. Where do you call it?'

I struggled to understand what she was talking about, and then I remembered the psychic fair. I'd told a few people about contacting spirits. I was surprised anyone would remember; that was over two weeks ago now. Perhaps she was hard-up for business.

'Thanks, but no.' I leaned against the open door in a significant way. 'I'm sorry, I don't have time –'

'I can feel spirit here,' said Alice Swanley. Uncannily, she was looking at my handbag, where I had some of the tapes. I felt like pulling the bag away to protect them from her.

She continued to address the invisible sprites she imagined must be hiding behind the sideboard. 'A lot of people can conjure spirit up, and for a while they think it is a plaything. It takes a professional to bring it under control. You may already have felt spirit stir and wondered what it was.'

'Thanks for your help,' I said, 'but I've got a busy day.' Once again, I laid my hand meaningfully on the door.

Still, Alice Swanley didn't take the hint. She began to wander the room, placing her hands on objects, as if blessing them or assessing their temperature. She did the violin case, the arm of the sofa and several of Jenny Tollderson's cat pictures. Most of the cats were dead, but if she felt them stir she didn't say.

'You may believe you have control, but spirit is capricious, like a child. It feels its way, content in the boundaries you draw, and then tests its bonds. Usually spirit is much stronger than you think.'

I noticed she said 'spirit'; not 'the spirit' or even 'spirits'. It was a curious affectation; at once primitive and also stuffy, like the jargon of grants boards. It said this word is belittled by a definite article. We wish it to be regarded as grave and cosmic.

She passed the phone, then laid a questing hand on my bag again.

This time I crossed the room and took it from her.

'Miss Swanley, I have to go out; this isn't a good time.' It wasn't a white lie; I had arranged to see Eleanor Lear this afternoon.

'Miss Lear, you are on dangerous ground if you think you can be so casual. You could seriously come to grief.'

She rounded on me with a stare. 'Last time a family's whole house was invaded. They had read a book about mediums and one of them had contacted a dead relative. They started hearing noises at night and seeing shadows, until there was only one room where they could sleep. They called me because there was loud rapping on all the floorboards, even though they had carpets everywhere. At first they wouldn't let me in, they were so scared. As soon as I was through the door I saw it. It was like a shadow, but pale. When it saw me it laid a stench and sank into the floor, only a head and shoulders visible. I spent the rest of the night battling with it, and eventually I was able to lead it from the house.' She paused. 'I was nearly too late. I almost didn't manage it.'

It had all been rather impressive until the brow-mopping at the end. 'Good, good,' I said, and emphasised the door.

She affected a sad expression. 'I don't want your money, Miss Lear. Spirit doesn't change allegiance by a transaction done in coin. You must transfer spirit formally to me. Then you will be free.'

I said nothing and hoped silence would make the point that subtler hints had failed to.

She finally stumped to the door. 'What you don't want, Miss Lear, is a visitor you can't get rid of.' She bustled off down the drive, the purple vanishing from her coat in the weak winter light.

I closed the door and put my bag down again on the hall table. Next to it was Jenny's phone message pad. *Andrew/Andrea (?) called. Saturday 9th.*

Alice Swanley should have come round last night. If she'd caught me just after that call she might have had a sale.

Eleanor had asked me to help with her sight-reading technique. She lived in a dinky white cottage, much like Jenny's.

I rapped on the bright brass knocker and heard footsteps clattering to the door. Bolts were drawn back, and a chain, and a deadlock turned. The place was secured like a fortress.

'Are there a lot of burglaries around here?' I asked when she finally released the door.

Her Noh mask eyebrows bunched together, not understanding why I'd asked.

'All the locks?'

'I like to know who's calling. Sometimes I have a bad feeling about somebody and I pretend I am not in.'

'Oh, have you had Alice Swanley here too?'

Eleanor took my coat and put it on an aristocratic padded hanger. 'Alice Swanley the clairvoyant? Oh dear, are you having to consult her? Do go in.'

Ah, I'd strayed into territory that she took seriously. I should have known. 'No,' I said. 'I think she was doing her Sunday rounds.'

I went, as directed, to the lounge. Eleanor was obviously one of those people who bought furniture regardless of whether they had space for it. The room was stuffed – three-piece suite, writing bureau, coffee table, dining table and Chippendale chairs. I was still searching for the piano in all this when she crossed the room and whipped away a paisley cloth.

She folded the cloth onto a chair and settled on the piano stool, then moved her fingers in intricate rippling motions. I'd nagged her about warming up and now she began every key-smashing session with this dactylic gurning.

'Some people say Alice Swanley's quite good. I think it must be very hard to make a living by clairvoyance.'

The question had to be asked: 'Do you use clairvoyants?'

'Oh no. In the Lear family, we're close down the generations so contact isn't a problem. When I've needed it I've felt a sense of the old Lears looking after me. Of course I wouldn't use ouija boards or cards, it's more of a general feeling. Like Ronald in the Antarctic talking to his ancestors. And Sir Bertrand on his famous expedition through the desert to find the mountains in Italy. He came across a pair of climbing boots, exactly his size, sitting side by side in the sand.'

She kept making claws with her hands, like someone trying to be a monster on Halloween. She had no idea how funny that looked while talking about dead spirit guardians.

When we broke for tea, she served it in dainty cups that were faintly see-through, as though fairies had made them from birds' eggs. The tea, though, was a stern economy brand, strong as Bovril. Surely those cups were made for the lightest Earl Grey.

There was also a salt cellar. Eleanor ground a little over a digestive biscuit. 'A little salt really brings out their flavour,' she said, and threw a pinch over her shoulder. Her right shoulder.

'Isn't it supposed to be your left?' I said.

She looked at the carpet. 'Oh dear. I was never very good at left and right. Do you go to church?'

I was getting used to Eleanor's style of conversation. It was like her driving: full of sudden turns. 'No, I don't go to church.'

Eleanor set the cup down. 'I never got on with the Church, either. Ever since I was at school and my class had to do a painting for the chapel. I had painted Jesus holding something in his left hand. The vicar was furious and said Jesus used only his right. It quite put me off.' She took another sip. 'But this is a Lear thing.'

Yes, I thought it might be.

'Have you explored Ixendon yet? Geoffrey Lear – Sir Bertrand's grandson, as you know – did a painting for the cathedral there. One day they telephoned him and said, "Will you come and take it away? It's very big and nobody likes it." So cruel of them as he was such a devout man. But like most of the Lears he had to find his own way.'

I smiled, looking at my cup. I had a story about Lears finding their own way. My Lears. Our claim to the name didn't go back very far at all. My great-grandfather had started life as Leach and changed to a name he preferred. The name Lear was hijacked, not bestowed in blood.

I was going to tell her about old Leach but something else came out instead.

'People used to ask who I took after. Which aunt, which uncle might be so musical. There wasn't anyone.'

I thought Eleanor would reciprocate with yet more fantastic Lears but she put down her cup and listened.

'I think it started when I was four. I heard Beethoven's Piano Sonata 14 in C sharp minor.'

Eleanor's eyes creased at the name.

'That's the Moonlight. At home we had an upright that nobody played, and I went to it, found the first notes by ear and felt my way through what I remembered.'

'You'd never played the piano before?'

'No. Then I discovered the sheet music in the library. It was ridiculous. The key signature was full of sharps. I remember I thought it looked like barbed wire. The timings were meaningless to me. I had to keep counting the stave and the ledger lines, and cheat with the pedal to play the octave. But every day I inched through it, bar by bar, because when a chord or arpeggio came right it was like magic.' I shrugged. 'It was just something I had to do.'

'Your parents must have been delighted when they heard you.'

'They were at work so they didn't know. The au pair reported to them what I was doing and said I should have lessons.'

Eleanor looked over her cup of inky tea. 'But then they must have been delighted.'

'I think they got more than they bargained for. Once they came to one of my competitions. I was winning quite a lot of them and they probably imagined they would be treated like royalty. But they found themselves sitting in a cold hall for hours with all the other parents. They couldn't agree who should stay to drive me home. It was easier when they didn't come to watch me play.'

'They must have been proud,' said Eleanor firmly.

'They said they were, sometimes. There was an evening when some new business partners came for dinner. I'd just won my place at the RCM and it was quite the topic of conversation. But when the visitors left, my parents made it clear I was to work in the business once I'd finished my music course.'

Eleanor's cup was midway to her lips. She put it down hurriedly, as though she'd forgotten it was there.

I reached for the teapot, refilled her cup and gave a bright smile. 'So yes, you're right. Lears have to find their own way.'

CHAPTER 41

'I just wanted to apologise,' said Gene's voice.

He rang on Monday at lunchtime. The weather was filthy and Eleanor and I were in our teaching room, roasting ourselves by the electric fire and picnicking on shop-bought sandwiches.

I mouthed 'Excuse me' and turned away to speak to him.

'Apologise for what?'

'Saturday. I must have been coming down with something. Look, are you free tonight? Not for that,' he added quickly. 'I need someone who can read a map.'

Not for that. I tried to sound perfectly non-reactive. Not fazed, intrigued, pleased, disappointed.

'Don't you have satnav?'

'Never needed it.'

'What time?'

'Seven. Oh, and we'll go in mine.'

That did make me smile. 'Scared of my driving?'

'I love your driving, but the paintings won't.'

Eleanor was doing her best to look like she wasn't listening, sprinkling salt on a glistening gherkin. What gave her away was the sharply arched eyebrow cocked in my direction.

'Somebody nice?' she said as I turned back towards her and put the phone down.

She made it sound so simple.

'Old school friend,' I said. And that made Gene sound very straightforward indeed.

The paintings were the ones Gene had talked about the other night, based on the accounts of people he'd hypnotised at the old folks' home. Four large canvasses wrapped in red ambulance blankets were laid in the back of his black VW.

Just in case I'd been having any doubts about what he'd told me.

He was driving, I was reading the map, trying to find four houses spread around Vellonoweth. It was raining hard, the kind of thick, syrupy rain that turned the windscreen to melting glass and oncoming headlights into sliding smudges. Streetlamps threw teary reflections over the map on my knee. My breath made clouds on the glass of the passenger window as I tried to find number twenty-two in Rectory Lane.

Finally I spotted it, beside an imposing set of stone lions that the small brick house couldn't possibly live up to.

Fortunately the householder's taste for grand accessories worked in our favour. Over the driveway was a lychgate with a roof like the entrance to a churchyard. We swung in under it and opened the hatchback in comfort.

Gene pulled the blanket off the top picture. It was a jumble of shapes and human figures in shadowy outline. There were also outlines of guns, like a poster for a family saga set in World War II.

'It's a bit apocalyptic,' I said. 'Who was the patient – General Patton?'

Gene took his glasses off and poked away a smudge on the lens. 'He used to be a coastguard. He remembered ships going down in the bay during the War, when there were gun emplacements in the hills.' He put the glasses back on again and looked balefully at the rain. 'And it's a watercolour.'

I dashed to the front door, which was answered by a smart-looking man who was just shaking out a wet overcoat. I explained what we were delivering and he splashed out with bin liners.

We rushed the painting in and propped it in the narrow hallway. A woman in a Snoopy apron came out of the kitchen, wiping her hands. The patient must have been her father because she gasped as she saw the picture and backed away for a proper look.

'Oh that's nice. How unusual.' She pulled her husband to stand next to her and pointed at the figures. 'Look, they've got the war in there and Alex and Eve.'

There was a thump from upstairs and small feet chasing each other. 'I'll go and get them,' said the husband. As he went up, calling for Alex and Eve, the woman said: 'Are you the artists?'

'No,' I said, 'just doing the deliveries.'

The woman looked disappointed. 'Well tell the artist it's lovely.'

We got back in the car, looked up the next address and launched once more into the scrum of traffic and water.

'You know,' said Gene as we joined a line of red brake lights queuing for the main road, 'at this one we should say you're the artist.' The indicator light flashing in the dashboard made tiny green points in his glasses.

'Left after the junction.'

'I'm serious,' he said.

I'd assumed he was joking. 'Why would we do that?'

'They want to meet the artist.' He swung the wheel.

'But I'm not the artist.'

A motorbike swerved towards us, a helmeted shape hunkered low against the rain like a leather-covered foetus. Gene braked hard, flicked the car into first and powered out of the way. 'It's more special for them if they meet the people involved in the picture.'

'They're meeting you. You did half the work.' I pointed left. 'Take this filter lane.'

'They don't understand about that.'

I said: 'They could meet the artist if they wanted to.'

The chunky rear bumper of a 4x4 loomed up fast. We nipped around it and halted at a red light.

'They won't get round to it; the moment's gone. Tonight is the special occasion, when the picture's unveiled. It has more impact if you're the artist.'

'I'm not the artist and we don't have to make an impact. Those people in Rectory Lane were quite happy.'

We were near the next house. I opened the window a crack and peered at gateposts and garden walls. 'Number fourteen, it's the one with the white car.'

I put the window up, sealing out the road noise, and sat back in the leather seat. 'If you tell them I'm the artist I'll tell them I'm not.'

Gene turned into the drive and pulled on the handbrake. 'You won't have to say anything.'

'Yes I will. What if they ask me technical questions? Why I used certain colours. What I left out.' I pulled my seatbelt off. 'I can't believe I'm even discussing it. I'm not the artist and I'm not taking the credit for someone else's work.'

'Just wing it. You've got artist hair.'

In the house, a face was inspecting us through a latticed window. It turned away to raise the alert.

We took the canvas into the hall. Mother in her sixties, son and daughter-in-law in their thirties stood ready, giving each other little anticipating looks. At the moment I pulled off the cover and mother and daughter clasped hands.

'Oh look,' said the daughter. Mother's hand was on her collarbones as though there was a lump somewhere there.

Gene and I played eye contact poker. I'm going to say it, said his twitched eyebrow.

Just don't, said mine.

'That's Olivia and Meg,' said the son, and moved close to the painting to examine the two child silhouettes who sat making daisy chains under a stormy sky. He turned to us. 'That's so clever, thank you.'

I refused to look at Gene. Mercifully he didn't say a word about the artist. We rejoined the traffic with integrity intact.

'I don't know much about art,' he said, the leather wheel skimming through his palm, 'but that artist seems to like painting children in shadow.'

'Shadows and big, glowing skies. It's a distinctive style. She probably eats too much cheese before bedtime. You know what? I could murder a really psychoactive camembert. Whenever I leave London that's what I miss. '

He clicked his tongue. 'You see, you do think like an artist.'

I ignored him. 'Take the next right.'

By the time we had delivered the third painting, the car smelled of wet clothes instead of leather and exotic wood. Gene's fringe was like wiry grass. My thicker curls, usually resilient to showers, were shrinking to my head.

The fourth destination was in a road of low-roofed bungalows and bonsai hedges. We splashed out to the boot. Gene pushed back the discarded ambulance blankets and looked at the remaining canvas for a long moment. It showed a ship keeling on turbulent waters.

A label was attached to the blanket. *22 Rectory Lane*.

'Gene, that's the wrong picture.'

He ripped the label away and scrunched it. 'No it's not.'

'It is.' I pointed to the sign on the close-mown lawn. 'This is Parma House, Parma Avenue.'

He shrugged, hands around the canvas. 'They'll never know.'

'But the picture won't make sense. The people at Rectory Lane were the coastguards. That's why there's a ship on it.'

'They'll make sense of the ship somehow. They're bound to know someone who's a coastguard or on the lifeboats. Anyway-' he glanced at the front door, where a face was peering out curiously – 'they don't know what their father said. They probably haven't had a coherent conversation with him for years.'

He hunched into his jacket and splashed to the door with his wide red parcel. The family welcomed him in.

I slammed the boot and got back in the car.

He came back ten minutes later, shaking rain off his hair. As he got in I put my elbow on the window sill and looked out through the glass away from him, my chin resting on my hand. He started the engine and did a three-point turn to leave the drive.

I stayed quiet until we reached the T junction. Then I said 'Did anyone get the right painting?'

His foot slammed onto the brake. The tyres screeched. We stopped dead. A horn howled behind us.

'Jesus,' I said.

He launched the car into a squealing getaway. 'They were fine about the fucking ship. Shall we go back, tell them it's the wrong painting, drive to Rectory Lane and tell them they've got the wrong painting too? They've bonded with them. They've made sense of the guns and kids and horses and sunsets. Think what would happen if I told them now.'

I looked out of the window, away from him. 'That isn't their picture.'

He said nothing. For a while he drove in silence, slaloming aggressively around the other traffic. His mouth was a tight line, holding in the thoughts he wasn't allowing himself to say.

On a quieter stretch of road, he spoke.

'They were four poor old people who no one's managed to talk to for years. And I mean no one. It's like getting data off a computer that's been completely fucked by a virus. You don't just play them womb noises or twirl a pocket-watch in front of their eyes.'

He turned onto the hill towards the cottage. The street lights thinned out and he flicked full beam on. White raindrops whirled around us like a force field.

He took his hand off the gear lever and gave me a nudge. 'We all mess up from time to time, but what harm was done? What awful thing have you done and not admitted to?'

That probably amounted to an apology, but I didn't feel like letting him off.

'Come on, tell me.'

'Nothing.'

'Not ever? You're not that well behaved.'

I bit my lip, thinking for a moment. Then I said: 'I cut the hairs on Charlie's violin bow.'

Gene gave me a roguish grin. 'That's nice.'

'It was very satisfying. I used nail scissors. Slowly, so I could feel each hair split. It was an expensive German bow too. Rehairing would have cost a fortune.'

'And you chopped it in half?'

'I trimmed off a millimetre on each side. Enough that Charlie would spend a frustrating day wondering what was going so wrong with his playing.'

In the window I could see his reflection. His glasses like fine black wires, his lips twitching as he played with a smile. 'No you didn't.'

'Fuck,' I said, and looked at the floor, shocked to hear myself use such language. He was right, of course.

CHAPTER 42

I woke to the feeling of needles in my skin. The cat was prowling up the bed, digging in its claws. Its mouth opened in a demanding miaow.

I felt weak as a mouse. Bonelessly exhausted.

Hadn't Gene said he'd been ill at the weekend? Lovely, he'd given me his flu.

The cat jumped off the bed, its tail pert with the thought of breakfast. I stumbled downstairs and fed it, the duvet around me like a turtle shell.

I crawled to the sofa and fell into a dream where I was trapped in a white decompression chamber, monitored through a window by people in white gowns and masks, which made them unable to communicate except with their eyes. I needed to recuperate, they made me understand through flicks of their doe-lashed orbs, because I had been constantly regressing and surfacing. An alarm sounded.

I opened my eyes. I could still hear it. It was my mobile.

My voice was like a car too old to start. At the third attempt, it rasped into life and I managed hello.

'Sally says, where are you?' It was Eleanor.

'I've got a flu thing.'

'My dear, you sound dreadful. You can't possibly teach like that. Is there anything you need?'

'Just sleep, I think.'

Back into dreams again and those eloquent eyes were still tending me, insisting I serve out my time. It's not me you need to cure, I told them, although they seemed to have no ears, just smooth heads under fabric. What about Gene?

And there he was, a slim-shouldered figure locked behind a porthole of glass. He spoke to me through a crackly radio. 'I've been here for years.'

I awoke to another phone. The house phone, on the opposite side of the sofa. I twisted round, took the pen and pulled the receiver into the duvet.

'Hello, this is Jenny Tollderson. Is that Carol?'

'Hi Jenny.'

She had phoned to check on Verdi, to see if I was still okay to stay for a while (yes, if I could spend the whole time sleeping) and to reiterate that if the washing machine gave me trouble I was welcome to use Jean Dowman's next door because Jean came and helped herself to her, that is Jenny's, runner beans.

After long, long minutes I lowered the receiver onto the table, wrote Jenny's name on her own message pad and sank into another doze.

All afternoon I slept, woke, slept. Each time the light was dimmer as though the day was struggling to stay alive. Gradually I began to hear the wet swish of rush-hour traffic.

When I next woke I had a text. *Are you up?*

It was from Jerry. The time was one in the morning but the text was recent.

This was unusually late for him to be looking for a chat. I called him.

'Hey,' he said. His voice sounded frail. 'I had another attack.'

I sat straight up and clutched the duvet around me. 'When?'

'About half an hour ago. It's all right. It's gone now. I got through it.'

A lone car rattled past in the road outside. 'Is Tim there with you?'

I guessed he couldn't be, but I had to ask. Did Tim even know about the attacks?

'He's away at a conference. I'm glad actually. I think he'd find it too freaky. Now I know I can cope. It's a good thing.'

I didn't know what to say. I tried a joke. 'So does Anthony Morrish have to give you your money back?' Then I wondered if I should have said that. I hoped we were playing by the rules of red feet in bed.

'It's okay. I know what it is now. Sometimes Ruby still needs to scream.'

'Jesus. How bad was it?'

'Average.' He gave a short, dry laugh. 'At least it was no worse.'

The temperature in the room had dropped into deep nocturnal cold. I burrowed further into the duvet, covered all my skin except my face and my hand on the phone.

'I thought you were okay,' I said. 'This shouldn't happen.'

'I have to make my peace with it. It's part of the process. And I also have to remember that Ruby was more than a murder victim. She had a life. She has a lot more to offer.'

I couldn't answer. I made a small sound so that he knew I was still here.

He gave a long sigh. 'It's funny, this business we've got ourselves into, isn't it?'

'You're damn right about that.'

'And yet I find it makes sense of things. Don't you?'

I laughed. 'Except for the things that make no sense at all.'

'They will, petal. You're just coming at it all backwards.'

I found myself wide awake. The clock on my phone said five in the morning.

For an instant I thought I was at Gene's. Then I saw Jenny Tollderson's sprigged duvet and remembered.

The flu must have gone. I felt bright as a firework.

I sat up. On the floor beside me was Jenny's A4 phone pad. I picked it up to put it back where it belonged.

It was covered in writing.

Not the orderly list of phone messages. This was mad paragraphs, going up the page at a wild slope, heedless of the ruled grey lines.

Sometimes you only realise you've cut yourself when you look down and see blood. My right hand began to stiffen, as though it was turning into a claw. I straightened the fingers but it protested with a cramped, weary ache.

I'd written all this.

A prickling started at the back of my neck. I knew immediately what this was. No wonder I'd thought I'd woken up at Gene's.

A great ream of the pad had been used, flipped over the top like a curling scroll. I hooked back through the pages, looking for where it started. Passages made vivid, startling sense, as though reloaded in my brain. But moments before I hadn't known I had experienced them.

I came to the phone list on the first page, and my befuddled entry: *Jenny*. That had been quite early in the day, or at least there had been light outside. When could I have written this? Between bouts of feverish waking? After I talked to Jerry?

I looked at the altered hand. Then plunged in to see what I had done.

The first few lines seemed to be more dreams. Perhaps I was warming up.

I'm in a street in an old city under a cold sky, with a friend looking for blood on a wall.

I meet a man who has known me for a month and nineteen years.

If you become ill, your body appears in ghostly outline.

But then, like a breeze filling a sail, it picked up a new, stronger course.

ANDREQ

I am in v strange place.

A power station in the dunes, made of glass and fed by sun. Nothing else for miles.

Above the sand you see slender towers of glass, like masts of a buried ship. Sandy winds have rounded the edges, so that the towers have waists and contours like bones.

Beneath the sand it is huge. (Unreadable)

There are many of these power stations. Each for a different facility in the sea domes. Force fields to stop the sea destroying gardens. Signals for phones. Channels for broadcasting. Heavy-duty power for deep-level trains.

Rich pickings to be made if you build a station that invents a new luxury. A current to disperse debris in the red season, perhaps.

But easier to muster a pirate army to invade a station owned by someone else.

The civilised comforts under the water come from a blood economy here.

It's like the world is two halves. Up here we have sieges, sabotage, battles. Down in the sea, nothing changes. No years. Just season after season. We keep them that way; they keep us this way.

Many of the station crew are armed guards. Scarred, flint-eyed and silent, they walk the sandy corridors, fingers drumming on a gun. Sprint to challenge a suspicious noise; protect their stolen ship from others who might steal in.

The rest of us crew the turbines. Mend the cables. Monitor the supply to the quiet, blue world. Sweep away the sand that trickles and bleeds out of the walls and threatens to stop the machines.

The station bears the scars of past attacks. Bulletholes in the walls, which sand pours through. So many rooms half-filled, going back to the desert. We find the doors that open into sand and melt them shut. We build new rooms. An explosive charge that sends the hollow bones ringing, and we have a new cave of glass, ready for decoration.

The station is building new bones, shedding smashed ones, like a tumour of coral.

When there is wind we hear the dunes drifting. A sound like hoarse breath on the glass bones that reach into the sky. The landscape above us is moving. You look out of a camera to the outside and each time the hills are in a different place.

Perhaps we are travelling too, vibrating in random directions with the joy of all this power we are generating.

When the sun is very bright the whole structure trembles, and settles deeper in the sand. One day we will touch the rock bed at the bottom and rest like a wreck.

No one xeches here. No one soothes. Off duty we doze in

sandy staterooms, eating, drinking, playing games which turn into fights. No one spends time on introspective arts. Here, there is either conscious activity or sleep, no in-between.

Do I miss it? The sight of a xeching person has a calming quality. The head tilted upwards, mind tripping on light seen without eyes. Or is that like a blind person wondering if they miss colours?

I take walks around the station. Look for places to be alone. I find an abandoned apartment where the glass walls are painted with bright murals like orange and purple graffiti. Bullets have made white stars on the garish surface, through which sand slowly hisses. Sand fills one corner of the room in a diagonal dune.

I scrape away a patch of paint, down to the raw glass. It reveals a wall of grains, with traces of old life. Tiny, fishbony skeletons. Bleached husk of a creature with a nose like a sword. A pair of human feet, end-on, mummified like dried fruit in the sand.

Every day the slanting dune slides further in. Each time the station settles I see it shake and grow.

CHAPTER 43

It was nearly six o'clock when I finished reading. The first cars were stirring outside. Reassuring sounds. I went to the window and looked out. The sky was pale. Night was vanishing.

Oh dear, Gene. It seems you've missed a bit. You don't know I carried on without you.

Although I wish I hadn't. I would rather not do it alone.

How could it have happened? Did it surge up out of the fever, maybe because I was chatting so late with Jerry?

I checked my phone. Jerry hadn't tried me again. I sent him a text. *Hope you slept well. Call any time.*

Outside, the trees were shaking their heads. It was going to be a windy day. A gust caught the dead leaves on the drive and stirred them in a circle, round and round, like glitter in a snow-globe.

I was back in harness. Sally came up between lessons and said there was a client downstairs who had asked to talk to me.

The client was standing by the CD rack, turning it with a long finger. A tall man, wearing a bulky overcoat that made his narrow head look small as a Q-tip.

He turned towards me and the open front of the coat revealed a greenish corduroy suit and a bright green bow tie. 'Miss Lear, how nice to see you. We met at the fete.'

The dapper professor. He didn't have to remind me where I'd seen him before. You wouldn't forget dress sense like that.

With an air of delivering news that was extremely important he said: 'My name is Richard Longborrow, and I have to express my admiration for what you have achieved so far. But I suspect you have been besieged by people telling you that.'

I hadn't thought my singing clients were that fond of me. He offered me his hand so I shook it and thanked him. His palm was cold, like a hand of marble.

'You'd like lessons?' I said.

'Miss Lear, you probably don't realise how much you're going to need help.'

'Help?'

'With the spirit you are contacting.'

This wasn't about singing. He was another spook touting for business. The Vellonoweth chamber of commerce, supernatural division, must have decided it was time for a sales drive.

'Mr Longborrow,' I said, 'if you'd like to learn to sing, I can give you lessons.'

At the counter, Sally was looking at her laptop with the kind of concentration that suggested she was pretending not to watch.

Richard Longborrow put his long fingers together in a steeple. 'Miss Lear, I can see you would like to continue your work in peace.'

I can't stand being called Miss Lear. 'Carol,' I said.

'Carol,' he repeated. His satisfied tone at being given this permission made me feel like taking it back.

I glanced at my watch. 'If there's nothing else I can help you with, I have to prepare for my next client.'

Richard Longborrow gave a nod, as if this conveyed something extremely important to him, although I couldn't imagine what. He put a finger on the CD rack and turned it slowly. Like the cogs clicking in his mind.

'Can I ask – and this is just a casual enquiry – who else has been talking to you about this?' He took a CD of Faure's *Requiem* out of the rack and turned it over to read the back.

Sally had stopped watching. Now she didn't think I was wasting time; he looked like he was going to buy something. And there was no way she would let me abandon him.

Richard Longborrow carried on talking to Faure's *Requiem*. 'You must have been contacted by Alice Swanley, am I right? Alice is a clairvoyant. That would be the wrong path for you to seek help.' He had picked another CD, Chopin Etudes. 'What do you think of this recording? Is it a good one?'

I remembered the backbiting at the fete. Clearly Alice Swanley was one of the people his clique didn't approve of.

'It's a beautiful recording,' I said. If I ignored the rest he'd probably give up.

He kept the Chopin and the Faure in his palm and looked again at the rack. His fingers dawdled over a Deutsche Gramophon reissue of Mozart concertos.

'That one's excellent,' I said.

'Miss Lear, you probably don't realise, because you are inexperienced, how wilful spirit is. This kind of journey can be very hazardous without expert help. Even if you are – ahem – Royal College trained.'

I supposed I was meant to feel unmasked. But his manner was so preposterous. He looked at the disc as he talked, like a spy master pretending he wasn't giving important orders to the person standing next to him.

I gave a tight smile and looked pointedly at the CDs too.

He continued. 'You've probably gathered that I am, in fact, a medium.' He made the statement with gravity, as though revealing something of such importance that I would go down on one knee.

'Miss Lear, I can do something for you. I can keep away unsuitable people who might wish to mislead you.'

He rotated the rack again, slowly like a new thought. 'There is a code among those of us who work with spirit. I will make it known that I have taken this spirit as a psychic colleague, and everyone will know it is in good hands. As I said, this is a hazardous journey without expert help. It can easily get out of control.'

It already has, I thought. But I doubt you can help with any of it.

Richard Longborrow smiled and swallowed, and a small mole slid up and down over his adam's apple. 'You may find more enlightenment on the international computer network. Conduct a search, if you will, for the musician channeller Willa Barry.'

He selected another CD from the rack, which he didn't even seem to have looked at. 'It was nice to talk to you. Do think about what I said.'

He walked at a ponderous speed, like a browsing elephant, to the counter.

For the next lesson I let Freda Worth and Eleanor holler and hammer like blacksmiths. I was thinking. Not about Richard Longborrow or his psychic friends, but Willa, the girl with the extraordinary piano. Being told her full name made her real, findable and intriguing all over again.

After the lesson I needed to order some music for Freda. I found Sally's laptop, sitting among the stacked boxes of new violin strings. Once I'd done my duty, I opened Google.

My fingers drummed out Willa's name in a split second. Not bad, I still had dexterity. Gene would probably tell me to slow my typing down.

There was one entry. *Willa Barry: composer who uses spirit as muse.*

The site was called *The Scrying Glass*. There was a short biography of Willa. Music degree at Edinburgh university; it was obvious she'd had a classical education. A section about her instrument, the seventeen-note enharmonic keyboard, which was on loan from a local collector. And a list of podcasts.

Her performances had been recorded. How exciting.

There were no names, only dates. Tallying them with the calendar on the desk, it was clear that one of the podcasts was the day she did Andreq.

I couldn't download it here, and in the cottage there was no internet, but Jerry was good at fudging with sound files. And he might like to hear that crooked instrument too.

I moused over the contents bar to see what else there was.

Users were invited to review podcasts they had listened to. There were a lot of comments on Andreq's music.

I know the other spirits Willa has used, said someone called MissMoon, *but where has this one come from? Anybody?*

It was someone new, replied someone called Spiritdancer.

Nice to have another release but I'm not sure about this one. SecondsightSandy.

I was at the concert and I think I saw her (round of applause, please!). It's the replacement singing teacher Sally's been using. She's from London. Name is Carol Lear. (Just call me Sherlock!!) Sorry to those not in Vellonoweth or the surrounding area, that won't be terribly significant or useful. BlackZak.

It was one thing to be doorstepped, and perhaps even accosted in the shop. But these people were talking about me, using my real name, in an online forum. And they all knew where I worked. That was uncomfortable.

I read on.

BlackZak, you guys seem to have a great community. Fairyweed7.

Good sleuthing, Sherlock. Spiritdancer.

There's more to know. Listen up, folks. This spirit is from the future. Yes, read that carefully. What a thing to mess with. Anyone know if this Carol Lear has a spiritual pedigree? BlackZak.

How does that future stuff work, then? Spiritdancer.

Never heard of her. Paul123.

Richard Longborrow's rambling sales pitch began to make sense. Not the talk of psychic hazards. His hints about legitimisation.

Does the singing teacher know what it takes to be a custodian? Indigochild.

This is the question that I want answered. Paul123

Why isn't she part of the community? Who is mentoring her? She shouldn't attempt this without guidance. It's dabbling. Rune-Maid

Wondered when you'd join us, Rune-Maid! Indigochild.

Wish I could be there with you guys. Fairyweed7.

It went on for three pages. No discussion of the music; just who is Carol? She has no business dabbling like this. There were ten other files of Willa's music on the site but each had only a few comments.

My phone trilled, announcing a text. It was from Gene.

Found a shop in Ixendon with psychoactive cheeses. Can I interest you in a night of bad dreams?

Bad dreams? Worse than the ones you give me already?

I texted back. *Perfect. Let's live dangerously.*

I put the phone down and went back to the screen. Gene wouldn't worry about a bunch of spiritualists getting in a twist. He'd leave them to enjoy being cross.

I exited from Willa's site and carefully nuked the browsing history, in case Sally had views on it too. Willa's podcasts were also on iTunes, untainted by opinions from Vellonoweth. I logged onto gmail and sent Jerry the links.

The system alerted me to an engorged inbox, collecting since the day I left London. Invitations to recitals been and gone, a dodgy attachment from Charlie that had to be a virus, bulletins from *Andante* magazine. I deleted hundreds of messages, while a nagging ache started in my hands and spread to my heart. The day-to-day life I'd been missing, saved up in the ether and served in one devastating hit.

CHAPTER 44

Gene was reading the mass of A4 pages I'd written the night before, his head at an angle as he worked through the slanted text.

We were sitting at the table in the cottage kitchen. Rain made the windows into liquid screens of indigo. A gutter outside pattered like a waterfall. The smell of wet coats mingled with the farmyard musk of an almost liquid camembert.

I'd turned off the blaring striplight in the ceiling and used just the lights under the kitchen cupboards. The low illumination emphasized the lines of Gene's cheekbones. The rain had sharpened his hair. As I sipped wine and watched him read, I thought how he looked like he belonged in a 1930s musical.

White teeth bit his lower lip. 'I don't think all this writing did your hands any good. How did it happen?'

'You gave me your cold. Obviously it came with extra benefits.'

He didn't smile. I picked up the inedible end of a baguette and tore it into tiny pieces.

All this time I'd been wishing I was back in London. But what would I go back to? Not practising. Deleting every new opportunity that arrived. Like those emails. The newsletters from the professional societies. The friends' concert invitations because it was too awful to go. The tip-offs about a freelance orchestra looking for a pianist for their Gershwin concert.

In London I would be a failure.

Gene turned over another page.

'Did you know it was happening?'

'Not until I read it. With the others I kind of knew about them at the time.' I tipped my head, trying to catch his eye behind the fine wire glasses. 'Haven't you ever asked anyone how it feels?'

If he caught the nudge in my voice, he chose to ignore it.

An ache had started in my right hand. I squeezed the web of flesh between my thumb and forefinger. Gene flicked his eye in my direction. He noticed that all right.

I folded my arms and rested my head on them. 'Sorry, I'm not very good company tonight. You can take those away if you want. Bedtime reading.'

He could make whatever he wanted of that remark. In fact I hoped he'd ask what I meant.

Some days I felt completely transparent. Like one of those fish that's just a heart. Spleen. Whatever.

He flipped more pages over, saw there were plenty left and put them aside. 'This isn't good.' He looked at my hand again. 'It's injuring you.'

I suddenly got an inkling of what he might say. It put cold steel in my heart. Don't you dare suggest we stop.

But why? It wasn't making me better. Look at me trying to knead the pain out of my hands. And that was just from writing.

No, we couldn't stop. Sometimes I needed it, sometimes he needed it, but it's what we did to survive in this place.

'If this was a piece of music,' Gene said, 'instead of you playing it, it's playing you.'

I wanted to banish that secret, evaluating look from his face. 'Music does play you. That's how you know you're doing it properly.' I gave up on the baguette and threw it on the plate. 'So what do we do now? Get out bell, book and candle?'

Otherwise, what do we do? Hey, I have an idea – we swap places and you do the talking, then I can study you.

There was a rap on the front door.

I went to answer. Eleanor was outside, under a grey umbrella glossy with rain.

'You left these in the shop.' She handed me my white gloves.

'Come and dry out,' I said. I led her through and made room on the kitchen floor for her to prop her dripping umbrella. It was exquisitely made, with a mother-of-pearl handle and a silk tassel, like an Edwardian heirloom.

'Can I offer you tea or something stronger?'

'Just tea is fine.'

Gene greeted Eleanor with an enigmatic smile. 'Carol's always leaving her gloves.'

Eleanor's brows lifted. 'Carol, I didn't know you knew my medium.'

Her medium? Oh lord. 'You know each other?' I said.

'Just physiotherapist will do,' said Gene.

I folded away the pages of my extracurricular regression and slipped them onto the worktop, out of sight.

Eleanor smoothed the back of her skirt and sat down. 'I've had physiotherapists before and they've been useless. Dr Winter here cured my sciatica. It was referred pain from an accident suffered by the wife of Sir Bertrand, who fell from a horse while hunting. Dr Winter homed in on this with such remarkable perceptiveness.'

Of course he did. I turned and bustled with mugs and tea bags. I had to stop this before she brought out the other old Lears, which he would probably feed on like a raptor. Especially if she made them mine as well. I felt like a schoolgirl trapped with a fond, silly aunt who was steering us all to social death.

'How does everyone like their Earl Grey?' I asked.

'Two bags for me, please, or I can't taste it,' said Eleanor. 'I wonder, Dr Winter, if you have felt tremblings from ancestors of your own?'

I banged the lid on the tea caddy, hoping to warn Gene off.

He said: 'When I was young I saw dead people looking after me.'

Eleanor gasped and almost clapped her hands.

He met her astonished eyes with a steady gaze. 'I found out I was adopted. That was why my parents called me Gene.'

I brought the mugs to the table, only just managing to keep their contents under control.

'Gene,' repeated Eleanor, savouring the word like good wine. 'Of course. They must have speculated about what you really were. What a clever name to call you.'

She couldn't be happier. Family, heredity, mystery – this

pushed all her buttons. It probably did no harm that Gene's cheekbones looked so aristocratic and the wet hair so 1930s, and that Eleanor was probably imagining his slim frame in a tuxedo although she was old enough to be his mother.

'And your dead people, they must have been your real family? I suppose they felt bad about leaving you. That's nice.'

'Oh yes,' said Gene. A nudge with his foot told me, in case I had any doubt, that he was making it up.

Once they'd disposed of the tea I pleaded tiredness from my cold and showed them, still chatting, into the dripping night. She was so tall they were about the same height, and sheltered him under her tasseled umbrella to his black VW.

As I was clearing away cheese and tea wreckage, Gene sent a text.

Chill. She thinks that makes me a better healer.

Another arrived shortly afterwards.

Muscle wastage makes pain worse. Go swimming.

I began a reply. *Go* – but keying various choices of infantile verb and fending off the predictive text made the pain worse.

Several hours later I was lying looking into moonlight. A steady throb of pain kept me awake like the bass of a neighbour's party music. Perhaps he was right about swimming.

Vellonoweth leisure centre had a pool. I walked down there before work. Slipped in and plodded up and down the lanes of blue water.

I thought it would be soothing; lenses out so a safe cocoon of myopic oblivion. It wasn't. It left me alone with my thoughts, writhing like snakes on a spear.

Gene had cured Eleanor. But he wasn't clever enough to cure me. That was the real point of this, to be able to play. To get myself back. Jerry was cured for months and although he had a relapse he was much better. When the new attack came, he seized it, defeated it and carried on.

I swam fast, my front-crawling arms slicing through length after length. Everyone else was better. Why not me?

CHAPTER 45

I swam again the next day. Twelve fast lengths, fuelled not by fitness but by fury.

This morning the script that kept my arms turning was different. If Gene had told me about swimming earlier, I might be cured by now. Hell, if Dr Golding had told me to swim, I'd be reclaiming my Yamaha right now.

Up and down the blue lanes, shrinking away from the caress of a stranger's limbs passing close and fast. Swimmers don't mind how close to you they get. Ploughing this same furrow of thought until I hauled myself to the showers.

The next morning, as I hurried across the leisure centre car park, eager to get my twelve lengths of tedium out of the way, a figure fell into step beside me and asked me how I was this fine day.

I had no patience for another obfuscated exchange with Richard Longborrow. My first thought was to say hello and hurry inside, but his eye had a seeking sort of glint.

No, I thought. This has to stop.

I turned and faced him. 'Mr Longborrow, what do you want?'

'Miss Lear, your work has tremendous potential. Many of my clients are asking about it. Of course I'm waiting until you give the nod before I say or do anything. Some of the people you might have gone to wouldn't understand how this should be handled.'

'What,' I repeated, 'do you want?'

'You would need background to understand. My clients are working in a number of ways, deepening their spiritual journeys. Since you brought your spirit to the fete there has been much interest. Many of my clients are practised with past lives but have never jumped to their timeline in the future. They are talented and our work is very advanced.'

I took a breath to ask my question for the third time.

'Miss Lear, I'm coming to that.' He gave his tie a tweak. This morning his neckwear was dark blue with small yellow stars, which accompanied a corduroy suit the colour of mustard.

'Miss Lear, my most urgent question is this: how can you assure me that you are genuine?'

Genuine. I had to look away to compose myself. A man in a yellow suit and a stars bow tie, who was trying to hustle me to use his services, was accosting me by the entrance to the swimming pool, asking if I was genuine.

I looked him in the eye. 'It's not genuine. Not at all. Go and break the news to them. Now, if you'll excuse me.'

I turned away. He pulled the door open and held it for me.

'Miss Lear, allow me to be the judge of authenticity. You lack the experience to know the nature of the spirit you are contacting. I will conduct your next summoning. When shall we set up a demonstration?'

'There is no spirit,' I said. 'It's not genuine.' I started down the stairs, into the chlorinated fog.

He followed. 'Perhaps you have had an unsettling experience and lost confidence. This is understandable in such a volatile situation.'

Then, fortunately, the turnstile allowed me to leave him behind.

The water swallowed me. My soles found the walls, pushed off. My arms gathered the water and I started to stroke away. Here was where my jumbled thoughts would untangle, align as if passing under a magnet. Ready for it, here comes the rage like warp drive.

No anger. Just this thought. I used to make music. Now the only people who wanted to partner me, who reacted to what I did, were shoddy tricksters.

Jerry phoned as I went back for more the next day.

'You're going swimming? But you hate swimming.'

'Yes. I still hate it,' I said.

The connection was awful. Jerry said something but it sounded as though he had tape over his mouth. It didn't help that rain was falling in a thick curtain, and I was straining to hear him over the beat and swish of the wipers.

He came through clear again. 'Interesting you're drawn to water now.'

'I'm not drawn to water now. I've been told to do it.'

He vanished in static and road noise, then came back. 'What made Andreq live under water?'

'Don't read anything into it. I'm following orders.'

The wind caught a dustbin and hurled it into the road in front of me. I manoeuvred the car round it.

As the lights changed and I turned for the car park, the ether started a new mischievous game. Jerry's voice suddenly boomed like thunder. 'He must KNOW YOU'RE THERE. He must be DREAMING YOU. Think what RUBY DID TO ME...' Then his voice went tiny, crystal clear and no louder than a thought. *'What are you doing to him?''*

I parked and cut the engine. 'Great, I'm nothing more than somebody's past?'

Whisper. *'Not necessarily. We live many lives.'*

'That's New Age bullshit.' I pulled my bag off the passenger seat and got out of the car.

Time for blue oblivion.

In the pool, I unload and re-sort. Feel the press of water as I push off.

Jerry, you sweet gullible fool. You were so lucky, you hit the jackpot with Ruby, or pretty damn close.

End of the lane. Turn. Nearly crash into a goggled head. He tuts and plunges away.

Somebody else gaining on me untidily. Defend my face against splashing.

Jerry, while I battle these intolerable waters, I'm going to tell you some truths. Remember what we found on the wall in east London? Ruby is all Anthony Morrish and a muddle in your head. Andreq is just me and Gene. It always has been.

Swimming is like entering a half-dreaming state. Sometimes it doesn't come out the way you thought it would. The home truths, as I repeat each lane, are cruel.

If I'm somebody's past, if I was delivered into a future life, I know the rules. It means this life is done. It's all over.

CHAPTER 46

A strip of four pictures from a photo booth. Jerry and Tim, cheek to cheek, their faces bleached by flash. They were growing beards, each a neat shadow around the jaw.

It was Saturday morning and Jerry had sent a parcel with my first two Andreq tapes. He'd also included a CD. With clever audio witchery, he'd made a disc of all Willa's podcasts, not just the Andreq one.

But the photo held my attention more. Jerry looked more masculine, vital. As though he and Tim had made a pact of belonging together, stamped with each other's mark.

I got a call from him as I walked home after an averagely awful day. 'Hey,' I said, 'hello bearded man.'

'Guess where I am? Christian Street.'

His smile warmed his voice and I could see it, wide and genuine, how it turned his eyes into wicked sloes. I tried mentally to add the beard. That was harder to see.

I could hear the Docklands railway in the background. It added a welcome rattle of civilisation. I had just walked past the last streetlamp and the only things I could see were the edge of a thick wood and the white line on the edge of the road. The cold was inching into the crevices of my scarf.

'What are you up to at Christian Street?' I said.

'Tim's with me. We're putting flowers here for Ruby. I thought you'd like to be here too.'

Had he told Tim?

And had he left anything out?

It wasn't for me to ask. They had beards now.

I heard feet stamping, like someone trying to keep warm. So it was cold there too. But cold in the city was bearable; not eroding, isolating, like here.

'Honoured to be invited. What did you get her?'

'Violets. For *V loves B*.' I heard a rustling. 'I'm putting the bouquet down. Rest in peace, Ruby. We're looking after you now.'

There was something ceremonial in the way he said it. 'Do we say amen?' I replied.

Tim's voice, slightly in the background, called out: 'And thank you, Ruby, for our five-figure book deal.'

Some scraping and scuffing, as if a hand was muffling the mouthpiece, and grumbling. So much for my imagined picture of two heads bowed respectfully in front of the white wall. Then some laughing and good-natured joshing. Grumbles had been sorted out.

A five-figure book deal. Jerry's visit to Anthony Morrish was turning up ace after ace.

A glare of headlights appeared behind me, throwing my walking shadow onto the pavement in front of me. The car passed and I was in darkness again.

Jerry came back. 'Sorry about that. We got a deal. A big one.'

'Sounds as if you should be leaving rubies, not violets,' I said. 'Tell me all about it.'

The north and south pole, apparently, drift and wander. Every 500,000 years or so they reverse. If north becomes south and south flips to north, the planet loses its protective UV shield. For several generations we'd have more sunburn, cancers, radiation. Large areas of the civilised world would be no-go deserts and we'd have to find ways to live away from sunlight. The last pole switch was 780,000 years ago, according to geological records, and the next one is already a good 250,000 years overdue –

A brisk knock at the door brought me out of the *Observer* science pages.

It was Jean Dowman, in a tartan skirt and ironed blouse; smarter than the prickly jumpers she wore to her lessons. I guessed it must be her church outfit.

'Jenny's asked me to check if you needed anything, such as the washing machine.'

She wouldn't really want me to use her facilities. Singing lessons now proceeded with polite hostility. Each time I made a suggestion she nodded as though she was really saying 'no'. I now made only superficial adjustments and sometimes she deigned to act on them. The sugar-borrowing had stopped. I could only conclude that she'd come round today to keep a promise made to Jenny.

'That's very kind,' I said. 'I'm managing.' In the doorway to the kitchen were two bags, prepared for a trek to the precinct later.

She spied them. 'Oh don't go to the launderette. Come to ours.'

If my laundry bags had been tucked away in the kitchen we could both have bowed out. Now we had to go through with it.

I hauled my bags next door. Jean showed me through a living room that was the looking-glass reverse of Jenny's. Built on the back of the kitchen was a conservatory. Jean's washing machine was here, battling for space with her seed trays.

'Just press go,' she said. 'It couldn't be easier. Help yourself to washing powder.'

I knelt on the floor and loaded my clothes. By the washing machine was a big hole in the skirting board stuffed with a couple of balled socks, but not tightly. Through it I could see a parallel hole from the kitchen to the lounge. When the doorbell rang and someone in grey trousers admitted two more pairs of legs I saw and heard that too.

Jean came into the kitchen and started taking cups and saucers out of the cupboards. 'Carol, why don't you go through to the other room? We're having tea.' She peeled cling film off a plate of sandwiches.

I went into the lounge. A sturdy-girthed couple were chatting to William Dowman. William introduced them: Delia and Stephen Pidgely, neighbours from Nowethland. Like Jean and

William, they were turned out in Sunday best; Delia with a pearl brooch on her navy jacket, Stephen had a blazer.

They stopped talking as I entered. I guessed my jeans and black jumper made me look like the gardener. I explained myself briefly, but they continued to stare at me in uncomfortable silence, even after I sat down.

I tried to get the conversation started again. 'How do you know William and Jean? Are you singers?'

'Oh no,' replied Delia. She spoke very softly. It was the sort of voice you felt you'd always be straining to hear.

Jean came in with sandwiches. Delia handed round plates.

'Let me help with that,' I said.

Jean shook her head. 'It's all under control.'

Tea and sandwiches were distributed, people added sugar and stirred. Then once again, they lapsed into silence, eating and sipping with unusual concentration. They all looked very awkward.

Finally, Stephen spoke. 'William, how is your rewiring going?'

'They said they'd be finished last Friday,' said William. 'I made them rig up a temporary circuit for the weekend, but they've left holes everywhere and managed to crack the plaster upstairs.'

He looked upwards and so did the rest of us because we needed something to do. There was a black wire running along the skirting board and up the wall to a candelabra-style light with pink fringed shades.

They managed chit-chat about power cuts, but it sounded as though they were eking the subject much further than it would go. It was obvious that if I hadn't been there they would have been talking about something else.

Perhaps if I left for a few moments they could regroup. I asked about the bathroom and was directed to a little room tucked away under the stairs.

I had barely closed the door when a voice said some words quietly and very quickly. Then everyone said a word in unison.

It sounded like 'Amen'.

They had been waiting for me to leave so they could say grace?

There was a large hole by the skirting board. I could see a tartan pattern beyond. The lounge sofa.

A male voice said: 'Just think, this has been going on next door to you.'

Jean said: 'I thought there was something strange about her. She's been teaching me, you know.'

Believe me, I thought, it was as bad for me as it was for you. And what was this 'something strange'? The visit from Alice Swanley? I was trying to get rid of her.

'Shh,' said William. He'd realised I might be able to hear.

I ran the taps. Sure enough, they started talking, quite loudly. They'd been listening for when I couldn't hear them.

I wished I could make out what they were saying, but all I got was a tangle of voices. Raised voices.

I washed my hands and went back in.

They were quiet again. But they were all watching each other, as though they were waiting for a cue.

Delia broke the silence in her near-whisper: 'Do you go to church, Carol?'

I could feel how heavily the question was loaded. It could have knocked another hole in the wall.

'No,' I replied. They remained silent, looking at me. Like four teachers demanding a fuller explanation of wrongdoing. I added: 'It's not my sort of thing.'

I could see mouths swallowing, eyes flicking. Delia gave a nod as tiny as her voice. Suspicions confirmed.

Stephen became positively chatty. 'Ah yes, but *plus ca change*. I wasn't keen when we got a woman priest, and I thought, oh blow, I can't go to her services. But it was getting so that there were fewer and fewer we could go to, so we decided to risk communion; we thought she couldn't do much harm with that. And we were rather impressed. She said a prayer for the people in the boat that went down. She put so much emotion into the words, far more than a male priest would. So there you are.'

He sat back, with a smile that suggested he felt he had been excellently daring.

Delia and the others nodded and murmured.

William said: 'So Carol, what do you think about that?'

They all swivelled to me again. Another demolition ball swinging my way.

I didn't have any religious views. I didn't have an opinion about it at all. I said: 'That's interesting.'

The washing machine was rumbling, mulling my clothes this way and that. No sign that it was finishing.

William spoke. 'Stephen, I know it's not fashionable to say so but the Church of England has wimped out over this. We don't need women priests. Carol, I would have thought you would have had a opinion on it. What do they think in London?'

What on earth was going on? Were they trying to bait the heathen into a feminist lather by being stuffy about women priests? My private view was that they could ordain whoever they pleased.

And what was behind this really? Did Jean have a grudge because she didn't get a part in the Vellonoweth musical and was now setting her God-squad friends on me?

They were staring at me; my turn with the talking stick again.

'Interesting,' I said.

'You do realise we don't belong to any strange cult,' said Stephen. 'We're just Church of England.'

The washing machine was revving into a new phase. I excused myself and went to check.

As I closed the kitchen door, they started again.

Putting my ear to the hole I heard whispering. No individual words, but they sounded more urgent than the first time.

A light on the washing machine indicated it still had twenty minutes to go. I couldn't stay out here for that long. I would have to face another round.

As soon as I set foot in the lounge, Delia's face turned dark, furious red. It was startling, like a stop-motion film of a sky darkening.

'You are taking a step back into superstition. You don't know what it's like to live in fear.'

Her voice was reedy and shrill, like an animal having its throat cut.

I'd intended to reply calmly, hoping to quieten her down, but it's hard to be logical when someone's screaming at you with a thunderous face, even if they're talking rubbish. The words skidded out of me, just as anxious and high.

'I'm not living in fear. Why do you say I'm living in fear?'

William intoned in a loud voice. 'African witch-doctors can cause someone's death by pointing a stick at them. In the Middle Ages it was the same. We don't know how lucky we are to have eliminated superstition from our lives.'

Stephen followed, his hand scrubbing worriedly at his chin: 'The man who had been dabbling with ouija boards was living in so much fear that he had to get a priest for an exorcism. The priest called on all sorts of devils and demons but missed the right one. After he had gone the man hanged himself. It's all very well to have a bit of fun but what you are playing with is black magic.'

I tried to speak, but Jean drowned me. Her eyes and mouth were scrunched slits under furious hair. 'Some people think they're going to have a bit of fun and before they know it they're in too deeply. Not even an exorcist can help.'

Stephen spoke again. Fury enlarged his voice like a wide organ pipe: 'All the forces of evil want is to make you live in fear and terror and do dreadful things. The Reverend said lives become ruled by superstition, then by fear, and that's how evil gets in.'

The Reverend. They'd got the vicar in on this too.

I flew to the conservatory and shut the door. Would someone bang in after me, drag me back for more?

They didn't.

I sat on the floor, knees hugged like a foetus. I heard unbelievable mayhem in the room I'd just left. Weeping, feet pacing, soothing noises. Then their voices rose again into another swell.

I watched the washing machine dial and tried to tune them out. Gradually it inched to the finish and I unloaded.

Behind me, the door opened. I looked round sharply, still expecting a grabbing hand.

Jean stood there. She said nothing, just regarded me with stolid tolerance.

I heaved myself to my knees and stuffed my clothes into my bag. Not a position of advantage, especially while revealing girl boxers, bras, music T-shirts and jeans. I got the bag shut and spoke to her politely. 'Thank you for the tea and for letting me use your machine.'

She turned without a word and walked through the lounge. I followed, looking at the flowered carpet.

William, Delia and Stephen regarded me silently, teacups poised on their laps. No one moved a twitch. Walking the length of that sofa to the door took a very long time.

I let myself in through the front door on the other side. I put my clothes away. And that's when the reaction came.

I sat down hard on the stairs, shaking violently. I looked at the walls, convinced this couldn't be coming just from me, the whole building must be trembling. I'd surely hear a vase topple or see Jenny's watercolour at the bottom of the stairs crash to the floor. But the picture remained fixed to the wall, perfectly still. There was no earthquake. The cottage was as solid as stone.

Next door they started again. I could hear it; a background of outrage lapping at the walls like a malevolent sea in a harbour. They were braver once I wasn't there; I heard it. An animal understands human speech through tone more than vocabulary, and so I understood those voices, humming just above audible range, on and on.

CHAPTER 47

Jean Dowman was booked as my first client that morning. She surely would cancel. That would mean Eleanor and I would have a free hour. We would practise sight-reading. Her concentration would skip into the bluebells and she simply would not care that she didn't do it well. She would laugh at how the musical gene had missed her and we'd have inky Earl Grey instead.

The snakecharmer pipes tooted as I pushed open the door. Sally was behind the counter, pricing a pile of sheet music, treble clef brooch boasting on a blue angora jumper.

She kept her eyes on the music books. 'No pupils today.'

Her rhythm with the pricing gun never faltered; stamp – slide to new pile, stamp – slide.

'Is something wrong?' I said.

Stamp – slide, stamp – slide, like a printing press. 'Felicity will be starting again next week and her pupils are taking this week off. It's not good for them to sing too much, they will damage their voices. And Eleanor's playing for Kitty the clarinet teacher this week. Thank you for your help. Here's your cheque.'

She put the cheque on the end of the counter. The phone rang. She turned away and picked the receiver up, preferring to look at the wall than at me.

There was no point in arguing; the politics were clear and a freelance has no power anyway.

In less than a minute I was walking out of the shop and looking at the grey precinct.

I could leave right now. Fling my two bags into the car, set off into the hills. Slip away from this town, put this odd interlude behind me. Find the A303 and sail back to London.

Jenny must be about to call, telling me to leave. To save her the bother I phoned her while I was walking up the hill.

There was no answer.

I reached the cottage, checked the house phone to see if she'd called there. Nothing.

It was bound to come soon, though.

I would write a note asking the Dowmans to take over feeding the cat until Jenny got back. Not asking, telling; they'd cost me my job. I bent down to collect the post from the doormat and found myself on eye level with the cat, who was curled under the sideboard. It opened its agate eyes and dared me to desert it.

How eloquent these animals can be. Jenny wouldn't have installed me, a total stranger, if she had trusted the Dowmans to look after the cat. So I couldn't go until I'd asked her about it in person.

Somehow I was relieved.

The sunlight slanted in through the sprigged curtains, so much brighter outside than in. It beckoned me to enjoy my last few hours of Vellonoweth in the open air.

I walked up to the park.

The day was so still that the trees and shrubs seemed to be holding their breath. I went down the steps to the gravelly beach, listened to the liquid thunder of the waves foaming into the shingle, looked out into the heaving sea. No matter how serene it was skyside, the ocean swelled and beat in its own time, like a heart.

Over at the end of the causeway, a red light twinkled on the radio station mast. After I came back from the pool this morning I'd dressed to the accompaniment of a man reading essays in German to a soundtrack of birdsong. Perhaps there were some things I'd miss.

My phone rang.

Here it was, my expulsion. I ran, slipping up the tiny stones, into the shelter of the cliff to answer it.

It wasn't Jenny. It was Gene.

'When's your lunch break?'

'Any time you like. My contract's finished.'

There was a pause. Was he shocked? 'That's a bit sudden.'

I didn't need to go into the reasons with him. 'The teacher's coming back. They don't need me any more.'

'How quickly can you come and meet me? I'm at the nursing home next to the Railway Hotel.'

Fifteen minutes later I reached the hotel. I passed its drive with the wire fence where Eleanor nearly launched us into the railway cutting. A few more yards down the pavement and the nursing home began, with a gold-lettered sign like a public school. There was a drive with plants chopped brutally to stalks for the winter. White handrails enclosed a concrete ramp to the front doors.

I went in.

When I'd been in the Railway Hotel next door, it had been a grotto of cobwebs and royal icing plasterwork. This side was less Miss Havisham, in clean pastels with a strip of Grecian-looking border.

On the reception desk was a stand of leaflets. They showed a canvas of swirling skies and the outlines of two German Shepherds with a gowned figure like Disney's Cinderella.

Reminiscence Project: Residents talk about their lives to an artist. Inspired by their stories, the artist paints a unique picture to form a valuable and cherished heirloom for generations to come .

Buyer beware, I thought. Those memories you are cherishing could be those of a complete stranger.

Gene wasn't there. I introduced myself to the receptionist. She replied with an efficient smile. 'Mr Winter the pain therapist?'

At that moment, he came out of a passageway.

'Miss Lear, nice to meet you.' He held out his hand, as though I was a colleague.

'My pleasure,' I said, taking his hand.

What was going on?

'It's this way,' he said, still formal and professional.

I followed him down a corridor. He opened a door and

switched on a light. There was a bed in the room, stripped back to an orange mattress. A desk, a wardrobe. Like a college study bedroom.

He turned the latch to lock the door.

'So we're not doing lunch, then?' I said.

'On duty,' he said.

He didn't look as though he was working. Or at least he wasn't wearing a white coat, just his usual knotty sweater and jeans.

He leaned against the door. 'I need a favour. There's a patient here who needs to see a regression.'

'Someone who needs to see a regression? How do you mean?' I sat on the bed.

'She's been asking me about it since I started treating her. She doesn't want it done on her – her entire system is swimming in morphine anyway and she can't speak for sustained periods, but she keeps saying she wants to see one. She believes in reincarnation and wants to see proof.'

Morphine, pain, a woman who couldn't speak? Several bizarre things in an already derailed day. And I had an unforgiving suspicion that he wasn't telling me the whole story.

'Is it one of your Alzheimer's people? I thought they could barely talk.'

'Sorry; I'll rewind. Forget the paintings, it's nothing to do with that. This is pain management. This lady's in the final stages of cancer. Some of her pain is no longer responding to morphine. More drugs won't help. She needs something else.'

'Something else to treat the pain?'

He nodded.

'Proof of reincarnation is going to do that?' It sounded mad.

He pushed his sleeves up. The colour of the jumper emphasised the fine black hairs on his arms. 'She's scared. The fear is magnifying her pain. This is what she needs.'

'And you want me to –?'

He nodded.

'Me? Isn't there someone else you could use?'

He folded his arms, looked at the ceiling. 'There are her

relatives, but they're strict Christians, they'd never agree. There's a nurse – who keeps wanting me to do her anyway. She's going to be another Egyptian princess buried alive who can talk to cats.'

I picked at a big stitch in the mattress, like a staple made of cord. 'She might not be. She might be a beautiful heiress who's the toast of Jane Austen's England and has fifteen grandchildren.'

'No. I know exactly what that nurse has got brewing, even if she doesn't. If she goes into a big number that old lady will be so frightened that nothing will keep her comfortable.'

I kept looking down at the mattress. Smiled nervously. 'You're doing a fine job of frightening me. You can stop now.'

Click. He unlocked the door. 'Come on.'

'What? Have we got to do it right away?'

'Her relatives are coming in an hour. I've got to be finished by then.'

He wasn't kidding. This was completely genuine.

I walked, feeling unreal, to the open door. He put a hand on my arm. It wasn't reassuring, it felt like flames.

'It'll be all right,' he said.

CHAPTER 48

I walked behind Gene down a corridor. My feet moved automatically. More faux-Grecian mosaic, a few pictures on the walls. Grainy carpet. Gene's back, the hem of the knotty jumper skimming the pockets of his black jeans. Everything I saw jumped at me in bewildering detail.

He stopped at a door and knocked. A nurse opened it, in white uniform and pastel cardigan. We went in.

I was expecting a bed but it was a common room. Chairs of assorted vintages, magazines and jigsaws on the tables, a TV, a half-finished Scrabble game, some heavy mahogany cupboards.

The nurse bent over a wheelchair, made adjustments to the covers and lifted a wrist that was as pale as a leaf kept out of the sun. She checked the pulse against the watch on her breast pocket then laid the hand on the tartan knee cover and moved away.

I saw a face that was putty grey, the skin clinging like a film over her skull. Her shoulders were huddled in a yellow angora shawl.

Gene moved around the room. He drew the curtains and put a lamp on a low table. When he switched it on the shadows flowed like water into the hollows of the woman's face.

He moved a table close to another chair and put a Dictaphone on it. Ready for me.

Feeling a little unsteady, I sat down. Could I do this?

The nurse said: 'She might be a little unfocussed because we increased her morphine this afternoon.' She gave me a long, glaring look. Then she quietly left the room.

Gene clicked the Dictaphone.

Quiet and efficient, like an ordinary medical team, we began.

Tape 6

The dune grows behind me, grain by grain. In my hand is sandpaper, rubbing on the glass wall, slowly shaving the mural to dust.

The noise is hypnotic, like dry hands brushing together. The result is addictive. The paint becomes powder; red, orange, purple. I stroke it away. It stains my fingers.

It's a good place to be alone. And roll ideas in a circle, over and over.

Under the colour the glass is cold like limestone. At first it keeps a blush of pigment. Keep going and it clears to the shade of the sand outside.

Sand starts to trickle from a wound in the wall. I run my fingertips over it and feel a dip, like a hole in a shoe.

'Too hard,' says a voice. 'Be more gentle.'

It is Ruhul. He leans against the wall, lazy, watching me.

He is one of the guards, and he seems to feel the urge to guard me when I want to be alone. A gun hangs off a holster at his tilted hip.

He is another addict of the sandpaper. We are good at being alone together.

His skin is black as an eel. He trails dark fingers along the glass to the table where I have laid some spare supplies.

Because I thought he might call.

He begins to work.

The dry-hand sound of sandpaper on glass. Ruhul's ebony fingers become dabs of colour, like an exotic animal. He sweeps them up one arm and admires the warpaint it leaves. He goes on with the scraping.

He likes to ask me about my life playing 'games of soothing'. I like to ask about life in the company of a trigger. How he met the bullet that has drilled away the edge of one cheekbone. He talks about retiring to a quiet, blue place, perhaps with time for soothing.

What we talk about doesn't matter. So long as there is this back and forth, this crisp, dry planing, this fall of pigment and the gradual spread of the window into the sand.

Ruhul has wavy staves of warpaint on his skin. That matters too. I keep looking to check.

We are treading towards the same corner. It is a squeeze, made tighter by the foot of the dune. Ruhul moves behind me to step past. The light throws his fractured shadow on the scraped glass.

He puts his hand on mine.

The sensation is startling. Cold glass under my palm. His warm skin on the other side.

I turn.

He is very still. Afraid he's misjudged everything. He drops his hand.

The silence crackles.

'So,' he says, 'if I lived in San Otanne would I have to play games of soothing?'

'Games of soothing. If you like.'

The words are not important. Really the conversation is happening through my eyes watching his mouth and his watching mine.

He begins a soft humming, far down in his throat. The sound gathers us together and becomes a tongue.

Ruhul. The sound of his name is a restless, tumbling sea.

CHAPTER 49

Gene brought me round. I was on my feet, wandering between the chairs. He took my arm and guided me to sit down. I did, feeling I should get up again. The old lady in the wheelchair thanked us. That kept me in the chair because I didn't want to break her.

Gene kept looking at me. His eyes were strange and black. I thought, belladonna.

The nurse came. Things were said, the patient handed over. I kept looking at Gene's belladonna eyes. He pushed the rough sleeves of his jumper up his arms. I heard the scratch of the wool, a mere grain of noise, but I heard it. The solid click as he removed the tape from the machine, the whisper of denim as he slid it into his back pocket.

'We'd better get her out, she looks like she needs air,' he said.

I thought he must be talking about the old lady. Then his smell of exotic wood came close to me and he pulled me to my feet. He was talking about me.

I was outside the room, walking along the corridor. Grecian border square-waved along the wall. Once I was moving, I walked fast. Because he was.

A nurse passed us, clipboard held in blue cardiganed arms. He moved closer to me to let her go past. His shoulder bumped against mine. The rough material of his jumper scratched on my leather jacket.

We reached reception. He said stuff to the receptionist, professional things.

I said nothing. Just moved when he moved.

We went through the swing doors, down the wheelchair ramp.

It was windy outside. The trees in the car park were rippling; no, they were bending, that wind was strong. Long-dead leaves drifted in a shoal across the gravel. The sun had gone and it was freezing cold.

The wind was behind us. It pushed like a hand in the back. He began to run. I ran. I didn't know where we were going, I was meant only to follow him. Down a road, around a corner. Shapes floated with us. An umbrella snatched from somebody's hand, a sheaf of papers from a dustbin, dead winter leaves. This was going to be a hell of a storm.

Through a gate. He got the key in the lock. Quick around the door. Slammed it to kill the noise.

The sudden calm. No wind any more. Just breathing.

Belladonna eyes.

It started down there in the narrow box of space between the front door and the stairs. I don't know how long we were there for. Somehow we managed to get up to the first floor and fall into his flat.

Such relief to really be up close, able to manipulate his reactions as much as he manipulated me. No more games, no more barriers, just complete obliteration. Necessary and beyond control, like nuclear fusion. A hurricane to clear the decks and start again from zero.

Chapter 50

I can smell his skin. I open my eyes. It's dark. The wind throws nails of rain against the windows. We are in his bed.

Gene is lying beside me. His face is in shadow. A sheet clings to the outline of his body, moving as he breathes.

Everything is too clear for night. My eyes feel full of sand. My lenses are probably ruined.

But what a way to go.

I push myself up on an elbow and look at him. While I have twenty-twenty vision I'm going to make the most of it. How amazing to be here with him.

He twists over and pins me like a judo throw. His face is above me, in shadow. I look for his eyes. They are a sliver of white, like mother of pearl. Restless, questioning.

Pressed under the bridge of his arms, I smile. 'You're always watching, aren't you? Never let your guard down.'

His face comes closer.

'Don't you dare hypnotise me now,' I say on a gasp for air. 'I want to remember this.'

He pulls back, looks at me thoughtfully, then strokes one hand over my eyelids, closing them.

'I want to show you something. Stay there. Keep your eyes closed.'

I feel him move away, leave the bed. The sweat from his touch leaves cold prints on my skin.

The bed gives as he climbs back on and prowls over like a puma. My skin prickles at his warmth.

One hand is placed over my eyes. The other pulls at my shoulder. Sit up.

I do. A band of silk makes a mask over my eyes and nose.

I try to investigate.

'Don't touch.'

He moves behind me. Glassy fabric brushes against my

back as he ties the band. He is wearing a silk dressing gown. An exquisite idea.

I want to see him in it but the band is a blindfold.

More silk settles on my shoulders.

He guides my arms into sleeves, then clambers around me onto the floor, pulling my hand.

I get up. His hands fasten the robe then he gets behind me, steering me. My feet navigate a rough textured carpet. A few paces and there's the metal runner between the carpets in two rooms.

'Why the blindfold? It's dark anyway.'

'Shh. You're in the doorway.'

One stride; two. I try to remember the layout of his flat. Bathroom to the right, lounge to the left. Where are we going? More strides, then he turns me left and whispers.

'Stop.'

I try the blindfold but his hand says no.

Noises. A metal bar, like a fire door opening. A smell, like beeswax polish and the old tea scent of antique fabric. He nudges me forwards.

The texture under my feet changes. It's wooden floorboards. Dusty, with wide gaps between. Like piano keys.

He's taken me through the fire escape into next door.

'What are we doing?'

His answer is to lead me onwards. For a moment I'm disorientated and don't want to go. Then something makes me feel warm, like it's right to be in here.

I don't believe in atmospheres or auras, but this room has one. It must be a smell or a noise. I can't walk any more until I know. Must take this silk off my eyes.

He stills my hands. Still as lead. He could whisper the fear away from a panicking bird.

His silk gown rustles. He puts something in one of my ears. A headphone.

It comes alive with a faint hiss. Timpani, trembling into life. An orchestra answering with an emphatic A, as though all the instruments are snapping their eyes open.

Then, tumbling out of it, the piano.

Grieg's piano concerto in A minor.

'You've been listening to this?' I fall back deliciously against him like a sweet memory of being sixteen. My eyelids flutter on the silk binding, wanting to open.

Gene puts his arms around me, pinning me still. Blindfold stays. Closes his fingers around my right hand which is trying to play the air. I feel the familiar burn of pain in my wrist and so I surrender.

He must have the other headphone because I can hear it as a fuzzy echo.

The Grieg halts, skips to something else. No more the anguished questions of A minor. Now G major, grounded and resolved. A Rachmaninov prelude.

Everything disappears except Gene's solid warmth behind me. His silk arms, his head leaning on mine. We stay there, the notes streaming around us, like Klimt's lovers in the fireflies.

It is so long since I listened to music properly. I haven't dared. But at this moment, it is sweet, not bitter. Because it is not what matters now.

The prelude rises and rolls and the last note exits into silence.

Gene removes the headphones. Still he stops me taking off the blindfold, puts a finger to my lips. Shh.

He's such a showman. What's he going to do now?

There is a noise like an object being put on a wooden box. It echoes. A faint metallic resonance.

I tear the blindfold off.

We are standing at a piano keyboard.

Gene sits on the bench and pulls me down beside him. He's stolen my balance and the ground is heaving under me. I fall against the bench.

The strings inside the keyboard reverberate again.

That's what the aura in the room is. Two hundred steel strings in an iron frame.

The keys are waiting. A strict row of black and ivory, smudged like old light switches with the prints of many fingers.

Welcome home. I knew you'd be back. Come and tell me everything.

I shove it away and stand up. The stool scrapes on the floorboards. The steel strings ring. Like the piano is disappointed.

Other instruments stare out of the walls. A double bass in its case, like a bulbous coffin. Violins stacked on shelves in battered black cases. Antique piano stools with bald tapestry.

The door to the flat, revealing a wall and another door beyond, and, like a distant smile, the white basin in Gene's bathroom.

In front of me, that piano.

Gene pulls me back onto the stool. I don't look at the keyboard. I look at him.

The moon turns his hair intense black, spills a mercury sheen on his silk robe.

He whispers. 'You could play. There's nobody in the building. They've all gone home.' He trails his fingers along my collarbone. Stops in the hollow in the middle. He smiles, as though he has had a ravenous idea, looks at his fingers between the V at the front of my robe. 'Or we could see how comfortable this bench is.'

The piano sings a soft harmony to his voice. His fingers slip down my breastbone, putting flames on my skin.

He pulls his hand away. Puts his elbow on the dark wood of the piano case, tilts his head on his hand. Flicks the iPod. 'Play that thing by Grieg.'

I stare at the keyboard.

Grieg, says the piano. My wrists hurt.

'Play it like you did at Kate's party.' A lean leg slides against mine, the razor edge of his shin bone. 'Or I will have to do now what I wanted to do then.'

Something starts to shake deep inside me. I kick his leg away, get up, lose my balance because his weight stops the stool moving back, stumble against the piano.

It answers with a shimmering growl.

I clamber over the stool, shouting, barely able to form

sentences. 'What the hell did you do that for?'

My cry hangs in the metal wires. And in the violins and basses that sleep against the walls.

He stands up, reaches for me. I am already away from him, pushing past an antique Chesterfield to get to the fire door and the sensible world.

He follows me through on athletic strides. 'Carol, listen. You've been desperate to play. You need to get it out of your system. It's like a bereavement, you need to say goodbye.'

I reach the bedroom. Tears are turning my vision to liquid. My clothes are a comet tail on the floor. I snatch them up.

He puts a hand on my arm.

'Carol, talk to me. This is no good.'

No. You want my reaction. You want me to scream at you. It's all about control. It's all tricks and games.

I push past him into the bathroom, barge the door shut, fling the clothes down. I start dressing, ripping my clothes away from his. Those dark jeans are tangled in mine. The intimacy is false, fake. I throw the jeans away from me, hard at the wall. The metal belt buckle crashes into a glass shelf, then the whole lot smashes into the bath. I haul on jeans, jumper, slam feet into boots.

'Carol? The regressions are getting darker. Don't you see? Something's building.'

This is just a game to him. An arrogant theory of pain. He wants a reaction? I'll give him a reaction.

I pick up an antique tooth mug from the basin and chuck it into the bath. It shatters, mingling with the remains of the glass shelf. I grasp the handle, now a hook of glass with jagged edges, and pull the door open. Just you dare charm me into making peace.

He isn't there. I go out into the hall. Put the light on. The tea chests are in the living room, still not unpacked. Freak. The iPod and the Dictaphone are on the table. That tape's mine. I'll pick it up before I go.

A sound. I carve the air with my glass claws.

Something rushes me from behind. I hit the frame of the

bathroom door. My ribs smash the air out of me. Gene is jammed up behind me, pushing me into the wall with his body.

He has my left hand, holds it against the door frame.

Elbows the door shut until it traps my hand.

His voice is in my ear. 'When I was a kid my parents had terrible rows. I remember my father shutting my mother's hand in a door. And then weeping all the way as he drove her to hospital.'

He increases the pressure. The edge of the wooden door begins to bite into the long bones of my hand. I can see it creasing the flesh. It's like a knife already.

'So drop the glass before you have to see me cry.'

I let my weapon fall. As it goes I hope it will spear his bare foot. It clatters onto the floor and spins against the skirting board.

He keeps me there a few seconds longer. To demonstrate who has control. He's breathing fast. His chest rising and falling pushes me painfully against the wall. His sharp hip bones – and something else – press into my back.

He closes his lips languidly on my neck and gives me a tiny bite. 'Thanks for a great evening.' With one foot he kicks my pathetic dagger into the far corner. Then he backs away and releases me.

I don't look back at him. I go down the stairs, pull open the front door and leave.

4:

The Storm

Chapter 51

I reach the cottage like a sleepwalker and capsize into bed. My brain begs for rest. My hands want me awake. A bitter throbbing pulse, sharp as a siren, which defies any dose of Nurofen. This is what my hands do when they feel abused and upset.

Like the day Karli blew in with his impossible offer.

Gene put me in front of a keyboard. That's all this was, a sick power game. How could he?

I remembered his weight crushing me into the wall. My hand trapped in the jaws of the door. He might as well have done the job properly.

I wanted to call Jerry. But it was four in the morning. Anyway, what would I say?

How would I explain today? The old lady, where it started, what led to what?

My mind flashed up a protective wall. Not ready yet.

But it must be examined. Take another run at it.

Try starting right from the beginning. That seemed gentle enough to manage.

The night I saw Gene listening to my tape on the Dictaphone. While I slept my voice whispered to him in the dark; and I wished I was there too. Finally being able to maul him all I wanted was incredible, but it was a game to him. It wasn't surrender, it was another performance.

How could I have thought it would be otherwise? He'd shown me often enough.

Games of soothing, Andreq said. That's very good. Games is exactly what they were.

It's a game I don't have the stomach for.

And what does that make Andreq?

Not my soothing oblivion, my cure, not even my future fate. More like my betraying, messed subconscious. As I was talking about seductive hands, shielded guns and paint on skin, Gene must have laughed himself into fits.

I fell into a doze. My arms kept startling me awake.

I lay there, very still, waiting for it to go away. Looking at the dark ceiling. More ghastly feelings crowded in, clamouring for attention in my pain-sharpened brain.

That poor dying woman. What did we do? Did she mind?

She was drugged. Maybe she didn't know.

And the piano, its orderly pattern of black and white.

That was what I needed. That is always how I restore control. Don't think about the problem, put your hands on the keys and after a while it is gone. If it comes back, you know what to do.

He put me at a piano. Well, if I was sitting at one now, I would be on my own. He wouldn't be there. There was a time when I'd wanted very much to play for him. But he's taken too much, he doesn't get that too. This is strictly me and the piano, because that endures.

But I am not with my piano. There is no release.

I got out of bed. I had no plan in mind, but lying there was intolerable. I wrapped myself in a blanket.

What next? How about downstairs?

In the moonlit lounge, Jerry's CD of Willa's music was on the sideboard. I took it with headphones, made a burrow on the sofa and let it begin.

I was listening, but not as a passive receiver. I was playing alongside her. Lightening her touch on the low notes, getting harder with the mid range, sharpening attacks.

My nervous system was preparing to perform, as if by the command of nature, like spring awakening buds and hormones.

While my playing instincts woke up, the pain beat a metronome in my bones.

I snatched the headphones off. I felt sick.

What do they say? Addicts never recover. A trigger can always send them back down.

Which he, of course, would know.

Through the window the moon cast a silver shadow on the hill. Beyond that, several hills on, was the smothered core of

Vellonoweth Hall. Which could become, thanks to an environmental catastrophe or a tornado in my brain, a glass power station in the sand.

Soothing games. I feel peeled raw. Full of howling feedback. And nothing that could take it away.

I looked at the tapes in my holdall, wrapped in a bag from a music shop in London, along with the foolish article from the science pages about the poles changing. I had only two of the tapes, from early on. The rest were at Gene's. So he could study them, the freak, and –

A sudden feeling like an axe blow.

Gene also had the tape from last night. That tape. He had no right to it, I should have got it, he wouldn't really have hurt me.

Yes, the door was closing on my hand. Yes he would.

CHAPTER 52

I woke at midday. Was it time to go yet? I wanted to, as fast as possible. And not think about the reasons why until I was a long distance away where it might be safe to start unravelling.

I fed the furious cat a double breakfast and checked both phones.

Jenny still hadn't called.

Eleanor phoned, on her lunch break. I chatted without knowing what I talked about, but it was good to hear about the clarinet lessons she'd been accompanying and to imagine her pick-axe touch on the keyboard. Really, it was a lot simpler to do music her way. The world carried on so normally. I asked her where I could buy a present for Jerry's birthday. She recommended Ixendon and added she might drop in there later herself because a girl called Willa Barry was playing at the Iron Horse pub.

Willa Barry. Very small world.

I got in the car but when I grasped the wheel, my wrists told me to let go. I turned the engine off and took the key out, defeated.

And today there would be no easy cure, like there had been after Karli's call.

I took the bus to Ixendon, like a normal person shopping, browsed in the antiques shops, ended up in the secondhand bookshop. I enjoyed myself, happily deliberating between getting Jerry a book about Jack the Ripper or one on English eccentrics. In the index of the latter, I found an entry for a Montmorency Lear who had built a small monastery in Cornwall. My spirits climbed even higher. I got it as a surprise for Eleanor. I drifted into another section and a title caught my eye, a name in fine gold lettering on a cloth-bound cover: *Jerry Williams*. It was a novel, written in the 1960s about an artist in Vancouver. Williams was Jerry's surname. He would love it.

Lives repeating through history and time.

The most unexpected thing can throw you what you're trying to forget.

Andreq, you've found your lover. Enjoy him. I wish...

No, don't wish. It was just another collaboration that took a wrong turn. Andreq, whatever you are, if you're taking calls, I'd rather be you right now than me.

Dusk had fallen by the time I left the shop. The cobbled lane outside was called Melancholy Walk.

Oh please. I was doing fine all day and now it's coming undone.

The wind blew freezing dots of rain onto my skin. I passed the Iron Horse. Its front window was a Dickensian-looking bay with swirly panes like the bottom of a bottle. A figure carrying two drinks slid around the curves in the glass like a flying spirit.

It took more than a bit of ancient glazing to disguise the long neck and punctuating eyebrows. Eleanor. There for Willa's concert.

Could I cope with company? I wouldn't be at my best. And if Eleanor asked why I was so quiet, what would I say?

But the music. It would be nice to hear Willa again, to lose some hours with a living, real musician. For the contact that couldn't cross to a mere CD. And to see what she would do with the instrument this time.

The spiritualists might be there. Did I feel up to them? They might not be. Eleanor wouldn't tolerate organised witchery. So there could be others who just wanted to see a talented girl play. And once we'd seen the concert, that would give us safe topics to talk about.

If it looked too worrying, I could leave.

I tucked my white leather bag, heavy with the books, under my arm, and walked back to the Iron Horse.

The pub was stifling, like an over-thick coat. Eleanor was in the corner, wearing a beret pulled down over her forehead like a stretched black mushroom. She was talking to a figure with a black shawl around her shoulders like a tiny Spanish widow. Willa.

It looked like they were friends. Yes, this would be all right.

Eleanor beckoned me with a raised glass. As I made my way over I spotted a face from the psychics' fair – a thickset woman with upbrushed hair. The one who sold the creepy old 'artefacts'.

So maybe it was another spirit-calling. I checked for cronies but she seemed to be alone. I kept my focus on Eleanor.

Eleanor performed introductions but Willa remembered me anyway. Her strong player's hand shook my disused one. She didn't do it hard, but her grip had brutal results.

I gave Eleanor the book. 'Take a look at the page I've marked,' I said.

She riffled the pages open and clapped a hand to her mouth. 'Oh my. Wherever did you find this? You clever girl.'

It felt like the first good thing in the whole day.

Willa looked over Eleanor's shoulder at the page about Montmorency Lear. 'I'm going to do a Lear tonight,' she said. 'I've been working on Eleanor. She's always said what a remarkable family they are. She just has to decide who to give me.'

Okay, we were veering into summonings. But if it was Eleanor, that was okay, wasn't it?

Eleanor shut the book, eyebrows pinching in a frown. 'I know who you should do, Willa. Carol has a spirit.'

How did she know about it?

My face must have said as much because Eleanor patted my hand.

'I read about him on the web. While doing family research. I don't think any of my lot want to play music, Willa. Carol is the musical Lear.'

'No, you shouldn't do me,' I said. I couldn't; not tonight. It would stretch my limits too much. 'Willa, you've done him already. The audience will want a change.'

'I think you'd be surprised,' Willa replied. 'There's been a lot of interest on the discussion board.'

'I saw it. I don't think they liked it.'

'There's always the difficult minority. But the download

stats tell me it was very popular. Besides, I would like him to meet this instrument.'

She reached behind the chair and pulled onto the table a violin case. 'Please say yes, Carol. It will be all right.'

It will be all right. A short while ago someone else had said those words to me.

It was as though I'd had a limb severed and kept forgetting. It drained the fight out of me. I felt as weak as a feather.

While we were talking the pub had filled. I spotted a few more faces from the psychic fair, or clones of them in black and amulets.

I turned to Willa. 'I'd like him to meet your violin but I haven't got anything of his with me.' I hoped that would settle it.

'Don't worry. I know him already.' She checked her watch and stood up. 'It's time.'

She picked up her violin case and worked her way to the back room. As she went, some lads at the bar made remarks about her wispy clothes.

Eleanor downed her drink – a murky cocktail that looked like advocaat and tomato juice. She put the glass down with finality, unfolded her cashmere coat and put it on.

I stood up. 'Eleanor, aren't you staying?'

She picked up her tasseled umbrella. 'I don't really go for these organised things. Tell me what he does, though.'

'Eleanor, she's only going to play music. It's just a concert.'

Eleanor fastened her top button, which made her look militarily correct. 'I don't think spirits like being played with. In private is one matter; in public quite another. I came because Willa asked me but I always had my doubts.' She touched the handle of her umbrella to her beret brim, as though saluting me goodbye. 'I'm sure it's all right when you do it; it's not for me. Tell me about it tomorrow. And thank you very much indeed for the book.'

I didn't want to do this either.

As Eleanor left, so did the one person who made me feel safe to stay.

I'd have to tell Willa I was going. I went to the theatre doors.

She was on the stage, kneeling at her instrument case. Her expression was tightly focussed.

It was too late to disturb her. I would have to leave and explain another time.

She stood up and lifted the violin to her collarbone.

Her right collarbone.

Her violin was left handed. Reversed. Like a looking-glass.

I leaned in the doorway, unable to move.

'This is Andreq,' she said, and sliced the bow down the open A string in a long, annunciating note.

The violin was a lovelier fit for her than the keyboard. It let her explore her curiosity about quarter tones and microtones in thrilling runs, like Arabic voices calling the faithful to prayer. Obviously she was self-taught as her fingering was awkward and her elbows waved like wings. But the music soared.

Why wasn't she playing in better places than this?

While she was still playing, two men walked onto the stage behind her, carrying a table.

My mouth fell open. She hadn't finished her piece.

Willa seemed to be expecting them. She saw the two men and southpawed a last, long note, sliding down through the microtones to the very tip of the bow.

One of the men came back on with a chair and an elderly woman walked stiffly onto the stage and sat in it.

Willa slipped away, quiet as a stage hand.

The woman tipped a bag of stones onto the table. 'Friends,' she said, spreading the stones with gnarled hands, 'now we are prepared I will perform the summoning.'

I dug my nails into the paintwork. Summoning? Who were they summoning?

Not Andreq, surely?

I looked around for Willa. For an explanation.

Willa had melted away.

CHAPTER 53

On the stage, a lone spotlight highlighted the woman's hair. It was dyed auburn but the roots were grey, giving the impression of a pelt attached to her scalp by invisible threads.

She started to sway in her chair, rolling the stones like a child playing with marbles. From where I was standing I had an uncomfortable view up her skirt, of strongly gusseted tights, like a tan-coloured cobweb.

What was she doing? Was she going to claim she was talking to Andreq? Could I stop it?

The woman raised her head to the navy blue ceiling and spoke.

'Ah, Christina, it is good to be with you again. Are you able to talk?' Paused and nodded, as if hearing a voice. Then: 'Christina is with us.'

The arrival of 'Christina' was greeted with reverent applause.

And as far as everyone was concerned, Andreq had departed with Willa. If they ever cared that he was supposed to be there.

The woman raised her hand. Silence was restored.

'Christina says, is there someone in the room who has recently lost something?'

A woman near the back raised her hand. 'I lost my gold watch. It belonged to my sister.'

The woman on the stage nodded, her eyes closed as if communing with something. 'Is your sister still with us?'

'No. She died last year.'

'Christina says your sister is with you tonight. You're not to worry.'

Enough already. It was every bit as bad as Eleanor had said.

I turned away to the bar. I spotted Willa near the back of the room, lips to a bottle of Beck's. I ordered another for her and one for myself.

Next to me was the heavyset woman from the psychic fair who dealt in temple furnishings. She was talking to a fat man in a black T-shirt. I caught names; the fat man was Zak and the dealer was Isabel.

Zak; the name seemed familiar.

He was inspecting a sword made of varnished wood, which Isabel seemed to be selling to him. It looked like a stage prop, or something to go with a pirate outfit. One of her funny relics.

As I waited for my change the runes woman squeezed in, holding a five-pound note and trying to catch the barman's eye. In the bright bar lights she looked like someone had animated Munch's Scream. Zak turned and they acknowledged each other with nods.

My attention was on my barmaid, who was waiting to use the till, when I heard Zak say: 'So Willa did Andreq again.'

Zak. I swallowed. That was why I knew the name. Was he BlackZak from the message board? And if he was, he had announced to all the world that I was the singing teacher in Vellonoweth.

I turned away from them and stared into the mirror behind the bar. I peered at the barmaid, trying to encourage her to go faster.

In the mirror I could see BlackZak and the runes woman.

The runes woman inclined her strangely hovering hair. 'It's a difficult case, the spirit Andreq. Mismanaged, I feel.'

BlackZak said: 'She's an amateur and it's very unsatisfactory. There are many people from the community who've offered her mentorship but she's thrown it back in their faces.'

My barmaid had now managed to get to the till and was prodding the screen, trying to find my order. Come on, I thought. Before these people realise I'm right beside them.

'Amateurs always go the same way,' said the runes woman. She looked at the sword, which Zak was tapping on the floor. 'What's that?'

'A Tai Chi sword.'

The runes woman squinted doubtfully.

Zak added: 'Its harmlessness is illusory. I once saw a man

in a competition get his arm broken when he was hit with one.'

The barmaid returned with my change. I took it and slipped away to Willa.

We settled in a corner and chatted. Inevitably, by the end of the first bottle I told her: 'You should be using your music properly, not wasting your talent.'

She gave me a patient look. 'People often tell me that. But I live the way I need to live. We all have to find what's right for us.'

She stood up, took the empty beer bottle from my hand and nodded to the instrument case. 'Look after him while I get a refill.'

Look after him. With the help of beer, the instruction became fluid. Him – the sinistral violin? The shred of Andreq that sang through it?

What's right for me, soothesayer? You said once that a soothesayer did whatever was needed. When you showed me your lover, was that your soothing for the echoes scratching in your soul? Could you feel me there? What did you think might happen when you made me tell Gene about your sinewy dance with Ruhul? Did you know what you'd done?

If that was your soothing then, how would you soothe me now?

It was past ten o'clock when we left. Willa headed for her home, walking away on the armadillo-back cobbles, violin case strapped to her back. I thrust my hands in my pockets and set off for the bus stop at the other end of Melancholy Walk.

The cold was bitter. My coat felt thin as a cotton T-shirt. A man in a bomber jacket was leaning against the window of the pub. He looked up from his mobile. 'Taxi?'

'Vellonoweth?' I said.

'Hop in.'

I flopped gratefully into the back seat while he sent a text, then we were on our way up into the hills. I leaned against the window and dozed.

When he pulled over, I lifted my head and reached for my bag.

Beyond my reflection in the glass, there were no buildings.

I sat up, suddenly very awake and sober as a straight line.

I hadn't checked his licence, I'd just dived gratefully in. Now here we were, stopped, in the boundless, dark moorland.

CHAPTER 54

The road was unlit; pitch black. The only lights I could see were a faint glitter in the distance; a village a long way away.

'Have we stopped?' I said. I meant 'why have we stopped', but the first word came out silent.

The driver said: 'This is where you get out.'

I slipped my hand into my bag. Closed my fingers around my keys. What was this? A mugging? Or worse?

'But we agreed you'd take me to Vellonoweth.' Another part of me thought: don't argue with him. Get out now.

But getting out seemed to be what he wanted; perhaps someone was waiting.

If I didn't get out he might drag me out.

At least if I was out I had a chance to run.

Run where?

He said: 'I'm not moving until you get out of this car.'

Headlamps appeared as white dots in the circles of condensation on the window. Another car was coming. I yanked on the door handle, scrambled out, slammed it and ran.

I waved my white handbag above my head so that the oncoming vehicle would see. Please stop, I prayed.

Behind me, the taxi driver started the engine. I prepared to hare into the heather, in case, but he sped off into the night without bothering with me again.

Just what was that about? He didn't even ask for a fare.

The other headlights slowed, swerved to the edge of the road. Thank goodness. I heard a crunch of tyres and saw the headlights tilt and nod as one side encountered the bumpy verge. The engine slowed to idle. I sprinted towards it. It was a yellow van.

Doors opened and closed and footsteps crunched.

Several figures were getting out. Black shadows moved across the van headlights.

Something about that made me rethink my eagerness to run to them. I paused.

One of the figures rolled up its sleeves. Another stood, very deliberately, in front of the headlights. A female voice called out.

It was the voice that not so long ago had been communing with Christina.

'So you've lost your way, have you?'

The runes woman, her grey roots a halo in the headlights.

I recognised another silhouette. Zak, rotund where a headlight caught him, otherwise camouflaged as night.

Of all the people to try to hitch a ride from.

'Not quite the same as London, here, is it?' said the runes woman. 'It's easy to get lost.'

I could see three more silhouettes behind. Altogether there were five of them.

I remembered the taxi driver sending a text before we set off. Was he a friend of theirs? Had they arranged this?

And what were they planning to do?

Zak folded his arms. 'Miss Lear. The singing teacher from London. Dabbling with spirit. From the future as well. For an amateur you're breaking some serious rules.'

He was holding something. The wooden sword.

In the distance I heard the drumming of a train passing, a very long way off. The noise carried easily across the empty hills.

There was no other sound. No cars coming.

A sick sensation turned in my stomach.

The runes woman spoke. 'You're not fit to have custody of spirit. You've no idea what you're doing.'

'It's not what you think,' I said.

A breeze whipped up. It went straight through my coat and lapped my shirt against the skin of my back. I squeezed my white bag tighter under my arm. Anything to feel warmer.

Zak was holding the sword out, testing its balance. His head was turned towards me, his expression in darkness. 'You think you're doing okay?'

'Yes,' I said. Because he had the sword.

'I don't think you're doing okay at all.'

'When spirit is with the wrong custodian,' said the runes woman, 'it is difficult to let go. Often you don't want to.'

She turned into the headlight beam. The Scream appeared in the downward sag of her deep-lined profile, like a torch discovering a death mask. 'Fortunately we are all experienced in exorcisms. If Christina has the strength.'

I would have laughed at them, just a little bit, if I hadn't seen Christina deployed so earnestly earlier on. I looked around me. The moor was black. Could I lose them if I ran away? Or if I couldn't, how bad could it be? It was just words, wasn't it?

Zak walked closer to me, tapping the sword in measured beats on the asphalt. He had more in mind than wordplay.

I heard a sound. Voices shouting.

About a hundred yards away, two points of light hopped over the brow of the hill. The voices became louder.

Coasting towards us were two young guys on bikes, their arms and legs ringed with fluorescent stripes. They were speaking in short, breathless sentences over the ticking of their wheels. The way cyclists chat if they're on a long empty stretch.

'What time have you got to be there tomorrow?'

'Not until six. I've got to wait all day.'

I ran out into the road, waving my white bag.

The front cyclist put on the brakes and skidded to a halt. The other swerved and ended up astride his bike on the ground. I wound up stumbling between them, trying not to tread on their legs, wheels or crossbars.

'Sorry,' I said, and kept saying it. Sorry.

I glanced back at the group in the headlights. Were they going to come after me?

They seemed to be staying near the yellow van. Zak, in the headlights, put his weapon behind his back.

But one of the cyclists saw him. He looked at his friend, as if wanting to check that he'd seen it too.

'What is this?' he said.

The other lad pulled his bike upright and wheeled it to me. 'Are you all right?'

A skirted shape stepped towards me. The runes woman called out in a voice like a parent taking charge of a child.

'She's fine. We're trying to help her. Thank you for stopping.'

I spoke to the cyclists, quietly. 'Are you going to Vellonoweth? Would you mind walking with me?'

The guys looked at each other.

The runes woman stood still and folded her arms. Behind her, Zak moved. The light from the headlamps silhouetted his cannonball gut and a slender shape beside him. The sword.

I looked at the guy in the red helmet. Hoped he'd seen.

'Come with us,' he said, and nodded to his friend.

The two guys began to walk down the road, one on either side of me, supporting their bikes with a hand on the junction of the handlebars. They matched their pace to me. I walked quickly, my eyes on the grey asphalt in front of their bike lights.

I glanced back, not quite believing they would let me go so easily. The cyclists did too. It wasn't just me who was spooked.

Behind, the van doors slammed and the engine started. Only then did we dare to speak.

'I'm Frank,' said the guy in the red helmet, 'and that's Neil.'

The patch of light in front of us widened like an atomic blast. The van engine roared, impossibly close.

I sprinted into the blackness at the side of the road. My feet rocked on an invisible minefield of hummocks and ditches. I crashed into the spiky grass.

I scrambled up again, sure the headlights would find me, but the van stayed on the road. Its red tail-lights climbed another hill and sank out of sight.

Frank and Neil were swearing. Their lights swung as they hauled their bikes out of the rough. I got up and stumbled back to the road, where they were squeezing tyres, inspecting their bikes' skinny frames.

'What the hell is their problem?' Neil demanded.

'I'm sorry,' I said again. 'Thank you for this. I hope I haven't damaged anything.'

'Are they friends of yours?' said Frank.

'No,' I said, 'they are not.'

I could still hear the van, its engine surging and slowing with the corners. But definitely going away.

We started to walk again. The bikes rolled along beside us, wheels ticking.

'What happened?' said Frank. 'Were they were mugging you?'

'I'm not quite sure,' I said.

'Do you want us to come with you to the police?' said Neil.

I hadn't thought about going to the police.

'Do you think I should?'

'Did they actually, well, do anything?' said Frank. His emphasis carried a weight of suggestions; rape, maybe.

'No,' I said. 'They just got threatening.'

'I don't think the police will be able to do much in that case,' said Neil.

A gust of wind rippled through my coat. I wanted to sit down, stop. I forced myself to keep my feet going.

'Thanks,' I said again. 'Thanks for stopping.'

Back in the cottage, I stood against the closed front door and let the warmth revive my bones.

My mobile was a blue glow on the sideboard where I'd left it charging.

There was a text.

Not from Jenny Tollderson. Or Jerry.

From Gene.

I took a breath and went to read it.

Where

That was all it said. There was another. No, three more.

Are

You

?

I folded onto the sofa, the phone in my hand. I banished the texts and scrunched myself up small as I thumbed to the options. *Reply?* No, no no. *Store?* No. *Delete?*

I sat looking at the point of no return.

Delete: are you sure? Yes No.

I left the phone and got up. I checked the front door. Then the back. I went upstairs to the bedroom and put the light on. A light from the Dowmans' house made a pale rectangle on their lawn. Shadows moved about. A door opened and closed.

Did they stop when they heard me move, look at each other and nod, or cross themselves?

I checked the windows were locked. Just to make sure, I opened them so I could shut them securely. The night air yawned with far-off sounds like the noise of static. I locked them tight. Went to bed.

I remember a song that said when you're in love all the colours are brighter. When you're scared it's sounds. In the trees. In the wind. Creaks in the ribs of the house. Sub-whispered conversations and movements next door. I jolted awake to every one, as though I was adrift in an old, unsteady ship that might split apart around me.

I'd put my mobile by the bed. I hadn't given it my verdict on Gene's message. I woke up the display and it asked me again.

Delete Yes No?

No.

Reply Yes No?

Yes.

Are you there?

I sent it.

CHAPTER 55

'Awake.'

Gene's voice, in my ear. We are in the bed in the cottage. He is beside me, propped up on one elbow, wiry hair falling over one eye, wrapped in the white sprigged duvet like a space suit. Next to it his skin is cement grey. The hollows of his collarbones and pectorals look as if he has been sculpted.

He mouths a word. 'Awake?'

I didn't think this would happen again, I thought it was ruined. I kiss him, stretch an arm out. Goosedown crackles as I reach for the tape player to turn it off.

He catches my arm and pulls it back to the bed. His bare knee slides over, sword-edge shin bone roughened by hairs. Hairs which I know make dark contours of his muscles. He puts a finger to my lips, says, very quietly, 'shhh', drags it out like a long note played *adagissimo*. Shhhhhhhhhhhhhhh.

The Dictaphone clicks and hums beside us. The tape makes a crisp, cellophane noise as it slides past the recording heads, listening.

It's like a dream of violent struggling, making no sound at all. Agony.

A cold wind wakes me. Half past three, says the clock. He's sitting in the window. A dark figure looking into the brooding hills.

He stayed.

I hear an owl cry, a shuddering flute. As if it is in the room. I find my glasses.

The window is open. Gene is dressed; jeans, knotty jumper. His feet are bare. His hand is dangling out of the window. Between his fingers is a glowing cigarette.

Yes, the soles of his feet are scarred with old burns. That is one of the things I know now.

My kimono is tangled in the duvet. I pull it out, wrap it on tightly and shiver over to sit with him in the window. It's a squeeze and the glass touches my shoulder. Through the thin material it is like ice.

'I don't think Jenny Tollderson will like you smoking in her bedroom.'

Smoke blown out in a long lazy pout like a flautist. His glinting smile. 'She's not going to think it's me.'

'Thanks.'

'And you're never going to meet her. So what's the big deal?' He inhales from the cigarette and breathes out through the open window.

'She's never going to know. That's what you do best. Does the owner of the antique warehouse know you've been slipping in there?'

'I'm very discreet,' he says, and looks rather pleased about it.

When I texted him he came straight over. I didn't think he'd still be awake, but actually in all the time I've known him he hardly seems to sleep.

I didn't tell him about the incident on the moors. Too complicated to explain quickly. And when he arrived he wasn't much interested in explanations.

I shiver, look at the white duvet thrown back on the bed and move to get it. He puts his bare foot up on the wall to bar my way. I push at the denimed leg but it stays like a closed gate.

'Gene, I'm freezing.'

He pulls me around so I am leaning against him. The skin of my back drinks up the warmth of his jumper, his smell. That makes me remember the other night, those arms and ribs and hips jamming me into the wall, my hand in the door. I shiver and this time it's not the cold.

I say quietly: 'Did your father really hurt your mother?'

He pulls me closer. I hear the fizz of the paper around the cigarette as he takes a drag. He breathes out.

'I didn't know what I was doing.'

I am shocked. He never does anything without being aware of it.

'Would you have hurt me?'

No answer.

A breeze makes the trees sing. I burrow further into his warmth. And have to ask something that may turn this very nasty.

'Do you want to hurt me? Sometimes I think you do.'

Silence. I have that sick sensation again, a turning dynamo inside. His arm is tight around my waist, its pressure is comforting and brutal like a tourniquet. But this way round, not looking at him, it's easier to talk to him.

'You said, the other night... something about that party – Kate Rafferty's and ... '

'..and what I wanted to do when I saw you play.' A small laugh, which shakes through me too.

Without being able to see his face I have to guess whether it's embarrassed or enjoying. It doesn't seem likely that it would be the former.

'Did you try to chat me up? Did I tell you to get lost? I'm sorry but it's a while ago and I can't remember.'

Another shaking in his chest, an increase of warm breath where his lips are close to my hair.

He says: 'I've got secrets and you've got secrets.'

Another drag on the cigarette. He sweeps my hair away from my neck and blows out the warm smoke on the skin, as though he is trying to leave a brand.

I think he would have hurt me that night. He's got it in him.

A deep breath, to slow the turning wheel. I try again. 'Did I do something and now you want to get even? Because I think there's something.'

He burrows his hand into my hair, scrunches it experimentally in handfuls. Not hard so it hurts. Gently, as if playing.

My hair used to be even longer then; half-way down my back.

'It wasn't that.' He shrugs, correcting himself. 'Well, it was; that day you played you looked completely wild. But I didn't want to just have you. I wanted to be you.'

A confession. After all the dodging and parrying he's put his sword down.

I twist, to try to see how this confession looks as well as how it sounds. Because I don't understand it, and a nasty, cynical part of me says he's making it up.

His grip tightens, keeping me where I am. The back of my ribs feel a heartbeat; his, fast. Getting faster. Nervous.

That's why I'm not allowed to see. Talking about this is upsetting him. It's real.

'I saw you play and I thought, how wonderful, to be so consumed like that. To let it take over you, total control. It wouldn't matter what else was happening, you could just do that.'

'You envied me?'

'Yes.'

What a bizarre idea.

Quietly, I ask: 'And what was it? What was happening?'

He releases my waist. Lifts my left hand. The one he'd tried to shut in the door. Mimes something chopping down across the fingers.

'Your father and mother,' I say.

His iron arm circles my waist again. His chin rests on my shoulder, pushes hard. As if I am empty clothes and he could fold me over. His heart is still hammering on my back.

'Did they hurt you too?' I ask.

He breathes out. A long, difficult sigh. Shifts position. I want to turn and do something comforting but his arm stops me moving, pins me where I am.

'At medical school people didn't know what to do with the patients who had intractable pain. It's an entire branch of medicine, pain that's officially incurable. Well you can cure it if you look hard enough, carefully enough. You don't treat the pain; you treat the person feeling the pain. And you've got to be careful because if you do it wrong you can make it worse. I found ways, wrote papers, went to conferences and presented difficult case histories.'

Difficult case histories. I flex my fingers carefully. 'Well don't tell anyone about this one. Your cure isn't working.'

I say it ruefully, meaning it mostly as a joke. He brings the cigarette closer to my face. Out of the corner of my eye I can see the glowing coal at its end. It is so close the fumes make my eyes water. He is holding it there deliberately. My stomach hardens into a knot. It's curious, this position; so intimate, so threatening.

I push it away. 'Don't get annoyed with me because you've lost your touch.'

He puts the cigarette to his lips. Takes a drag. Holds it at a sociable distance.

'I hate curing people. It used to be fantastic, especially the intractable cases. I'd see one or two really difficult ones every week. When you got them through it was such a high. Often they need to dig into some strange stuff. They hardly remember what went on, just a bit of cathartic sensation and it's gone, like giving birth. They don't know how bad it was. When I go to sleep those people are back again screaming. I haven't slept through the night for years.'

Lips to cigarette. Ribcage out, gasping the smoke in.

'That's so wicked of me, isn't it, to hate the people who need my help.' Cigarette again.

I lean against him, not knowing what to say.

'And then there you were one day in Guy's, seeing old Dr Goldilocks. Goldilocks who gets the broken musicians. He's dreadful by the way, like a bored mechanic. Anyway, I saw you there and I couldn't stop thinking about it. You, of all people, went wrong too.'

As always, when someone makes me aware of it, my nerves answer with white heat of their own.

Gene sucks the last out of the cigarette and tosses the butt out into the road. 'I haven't lost my touch. I just haven't finished.'

The end hits the flagstoned path, shakes off a few red sparks and stays there. A red dot, glowing.

'You're such a control freak.'

He moves my hair so he can rest his chin on my shoulder again. Whispers, like he's suggesting we sneak off somewhere to play. 'It's not me who's in control. That's the mistake most therapists make.'

'Watch it. Next thing you know you'll be getting out crystals.'

I relax against him. It feels so good to use his body like this. Too good, I never want to move again.

I whisper. 'Who have we created? Who's Andreq? Is it me or you?'

A short, ironic laugh. He rests his forehead on my shoulder. 'What's so funny?'

Hot breath through the silk of my kimono. 'Thank God we're only doing you.'

His hand slips onto my breast. Over my heart. It leaps as though it is the only organ in my body. On the path outside, the wind catches the cigarette end and rolls it backwards and forwards. Like a tiny bloodfish in dark water. A red organ, swimming alone.

That ESP trick of his again. And now he doesn't have to use any words.

No, the red dot is just a cigarette end.

I don't want to do this now.

Too much of the time I've spent with him has been diluted, half-removed oblivion. I've probably spent more hours like that or asleep in a room next door to him than I have awake and talking to him while we are ourselves.

I slip my fingers between his. Interrupt the warm connection with red organs. 'Don't do this. You hate it.'

A breeze comes in through the window and rakes down my arms. I shiver.

He turns so that his back shields me from the cold. The grip of his arms grows more purposeful around me. 'I always do things I shouldn't do.'

Chapter 56

Tape 7

On Ruhul's skin is a sheen of sweat like rain on ebony. He stirs and the covers cling to his limbs like webs.

'You never sleep,' he says. His voice is light, as though he left half of it unwoken.

'Why sleep when staying awake with you is so much better?'

The rest of his voice arrives. 'I have something to tell you.'

I look at him. Swallow. 'Okay. You look so serious.'

He props himself up on an elbow. 'Do you know what this power station does?'

I shrug. I'd never given it any thought. 'Don't ask me. I just shovel sand.'

'It makes xeching.'

I search his face. He returns my gaze steadily, with a nod. You can believe it.

'No,' I say sharply, and roll away from him, lie on my back. Study the ceiling, the constellation of white bullet holes.

I quote the physiology I was taught. 'Xeching is from the ancient sensory passageways of the brain...'

'Xeching,' says Ruhul, 'is all electrons.'

'Xeching... is ancient and natural –'

'Xeching is fireworks travelling down a wire. Electrical trickery. It was invented here. It's made by a machine.'

A profound rumble and the glass bones of the station sing. Sand shivers out of the bullet holes. The turbines are doing well today.

At their rather individual task.

I throw the covers off. I start to walk around. Sand grinds under my bare feet on the glass floor. I look back at him. 'Really?'

'There is,' says Ruhul, 'no such thing as xeching without this station.'

My fingers find the sandpaper. I go to the edge of the growing window. And try to make a little more of it clear.

After a moment, Ruhul is beside me too.

The station shakes. Sand whispers down the walls. The slanted dune creeps inwards, second by second, as it sends another xech undersea.

CHAPTER 57

It was morning. I was alone.

I rolled into the other pillow and buried my face in it. It carried a trace of his smell; exotic wood.

I opened my eyes in the white cotton. Like being a bird high up in a pale sky with the ground travelling far below. And no idea where to land.

What he said in the hollows of moonlight. No more hiding.

Like those two in that other place; what do we all do now?

I twisted again, onto my back. The window was open. The room was full of the scent of rain. I breathed it in like a forest. The echo of traffic came in, gathered from the surrounding roads by the damp air. A tang of cigarette smoke caught my throat. I drew it in, inhaled eagerly for more.

I thought it had all ended badly. But now...

I found my glasses. The tape recorder was beside the bed. Witness to fragments of what had happened; confirming by its presence that others had too. The tapes themselves had gone.

I grabbed my robe and went down the stairs. What other traces of him could I find?

My black poloneck was laid neatly on the sofa with my high-heeled boots, picked up from the floor when he separated his out. He had left so carefully.

There was nothing disturbed in the kitchen. No used mug, no water glass. Except for the smell of cigarettes and the ghost of his fragrance he might never have been here.

It was a wonder he ever let himself be captured on a tape.

I put the kettle on, found my phone and flumped on the sofa to write a text. *Are you okay?* That sounded wrong. *Are you there? See what I did there?* Idiotic. *Lov-* Whoa, don't scare him. We don't yet have a vocabulary. *Hello.* I sent that.

There was a crash in the kitchen, like a large parcel barging through a letterbox. I went out and the ginger cat was a stern obelisk sitting by its bowl. I fetched its foil pouch from the fridge. Gritted my teeth as I dug the spoon in.

The contours in the meat showed no sign of overnight drying. The crafty feline must have already persuaded Gene to feed it. I gave it a nugget, in admiration.

My phone, in the other room, came alive. I ran to it.

Tapes in the post. Blessings from the other side.

I thumbed in a reply. *Come and deliver them by hand, you idiot.*

It bounced. This primitive place.

I went to one of the open windows and tried again. Still nothing. Come on, I had it a moment ago. I walked around kitchen and lounge, watching for the signal to sneak back through the shadows and reflections of the hills.

Not today. Not even upstairs.

I threw clothes on and went up to Vellonoweth Hall, shielding my face from lashing rain. The signal bar suddenly filled and I zipped the message off.

By then my legs were carrying me, wanting to walk for ever. I was disembodied from lack of sleep but I couldn't keep still.

I dialled Gene's number.

A recorded message. *The mobile phone you have called is switched off or out of range. Please try again later.*

I went over the top of the hill and climbed down to the little bay. The sea was gunmetal grey, flinging up and down the pebbles.

My phone rang.

I answered, called into the receiver to hang on until I could hear, sprinting up the beach with the ebb and crash of the waves in my ears. In the shelter of the big cracked cliffs, it was quiet.

It wasn't Gene. It was Jerry.

'Gene texted me,' said Jerry.

'He texted you? What for? How did he get your number?'

'I thought you must have given it to him. He's had to go abroad but he wanted me to check you're okay.'

'He's gone abroad? Right.' There should be proper questions I could ask. But I could only repeat what Jerry was saying. Like in a dream.

'Carol? Tell Uncle Jerry, what's happened? Spill the beans.' I could hear the curiosity in his voice.

'Spill yours first.'

'I got a text. It was sent about an hour ago. *I've had to go abroad, check Carol's okay.* That's all it said.'

'Hang on, Jerry, I'll call you back.'

I rang Gene's number.

The mobile phone you have called is switched off or out of range.

There was nothing unusual in him vanishing for a few days. He wasn't the kind of person who kept in touch for its own sake. It was remarkable that he'd asked Jerry to let me know. Presumably he'd tried to tell me and the fickle ether had bounced it back.

But then I'd had that message from him. *Blessings from the other side. Tapes in the post.* What the hell did that mean?

The waves beat, up and down. A gravelly white noise rhythm.

Something about this wasn't right.

I rang the hospital and asked for Gene's department. The receptionist said: 'Mr Winter doesn't work here any more.'

I asked again, not sure I'd understood.

The receptionist filled in more details, brisk as a call centre.

'He was seconded to us for a few weeks until our new head of department, Mr Hammond, arrives. Mr Hammond will be here from tomorrow. He's very nice.'

She thought I was one of his patients.

'Do you know where Gene's gone? I'm a friend.'

She took this in her stride too. 'I'm afraid I cannot give out personal addresses. Mr Winter has gone to the practice in New Zealand –'

'New Zealand?'

'Yes New Zealand,' said the receptionist. 'Mr Hammond is coming over from there to take his place and to take over all Mr Winter's patients. He's very nice.'

She told me more too, to emphasise the irrevocability of it and the sweetness of Mr Hammond. Convinced I was a mere patient, perhaps with delusions about her relationship with her physician.

CHAPTER 58

I ran all the way down the hill to his flat near the hospital. I rang the bell but there was no answer.

I tried the antiques warehouse next door. It was a former coach house with a big pair of padlocked double doors and a smaller door in the middle. I tried the latch. It was open.

Inside was a jumble of old chairs in various stages of upholstery, big refectory tables sanded bare. A radio was playing and someone was whistling along.

The cocktail of smells came to me as though someone had bottled that evening; beeswax polish, wood glue and the old tea smell of antique fabric.

The whistling and the radio were annoying, intruding. At the same time I think they kept me sane.

I followed the whistling upstairs to a galleried landing. The floorboards were wooden and dusty, with wide gaps between the planks.

I remembered the feel of them under my bare toes.

The daylight that came down from a window in the roof showed layers of cleated bootprints. And was there also the secret print of naked feet?

There was the piano with its wooden seat. Not far away was a plain white door flush with the wall, marked with a green sign. The other side of the fire escape from Gene's flat.

I stared at it, seeing through it to the little corridor beyond, the bathroom, the mealy carpet.

I tried his mobile again. Perhaps I would hear it in the room next door. It didn't even ring, just repeated the recorded message.

I turned to the piano. The lid was open. It was a Broadwood, like the old Druid piano. In the daylight the mahogany case was badly scuffed, awaiting restoration. There was a scrape mark along the top that looked fresh. I remembered Gene pulling the iPod across, sliding it on the wood, the hum of the steel strings in the soundbox.

I wished the whistling would shut up.

It did.

'You can try it if you want.'

A man was standing in the workshop doorway, wiping his hands on a towel.

I shook my head, took a step away. No, not even if I had been fit to. I felt sick just looking at it.

'Have you seen the guy in the flat next door? I'm a friend of his.'

'There was a removal lorry here yesterday. I thought it was something for us but it took away some crates.'

Oh, I said. Thank you.

'I was here early this morning. I saw him leave in a taxi.'

'Do you know what time it was?'

'About six-thirty.'

Thank you, I said, and left.

New Zealand. Blessings from the other side.

My brain was in stasis. I passed the used car showroom by the roundabout. There was his slightly dented, black VW on the forecourt, for sale.

One domino pushed over others. I was being so naive. This had been planned all along. Removal lorries. Selling the car. Making arrangements to get a lovely Mr Hammond over from New Zealand. It was all fixed months ago.

I start walking up the hill. He can't have gone. Not after what he told me in the honest dark, freezing cold in the window. About home, about the party where we'd collided all those years ago. That cigarette hovering close to my face, the sadistic thread in his wiring – strangely not surprising and perhaps I understand where it was seeded. He likes control but probably can't help it with a start like that. No wonder he's so infernally, devastatingly clever at what he does.

Up to the park again. I keep trying his phone. As if the message will change. *Mobile is no longer switched off or out of range, he changed his mind.* Back down to the ocean, whose wide waves might sweep up any signal and bring it in, no matter how far away.

The water surges and retreats, like a great machine marking the passing seconds and minutes.

I thought this was a new beginning. Not an abrupt end.

Maybe it isn't an end.

Those tapes were on their way. What else might come with them? A note?

He'd said it himself – we hadn't finished.

The message does change. *The mobile phone you have called is discontinued. You cannot make calls to this number.*

When I felt able to talk again, I called Jerry back. Told him about New Zealand.

'Slow down. Did you and he have a thing?'

'It's complicated.'

Jerry's voice lifted in a big smile. 'I knew it wasn't the pussycat keeping you there. All this time you've been glued to him in a big bed.'

'Just two nights.'

'Two nights and he bolts without telling you? Forget him, petal.'

I couldn't speak. Could not answer him at all.

CHAPTER 59

Back at the cottage. I sank onto the sofa. It seemed only moments later that I woke to the sound of my phone.

I flew to it. My first thought, primitive, non-logical. Was it Gene?

No, said the display. *Jerry*.

Gene would be high in the air above a random continent. Sleeping it off like me. For the same reason as me.

I wished I hadn't thought that. My logical brain offered a reprieve. Of course it wasn't him. If he was on a plane, he was unable to call anyone, even if he wanted to.

'Hi Jerry,' I said.

'You sound fuzzy.'

'I was asleep.'

'Just checking in. Any news?'

Red feet in bed. I didn't deserve him. I melted back into the cushions and took a deep breath.

'His phone is disconnected.'

There was a pause. 'So you're a dark horse, aren't you?'

'I guess I am.'

'I thought there was something about him when I first met him.'

'That's understandable. He hypnotised you.'

'Not the way he did you. I could see this coming a mile. Champagne bubbles. Notes hanging in the piano. If he'd done me like that you wouldn't have had a look-in, girl.'

Sweet Jerry. Trying to make me think about the good times. In a moment he'd tell me it was a clear diagnosis of cold feet. And to wait for the thaw.

'How many regressions did you do?'

'I don't know. Quite a few.'

Jerry took a deep breath. The pause bristled with significance. 'Carol, you never see the signs until it's too late.'

I fiddled with the zip on the edge of the chintz cushion. 'Not everybody wants to be leaped on, you know. It was just hypnosis.'

'That's why he went.'

Jerry was such a romantic. Because he was in love, that must mean everyone else was.

With difficulty, I kept my voice even. 'It's not like that. He knew exactly how long he had here. It was all games. He timed everything for maximum chaos.'

'How do you know? What do you know about him?'

'Jerry, I didn't treat Gene badly. He's all about control, he does it for a living and he can't stop in real life.' I kneaded the cushion, dug my fingers into it like claws.

'Not everyone expresses their feelings straightforwardly. Carol, he knows you and he knows Andreq. That makes him desperately involved.'

I'd lost track of what was going on here. Or maybe I hadn't. Jerry said that so reverently, as though he wished his own hypnotist had been Tim.

So he wished Tim had been more involved with Ruby. I didn't need all this projected on me. Not today. I pulled the cushion close and hugged it hard.

'Jerry, the music world is full of people like him. You have to move on, find the next project.'

'And what if you don't have a next project? What then?'

That was nasty. That could knock over a bus.

I crushed the cushion harder. 'You think he's waiting in New Zealand for me to call and say, let's start again? Jerry, he's cut his phone off. That's what you do to disappear.'

'He had to do that, you dumb girl, because you can't take a phone contract to another country. But you didn't have to give up on Karli because he went abroad.'

Karli? How had we derailed to Karli? 'What's Karli got to do with it?'

'You could have kept up the relationship. We have wonderful inventions. Text. Email. Skype. Instead, what did you do the day he went away to America?'

'I don't remember what I did. It was nearly a year ago.'

'You didn't even go with him to say goodbye. You went to an audition.'

'Yes, I probably did go to an audition. I couldn't stop everything because he was leaving. I had to get on with life. And he didn't want a relationship. We were duet partners.'

'You know what Karli said to me once? He said "I've never known someone so involved with their instrument as Carol." For a musician to say that is quite something.'

'I didn't know you two were so chummy.'

'Carol, you're not a musician now. You're going to meet people who aren't. You're thinking Gene's like another obsessed automaton who plays an instrument, because that's what you like. Or that he'll help you play again. He's not. There's so much you're missing. Welcome to the ordinary world.'

The connection broke into silence. He'd hung up.

I dropped my hand to the sofa, numb. Then something inside me lashed back. I hurled the cushion across the room. The cat sprang up from nowhere onto the sideboard and froze in a spiky arch.

If I'd had something breakable to hand I would have smashed it, without a doubt. How dare Jerry. Especially bringing up Karli. He thought it was all so simple. He had no idea.

And as for being involved with their instrument? Karli was the worst I'd ever come across. On a day he had to perform, he wouldn't even speak.

I went upstairs. The sky was darkening again. Hail was pattering against the glass. Seeing the window sill drained all the fight out of me. I sat down and put my back against the icy pane, remembered the warmth of Gene behind me. Not even twenty-four hours ago.

I should have stayed awake the entire night like he did. If I hadn't slept, would he still be here?

He'd put me there; I had no choice.

Silently, I gave Jerry the real answer. Another obsessed automaton, a way to play again? I should have said you've got it so wrong. I now don't think of Gene that way at all.

The phone rang again. Wearily, I answered.

'I'm sorry for having a go at you, petal. Maybe you should come home.'

'I can't yet.'

'Sweetheart, it won't do you any good moping down there. Find someone to feed the cat. Or leave it to catch mice.'

'It's not that. I've got to finish a few things.'

He was right, though. Why didn't I want to go?

Because those tapes would arrive soon. This wasn't finished until they did. Maybe it would be tomorrow. Or – surely not – Gene wasn't posting them from New Zealand? How long might that take? 'Shit,' I said, out loud, which probably didn't make much sense to Jerry. Couldn't Gene just have put them through the door?

'All right. Be careful. Ruby sends her love too.'

'So do I.'

Ruby sends her love too.

I leaned against the cold glass and closed my eyes. I opened them again. Still here, numb except for my hands, trying to conjure up answers.

The tapes. When they arrived, what would come with them?

I suddenly saw. There wouldn't be a message. Or if there was, it would be one of his enigmatic flourishes, not the honesty of last night. The most truthful thing we'd done had been with us all the time. It was in Andreq – soothing, struggling to hide his secret damage and sitting alone with a bird on the shoulders of the world.

The Dictaphone was beside the bed. *'You never sleep,'* Ruhul had said last night. Who was Ruhul really talking to? To Gene, who doesn't sleep?

I wanted to run it again, and all the other things that passed in their sand hideaway, but Gene had taken it. To listen to as he crossed the clouds?

I found the tape from the very first time. Put it in the machine, pressed play and lay down. Gene was there, talking in a whisper that could fill a cathedral. The bubbles in the glass. I tried very hard not to think about Jerry's evaluation of that.

Maybe I could slip there on my own, go back to Andreq and Ruhul and see what else there was. Come and talk to me, Andreq. Come and tell me the real truth. Tell me everything I said to Jerry was cynical and wrong. Tell me it wasn't just games of soothing.

On the tape, my voice started. My second voice. Andreq arrived in his new world. My consciousness remained on the white ceiling, on the sky outside which was now dark, the hail spraying the window, the duvet white like a snowy field, the faint bite of Gene's cigarette smoke.

I hit Stop. This wasn't going to work.

I found Jenny's *Yellow Pages*. It had a few advertisements for hypnotherapists – the sensible, down-to-earth kind who offered to help with weight loss and giving up smoking. I crossed off anyone who made claims about past-life regression. No thanks.

This time, I would choose my collaborator carefully.

CHAPTER 60

I rang one of the numbers that looked properly clinical. The hypnotherapist was kind and encouraging until I mentioned what I wanted.

'I'm sorry, I don't think I can help you with that.'

The second gave me the same response. I asked for her reasons.

'Let me give you some advice. You'll be hard pressed to find a reputable therapist willing to take the risk. Our professional body has strongly advised us to refuse such work.'

Her professional body had advised her? How many requests of this sort did hypnotherapists normally get?

I'm sorry, she said. It would not be professional of me to continue this conversation.

Richard Longborrow. There he was in the shop, ponderously choosing a newspaper, when I went to buy milk. I saw him before he saw me, and could have slipped away. But here, if I wanted it, might be a solution.

I considered him in his overcoat with the velvet collar, the flash of violet neckband that was today's bow-tie.

Would it be so very bad?

Of course Richard Longborrow looked through the shelves and saw me. He came striding over, smiling with the assurance of someone greeting an old friend.

He spoke fast. 'Have you been trying to get hold of me? I've been trying to keep a slot open, saying to myself, Carol will want some time, but there's so much going on. So how are you?'

What a stupid question. Two hours' sleep was not a good look for me. I probably looked like I'd spent the night summoning devils or whatever he normally did.

Richard Longborrow fiddled with his violet bow tie. 'If you

have time, we could go for coffee?'

I had a choice: walk away or evaluate this properly. We went to the tea rooms in the back of the indoor market.

Richard had rooibos tea. He leaned back in his chair and spread his arms. 'Carol, I'm all yours. Tell me what I can do for you. Why have you made me wait so long?'

His eagerness made me want to push my chair back and run away. What happened to all that business about trying to protect his reputation? It didn't help that my coffee had been stewing in a jug and tasted like caffeinated engine oil. And left my heart trying to leap out of my throat.

'I thought I had to pass some tests,' I said.

He took a sip of tea and set it down in the cup daintily. 'I have the proof I need in order to proceed.'

'Proof?'

'I am now satisfied that you truly are a past life in contact with a future incarnation. The learning opportunity is tremendous.'

I curled my nails into my palm. I felt sick again.

'Carol, I'd say we know each other quite well by now. You know where I'm coming from and I've taken your concerns on board. We should go to my studio, I'll set up a tape and we take it from there.'

My throat-heart hammered like a sparrow trapped behind a window.

Richard Longborrow put his palms out, like a hostage negotiator demonstrating he means no harm. 'Of course, I don't want to rush you. Just say the word, when and where, and I'll take over.'

Take over Andreq? No. I couldn't.

'I'll think about it,' I said, and we paid up and left. I walked a little way up the hill and looked back to see him collecting a bicycle propped against the wall of the post office. He backed it slowly into the road, swung his leg over and coasted away in a thoughtful undulating path.

I walked faster, to get away from him all the more quickly. Someone like him wouldn't help. I shouldn't have asked.

It started to rain.

Back at the cottage and the mail had brought a yellow padded bag. Postmarked from Heathrow Airport.

The address was written in careful capitals. The kind of writing that gave nothing away. Deliberately anonymous.

I opened it in slow motion. Picked each staple open, in case there was something written inside the envelope, or a note that might be destroyed if I ripped it open. And to put off the moment when I'd find there was nothing.

There were five small tapes, neatly labeled with the dates.

That made the full set. There was no note. It was like buying something from an unknown person on Ebay; it just arrives, with no trace of the individual who had it before.

I went upstairs, fetched the tapes I had up there. Put them all together in a row on the bedcovers. There were seven. Our strange time together, condensed into a few hours. Tape 1-7; that was all Gene had to say, as if an anonymous guide is all he ever was.

Rat-tat-tat, from downstairs. Someone was knocking on the front door.

I peered out of the window. On the doorstep was a man in a black leather jacket, jeans and climbing boots.

He saw me looking out of the window and held his jacket out. On his belt was an identity card with a photograph. Although he didn't look like a meter reader.

I went down, put the chain across and opened the door a crack.

The man smiled as if he saw this kind of behaviour all the time. 'Could I have a word? It's about Gene Winter.'

CHAPTER 61

It's about Gene Winter. I imagined a car soaring off the edge of a mountain. A gleaming missile hanging in the air.

I dropped the chain end and it banged against the door. 'What's happened?'

'No need for panic. He's all right. As far as we know.' The man handed me a card.

Colin Neen, private investigator: prenuptial enquiries, surveillance, fraud, missing persons; unusual cases welcomed.

Missing persons? Who was looking for him? Apart from me.

I showed him in. He put himself on the sofa and opened a leatherette writing case that contained a notebook. Asked for a glass of water and began.

'I have been hired by the relatives of the late Mrs Maud Jeffries.'

He gave this information and paused to observe my reaction.

'I don't know her.'

'You met her in the Acorns Nursing Home on Monday, February the eighteenth. She died the next day.'

I gasped, because that's what such news makes you do.

'Her death was expected, Miss Lear,' said Neen. 'She had cancer.'

Yes, I remembered now. The shrunken lady, no more substantial than her angora shawl. The morphine pump, whatever that was. I never saw it but the very name was enough.

Those details came back, and with them a hard taste.

Jerry, you thought I was too cynical about Gene?

The detective's casual appearance was deceptive; his jeans were pressed with front creases and he wore a crisp shirt under the jacket. As though he would have been more at home in an army uniform.

'Mrs Jeffries's family want to take a case to the Chartered

Society of Physiotherapy. Not because she passed away. Mr Winter's not accused of helping her to die. But the family are concerned about the treatment given the afternoon you were there.'

At that last sentence, Neen watched me carefully.

The afternoon I was there. I should not have been if those were her last hours. I should certainly not have been wound like a doll and made to perform.

Neen added: 'The relatives are worried about medical misconduct. So can you tell me, in your own words, what happened?'

What happened? I didn't have much of it myself. I had a whirlwind of Ruhul and Gene, much too uncomfortable. The poor fading woman had hardly existed in the room for me. What did I say in front of her?

Misconduct, was that what they were calling it? The word seemed unequal to the shame. God.

But that explained why the other hypnotists were saying they'd been warned off.

Neen was looking at me, his pen poised.

'I'm sorry. I can't remember very much. I was hypnotised.'

A statement that was mostly – mercifully – true.

Neen smiled. His front teeth, upper and lower, were very white. The rest were greyer, like old underwear.

'Let me ask some questions. You were present with Mr Winter when he carried out the treatment in question?'

I folded my arms. 'Well, obviously. Why don't you find him?'

And when you do, give him a kick from me.

'We're aware that Mr Winter isn't contactable. I'm following up peripheral leads. The nurses filled me in on the reminiscence project, and Mr Winter's role. And the pain treatments.'

'It seems you know all about it.'

'It's always the way that the more people you talk to, the more you find out.' Neen looked down at the fingernails of his left hand. With his right thumbnail he began to clean under each one. As if they were good places to find information.

'The nurses said you were brought in for only one therapy

session. And from what I've heard you were up to something rather curious with Mr Winter yourself.'

He unfolded a piece of paper from the writing case and passed it to me.

It was a printout from Willa's website. The 'difficult minority', discussing Andreq. *Who is Carol Lear? What is this spirit? Has anyone else used him? When is he from? Doesn't she have guidance? Isn't anyone going to do something?*

When I'd seen it before there were three pages. Now it was eight. Eight pages. Still fulminating like Disgusted of Tunbridge Wells.

I handed the printout back, saying nothing.

Neen scratched behind his ear with the end of a pen. 'You must have guts to do a thing like that. I'd never get to sleep at night.'

His technique was like the sea. Push up the beach, slide back, push up again with the question in a slightly different way. Take away a little more each time. Now he was trying to flatter me into talking.

'Don't believe everything you read on the internet,' I said.

'Quite right, Ms Lear. There are better sources than the internet. Vellonoweth's a small place. The spiritualists are a close community. And that is why Mrs Jeffries's family are so concerned. They are devout Christians. If Gene Winter has a history of contacting the spirits of the departed, and he's imposed this practice on their grandmother, it's gross misconduct.'

Misconduct. I felt that complicated twinge again.

Neen's instincts were right. This case had more depths than his slimy brain would ever appreciate.

Where was Gene? Why was I taking the flak? I shouldn't defend him. I should throw him to the Christians. In fact, I'd pay to watch.

But there was something so dislikeable about Neen. To him, this was nothing more than information. To me, it was hard earned and private. He had no right to it.

Crisply, I said: 'Mrs Jeffries asked for the treatment. Gene was trying to help her. He said the morphine wasn't working any more.'

Neen looked at me pityingly. 'Why protect him, love? He's deserted you.'

Love. A word so carefully deployed. One minute: bad cop. The next: slushy cop with a hug and a hanky. Very sneaky.

I stayed totally still. 'Oh?'

'Look, love; I'm sorry. I can see you're having a rough time. And so are Mrs Jeffries's family. They are worried about what Mrs Jeffries has been exposed to. You have your sessions recorded on tape, don't you?'

How could he know that? I pressed my lips together.

Neen walked his fingers through his notebook. 'The nurse remembers a tape recorder. And –'

He dug into his pocket and pulled out a supermarket bag. Unrolled it and, holding it open by the handles, peered in. A fastidious movement, as though he didn't want to touch the object for fear of adding fingerprints.

'Dictaphone microcassettes, pack of three. Why don't you use digital?'

He'd grubbed through the bin. And probably made his other assumptions from what he found there.

I stood up. 'Get out or I'll call the police.'

'By law you no longer have any right to something you throw away.' A statement he had clearly used many times before.

I stood up. 'I have nothing more to say to you.'

I opened the door, but Neen packed up his pen and writing case thoughtfully, as though he was the one concluding the interview. He put the bag of 'evidence' back into his pocket.

'It would really help if I could hear those tapes. Set everyone's mind at rest. Just the one that involved Mrs Jeffries would be perfect.'

A smile. Close up, I could see even more clearly the difference between his white front teeth and the true ones behind. Some of them had tiny cracks like old china.

'No.'

'It's not for my benefit, or for Mr Winter's. Although you may not care what happens to him. Anyway, don't hesitate to call if anything else occurs to you. You've got my number.'

'Goodbye,' I said.

Outside, it was raining heavily. Water turned the flagstones on the path into a lake. 'I'll be in touch,' said Neen, and splashed to his car.

Maybe by the time he tried I'd be back in London.

I closed the door. Looked at the neat room. Glad to have ejected the disagreeable man.

Misconduct, he'd said. That old lady, struggling to make peace with her coming death. What had she heard?

One thing was sure. I'd stayed in Vellonoweth way too long. I went up to the bedroom, pulled my two bags out of the wardrobe and threw them on the bed.

The seven tapes were laid out on the duvet. I swept them together and put them in a bag. The envelope too, with Gene's writing in capitals, hiding himself so deliberately. It caught me, the way he could with a pause or a look or a word.

Damn him for this sordid mess.

This was over. It was time to straighten the cottage, get in the car and go.

CHAPTER 62

Forty-five minutes and my possessions were removed. Cushions were straightened. Washing-up put away. Bed made with clean sheets. Lounge hoovered. On my purge I found a book I'd borrowed from Eleanor. I would have to return that. I'd ask her if she could take over the cat until Jenny came back.

Rain was coming down in thick sheets. I borrowed one of Jenny's coats. Cars swished along the main road, headlights on, wipers sweeping at double time. Eleanor's white cottage stood out gleaming against the furious sky. I gripped the knocker and rapped.

The bolts were drawn and the door opened.

'My dear, what a day to be out.' She swept her arm backwards to pull me in.

Once inside I handed over her book, heavily wrapped. 'I can't stay long. I have to go back to London. I just came to give you this.'

She blinked, startled. 'You're going right now?'

'If my car will oblige. It might not like the weather.'

'You're mad to drive in this. At least have a cup of tea until it blows over. It's supposed to brighten up in an hour.'

Her court shoes tapped away into the kitchen and she put the kettle on.

Could I cope with talking? I couldn't be good company, I had too much in my head.

I took off the dripping coat and arranged it on a hangar. On the hall stand was a card with the hospital crest. An appointment, for a fortnight ago, with the physiotherapist Mr Winter.

That evening came back to me; when he told Eleanor he was adopted and his family called him Gene because of that. Complete baloney to make her believe in his curing powers.

I went through to the lounge, found a chair and sat down.

Or was that story lies? Was I the one who got the lies?

Eleanor talked to me from the kitchen. 'Where are you going? What are you going to do?'

'Carol? You fell asleep.'

Eleanor was sitting beside me. Her eyebrows framed the question.

I sat up. 'I'm sorry. I haven't been sleeping well. A few things have happened.' I shook myself, mortified. To lapse like that in front of such a queenly figure.

'You're going to drive up the motorway in this state, in this weather?' Eleanor rose from the sofa and went back to the kitchen.

Cupboards banged. 'I expect you're like me,' she called. 'Sometimes you need a bit of help.'

She returned and placed a brown medicine bottle on the coffee table.

It rattled as I picked it up. What was it, Pro Plus? Amphetamines? No; Valium.

I heard a metallic jingle. She had her car keys in her hand. 'I'm going to drive you home. You take a couple of those and get some sleep.'

She put on a rain hat with a big floppy brim and we dashed out to her silver car. Under our feet, the pavement was running with water.

As I put my seatbelt on Eleanor unhooked the chain from her driving mirror and put it into my hand. I'd thought it was a St Christopher. It was a locket, antique with a filigree metal border and an intricate chain like seaman's rope.

'Put that on,' she said, and executed a swift three-point turn.

I put the locket over my head, pulled my hair free of the chain. Inside was a tiny black and white portrait of a man in a hood surrounded by snowy fur. His face was dark with sun exposure.

'That's Ronald Lear,' said Eleanor, black gloved hands working the wheel. 'I think you need someone to look after you. Post him back when you get where you're going.'

I unlocked the cottage door. Back in its four walls with Ronald Lear's picture in a locket around my neck and a bottle of Valium in my hand.

I changed, put my soaked jeans and boots to dry on the boiler and inspected the bottle of Valium.

Diazepam. Do not drive or operate machinery. They were pink tablets. I shook out two and swallowed them. Sat on the sofa, wondering, what next.

There was a music manuscript book on the coffee table. That belonged on the sideboard.

I should replace it. But next to it was my bag with the tapes.

I don't know how long I stared before I unwrapped the tapes and removed the first. Then the Dictaphone.

I placed it on the table, connected the headphones. My hands were trembling. Valium not working very well, perhaps. I flipped up the cassette door, slotted the tape in and pressed Play.

The wheels spun in the little window, snagged the tape and the headphones came alive. Then Gene's voice began.

The room became bubbles, then dissolved.

Chapter 63

8

'*Squeeze the trigger* and remember the gun will kick,' says Ruhul.

I tighten my grip on the butt. The gun is much heavier than I thought. The bullet shrieks out before I'm ready. The recoil flings my arm up like a rag.

A white star bursts across the far wall. About a foot away from the red cross we'd painted as the target.

Ruhul folds his arms and looks unimpressed. 'Hmmm. You'd better leave the gun stuff to me.'

One final time we check our kit: water packs, insulating clothes and guns in holsters.

We're jumping ship for a more soothing life. We have a route planned through the old passageways of the station to the sand vehicles outside. And a gun each to give us the authority to escape with no trouble.

At least, Ruhul's will.

After that, we see where we get to. Perhaps somewhere blue.

The slanted dune has now claimed half the apartment. We close the door on it for the last time.

Ruhul listens, checks along the corridor, then leads the way to a service door.

Inside is a glass shaft, infinitely tall to the air far above. The other way goes infinitely down, to the long-abandoned roots of the station. Pipes run up the side. It smells hot.

Ruhul whispers. 'Silence from now.' In the narrow walls his voice is a desiccated echo. He steps onto a pipe and starts to climb.

I follow. Sand grinds under my palms. Slips under my feet. I watch Ruhul place his feet and hands, choose the same holds. The gun thumps against my hip.

Further up, the walls are cracked like eggshell. Our weight

on the pipes pulls the cracks further open. Sand hisses past us.

We reach a steel door. Into another shaft. Hand over hand; palms sore from sand.

The pipes are very hot; it must be near the surface.

Another hatch and we come into a room, which is humming with power.

Ruhul's face and hands are fawn suede. He pulls his gun out, goes to the door and checks outside.

I touch him on the shoulder. 'I thought we'd come out at the vehicles.'

'Something to show you first. Quick.'

He takes my hand and draws me into the middle of the room. There is a metal dome, held shut with clamps. He gives me a purposeful look and releases them.

I put my hand on the lid to stop him. 'What is it?'

'This is what stole your life. This is the heartbeat of the station. The core of xeching.' He hauls the lid open.

The core of xeching.

I feel slowed as I look at it. It's so simple. There are wires and metal boxes and in the middle of it a cylinder, about the diameter of my wrist. Inside that is a circle of vibrating buds like the stamens of a flower.

There it is quivering like a giggle, pumping out an electrical trick that travels down to the sea.

Ruhul thrusts his hand inside. 'Quick. We've got about a minute before they're in here with guns and all that. This is my gift to you.'

He pulls the cylinder out.

The casing starts to hum. An alarm like a snare drum starts to beat.

He puts the cylinder into my hand.

It doesn't weigh very much, this device. Even though it is a wedge between me and all the people I have known. It is no larger than my palm but it's a veil of shame that has made everyone hide me.

Ruhul moves to the door, glances out, then back at me.

'Come on. All your life you've been trying to keep up with it and it's just a bit of junk. Now you can stop feeling like you failed. Smash it.'

The alarm continues to beat. From far off I can hear shouts, footfalls.

Ruhul strides back towards me. 'I'll do it.'

I pull away. 'No. Don't.'

I need time. This can't be settled so quickly.

'We'll have the conversation about it later. Give it to me.'

The footsteps are not a faint patter any more. They are brighter. Louder. Still, I can't move.

'All right, you do it,' say Ruhul. 'But do it now. This is everything you've told me. Those special tutors, wicked doctors. Treatments that mean you can't sleep. Games you couldn't join in with other kids. The reason your family got rid of you. It's why every single day you've had to hide.'

'Yes it is.'

'Then destroy it. Then you'll be free.'

I can't. 'That's not the answer.'

He spreads his hands, impatient. 'Andreq, this is no time for soothing rubbish. Give it to me.' He strides back towards me.

I pull it away from him. 'No.' I look at it in my hand. 'If I smash this, it's still ruling me. I've got to make peace with it.'

Four more guns are suddenly in the room.

The guards have crept in like shadows. Their expressions are as still and deliberate as the weapons that are now watching us.

Ruhul's gun is down, exasperated with me. And now we've run out of time.

There is nowhere to go.

I lift my gun and point it deliberately at Ruhul.

The guards understand. I have the xech device in my hand. Ruhul, on patrol, heard the alarm first. He came in to stop me, but I was faster with my gun. I'm sure it's obvious.

I try to make my gun look steady.

In Ruhul's throat, a pulse flutters a response. I think he wants to shoot them, but there are four of them and two of us.

One, really, because if I fire who knows what I'll hit.

One of the guards takes his arm and pulls him back. He can step back into his guard role and no one will know.

As he slots into their line, a bead of sweat trickles over his collarbone and into his shirt. On his arm, the pores show pinpricks of bright colour. The ghost of warpaint drawn on his skin in a wavy line.

A guard steps up and snatches the xech device from my hand.

He backs away.

The guns around us stiffen.

'Let him go,' says Ruhul, but that won't stop them now.

I spin and run for the hatch. The bullets follow. I dive in. The only way is down, climbing fast.

Walls split and crack. Sand rains on me, loaded with glass spears.

A sudden blaze of fire across my chest. Then immense, oily warmth that keeps coming, like it's swelling from the centre of the earth. Sand arrives in a helpful cover.

I carry on down. My head gets lighter, as though it's made of air. I start to race the sand down the glass chimney. I've let go.

I'm falling as swiftly as the grains raining from the walls and roaring in my ears.

How far is it to the bottom? Perhaps there's time for a rest.

It's quite dark now. I must have gone a long way. The only things I know are black, and the rain of sand that travels with me.

There is dark, and there is sand. Dark and sand.

Dark and sand.

Dark. And dark.

Dark.

CHAPTER 64

The dark lifted. I came back to the sofa. But I was falling.

I gripped the arms of the sofa, tried to stop it. That did no good. The whole room was a lift, its cable snapped, plummeting down.

Must stop. I reached for the tablet bottle, knocked it over. Hoped I could stop it sliding into the swallowing sky. Shook out two pink pills and clung on. Let Valium handle the brakes.

We slowed, the room and I. We eventually stopped.

A manuscript book was on the coffee table, sprawled with writing.

My phone was beside it. I picked it up and started a text.

Andreq died. Dropping forever into the sand. So quiet, tho, not like you said. None of the screaming. Blessings to the other side.

I sent it to Gene.

It failed. He was unreachable. Silly me, never mind. I sent it to Jerry.

Damn this Valium. I needed to think but I couldn't grip anything. It just gave me slippery loops.

Rain was lashing against the window. Wind was frisking the trees. I put Radio Active on. It was playing American ballads, with warnings about a storm. I turned it off and tried the TV instead.

I awoke. The room was dark. The TV was showing the snow of an empty signal. That blank eye stared at me, sucking the air from the room, hissing of nowhere, letting go and vanishing into the dark. *And dark.*

In moments I was in the kitchen, fingers groping the tiled splashback for the lights.

The clock on the oven said two in the morning. My phone

was by the kettle. I tried another text to Jerry. There was no signal.

I walked to the window, up the stairs, commanding the signal bar to swell. Come on, let me reach Jerry. Don't keep me in this dark where no one can hear me.

Into the bedroom, the phone held out, trying to catch a cobweb of connection.

When Jerry thought he was dying at the hands of the Ripper, what did he feel like? *They hardly remember what went on,* Gene had said, *just a bit of cathartic sensation and it's gone, like giving birth. They don't know how bad it was.*

But much better to be Jerry than Ruby. Ruby didn't stand a chance.

Letting go, into the dark. Everything folding in, alone.

Was this what Jerry's panic attacks were like?

The Valium returned and put it at a distance; *que sera sera*.

I drifted downstairs again. I pulled two sweaters out of my bag, put on a big coat of Jenny's and went out.

An object like a mortar board was in the drive. The satellite dish, blown off by the storm. That must have blanked out the TV.

Fear levels returning to normal.

I put it inside the house, then walked up the hill. In a lay-by on the main road to Nowethland, I trapped a signal.

Jerry's phone was on voicemail. Of course. It was his birthday. It was two in the morning. He was probably nesting somewhere with Tim.

It started to snow. A fine dusting of white had settled on the black pavement, frosted the hedges and trees. I stayed out there. I liked the way it made the night benevolent and pale.

Gene had left me his trouble – and now his sleeplessness.

CHAPTER 65

I did eventually return to the cottage and sleep. I woke at ten.

The sky was heavy and grey, and I could feel the bitter chill even inside the cottage.

No, that chill wasn't from outside. There was something waiting to be remembered.

I had a sudden feeling, big as a nuclear explosion, suspended into infinity like the instant of a high-speed collision. Then felt like I was looking into the distance, not sure what I was trying to find.

Oh yes. Andreq died. People needed to know.

My phone was there. I wrote a text. I sent it to Jerry.

Then I saw I'd sent it already. The previous night.

I hauled myself out of bed and into the shower.

As I dressed, I brought myself back into the world with Radio Active. A programme about birdsong, interspersed with warnings about gale-force winds. They said not to drive, but maybe I could get far enough up the A303 to escape before it hit. Or I could stop somewhere.

I took the car to get petrol and made a stop at Sally's shop to get Jenny a replacement manuscript book. As I pushed open the door, I cocked my head for the Clavinova being tenderised. All was strangely quiet.

'Kitty and Eleanor are playing for the old folks' home today,' said Sally, spreading packs of guitar strings in a fan on the counter.

I bought the manuscript book and left.

Back outside the shop, the sky was darkening as if the day was closing down. I drove up to the cottage again and wrote final notes and instructions. A page for Eleanor about the cat. A note for Jenny with an explanation about her satellite dish, with date and time for insurance questions. The empty Valium bottle went in the bin. I sliced my pages out of Jenny's manuscript book and opened my overnight bag.

I must have been in a Valium gap when I packed. My kimono was on top, which I don't normally do because the embroidery snags in the zip. My bath bag was jeopardising two novels with oozing shampoo. I lifted everything out and repacked.

The Andreq material, which I'd had wrapped in a bag from a music shop in London, wasn't there.

It wasn't in the bigger clothes bag either. What a thing to forget.

I hadn't put them in the cupboards, or under the cushions, in the car, left them in the bathroom, stashed them inexplicably in the violin case or the empty washing machine. I hadn't sneaked them among Jenny's CDs or her regular-sized tapes.

I looked around the room, wondering where else to try. A shape caught my eye on the Oriental rug, beside the frilled skirt of the sofa.

It looked like a penknife or a cigarette lighter, although I didn't remember Jenny having anything like that. And I'd moved the sofa earlier as I'd hoovered. I picked it up.

There was a switch on it. I pressed it.

Out of the black handle sprang a vicious blade. I nearly dropped it. I stood looking at it in my hand; a curved edge of metal, one edge serrated and tapering to a daggerlike point.

My tapes had gone, and whoever had taken them had been carrying a flick knife.

CHAPTER 66

Colin Neen's business card was in the bin, under this morning's cat food wrapper and a suppurating teabag.

I called him. 'I'm getting the police unless you return those tapes right now.'

'Didn't I tell you yesterday, love? The trash in your bin no longer belongs to you.'

'Don't bullshit me. And I'm taking the knife to the police too.'

'Whoa, back up. Today I've been at the Acorns Nursing Home and the hospital in Vellonoweth. What's happened?'

Neen flicked the knife-blade in and out, looking at it thoughtfully. He'd arrived like an emergency service, less than five minutes after I spoke to him.

He closed the knife and put it down. 'It's illegal to carry these in public or outside the home. I'd say your visitor was a young male, possibly a gang of them because they like to swagger a bit with their tools. And it's obvious they didn't break in. Did you leave the door unlocked?'

I folded my arms. 'I live in London. I'm OCD about locking doors.'

'And the tapes have gone? Are you sure you haven't mislaid them?'

'I wouldn't mislay them.'

His smile went beyond the teeth that were capped and showed the marbled, yellow ones. 'People mislay all sorts of things. Diamond rings, passports.'

'I didn't mislay them.'

'Right, so who else has a key? Your neighbour?'

'I hope not,' I said.

Outside, Jean Dowman slammed her front door.

'Wait there,' said Neen.

Neen went out, hands in pockets, making a kangaroo pouch of his blouson jacket. Called to Jean Dowman, who was getting in her car.

Whatever question he had asked her, she answered in a shrill voice.

'She's playing with black magic. In my friend's house. You've no idea what it's like living next door to that kind of thing. I heard her screaming last night. I called Jenny's cousin. Her sons came and took it away.'

I watched from the door. Jean spat the words straight through Neen as though she was really aiming at me.

Neen asked the questions I wasn't calm enough to, as if a sensible part of my brain was operating him by remote control.

'What did they take away?'

'The tapes she records that thing on.'

'Where has she taken them?'

'I'm not going to tell you. It's gone now. Good riddance.' Jean slammed herself into the car, started the engine, wrenched through the gears and drove away.

Good riddance. How dare she.

Neen came back in. 'You've certainly made some friends while you've been here.'

'That's theft, isn't it?' I said. 'They came in and took my property.'

He looked around the room. 'Let's find this cousin. Where's the phone?'

'In the kitchen.'

He went through. I followed. 'Address book?' he said.

'Don't know.'

He took the phone off the wall. 'Who's on speed dial?'

I shrugged. I hadn't had to use it.

He pressed the first button. I heard a crisp voice. 'Veterinary practice?'

'Sorry,' Neen called into the mouthpiece as though it was a walkie-talkie.

Preset two yielded the doctor, despatched with equal

abruptness. Three was an answerphone. Neen listened: 'Who's Felicity?'

'Jenny's sister.'

Preset four was an answerphone too. Neen held the receiver out to me. 'You've reached Freda, John, James and Thomas Worth. We can't answer your call but please leave a message. God be with you.'

'James and Thomas,' repeated Neen. 'I wonder how old they are.'

Freda Worth. My yelling pupil with atrocious breathing. Why was she on Jenny's presets?

Neen tried preset five. It waited before connecting, and gave a foreign-sounding ringtone. 'Spain,' said Neen, and put the phone down. 'And that's the lot. Vet, doctor, and three private numbers.'

Neen poked the pile of post I'd left by the phone and looked at a catalogue. 'Arthritis nutraceuticals. Interesting.' His tone suggested he felt he'd now grasped the essential nature of Jenny from just these observations. I wished I didn't need his help.

I remembered. 'Freda Worth is the one we want,' I said. 'She's allowed to sing in the Ixendon festival because she's Felicity's cousin.'

'Good,' said Neen, and opened a cupboard. It contained mugs. Not what he wanted so he moved onto the next. He carried on, leaving doors and drawers open like a looting burglar, until he found telephone directories. He found W, scribbled an address and started for the door.

I beat him there. 'I'm coming.'

He checked his phone for messages and put it in his pocket. 'It's business, love. And there are people with knives.'

Everything was material for him to gobble or discard. Not my tapes. I folded my arms. 'I might have remembered something. I could tell you in the car.'

His car was a blue Toyota, with a smooth-hoovered interior

and an air freshener on a cardboard tree. I imagined him getting identity tags out of the glove compartment and pretending to be a taxi.

He revved like a boy racer, swung the car up the hill in the direction of Nowethland, then settled to a cruise speed, guiding the steering wheel with one nominal finger.

'You realise, of course, that I am in the employ of the Jeffries family. They are paying for information I find in the course of my investigations.'

'I am aware of that.'

I looked out of the window and tried to ignore him.

'I get the impression you think I will be shocked by all this business. Let me tell you that you wouldn't believe the things I've seen people do. I've never seen a normal, boring person who doesn't have a secret. A vice, a minor criminal conviction, a fraud, an addiction. Nothing surprises you after a while.'

He said it boastfully, as though this wealth of experience gave him gravitas and wisdom. I looked out at the rain, turning a barren field into Flanders mud.

'So you can tell me anything you like about Robert Winter and it won't shock me.'

Robert.

Neen's eyes flicked from me to the road and to me again, while his lazy finger toyed with the steering wheel. He was smiling just enough to hide the old underwear teeth.

Waiting for me to ask.

'Robert?' I said, hating to give him the satisfaction.

'That's right. Robert Gene Winter. He started using the name Gene in the sixth form.'

How did Neen know a thing like that? Not the Robert part; it wasn't hard to discover somebody's proper name if you were hobnobbing with their employers. But to know when they switched their first names? That took investigation to an indecent level. Was there anything that wasn't irrelevant to this man?

Robert Winter. I couldn't blame Gene for swapping. The holocaust name was much more exciting.

A corner and a gap in the hills gave us a brief view of Nowethland, a fan of red and grey roofs in the darkening afternoon, beaded with orange streetlamps.

'You know,' said Neen, 'some of the most bizarre cases I've seen have involved doctors. They get a God complex. And then they've got access to all these drugs –' He finished the sentence in a whistle.

'Gene's not a doctor. I think you need to get your facts straight.'

'Oh yes, I remember. Not a proper doctor.'

Was the rudeness deliberate, to bait me? Sorry, detective, that's too obvious.

'I looked at his CV at the hospital,' said Neen. 'He did research on pain. I found one of his papers. "Humans are infinitely sensitive to pain," he wrote. "The richer our inner lives, the more varieties of pain we can feel." I'd no idea these doctors were so poetic. They're usually too busy to even look at you when you go see them.'

A pause. What did he expect me to say?

Neen added: 'He published as Robert Winter. You'd never have found it, love. '

I looked out of the window, at the trees bending under the wind as the sky turned dark. Neen didn't deserve my reaction.

'Arrogant too,' continued Neen. 'One of his pet subjects was curing the incurable.' His voice dropped into slushy cop. 'Did it work, then?'

I kept my eyes on my tilted reflection in the wing mirror.

'And he was bedding you. The Chartered Society don't like that.'

'I wasn't his patient.'

'No, he was imposing treatment on you and abusing his position. A very murky area. So have you remembered anything about him or did you just want to come out for a gossip about your squeeze?'

I focussed on the vehicles going by with dipped headlights. To try to erase this man from the car.

Neen drove on, one-fingered. After a moment he spoke

again. Still slushy cop. 'Sorry, love. It's hard the first day you come off them, isn't it?'

He took his hand off the gear lever, grappled in his pocket and threw something onto my lap. The empty Valium bottle.

'He didn't get those for you, did he?'

The label read *Lear. Valium 5mg.*

I smiled. Allowed myself a small victory.

'Those tapes will be very informative,' said Neen. 'I am very much looking forward to hearing them.'

In the side mirror, my eyes tell him No.

CHAPTER 67

In a street of semi-detached gabled houses, Freda Worth's was conspicuous by the police car parked in the drive.

'So why are Plod here,' mused Neen.

We cruised past. He parked further down the road, zipped his jacket to the top and took a pack of Dunhills from a compartment behind the handbrake. 'You can come too. You'll be good cover.'

I'm coming regardless, I thought, and slammed the door. I followed him across the road and into an alleyway between the houses. The wind pinned my coat to my legs like a heavy sheet. I put my hand in my pocket, grasping my keys so the shanks poked between my fingers like claws. It hurt but I did it anyway. I should have brought the flick-knife.

Although I'd probably be as useless with it as Andreq was with a gun. And not as brave. Oh my heavens, not at all.

In the alleyway was a wheelie bin. I spotted it just as Neen lifted the lid.

I raced up to him, key-claws ready in my pocket.

'Empty, love,' he said, and left the lid up for me to see. A black interior smelling of rotten vegetables, a few sticky onion skins.

Neen held a cigarette out to me.

'I don't smoke.'

'I don't either but it's the best excuse for why we're here.' A show of white teeth and their grey companions. 'The alternative is smooching.'

How he liked to wallow in the subterfuges of his trade. He lit up, but didn't smoke the cigarette, just stood with it burning down between his fingers.

A gutter poured water from the roof in a fat stream. The smell of the cigarette made me think of a quieter night, sitting at an open window with Gene. Now I was skulking outside a house with a tawdry detective, trying to reclaim the only thing that remained of that.

I looked at my watch. It was now three hours since the tapes went missing. Perhaps they were in a bin somewhere, disinfected with holy water. Or hammered to smithereens.

That wasn't as bad as imagining the alternative. Someone inspecting the labels written in that deliberately undisclosing hand. Assessing the sorcery in Gene's voice and the depths in my altered one. I hadn't even shared those later tapes with Jerry. They weren't for anyone else to hear.

On the opposite side of the road, the wind tried to split a hedge into its separate trees. Freda's green front door remained firmly closed. With its mock-antique coach lamp it looked like a cheap Christmas card.

Finally the door opened. Neen started a new cigarette and puffed with purpose. One eye was on the two policemen, who were talking over their shoulders to someone who stood out of sight in the doorway.

'I'm afraid there isn't much we can do, Mrs Worth. Black magic may be distasteful but it's not against the law. But if you have evidence of an actual crime such as someone being hurt, we'll step in.'

Freda Worth said a grudging, disappointed goodbye and shut her front door.

Neen dropped his cigarette and squashed it with his boot.

'Unless I'm mistaken,' he said quietly, 'our Mrs Worth is not reassured by Plod. She might like to talk to someone who is more willing to listen.'

He walked around the corner.

I didn't want him to see her on his own. But if I was there too, Freda would never talk.

The next instant he darted back and flattened himself against the wall. He put his arm out, warning me not to move.

The Yale lock clicked open. Two youngish-looking men came out of the house in fur-hooded parkas.

One of them had a bag. A white plastic bag with a design of a piano keyboard in black. From a music shop in London.

Those were my tapes.

Neen pulled me back. 'No, love, they've got knives. We can pick a better time.'

The boys climbed into a white van. It started in a fog of exhaust. A quick three-point turn and they accelerated away. The van had a name on it: *Worth Builders and Decorators.*

We sprinted to the car. Neen did a U-turn while pulling on his seat belt, swerved around a car nosing out of a turning, and settled into a cruising position behind the van's lettered doors. We followed it along the main road, past the last amber street lamps and into the dark zone of the hills.

'So,' said Neen, 'the police were called to sort out a case of black magic. That's a bit of an extreme reaction to a few tapes.'

'Some people,' I said, and shrugged.

Neen's phone warbled. He pulled it out of his pocket and glanced at the bright screen.

What he saw there made his face crease into a big smile. 'Ah, good girl,' he said, then flicked a glance at me. 'Hold tight.'

He gripped the steering wheel, accelerated and tried to nip around the van.

'What are you doing?' I said.

The white van surged possessively into the middle of the road. Neen dropped back.

'Bolshy little bastard.'

Judging by his grin, that seemed to be exactly the reaction he wanted. He jabbed the accelerator and made another bid to pass. The van swerved and blocked again.

'Have you gone mad? They'll know we're here.'

'That's the idea.'

Neen pushed his bumper up close to the van as though his car was coupled to it like a train carriage. And he didn't pull back. We screamed along the middle of the road, twisting between hedges and around blind corners. I gripped the seat, waiting for an obliterating smash. Then Neen conceded defeat and tucked behind.

The van slowed and returned to its proper side of the road.

I let go. 'So what was all that for?'

Neen sat back and returned to his customary one-fingered steering. 'Now he thinks he's won a race. He'll be happy to keep us in his rear-view mirror and won't notice we're following.'

Neen took the phone off his lap and slotted it into a holder on the dashboard. 'Which gives us time for this.'

The phone screen showed an icon for an audio file. Neen tapped it and it began to play.

A voice started.

'You're relaxed, drifting in a pleasant place with no worries.'

I jumped as though a spider had landed on me. Those vowels; slightly northern on 'worries'.

It was Gene.

I looked at Neen. 'What's this?'

'It's the treatment you and Mr Winter gave to Mrs Jeffries. A nurse recorded it on her phone after she gave Mrs Jeffries her morphine. Seems she had a bit of a grudge. Wanted Mr Winter to do her instead. You can always rely on the woman scorned.'

I reached to snatch the phone. Neen put a hand out to stop me. 'Be a good sport, love. Everyone needs to hear.'

CHAPTER 68

Neen glanced at the white van, cruising steadily in front of us. But most of his attention was on the iPhone screen.

I sat in my seat as still as a pinned butterfly. Dreading what I would hear.

The tiny speaker made Gene's voice lighter.

'Let yourself sink into the chair. Everything falls away. Everything that has happened today. There will be no pain, no worry.'

It was curious how cautious he sounded. Compared with his usual style it was as though he was reading from a textbook. He didn't usually say *No pain*.

He must have been hypnotising Mrs Jeffries as well.

Then he said my name. He didn't usually do that.

'Carol, listen to me. Get up, take ten steps across the room and remove the curtain.'

Beside me, Neen licked his lips and swallowed.

I didn't dare move.

On the recording there was a sound like a chair moving. Then footsteps, something bumping against chairs. A heavy curtain landing on the floor.

Then another sound.

Metallic.

It was the yawn a piano makes when you open it.

Such a tiny noise, but I always knew it. And the shiver as you rest the raised lid on the front panel.

Sitting in Neen's car, I felt cold prickle through my entire body.

On the recording, Gene's voice drifted in, kind as an angel. 'After this you will feel no pain.'

I began to play the piano. Without a single note written in front of me. Just what was happening in my head and heart.

The music was thinned by the iPhone's speaker, but I fell

into it. It was Ruhul and Andreq, scraping away at a mural, companionably addicted. Coveting each other in looks and abandoned sentences. Daring to begin it with a hand on a hand. Spinning together in relief. All said in slow, soaring music, like a score for a ballet.

I looked away from the blue display and squeezed my fists into my eyes. Outside the car, the wind was rocking the hedges, hurling twigs across the road. Like the slow cyclone that seemed to be consuming my insides.

Gene had made me play. The regression I was so worried about was hidden in music, but damn him, he had made me play.

How had it happened? How had he concealed a piano from me?

Neen pressed stop. 'You just played music? Was that all?'

'Seems so.'

'I thought you couldn't play.'

No pain, Gene had said, at the beginning. Or was that for Mrs Jeffries?

'I paid for it later,' I said. 'Still am.' That explained why I'd had to mainline Nurofen ever since. I thought it was stress.

I had a sudden, appalling thought and turned to Neen. 'Did Mrs Jeffries die peacefully?'

'She did. She slipped into a morphine coma shortly after Mr Winter left.'

He'd said the morphine hadn't been working before. 'So he did help her.'

'Well, she was drugged.'

I remembered as Gene led me into the room. I was so nervous about the fragile state of that morphinated lady. I was watching him because he knew what to do. There could have been an entire orchestra in the room, dressed as elephants, and I would only have seen him and her.

The way he started. Was he talking to her, and at the same time cueing me to be careful? Maybe he didn't dare let me do a proper regression in case it scared Mrs Jeffries. So he sent me to the piano to say it all there.

Just as well. Or maybe it was what allowed me to really talk.

The night opened out in amber streetlights. We'd reached Vellonoweth. The white van glided through the precinct, past the Assembly rooms and the Railway Hotel, past the stacked towers of the hospital, then on again into the dark moors.

I asked: 'Have you got headphones?'

Neen handed me a white tangle.

I plugged them in and ran the recording again.

The lady in her morphine cocoon, and anyone who was listening, heard just a piano doing its best with worn felts and sticky keys. But on the inside it was Andreq, Ruhul, me... and Gene. I remembered Gene's face when he woke me. Like a startled fox. He looked so young; about sixteen.

Why didn't he tell me I'd played? He could have, that evening. Maybe he thought he'd cured me because he told me I'd feel no pain. Perhaps that's why he took me to the piano in the warehouse.

'Are you there, love, or have you gone into a coma too?'

Neen was talking to me.

'Sorry, what did you say?'

'Just curious, but what's it like, doing that other life stuff? Must be quite morbid, being a past, already dead.'

I folded the headphones away. 'No. It's like being twice as alive.'

CHAPTER 69

The rocking hedges continued to slip past the window. In front of us, the Worths' white van vanished around a corner like a fish, reappeared as we kept up with it. I took a deep breath and then a few more, and looked at Neen.

'I suppose you don't need to find those tapes now.'

Neen gave me his half-and-half smile. 'That session wasn't what you normally did, was it?'

'I guess not.'

'The Jeffries family still need to hear what it was supposed to be. With all the fuss on the internet. They're devout Christians.'

The van swung around corners, brake lights pulsing with the dips and gullies in the road. Going onwards, into the night, on a mission with my tapes.

What else was on them? If I had no idea that I played music on that tape, what else might I not have been aware of? I'd never played beyond tape two. Were there other truths to discover if I listened to what the Dictaphone heard? How much was Gene directing what was happening? Or were all the rest exactly as I experienced them?

I was grateful for Neen's persistence. We'd negotiate later about who got to hear what.

The van turned into a side road. Its rear end suddenly seemed to tip upwards as though it had plunged into a chasm.

Neen killed the headlights.

'What are you doing?' I said.

'Neen knows what he's doing,' said the detective. With one hand on the wheel, he reached into the back seat. Brought out chunky binoculars.

'They'll smell a rat if they know we've followed them down here,' he said. 'Fortunately we have night vision.'

He nudged a switch and a red light came on. Focusing the

binoculars, he turned after the van. Into the chasm.

We passed a triangular gradient sign. *1:4. Use low gear.* Neen put the car into first gear. We jerked to a stop, as if a chain had caught the back bumper. I couldn't see the slope but I was uncomfortably aware that my feet were pressed hard into the floor. We must be nearly vertical.

We inched down. Grinding sounds came from under the car, as though the wheels were fighting to go faster. Any moment I imagined the prayer that was holding us would snap and we'd go hurtling into the pitch black.

Far below was the van, like a small red-eyed creature daring us to follow.

Neen steered one-handed, watching the view through the black cones.

Where were we going? Why had the boys come here?

I took my eyes off the van. In the far distance were lights. Not amber like a town, but lone points of red and white, a long way away and blurred by mist. Closer to, but much higher in the sky, was a strong red light.

The road levelled out. Neen eased into a looser gear and handed me the binoculars.

I put them to my eyes. A landscape sprang out of the dark, like an X-ray of the night. We were by the sea. Those lights were tiny, ghostly fishing ships, rocking on the vast, grey horizon.

I pointed the binoculars at the hovering red light. It became a tall mast, shuddering between slender cables. I followed it down to a square building like a shed on legs.

Neen was looking towards the red light as well. 'What's out there?'

I put the binoculars down. 'It's the radio station.'

His face asked the same question I had in my mind. What were we doing here?

CHAPTER 70

The road flattened out beside a derelict cottage, which was no more than a battered wall with smashed windows. There were no other buildings. It continued into the sea, a causeway of ridged concrete reaching into the spray.

The van was on the causeway, rocking through the potholes, making its way to the spike-legged building. I trained the binoculars on it and got a jumble of green images. Eyes in the wing mirror, with pupils of white like a nocturnal hunting animal. A stripe leading down a sleeve. Hands in fingerless woollen gloves. A flick knife, the blade jacking in and out, limbering up.

'They've still got a knife,' I said, in a voice that didn't quite work properly.

Neen took the binoculars and looked. 'Probably just posing with it.' He cut the engine. 'I don't think the car will make it across. We'd better go on foot.'

When I tried to get out, the wind held my door closed. On a second push I climbed out into a salty, sleety gale.

Behind, a cliff rose up, a bulk disappearing into the black night.

Neen was looking at the red light on the radio mast. 'What kind of programmes do they make here?' he said.

'Some very weird shit, unfortunately. Whalesong and Himalayan chants.'

'Blimey,' said Neen, and set off splashing.

Once again I was grateful for his persistence. I didn't care about the reason for it.

Neen played the torch on the ridged concrete. One moment we could hardly run fast enough to keep up with the pushing wind. The next it stopped us like the end of a rope. Spray stung my face, the narrow line of exposed skin on my wrists where I couldn't get my hands all the way into my pockets.

We reached the building, got into shelter behind the Worths' white van. The wind vibrated through its metal sides like dull thunder.

'The Jeffries family must be paying you danger money,' I said.

Neen pulled something out of his pocket and offered it to me. His keys. 'Go back to the car. I'll take it from here.'

I shook my head.

Neen pocketed the keys again. 'He's not worth it, you know.'

Several other vehicles were parked beside the Worths' van. Land Rovers, scoured clean by the sea spray; another van.

Above us, the old fort shuddered on metal stilts. The buildings started on a platform about twenty feet above, a cliff of corrugated iron rising in corduroy stripes into the black sky.

Neen and I spotted the ladder at the same time. I got my foot on it first and started to climb. Through the rungs I felt the waves lashing the legs. Neen's footfalls chopped into the ladder below me.

I came out onto a metal deck. It was swimming in water and slimy rags of seaweed, and covered with wire netting to give grip. The radio mast rose into the sky, tethered by thick steel cables, which it seemed to be straining to break. The red light at the top was blurred and shaking. The struts made strange singing noises. Down below, the sea crashed and boomed.

A light illuminated a small door, like a hatchway in a ship. We ran to it, opened it. A young guy in a Kangol hat and skinny fleece came running up the steps. 'Can I help you?' His tone said, stop right there.

'We're here with James Worth,' said Neen.

The guy turned. We followed him down. Behind us, the door swung shut, sealing out the roaring wind. Our footsteps had sound again, clattering on the metal stairs.

The whole building creaked and boomed with the thunder of the waves underneath. A tannoy was playing the radio programme very quietly. With relief I registered it was swoony ballads.

A corridor, then more stairs. 'I'm Kit. IT man. They're all in the studio. Have you been here before?'

I didn't dare open my lips. For some reason I was feeling sick.

Kit must have noticed. 'This place sways about when it's windy. Get a doughnut from the galley. It helps.'

The corridor was decorated by framed photographs of grinning people sitting at mixing desks. All of the pictures were shaking. I looked at the floor instead and the sick feeling began to ease.

Kit stopped at a door marked *Studio: Quiet please*. Inside, there were glass partitions and another inner room with microphones, speakers and other equipment in racks on the wall.

First I saw the scarlet bow tie. Then the upbrushed black hair, the silver rattlesnake bangles.

Richard Longborrow and Isabel Caswell.

Of course. To dispose of a troublesome spirit, who else would you call?

They were in the studio, talking to a fat man who was sitting at a microphone. The pouches of his cheeks rested on the cushions of a pair of padded headphones.

Neen voiced the question that was in my mind. 'Are they making a programme?'

'Copying tapes onto CD,' said Kit. 'We've got all the old equipment here, right back to U-Matic and Betamax. Can convert anything you like, audio or video.'

I looked past Isabel and Richard at the machines on the wall behind them. Banks of tiny wheels behind glass, red lights next to each pair. On the desk in front of Isabel was a row of labels, written in neat block capitals. *Andreq 5*. A row of them.

Richard and Isabel were making copies of my tapes.

Chapter 71

Kit shouted 'hey,' but I pushed in through the double doors.

The DJ was inspecting an object on the desk. It was a cast of a pair of hands in a pale substance like tallow.

'What in Jesus are these?'

'They are spirit gloves,' replied Richard Longborrow. 'My grandfather was doing a séance and spirit thrust his hands into molten wax. I always have them with me when I am contacting spirit for the first time.' He loosened his bow tie and swallowed, his chin puckering like an ostrich, then put on some headphones.

Was he scrutinising talk of bubbles in a glass? A hanging note sliding into the horizon? Wondering which of his cronies would like them?

As the second door closed behind me the sound of the sea stopped. The studio was completely silent except for the show playing at low volume.

I snatched the headphones off Richard's head, then went for the whirring tape decks.

The DJ stood up and intercepted me like a bear. 'I'm Roger and this is my show. The rule is, don't touch.'

'That's stolen property.' I said. 'You don't have permission to copy those tapes.'

Roger scratched his fat cheek. 'I'm not doing the copying. These people are hiring the facilities. I don't know what they're using them for.'

Isabel wrapped a carrier bag around a stack of CDs and secured it with parcel tape. 'Miss Lear, I was called to help with a disposal. The boys certainly seemed glad to be rid of them.' She put the package on the floor. There were several others already there.

I looked at Neen. 'Stop them. It's theft.'

Neen picked up the headphones I'd torn off Richard. 'I'm

not the police, love.' He peered at the display on the laptop. 'How do I listen to this?'

I grabbed them. 'You don't.'

Isabel looked at Neen. 'Are you interested in buying?' Whenever she moved, her hair remained a solid mass, like the head of an Easter Island statue.

Neen nodded.

Isabel replied: 'The copies will be released on the market soon. But there's a waiting list, and I'll be selective about where they go.'

Released on the market? I suddenly realised what some of the paperwork on the desk was. Scans of the newspaper article I'd kept on the north and south poles. Articles from other magazines too, with mad-looking headlines about Atlantis. Authentication for the lucky buyers?

Next to me was a bundle of red and blue power lines. I yanked them hard. Several came out and I pulled out some more. The decks stopped.

Isabel whipped round with a look of fury.

Roger sat down and his chair creaked. 'Sort yourselves out, people. I've got a show to run.' He leaned to the microphone and began to speak in a slow, deep voice.

While he smoothed the way into the next song, Isabel picked up the pulled leads and tried to make sense of them. 'I can give you ten per cent. Our overheads will be less than I thought.'

'They're not for sale. Stop this now.'

Isabel looked at the leads and then at me. 'This is the problem with you amateurs. One minute you want to keep spirit because it's your true soul. The next you're ringing up in a panic begging me to take its artefacts away. There comes a point where you have to let people deal with it properly. I've found you those people, so be a good girl and take the cut.'

Neen reached into his pocket and brought something out. A cheque book. 'You could make your first sale now, Ms Caswell.'

'Who on earth are you?' said Isabel.

'I'd like a very special deal. How much for all of them?'

Isabel looked at him as though she was a doorman at

Claridge's assessing whether to throw him out. 'You're talking big money.'

'My client will pay a competitive price,' said Neen.

'Your client?' Isabel folded her arms the other way.

Neen handed her a card. Face down, like a secret move in a game.

'Neen,' I said, 'they're not for sale.'

He wasn't paying attention to me. He was watching Isabel. She read the card and looked at it, thinking.

'Folks,' said Roger, 'it is five minutes until I load up the Slow Hours and this studio is too full. Go and find the galley, fix yourselves a coffee. And tell Kit to come in and stop the weather service crashing.' He stood up and spread his arms wide, herding us to the door.

Away from the soundproofed studio, the building shuddered above the sea. Neen said in a tight voice: 'I'm going to be sick,' and barged through a door.

I waited, trying to convince my ears not to hear his retching above the sea grumbling outside.

What should I do? First things first. Let Neen get all the copies. That was neat. Sort out everything else as it came. I felt bile rising in my throat; gripped a handle on a bulkhead.

Footsteps came down the corridor. Short-striding legs, moving at a bustling pace. Pushing the bangles up her arms. I knew without having to look up that it was Isabel.

Neen came out of the bathroom, wiping his mouth on a tissue.

Isabel held the card out. 'Ten thousand pounds.'

Neen nodded. 'For all the tapes. Exclusively.'

I stared at Neen. 'Ten thousand pounds? The Jeffries family will pay ten thousand pounds?' I said.

Neen raised an eyebrow. A gesture that said, don't be naïve. He looked back at Isabel and reached for his chequebook. 'Done.'

A slow smile spread over Isabel's features. 'A pleasure doing business with you and Anthony Morrish.'

Anthony Morrish. I barely made it through the bathroom door. I heaved my guts into a steel lavatory. The sea reverberated even more through the echoey bathroom. Something was clattering, bang, bang, against the outside wall. The floor felt like it was moving. I pressed flush and the contents of my stomach swirled away with a trickle of blue disinfectant.

As my insides calmed, I assessed my options.

They didn't have the tapes yet. The tapes were still in the studio with Richard Longborrow.

I didn't know what I'd do after I got in there, but I set off with purpose.

I turned a corner. Someone bumped into me. A boy of about sixteen, smelling of pungent aftershave and wet fabric. His soaked parka had a stripe down the arm. I followed it down and saw fingerless gloves. A memory in green told me the rest.

Fingerless gloves held a flick knife.

He was solid and bony. I tried to push through him with my elbows.

The boy yelled at the top of his lungs: 'She's here!'

I squirmed past the boy and started to sprint.

Suddenly it was dark.

CHAPTER 72

The dark was total. It took the floor and walls away.

I stumbled; no idea if my feet were on the ground or if I was suspended from the sky on a wire. I fell against a wall of cold metal like the side of a ship. Sound groaned up the steel from the sea and ended in my bones.

Where was the boy with the knife? Where did he go? He had to be groping in the dark like me; white predator eyes and a flicking blade, about to touch me, about to lash out. What if he found me, in the dark, alone?

Roger's show, previously a rational thread in the thrash of wind and water, had vanished.

Now the only voices I could hear were shouts. And no light anywhere.

I froze and listened. I couldn't hear anything, he must have got away. There was just the insistent sea, the grumbling steel.

I couldn't stay where I was. I moved along the wall, staying low, fingers trailing along the rough carpet tiles so I didn't fall over. I moved a few paces, stopped to listen. Moved again.

It's so quiet. Where is everyone? Am I the last person here?

A voice calls out. 'Anybody there?'

I cry out to answer, then stop. Who is it? I forget my feet and fall. It is amplified in metal.

The voices rise in alarm.

'James?'

'Who's that?'

'Thomas is here too. What's happened?'

The boys. I stay very still.

'There are stairs here.'

Have they heard me?

Maybe not, they are talking all at once, trying to keep track of where they all are.

Another voice. Thicker, older. 'I'm Colin. I work for the

station. Thank God I've found someone.'

Neen. Thank God indeed.

'How do we get out?' says a boy.

'I don't know,' says Neen, 'I only started here today.'

Crikey I know a lot of good liars.

The fort's metallic bones grind. As if something above is stretching and waking.

'What happened to the lights?' Neen's voice.

'It was us.' One of the boys.

'It was you?' Neen.

'That exorcist woman who bought the tapes said she'd destroy them. She's making copies instead. Then the DJ threw us out of the studio so we went and found the fuse box.'

Their voices become softer, there must be a corner taking them away.

'Aunt Jenny's going to have to get the cottage exorcised because of what that woman did.'

'Just keep walking,' says Neen. He's trying to keep them calm.

Thank God, they didn't find me.

I scramble after them. I'm better to be with them or I'll never find my way out. I fall into metal walls, feel my way around the corner.

A colossal bang. As though a train has erupted through the wall. It seems to make time hold its breath, suspend us in black amber. Until our hearts come galloping back and tell us to scream, run.

I hope they can't hear that I screamed too.

Up above, a cry of metal, as though the ceiling is splitting open. An eerie roar like a set of cello strings breaking in a metal chasm.

'Keep going,' calls Neen. 'We need to get out.' He's trying to sound convincing, make the boys trust him.

One of them starts to mutter the Lord's Prayer. Very fast, as though he's worried he won't get all the way to the end.

The wind suddenly surrounds us. There's a hole in the black darkness, letting in the air and the stars. That's the door to the deck. A bright torch shines down. Illuminates heads, shoulders, in front of me.

I knew it couldn't be that dire. This is England, there are emergency services. Let reason return. People don't die in situations like this. I'm not a past life yet.

A voice rings out. 'This is the coastguard. We've lost the radio tower. We're going to evacuate you. I'm going to throw down life jackets. How many are you?'

'Three. There are three of us.' Neen's voice.

Three? There are four.

Another figure, bulky with oilskins, striped with glowing tape like a fireman. Throws packages down the steps. Voice through the loudhailer, rising over the storm.

'One, two, three. Put them on before you come up.'

The boys leap for the life jackets. I glimpse a striped sleeve, the fingerless gloves, a face I saw in green with white eyes.

Neen is next to me, wrestling his wet leather arms into a life vest. 'Stay down here,' he whispers. 'Until they get out of the way.'

'What on earth are you talking about?'

He pulls the jacket tight. 'If you go up those boys are going to hurt someone. Not just you. You'll be much safer down here.'

Safer down here? I don't think so.

The boys have their life jackets on. Stripes of glowing tape flash as they scramble to the light. Water sluices down the steps.

I go up immediately after Neen.

Outside, the radio tower is lying like a felled ship's mast across the deck and spearing out over the water, red lights still showing the way. Snapped cables coil on the metal deck like snakes. Salt water scours my face, through my clothes, lights up a stripe of pain across my wrist. I've cut myself.

People are trying to walk across the deck and can't beat the wind. They drop and crawl in their stripes, like bees. I start to crawl too, fingers gripping the netting nailed to the deck. Perhaps someone will give me a life jacket. The whole floor is shaking, like a table whose joints are loose.

Arms grab me, start dragging me. If this is rescue it's rougher than I expected.

I smell pungent aftershave. The arm has a stripe like the warning markings on a poisonous animal. I kick and scream but no human sound can be heard while the sea is laughing so loud.

More stripes arrive, but head to toe, not just the padded waistcoat of a lifejacket. Not dragging, helping me walk. Coastguards.

One by one we climb down the ladder, hurried along by the next feet descending from above. I can't see where the ground is, just feel the difference when my feet touch concrete. Another coastguard is waiting, grabs my arm as though I am an escaping shirt on a washing line. Puts my hands on a rope. I walk along the rope, which has knots. The rough surface under my palms. I can feel the tug of others following. It is as though the sea, the sky and the wind have mixed to form a new element that roars and beats around us.

Coastguard arms are waiting. They put a silver blanket around me and push me into a vehicle. Close the door.

CHAPTER 73

At last. The air is the air, and it isn't wet and moving any more.

We're in a long-backed Range Rover, the seats facing each other like a Tube train. Neen and Kit the engineer are already in the other seats, wearing silvered blankets. Kit's Kangol hat has gone and his fleece is see-through with water. He's dozing with his head against the window.

Neen is alert, guarding a set of large square packages on his lap. He has got what he came for. I look at them, wondering if I can do anything. The mere thought of his persistence makes me feel exhausted. Just undoing one of the tabs of parcel tape looks like too much effort.

I say to Neen: 'Did you get all of them?'

He nods. 'Yes.' Coughs a little. 'Kit took care of it.'

'And Anthony Morrish is buying.'

Nods again. 'He is.'

The weather still roars outside. It's a thick mass of moving salt water, like an aquarium. But inside it's warm, dry. The windows are bloomed with steam. It feels safe. There is time for conversations.

'Do you want to tell me why?'

'Anthony Morrish had a bet with Gene.'

A bet. It's one of those long moments where everything needs to shift position, get comfortable again. 'A bet with Gene?'

'They were on the same table at a psychology conference. Anthony was talking about his Ripper victims. Gene suggested they never existed. Anthony cited his impressive cure rate. Over eighty per cent. He cures more people than these doctors do. Gene said any competent hypnotist could make someone contact the spirit of a person who was clearly fabricated and could use it to cure them. Anthony said it was impossible.'

Not Robert any more. I'm allowed to have Gene back now. My treacherous friend.

Neen continues. 'A sum was agreed.'

'How much?'

How much for my soul.

'Two grand.'

'Now Morrish has just paid ten? I'm so glad my stock has risen.'

'Tony's got a book coming up. A TV show. The public will get confused.'

Tony. Morrish and Neen are close buddies, it seems. Not even Jerry calls him Tony.

I ask: 'And how does paying Isabel Caswell ten thousand pounds solve that?'

'Isabel is a businesswoman. She has the ear of grass-roots spiritualists. It's good for her and Tony to be friends. In a few weeks it will be known in the community that the Andreq tapes are a hoax. He'll be grateful, of course.'

Neen smiles, but he's too tired to stretch his lips much past the white teeth. 'I'll be checking. I do all the checking for Tony.'

I look at the tapes again, wonder if I can grab them. I could, but I'd get them to my side and Neen would snatch them back to his. This isn't the time to try.

'You do the checking?'

'Tony's a shrewd man. When someone applies to be treated, I make sure they'll give a good show.'

'Jerry?'

A smile two teeth wide. Very tired. 'I probably know more about Jerry than you do. He was one of our best ever. That's why Tony invited him to be involved in the book.'

I look at Neen sceptically and he offers more. 'Look, love, Tony's reputation is built by being careful. The medical establishment often have difficulties with his work. He didn't appreciate it when he was at a dinner and someone who wasn't even a doctor started talking about fakes.'

I could well imagine it. A sand-grain of pride prickles in my soul.

The passenger door opens. A coastguard helps Roger the DJ in, huddled in foil. His hair is plastered to his head. While the coastguard is settling him in he manages a joke about how he's got enough buoyancy to float his way back to shore. A real trouper.

Out of the front windscreen, out in the weather, a set of brake lights comes on. Red smudges in the tempestuous sky. They begin to move.

A coastguard gets in our driver seat, starts the engine. A deep, six-litre throbbing.

'This'll be a bumpy ride, hang on.'

The driver puts the wipers on, which make no difference to the visibility. Lets off the handbrake and begins to crawl forwards.

I look behind and I can't see the radio station. I can't even see the sea out of the side windows. I'm glad I'm not driving.

'So how did this bet work?' I ask.

'Gene was to give him an audio of the regression and tell us the identity of the patient. I would check them out and find out how their new incarnation was affecting them. Whether they were telling their friends, changing their job. How the cure was going. You know the sort of thing.'

'Are you now going to tell me you followed me?'

'It never got that far. He sent the audio – two in fact.'

'Did he.' It wasn't a question. It was an attempt to get rid of the bitter taste in my mouth.

'Oh it was clear what was going on with those mock-healers under the sea. Tony didn't appreciate that, I can tell you. If I wasn't such a nice person Gene would have had his legs broken. But he never told us who you were. And then he left London, so it seemed he'd had his fun and backed down. Or so we thought.'

Neen looks at me as though he thinks I will explain. I have no explanation to offer. And if I did, why would I tell him anyway?

Neen continues. 'And then Jerry started asking Tony for advice about a friend who was involved in something strange.'

Jerry. Always so worried about me.

I look at the tapes, bundled together in green bags. Neen's

got his foil blanket protectively over them, as though he's making sure they're warm. You can't keep those, you know. And I'm getting the impression that Gene didn't want you to have them either.

That little sand prickle again, this time a grain of strength.

When we get out of the car. Maybe that's the time.

I ask: 'What is Anthony Morrish going to do with all of these?'

'The key with these situations is how you turn it around. We'll have the option to make some publicity out of it. At a future date Tony could leak to the press that he unmasked a trickster. Show the public he's on the side of truth. Depends what his PR people say, of course. But the main thing is, he has control.'

'He's going to do that?'

Neen shrugs. 'It's up to him. I'm just the gopher.'

The Range Rover lurches. Our driver swears. The wheel jerks in his hands as though something outside is controlling it. The red tail lights in front of us slide sideways, like shooting stars. Our driver stamps the brake.

The vehicle slips along as though its wheels are liquid. But after a moment the tyres bite again and we stop.

In front of us, the lights of the other Range Rover are at an angle.

'They're off the causeway,' mutters our driver. 'Come on, Pete, get her back up.'

We watch. Through the swing of the wipers, the lights come into focus, blur into the spray again. There's a scream of spinning wheels trying to grip, roared down by the wind and the pounding sea. The lights shudder, give a lurch and come level again.

See, I knew we'd be fine. We're in vehicles; safe.

Our driver moves off after it, swearing.

I say to Neen: 'Why are you telling me this now?'

'You're a nice girl. You deserve to know what Gene Winter involved you in. You have no need to be loyal to him.'

I know Neen by now. He doesn't do things from kindness. 'You're going to ask me where he is.'

'Tony would like to clear up any misunderstandings.'

'I don't know where he is. The hospital wouldn't tell me. They protect their own.'

Neen waves his hand. 'I know all that. I traced him to the practice in New Zealand. He left after one day. They don't know where he is.'

'He quit?'

Neen nods. 'I contacted the medical association in New Zealand. He's not practising medicine any more. He's conned everybody.' Neen looks at me pointedly as if this will squeeze some truth out of me. 'Like I said, nobody has any need to be loyal to him. He's played you, like he played everybody.'

Played. Two barefoot intruders in a dusty warehouse. At last, nothing between us but silk. Then that metallic noise as he touches the piano. Its strings vibrating, small and chilling because I know what it is. The blindfold comes off and I can't look away. The grimed, age-veined keys, saying *don't look away, my girl. You're going to need me. There's another storm coming.*

'What's so funny?' says Neen.

I'm smiling. But I'm not going to tell him why because it's a very private joke.

I hate the piano.

When it went well with Karli, I didn't think about the piano at all. Afterwards I went back to the only thing I knew. A gap-toothed instrument waiting for me like a sour spinster aunt. But it's not life. It's not a way to live.

It's a *machine*.

Like Andreq with xeching, I've tethered myself to it. I defined myself by it. I thought the machine was me. I told myself I was communicating something essential, natural and noble. Really I was hiding, channelling the raptures and agonies of men who had been dead for centuries and throwing them into this instrument. I shut myself in tiny rooms that would never let out a sound I made. Instead of going out and having raptures and agonies of my own.

Performing can be a full, rich life. But I hadn't had a life.

All I had was a six-foot wooden box. I'd locked my future into it as a child, deferring the rich, full life to some indefinite date.

Like Andreq, I have to let it go. When I get back to London, I'm going to shut my piano in that garage and go out in the sun like everybody else. It's what I've been trying to do for years. I just never realized.

A lurch. Neen, Kit, Roger and I are thrown together into the channel that runs between the seats. An impact that I register after it's happened, feel not as if it connected with the metal skin of the vehicle but went straight to my actual bones.

Then around the windows, something thicker than the raging spray. Water.

Roger the DJ pushes at the door. Shouting. It won't move. The driver's shouting too.

'Wind down the window. Equalise the pressure. Or the water will hold it shut.'

Neen is scrabbling for the door handle. 'We've gone in,' he is saying, very fast like he's trying to keep calm. Kit, knocked awake, is looking around bewildered.

We have gone off the causeway into the sea. We are five people, in a capsule of limited air, going down in the water.

The driver is still shouting about opening the windows. I find a handle. Turn.

Water pours in, a blaze of black cold, greedy for our air. We are all screaming, to finish its work even faster. I feel the door tip open. Tumble into the heaving liquid.

I don't know which way up I am, everything is water. It closes over my head. I bully it away. Give me air. I'm spluttering, gasping. My mouth stings.

I try to swim, but the waves are operating my arms and legs. Debris tantalizes my fingers, inviting me to grab hold. They are solid things but small, like a shoal of fish. Nothing substantial anywhere. Like being loose in the sky, great depth underneath. Have to fight or I'll fall.

Under again, wrestle back up. Cry for air. Such an effort just to stay breathing. I don't know how long I can carry on.

Thank goodness. Something that will hold me. I'm not

letting go. The water heaves us up and down but we are joined. Wherever this thing takes me I am going.

Small plastic things nudge against my arm like feeding fish. My tapes. Loose tape curls around my hands. Or is it seaweed. Andreq, come to say goodbye.

Until next time?

Perhaps I am on a couch in a blue studio, a soothesayer guiding me towards last moments. I apologise for what I am about to put him through. I might scream. *A bit of cathartic sensation and it's gone. They don't know how bad it was.*

I hope he is prepared.

CHAPTER 74

I'm lying in bed. Secured between rough, dry sheets, like I've been tucked into an envelope. Warm. Drowsy.

My senses keep shuffling. One moment I am moving on a boat. The next I am sinking through the floor. Synapses re-entering the world after hypothermia.

I have a bandage over my right arm. I move my hand, seeing if that will tell me why. It feels curious, like a zip has been put into the skin under the bandage. No pain, just tightness, like stitches.

Whatever they've given me, it's good.

The hospital room is white. The other beds are empty, freshly made. A slow day.

The window next to my bed faces the sea. Outside the sky glowers, as though gathering strength to repeat the previous night's storm. From time to time it throws hail at the glass.

Opposite my bed is a window into the corridor, at an angle to the first. Together they make a ghostly kind of mirror. It reflects the sky, and when people go past in the corridor they slide across in a flat outline like a Pepper's ghost.

So far I have seen Roger the DJ, walking fast and irritated, a mobile under the folds of his chin, rolling a cigarette at the same time. A nurse followed him and confiscated it.

I saw Kit the engineer, subdued, holding onto a spiky-haired girlfriend.

The wind and rain settle to drizzle, a soft sound, steady and gentle.

I'm wearing glasses. My contact lenses disappeared into the sea, slid away with Andreq and my shoes and my watch and my keys and my wallet and my phone. A nurse brought a box of glasses from the hospital lost property and told me to find a pair I could see through.

Where did they come from, I asked.

'Never mind that, or what they look like,' she said. 'Just find some you can use.'

Wire John Lennons were tangled with heavy black frames. Each one I looked at suggested a face and a life. Half-moons: when I'm sixty-four. Strong black arms and surrounds: smoke in a Soho cavern. Blue-tinted with one lens shattered into a spider web: desert sun through a sand-scoured windscreen open to the sky. I lingered on those, only the nurse whipped them away, saying they shouldn't be there, they were no good to anyone.

The best match for my myopia were some small square frames with a greenish tint like a stagnant pond. Not sure who that is, but for now it's me.

I saw the reflection of Richard Longborrow slip by, walking slowly across the background of the sky. His collar was open, with no bow tie, and he was staring at his shoes.

I saw Thomas and James Worth leave, walking slowly between parents who linked their arms around them tightly like bodyguards.

I take off the tinted glasses again. The white paint on the walls is tinged with a colour to soften it, which sometimes seems blue, sometimes pink, sometimes peach and sometimes green. Or perhaps it's hypothermia making sense of green glasses.

A figure steps closer out of the blur. 'Carol?'

'Gene?'

I scrunch my eyes, trying to see. Put the green lenses back on.

No, just the nurse. Not the one with the box of dead men's glasses; a male nurse who'd been in earlier. He takes the chart from the end of the bed and lifts my wrist, checking my pulse.

The nurse chats to me, fingers monitoring my artery, one eye on his wristwatch. 'It was a hell of a storm last night. We've had so many road accidents. The sea was throwing rocks through people's windows. A wave hit the lighthouse and stopped the light revolving.'

'What about the radio station?'

'Half its roof has gone. The mast took it off.' He lets go of my wrist and updates the chart. 'I think we'll be using broadband a lot more from now on.'

'Did everyone get out?'

'Yes. The coastguard got everyone.'

He takes a penlight out of his pocket and shines it in my eyes. 'Do you have any next of kin, someone we should contact?'

I haven't even thought about that.

The nurse knows I'm not compos mentis. Tries to jog my memory. 'When I came in you thought I was someone...'

'Gene.'

It feels good to say his name.

Gene: next of kin. What a funny idea.

'Should we try and contact...?'

'No.'

'If you're sure,' says the nurse, and leaves.

I take off the glasses and rub my eyes. The white room is filled with pink, green and blue clouds. I feel so tired.

Presently I put the glasses on again.

I try to read a magazine but the text keeps swimming. Instead I sit back with it spread on my lap and doze.

A noise.

It's the glasses nurse, seeking my attention. 'Two of your friends have come looking for you. The registrar doesn't think you're well enough to have visitors yet. But they wanted me to let you know they'll pick you up when you can go.'

I put the green glasses on. 'Who are they?' As if she'd know, but I have to ask.

Fortunately, like the other nurse, she's used to talking to the temporarily confused. 'Thinnish guy, shaved head, red jumper.'

Jerry. All the way from London.

'Tall woman, fifties-ish.' As she thinks about how to describe her she indicates a dramatic eyebrow on her face.

Eleanor.

The nurse notes my recognition approvingly. 'They've gone off together to the canteen.' She makes a note on her clipboard and holds out a plastic cup of medication. I swallow the two capsules, sip water to chase them down.

Jerry has gone to the canteen with Eleanor. Without doubt she will soon be telling him about Lears past and present. Jerry will love all that. Geoffrey, the tortured painter. Ronald, the explorer who made the Antarctic sound like a gentleman's club. And Sir Bertrand, provided with mountaineering footwear by kindly dead guardians. In return, Jerry will tell her about Ruby Cunningham and they might even swap stories about a remarkable Lear from the future. Two people who want their lives to be a continuum through the centuries.

The nurse ticks more boxes on her form. Now I am sorted, claimed by people from the living, healthy world. No longer a washed-up waif with no keys, no phone and no glasses. Now I have context.

'It's nice that they found you at last,' she says, finishing her notes. 'Is it your brother? Mother?'

'Just some of my bizarre family,' I say, and I'd never have thought those words would make me smile so much.

The nurse goes.

I drift. The smell of the sea comes into the room. The storm has come up again. Rain and hail trying to get attention, throwing handfuls of gravel at the glass. And a tree branch, tapping like taloned claws, tapping away. Let me in. Like someone outside watching.

And so, Gene, I was the subject of a bet. Used, like a life remembered by one of your patients. Fed lines so you could goad a trickster. Drowned then discarded.

You could have won, you know. Stolen Anthony Morrish's crown, got the book deal, the TV show. Had an endless supply of playmates whenever you felt like a control freak game. Why didn't you go the whole way? Lost your nerve, did you? You said you hadn't finished. Have you finished now?

And, come to think of it, when did it start?

Was the Anthony Morrish bet in your mind all along? From when? That first meeting in the hospital, at the basement theatre in King's Road, on that first night when you talked so bewitchingly of time machines?

That stops me, like a vast computation. Too drowsy to do it. I take off the glasses. Rub my eyes. The colours are back, shapes sliding over the real world.

Is that what a xech is like?

Recharge. Reset. Calmer.

Maybe that first time was just another tired night helping a patient, on autopilot, and he barely even registered who I was.

That wouldn't be surprising. The first day at the hospital I didn't remember him much either.

I do now. He always wore the same black leather jacket, even in summer. He looked as though he was cold, or trying to keep something out.

He's changed a little as he's dropped youth. His features have become sharper. The intensity is more under control. Back then, when he was sixteen, he was intimidating. He looked aggressive, as if he might self-destruct. Disturbed by the violence happening at home? Impossible to know, but he'd really learned to inhabit that name.

I wasn't the only performer at Kate's party. Some of the others sang, played or recited too, but they were rank beginners. I'd been doing it for years, been running harder. Running for my life.

Does Gene, watching quietly, recognise a comrade on the same battlefield? Someone who needs her art like a mad love to sweep her away to a new life?

Does he go to medical school, also looking for his purpose, his escape? Finds it in a lecture on incurable pain?

A vanquishing power that defies science, they tell him. Well, he's way ahead on that. He knows it doesn't start with the closing of the door on the hand, but with the door opening, the hand being placed.

So much to learn, it gobbles up the years. Understanding more, guiding these patients to the rope and the axe, connecting with their inner lives where this unkillable pain is really rooted. The more tricky the better, when you hit the sweet spot nothing's so good. It's only when he stops that the payback comes.

Gene is just like I was, channelling the raptures and agonies of dead composers.

And then he meets, once again, the person who all that time ago showed him the way.

How fascinating that it didn't work for her.

So now what will he do? Go searching for another trapped soul? Has he had a string of people like me? He's got a whole new hemisphere to hunt in now.

And what does all this make Andreq? A bet between two hypnotists, a trick played on a gullible innocent? An ego trip for a burnt-out *idiot savant* therapist?

That's what Neen would say.

I think the bet was nothing. The big showdown isn't Gene's kind of game. The intimate conquest is more his style. Much better feedback. I imagine Gene sized Anthony Morrish up and thought, *you're irritating, I know how to get through to you*. He had fun with Morrish, but then he had no further interest in it.

Gene, why didn't you take me to the end in one go? Normally that's how it goes. In the chair, hello you married Henry, off with your head, feel better now. All over in an hour.

You did eight hours; that's aeons.

Was it because this time, they were talking to you too?

Was that why you kept the other tapes for so long?

I don't think you'll go hunting for another victim, even with your twisted sensibilities. I think you were well past the point where you needed to stop. You were already trying to escape; first running away from London and then from this entire half of the world.

Andreq knew. He told you you couldn't continue. That night you'd been hypnotising those people with Alzheimer's and could barely fight your way back. When he refused to soothe, that wasn't a message for me. It was for you.

Could this have gone differently? That night in the warehouse, when you took me to the piano, were you expecting I'd want to play? What you said was, *You need to say goodbye.* Were you offering me a choice? If I'd chosen to trust you, to understand what you were showing me instead of lashing at you with a fist of glass...

Andreq and Ruhul might certainly have preferred to be left at that point, to live as ordinary, uncomplicated lovers.

Would we have put all the rest of this aside?

The reflections are like infinity mirrors, you could go mad.

Andreq, I'm sorry that you were the sin-eater for Gene and me. I don't know how much detail you were getting, but we probably caused you no end of trouble.

The nurse had offered to find Gene. I should have said yes. Go forth and seek him. He's next of kin and more. And then by magic he would be standing here, because no one can resist a summons on such authority.

No, I think it would take higher powers than that to find him. He wants to be lost.

In the Pepper's Ghost window, shadows come creeping behind the clouds. The trees are growing restless.

Andreq is vanishing. The sea has him now. Long curls of tape unravel through the fathoms.

What were you really?

Would Ruby be able to tell anyone what Jerry is?

No, that's not the right question.

You're not down in the ocean. You're Gene and me. We made you. One soul who showed us how we have been travelling all this time on conjoined journeys. Who let us tell the truth about ourselves, who made us twice as alive. Our real relationship wasn't with each other. It was with you.

Glasses off. Blink. Here it comes, the slipping colours of the xech, like a lava lamp. It is nice, and all it is is a bit of electrical small-talk between eye and imagination.

What do I want now?

What will I do?

Big questions, but suddenly not so scary. Quite simple, in fact. I'll go exploring too. I've never travelled except to play – and that meant dingy concert halls and the dismal treadmill of

England's motorways. But I can break old habits. The future isn't written yet. We all get a chance to fix our mistakes.

I could do desert sun through a sand-scoured windscreen open to the sky. Join the continuum of marvellous adventuring Lears. I can start a friendship or a love affair without music as a go-between. Maybe I won't climb mountains, but on the other hand, why not?

It's time for me to find out which Lear I'm going to be.

Also by Roz Morris

Lifeform Three

Misty woods; abandoned towns; secrets in the landscape; a forbidden life by night; the scent of bygone days; a past that lies below the surface; and a door in a dream that seems to hold the answers.

Paftoo is a 'bod'; made to serve. He is a groundsman in the last remaining countryside estate, once known as Harkaway Hall and now a theme park. Paftoo holds scattered memories of the old days but they are regularly deleted to keep him productive.

When he starts to have dreams of the Lost Lands past, Paftoo is thrown into a nocturnal battle for his memories, his soul and his cherished connection with Lifeform Three.

'Beautifully written, meaningful, top-drawer storytelling. An extraordinary novel in the tradition of great old-school literary science fiction like Atwood and Bradbury'
LEAGUE OF EXTRAORDINARY AUTHORS

Available now in all formats

CONTACT THE AUTHOR

www.mymemoriesofafuturelife.com

You can also find Roz Morris online at www.rozmorris.wordpress.com, on her blog www.nailyournovel.com, and on Twitter as @Roz_Morris.

If you enjoyed this book, would you consider leaving a review on line? It makes all the difference to independent publishers who rely on word of mouth to get their books known.
Thank you.

If you also feel the urge to make things up, you might like Roz's writing books:
Nail Your Novel – Why Writers Abandon Books and How You Can Draft, Fix and Finish With Confidence
and
Writing Characters Who'll Keep Readers Captivated: Nail Your Novel 2
Available in print and on Kindle.

Printed in Great Britain
by Amazon.co.uk, Ltd.,
Marston Gate.